The Folio Book of Comic Short Stories

THE FOLIO BOOK OF

Comic Short Stories

SELECTED AND INTRODUCED BY

David Hughes

ILLUSTRATED BY

Paul Cox

The Folio Society

LONDON 2005

Typeset at The Folio Society in Plantin Light with Cerigo display.
Printed on Voluprint paper by Cambridge University Press and
bound by them in quarter cloth and paper sides, blocked and
printed with a design by the artist.

Contents

Illustrations

vii

Introduction

I have chosen these stories on the strength of an imperative: make me laugh. When asked by The Folio Society on a less than solemn occasion to edit this volume, I decided, with a frivolity inspired by the moment, in favour of a policy of never asking why any of these writers made me laugh. I knew if I did I would find them at once unfunny: comic stories do not benefit from gratuitous comment.

So this is not an essay on the nature of humour. No definitions of comedy seem either appropriate or possible; they just wreck the fun. Were I to devise a thermometer which, stuck under the tongue in my cheek or pressed to the nerve of the funny bone, would measure how close I was to being carried off to hospital with a damaged ribcage, or into intensive care for an operation on the tear-ducts, I still wouldn't know quite what it was that set me off into hysteria (I think it's a touch of Wodehouse, doctor), the shakes (another attack of Leacock), groans of agony (I'm a martyr to Amis, sister), pain more exquisite than pleasure (believe you me, nurse, a dose of V. S. Pritchett's just like an iron band round the chest), or even that acute amusement (Spark, doc, that's what I've got) which is sometimes a surer measure on the scale of comic eruption than pure merriment. Given that one man's maniacal laughter is someone else's clinical depression, he who selects for others is bound to be wrong about any generalisation he utters. Yet in matters involving a risk to life as threatening as a sense of humour, I would far rather be ill than cured.

I thus sat at home in hilarious Kennington and decided to throw, on paper, the party to end all parties. I would banish such trivia as gloom and doom and feel free to invite anyone, whenever in the modern era they happened to have had their

Introduction

being, as long as they were good company. The mind of every anthologist is equipped with a bouncer to keep out the bores. It was a magisterial pleasure to be able to pull the heavy on Henry James, give D. H. Lawrence the elbow, frog-march Aldous Huxley into the thickets of the intellect, and bury the whole of Bloomsbury under the very restaurant where The Folio Society had just treated me to an editorial riot of a lunch. ('Lunch' is the Recreation cited in *Who's Who* by Keith Waterhouse, the wittiest of men, though I found no short story that did him as much justice as that tasty mono-syllable of wit.)

   Like any anthology of the best of a literary culture busy rounding itself off (or dying, if you detest euphemism), this mouth-watering book at your disposal is as full of gaps as of teeth. The numbers at our party had, inevitably, to be kept down, but it is also the truth that if you invite too many guests (or the wrong ones) they invariably compete with each other, rather than contributing to the party as a whole. I decided that this guest list of genius I was compiling should amount to an autobiographical reflection, not only of my response to the convulsive humour of the written word, but of any good story's ability to set fire to life.

   Usually we remember the place where, whether in youth or middle or old age, we first added this author or that to our inner library. Associations add to the pleasure of discovery; they bring back the moment when you opened a particular page not knowing what to expect and delight kicked in. I sus-pect that this is truer of comedy: it always escapes me where I first read *Sons and Lovers* or *The Golden Bowl*, but Dickens and Richmal Crompton bring back lolling in the beech-woods in Hampshire during the war, Oscar Wilde haunts rooms high up in an Oxford College, while that bearded sage of a humorist from Canada, Robertson Davies, is, oddly, eternally present in Sloane Street, London, where I once interviewed him.

   All these stories share a genius for setting off life's fireworks – from the bush-ranger Henry Lawson's arousing tale of a ventriloquial rooster out in the post-convict outback, to Muriel Spark's sardonic encounters with flying saucers – Spode, naturally – in 'Miss Pinkerton's Apocalypse'. They testify to life's power to twirl things around in so artful a fashion as to assure us that the western world consists of a ridiculous past, exemplified by the Trollopian ladies making as free as pop groupies with a pair of breeches in 'The Relics of General Chassé'; a present that is immeasurably to be mocked as in the way Elizabeth Bowen kicks it around in 'Shoes', and a future that exists only if you poke fun at it in advance as Kingsley Amis does in 'The 2003 Claret', written two decades earlier than that date. The pleasures (and pains) of the flesh are there in James Thurber's cautionary tale of matrimony, 'The Curb in the Sky' ('When Dorothy grew up she became quite pretty and so even more of a menace'), and in Damon Runyon's incomparable 'Piece of Pie', in which Miss Violette Shumberger eats valiantly for America. Whole worlds crumble: Evelyn Waugh sends up the cinema in 'Excursion in Reality', Stella Gibbons mocks journalism in 'The Great Mammoth Story' and Sophie Chattel-Monkheim, the heroine of a marvellous 'Saki' joke and a Socialist by conviction rather than at heart, is forced to decide between her entire household staff and the only man in the world who can cook a 'Byzantine omelette'.

There are risks. Most funny men live unfunny lives. Tony Hancock bore with his own humour for only so long as it took to decide on taking his own life. Without the jokes Peter Sellers dissolved into a ghost of himself. The dry comedy of Alec Guinness's acting was inspired only by the gloom of his inner disposition.

Writers are also actors, on page rather than on stage. Only out of misery, perhaps, does humour spring as a last gasp of the positive in a hopelessly negative world. I did promise not to theorise, for fear of missing the jokes, but I can't help but notice that Evelyn Waugh's humour line by line, which in

Introduction

'Excursion in Reality' has a bland ungentlemanliness of asperity in its composition, was shadowed by a melancholia that burst now and then into drunken quarrel. His rudeness, to the club staff no less than to his fellow-members of White's, was matched only by greed and a scorn for his children – Waugh was on the sombrely knotty side at home, hard to live with, rising into comedy only alone at his desk pen in hand, and even then fretting. Kingsley Amis, for that matter, could not even live with himself, for fear of the dark and the death it concealed. Dorothy Parker enlivened, with one-liners as black as a bin-liner, the *New Yorker*'s round of writers that daily gathered in that little bar at the Algonquin on West 44th Street, but did she or any serious writer ever laugh at their own jokes? Indeed, isn't the result always funnier if you are a serious writer in the first place, rather than a self-appointed comedian whose buffoonery can so easily turn him into a joke? See how easy it is to get befogged by speculation and bogged down in platitudes.

My late literary agent, a paragon of cunning and charm named Giles Gordon, acute negotiator and fine friend, lured me into a big bang of a comic moment. For ten years from 1986 he and I edited for the publisher Heinemann a yearly volume, never less than 300 pages, of Best Short Stories. Our two or three meetings a year – rituals, in a word – grew increasingly intemperate and scandal-mongering. At the time, he was slipping stories of the book trade into the satirical magazine *Private Eye* and I was writing *But for Bunter*, a novel about the real-life model for Billy Bunter, in which the famous schoolboy fatty lays claim to being entirely responsible for the absurdity of the twentieth century. Giles and I had a hugely funny time, but our meetings told us nothing about definitions of comedy except that it was indefinable. As often as not, shows on television purporting to celebrate humour are so unfunny as to be ludicrous, and I have no doubt that others, watching our antics, would have found our behaviour anything but amusing.

xii

Our annual conferences became cumulative; one joke
built upon another. Our mood usually took off in the Garrick
Club so that more sober members, if any, cast our rowdy
table a glance. After a month of further reading we would
assemble our choices at Bertorelli's in Covent Garden, where
on one occasion we had to shift tables because an author
whose story we were likely to reject was lunching next to us
with his agent. Our final choice was made by tradition at
London's oldest wine-bar by Charing Cross, called Gordon's
(no relation). This time Giles brought the stories in a super-
market plastic bag, which we put at our feet to subject them
one at a time to final analysis. We were on sherry, which Gordon's serves in tumblers. I remember with care placing the
stories back in the plastic bag. It was my turn to deliver the
finished article to Heinemann after the weekend.

When I reached home with the plastic bag to put the stories in reasonable order for the press, I found I had to choose
whether a frozen pizza should precede a vac-packed salami
on the contents page or whether the book was to be rounded
off with a tin of cat-food. For I had picked up a plastic bag of
identical size and weight which, as in a spy story, someone
looking forward to his supper had placed adjacent to mine
on the floor. He would dine off juicy slices of Alice Munro or
Rose Tremain; I could hope only that he would return them
when Gordon's reopened on Monday morning. I spent a terrible weekend. It turned out that insult was added to injury:
he had not bothered to take my plastic bag at all.

I have had just such fun with this book without as much
sherry; nor was I alone because my wife Elizabeth has helped
me with the winnowing. In affection we dedicate it to Giles
Gordon, without whom many successors to those contributing to this volume would have been the poorer and the less
wise.

So bring them on . . . Dickens (his laughter anarchic, liber-
ating, harsh, as Peter Ackroyd's vast life puts it), Saki (master
of the blackly minimal), Richmal Crompton (the champion of

Introduction

every boy who ever thought a handkerchief was for blotting ink and carrying frogs). Bring them on together with their best asides – which is what a short story often is – and let them perform their twists of anecdote and turns of plot, to a crescendo of applause on the platform of this magnificent hall hired on your behalf: viz, the handsome book in your hand.

This, above all, this was to be the pleasure of your anthologist: given a free hand to set up a feast, a festivity, for the humorists he first met on the page, who with brevity made sense of life, set it on a roar, strained the diaphragm, touched off a good weep of joy, and furnished forth the party of a lifetime.

DAVID HUGHES
2005

The Lamplighter

CHARLES DICKENS

'If you talk of Murphy and Francis Moore, gentlemen,' said the lamplighter who was in the chair, 'I mean to say that neither of 'em ever had any more to do with the stars than Tom Grig had.'

'And what had *he* to do with 'em?' asked the lamplighter who officiated as vice.

'Nothing at all,' replied the other; 'just exactly nothing at all.'

'Do you mean to say you don't believe in Murphy, then?' demanded the lamplighter who had opened the discussion.

'I mean to say I believe in Tom Grig,' replied the chairman. 'Whether I believe in Murphy, or not, is a matter between me and my conscience; and whether Murphy believes in himself, or not, is a matter between him and his conscience. Gentlemen, I drink your healths.'

The lamplighter who did the company this honour was seated in the chimney-corner of a certain tavern, which has been, time out of mind, the Lamplighters' House of Call. He sat in the midst of a circle of lamplighters, and was the cacique, or chief of the tribe.

If any of our readers have had the good fortune to behold a lamplighter's funeral, they will not be surprised to learn that lamplighters are a strange and primitive people; that they rigidly adhere to old ceremonies and customs which have been handed down among them from father to son since the first public lamp was lighted out of doors; that they intermarry, and betroth their children in infancy; that they enter into no plots or conspiracies (for who ever heard of a traitorous lamplighter?); that they commit no crimes against

I

the laws of their country (there being no instance of a mur-
derous or burglarious lamplighter); that they are, in short,
notwithstanding their apparently volatile and restless character, a highly moral and reflective people: having among
themselves as many traditional observances as the Jews, and
being, as a body, if not as old as the hills, at least as old as
the streets. It is an article of their creed that the first faint
glimmering of true civilisation shone in the first street-light
maintained at the public expense. They trace their existence,
and high position in the public esteem, in a direct line to the
heathen mythology; and hold that the history of Prometheus
himself is but a pleasant fable, whereof the true hero is a
lamplighter.

'Gentlemen,' said the lamplighter in the chair, 'I drink
your healths.'

'And perhaps, Sir,' said the vice, holding up his glass, and
rising a little way off his seat and sitting down again, in token
that he recognised and returned the compliment, 'perhaps
you will add to that condescension by telling us who Tom
Grig was, and how he came to be connected in your mind
with Francis Moore, Physician.'

'Hear, hear, hear!' cried the lamplighters generally.

'Tom Grig, gentlemen,' said the chairman, 'was one of us;
and it happened to him, as it don't often happen to a public
character in our line, that he had his what-you-may-call-
it cast.'

'His head?' said the vice.

'No,' replied the chairman, 'not his head.'

'His face, perhaps?' said the vice. 'No, not his face.' 'His
legs?' 'No, not his legs.' Nor yet his arms, nor his hands, nor
his feet, nor his chest, all of which were severally suggested.

'His nativity, perhaps?'

'That's it,' said the chairman, awakening from his thoughtful attitude at the suggestion. 'His nativity. That's what Tom
had cast, gentlemen.'

'In plaster?' asked the vice.

'I don't rightly know how it's done,' returned the chairman. 'But I suppose it was.'

And there he stopped as if that were all he had to say; whereupon there arose a murmur among the company, which at length resolved itself into a request, conveyed through the vice, that he would go on. This being exactly what the chairman wanted, he mused for a little time, performed that agreeable ceremony which is popularly termed wetting one's whistle, and went on thus:

'Tom Grig, gentlemen, was, as I have said, one of us; and I may go further, and say he was an ornament to us, and such a one as only the good old times of oil and cotton could have produced. Tom's family, gentlemen, were all lamplighters.'

'Not the ladies, I hope?' asked the vice.

'They had talent enough for it, Sir,' rejoined the chairman, 'and would have been, but for the prejudices of society. Let women have their rights, Sir, and the females of Tom's family would have been every one of 'em in office. But that emancipation hasn't come yet, and hadn't then, and consequently they confined themselves to the bosoms of their families, cooked the dinners, mended the clothes, minded the children, comforted their husbands, and attended to the house-keeping generally. It's a hard thing upon the women, gentlemen, that they are limited to such a sphere of action as this; very hard.

'I happen to know all about Tom, gentlemen, from the circumstance of his uncle, by his mother's side, having been my particular friend. His (that's Tom's uncle's) fate was a melancholy one. Gas was the death of him. When it was first talked of, he laughed. He wasn't angry; he laughed at the credulity of human nature. "They might as well talk", he says, "of laying on an everlasting succession of glow-worms"; and then he laughed again, partly at his joke, and partly at poor humanity.

'In course of time, however, the thing got ground, the experiment was made, and they lighted up Pall Mall. Tom's uncle went to see it. I've heard that he fell off his ladder four-teen times that night, from weakness, and that he would certainly have gone on falling till he killed himself, if his last tumble hadn't been into a wheelbarrow which was going his way, and humanely took him home. "I foresee in this," says Tom's uncle faintly, and taking to his bed as he spoke – "I foresee in this", he says, "the breaking up of our profession. There's no more going the rounds to trim by daylight, no more dribbling down of the oil on the hats and bonnets of ladies and gentlemen when one feels in spirits. Any low fel-low can light a gas-lamp. And it's all up." In this state of mind, he petitioned the government for – I want a word again, gentlemen – what do you call that which they give to people when it's found out, at last, that they've never been of any use, and have been paid too much for doing nothing?'

'Compensation?' suggested the vice.

'That's it,' said the chairman. 'Compensation. They didn't give it him, though, and then he got very fond of his country all at once, and went about saying that gas was a death-blow to his native land, and that it was a plot of the radicals to ruin the country and destroy the oil and cotton trade for ever, and that the whales would go and kill themselves pri-vately, out of sheer spite and vexation at not being caught. At last he got right-down cracked; called his tobacco-pipe a gas-pipe; thought his tears were lamp-oil; and went on with all manner of nonsense of that sort, till one night he hung himself on a lamp-iron in St Martin's Lane, and there was an end of *him*.

'Tom loved him, gentlemen, but he survived it. He shed a tear over his grave, got very drunk, spoke a funeral oration that night in the watch-house, and was fined five shillings for it, in the morning. Some men are none the worse for this sort of thing. Tom was one of 'em. He went that very afternoon on a new beat: as clear in his head, and as free from fever as Father Mathew himself.

'Tom's new beat, gentlemen, was – I can't exactly say

where, for that he'd never tell; but I know it was in a quiet part of town, where there were some queer old houses. I have always had it in my head that it must have been somewhere near Canonbury Tower in Islington, but that's a matter of opinion. Wherever it was, he went upon it, with a bran-new ladder, a white hat, a brown holland jacket and trousers, a blue neck-kerchief, and a sprig of full-blown double wall-flower in his button-hole. Tom was always genteel in his appearance, and I have heard from the best judges, that if he had left his ladder at home that afternoon, you might have took him for a lord.

'He was always merry, was Tom, and such a singer, that if there was any encouragement for native talent, he'd have been at the opera. He was on his ladder, lighting his first lamp, and singing to himself in a manner more easily to be conceived than described, when he hears the clock strike five, and suddenly sees an old gentleman with a telescope in his hand, throw up a window and look at him very hard.

'Tom didn't know what could be passing in this old gentleman's mind. He thought it likely enough that he might be saying within himself, "Here's a new lamplighter – a good-looking young fellow – shall I stand something to drink?" Thinking this possible, he keeps quite still, pretending to be very particular about the wick, and looks at the old gentleman sideways, seeming to take no notice of him.

'Gentlemen, he was one of the strangest and most mysterious-looking files that ever Tom clapped his eyes on. He was dressed all slovenly and untidy, in a great gown of a kind of bed-furniture pattern, with a cap of the same on his head; and a long old flapped waistcoat; with no braces, no strings, very few buttons – in short, with hardly any of those artificial contrivances that hold society together. Tom knew by these signs, and by his not being shaved, and by his not being over-clean, and by a sort of wisdom, not quite awake, in his face, that he was a scientific old gentleman. He often told me that if he could have conceived the possibility

5

of the whole Royal Society being boiled down into one man, he should have said the old gentleman's body was that Body.

'The old gentleman claps the telescope to his eye, looks all round, sees nobody else in sight, stares at Tom again, and cries out very loud:

' "Hal-loa!"

' "Halloa, Sir," says Tom from the ladder; "and halloa again, if you come to that."

' "Here's an extraordinary fulfilment", says the old gentleman, "of a prediction of the planets."

' "Is there?" says Tom. "I'm very glad to hear it."

' "Young man," says the old gentleman, "you don't know me."

' "Sir," says Tom, "I have not that honour; but I shall be happy to drink your health, notwithstanding."

' "I read," cries the old gentleman, without taking any notice of this politeness on Tom's part – "I read what's going to happen, in the stars."

'Tom thanked him for the information, and begged to know if anything particular was going to happen in the stars, in the course of a week or so; but the old gentleman, correcting him, explained that he read in the stars what was going to happen on dry land, and that he was acquainted with all the celestial bodies.

' "I hope they're all well, Sir," says Tom – "everybody."

' "Hush!" cries the old gentleman. "I have consulted the book of Fate with rare and wonderful success. I am versed in the great sciences of astrology and astronomy. In my house here, I have every description of apparatus for observing the course and motion of the planets. Six months ago, I derived from this source, the knowledge that precisely as the clock struck five this afternoon a stranger would present himself – the destined husband of my young and lovely niece – in reality of illustrious and high descent, but whose birth would be enveloped in uncertainty and mystery. Don't tell me yours isn't," says the old gentleman, who was in such a hurry to

6

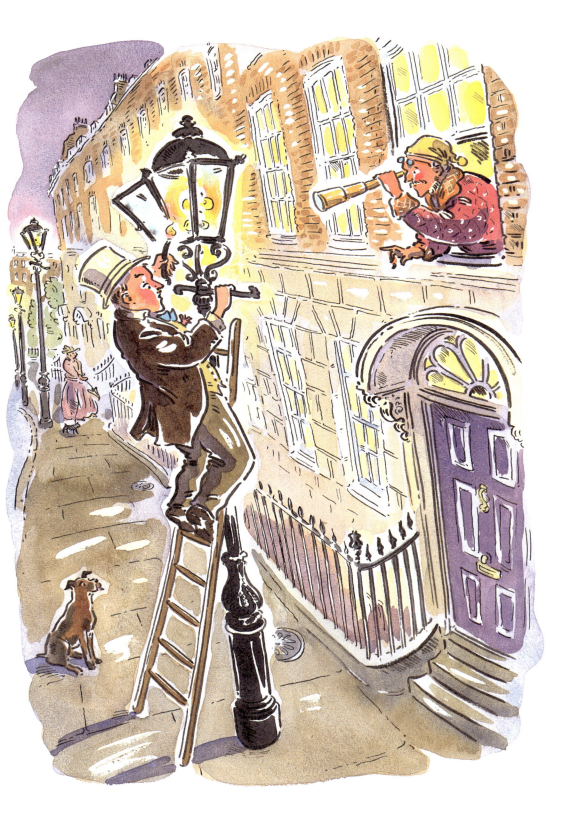

speak that he couldn't get the words out fast enough, "for I know better."

'Gentlemen, Tom was so astonished when he heard him say this, that he could hardly keep his footing on the ladder, and found it necessary to hold on by the lamp-post. There *was* a mystery about his birth. His mother had always admitted it. Tom had never known who was his father, and some people had gone so far as to say that even *she* was in doubt.

'While he was in this state of amazement, the old gentleman leaves the window, bursts out of the house-door, shakes the ladder, and Tom, like a ripe pumpkin, comes sliding down into his arms.

' "Let me embrace you," he says, folding his arms about him, and nearly lighting up his old bed-furniture gown at Tom's link. "You're a man of noble aspect. Everything combines to prove the accuracy of my observations. You have had mysterious promptings within you," he says; "I know you have had whisperings of greatness, eh?" he says.

' "I think I have," says Tom – Tom was one of those who can persuade themselves to anything they like – "I've often thought I wasn't the small beer I was taken for."

' "You were right," cries the old gentleman, hugging him again. "Come in. My niece awaits us."

' "Is the young lady tolerable good-looking, Sir?" says Tom, hanging fire rather, as he thought of her playing the piano, and knowing French, and being up to all manner of accomplishments.

' "She's beautiful!" cries the old gentleman, who was in such a terrible bustle that he was all in a perspiration. "She has a graceful carriage, an exquisite shape, a sweet voice, a countenance beaming with animation and expression; and the eye", he says, rubbing his hands, "of a startled fawn."

'Tom supposed this might mean, what was called among his circle of acquaintance, "a game eye"; and, with a view to this defect, enquired whether the young lady had any cash.

7

' "She has five thousand pounds," cries the old gentleman. "But what of that? what of that? A word in your ear. I'm in search of the philosopher's stone. I have very nearly found it – not quite. It turns everything to gold; that's its property."

'Tom naturally thought it must have a deal of property; and said that when the old gentleman did get it, he hoped he'd be careful to keep it in the family.

' "Certainly," he says, "of course. Five thousand pounds! What's five thousand pounds to us? What's five million?" he says. "What's five thousand million? Money will be nothing to us. We shall never be able to spend it fast enough."

' "We'll try what we can do, Sir," says Tom.

' "We will," says the old gentleman. "Your name?"

' "Grig," says Tom.

'The old gentleman embraced him again, very tight; and without speaking another word, dragged him into the house in such an excited manner, that it was as much as Tom could do to take his link and ladder with him, and put them down in the passage.

'Gentlemen, if Tom hadn't been always remarkable for his love of truth, I think you would still have believed him when he said that all this was like a dream. There is no better way for a man to find out whether he is really asleep or awake, than calling for something to eat. If he's in a dream, gentlemen, he'll find something wanting in flavour, depend upon it.

'Tom explained his doubts to the old gentleman, and said that if there was any cold meat in the house, it would ease his mind very much to test himself at once. The old gentleman ordered up a venison pie, a small ham, and a bottle of very old Madeira. At the first mouthful of pie and the first glass of wine, Tom smacks his lips and cries out, "I'm awake – wide awake"; and to prove that he was so, gentlemen, he made an end of 'em both.

'When Tom had finished his meal (which he never spoke of afterwards without tears in his eyes), the old gentleman hugs him again, and says, "Noble stranger! let us visit my

8

young and lovely niece." Tom, who was a little elevated with the wine, replies, "The noble stranger is agreeable!" At which words the old gentleman took him by the hand, and led him to the parlour; crying as he opened the door, "Here is Mr Grig, the favourite of the planets!"

'I will not attempt a description of female beauty, gentlemen, for every one of us has a model of his own that suits his own taste best. In this parlour that I'm speaking of, there were two young ladies; and if every gentleman present will imagine two models of his own in their places, and will be kind enough to polish 'em up to the very highest pitch of perfection, he will then have a faint conception of their uncommon radiance.

'Besides these two young ladies, there was their waiting-woman, that under any other circumstances Tom would have looked upon as a Venus; and besides her, there was a tall, thin, dismal-faced young gentleman, half man and half boy, dressed in a childish suit of clothes very much too short in the legs and arms; and looking, according to Tom's comparison, like one of the wax juveniles from a tailor's door, grown up and run to seed. Now, this youngster stamped his foot upon the ground and looked very fierce at Tom, and Tom looked fierce at him – for to tell the truth, gentlemen, Tom more than half suspected that when they entered the room he was kissing one of the young ladies; and for anything Tom knew, you observe, it might be *his* young lady – which was not pleasant.

' "Sir," says Tom, "before we proceed any further, will you have the goodness to inform me who this young Salamander" – Tom called him that for aggravation, you perceive, gentlemen – "who this young Salamander may be?"

' "That, Mr Grig," says the old gentleman, "is my little boy. He was christened Galileo Isaac Newton Flamsteed. Don't mind him. He's a mere child."

' "And a very fine child too," says Tom – still aggravating, you'll observe – "of his age, and as good as fine, I have

9

no doubt. How do you do, my man?" with which kind and patronising expressions, Tom reached up to pat him on the head, and quoted two lines about little boys, from Doctor Watts's Hymns, which he had learnt at a Sunday School.

'It was very easy to see, gentlemen, by this youngster's frowning and by the waiting-maid's tossing her head and turning up her nose, and by the young ladies' turning their backs and talking together at the other end of the room, that nobody but the old gentleman took very kindly to the noble stranger. Indeed, Tom plainly heard the waiting-woman say of her master, that so far from being able to read the stars as he pretended, she didn't believe he knew his letters in 'em, or at best that he had got further than words in one syllable; but Tom, not minding this (for he was in spirits after the Madeira), looks with an agreeable air towards the young ladies, and, kissing his hand to both, says to the old gentleman, "Which is which?"

' "This," says the old gentleman, leading out the handsomest, if one of 'em could possibly be said to be handsomer than the other – "this is my niece, Miss Fanny Barker."

' "If you'll permit me, Miss," says Tom, "being a noble stranger and a favourite of the planets, I will conduct myself as such." With these words, he kisses the young lady in a very affable way, turns to the old gentleman, slaps him on the back, and says, "When's it to come off, my buck?"

'The young lady coloured so deep, and her lip trembled so much, gentlemen, that Tom really thought she was going to cry. But she kept her feelings down, and turning to the old gentleman, says, "Dear uncle, though you have the absolute disposal of my hand and fortune, and though you mean well in disposing of 'em thus, I ask you whether you don't think this is a mistake? Don't you think, dear uncle," she says, "that the stars must be in error? Is it not possible that the comet may have put 'em out?"

' "The stars", says the old gentleman, "couldn't make a mistake if they tried. Emma," he says to the other young lady.

' "Yes, papa," says she.

' "The same day that makes your cousin Mrs Grig will unite you to the gifted Mooney. No remonstrance – no tears. Now, Mr Grig, let me conduct you to that hallowed ground, that philosophical retreat, where my friend and partner, the gifted Mooney of whom I have just now spoken, is even now pursuing those discoveries which shall enrich us with the precious metal, and make us masters of the world. Come, Mr Grig," he says.

' "With all my heart, Sir," replies Tom; "and luck to the gifted Mooney, say I – not so much on his account as for our worthy selves!" With this sentiment, Tom kissed his hand to the ladies again, and followed him out; having the gratification to perceive, as he looked back, that they were all hanging on by the arms and legs of Galileo Isaac Newton Flamsteed, to prevent him from following the noble stranger, and tearing him to pieces.

'Gentlemen, Tom's father-in-law, that was to be, took him by the hand, and having lighted a little lamp, led him across a paved court-yard at the back of the house, into a very large, dark, gloomy room: filled with all manner of bottles, globes, books, telescopes, crocodiles, alligators, and other scientific instruments of every kind. In the centre of this room was a stove or furnace, with what Tom called a pot, but which in my opinion was a crucible, in full boil. In one corner was a sort of ladder leading through the roof; and up this ladder the old gentleman pointed, as he said in a whisper:

' "The observatory. Mr Mooney is even now watching for the precise time at which we are to come into all the riches of the earth. It will be necessary for he and I, alone in that silent place, to cast your nativity before the hour arrives. Put the day and minute of your birth on this piece of paper, and leave the rest to me."

' "You don't mean to say", says Tom, doing as he was told and giving him back the paper, "that I'm to wait here long, do you? It's a precious dismal place."

' "Hush!" says the old gentleman. "It's hallowed ground. Farewell!"

' "Stop a minute," says Tom. "What a hurry you're in! What's in that large bottle yonder?"

' "It's a child with three heads," says the old gentleman; "and everything else in proportion."

' "Why don't you throw him away?" says Tom. "What do you keep such unpleasant things here for?"

' "Throw him away!" cries the old gentleman. "We use him constantly in astrology. He's a charm."

' "I shouldn't have thought it," says Tom, "from his appearance. *Must* you go, I say?"

'The old gentleman makes him no answer, but climbs up the ladder in a greater bustle than ever. Tom looked after his legs till there was nothing of him left, and then sat down to wait; feeling (so he used to say) as comfortable as if he was going to be made a freemason, and they were heating the pokers.

'Tom waited so long, gentlemen, that he began to think it must be getting on for midnight at least, and felt more dismal and lonely than ever he had done in all his life. He tried every means of whiling away the time, but it never had seemed to move so slow. First, he took a nearer view of the child with three heads, and thought what a comfort it must have been to its parents. Then he looked up a long telescope which was pointed out of the window, but saw nothing particular, in consequence of the stopper being on at the other end. Then he came to a skeleton in a glass case, labelled "Skeleton of a Gentleman – prepared by Mr Mooney" – which made him hope that Mr Mooney might not be in the habit of preparing gentlemen that way without their own consent. A hundred times, at least, he looked into the pot where they were boiling the philosopher's stone down to the proper consistency, and wondered whether it was nearly done. "When it is," thinks Tom, "I'll send out for six-penn'orth of sprats, and turn 'em into gold fish for a first experiment." Besides which, he made up his mind, gentlemen, to have a country-house and a park; and to plant a bit of it with a double row of gas-lamps a mile long, and go out every night with a French-polished mahogany ladder, and two servants in livery behind him, to light 'em for his own pleasure.

'At length and at last, the old gentleman's legs appeared upon the steps leading through the roof, and he came slowly down: bringing along with him, the gifted Mooney. This Mooney, gentlemen, was even more scientific in appearance than his friend; and had, as Tom often declared upon his word and honour, the dirtiest face we can possibly know of, in this imperfect state of existence.

'Gentlemen, you are all aware that if a scientific man isn't absent in his mind, he's of no good at all. Mr Mooney was so absent, that when the old gentleman said to him, "Shake hands with Mr Grig," he put out his leg. "Here's a mind, Mr Grig!" cries the old gentleman in a rapture. "Here's philosophy! Here's rumination! Don't disturb him," he says, "for this is amazing!"

'Tom had no wish to disturb him, having nothing particular to say; but he was so uncommonly amazing, that the old gentleman got impatient, and determined to give him an electric shock to bring him to – "for you must know, Mr Grig," he says, "that we always keep a strongly charged battery, ready for that purpose." These means being resorted to, gentlemen, the gifted Mooney revived with a loud roar, and he no sooner came to himself than both he and the old gentleman looked at Tom with compassion, and shed tears abundantly.

' "My dear friend," says the old gentleman to the Gifted, "prepare him."

' "I say," cries Tom, falling back, "none of that, you know. No preparing by Mr Mooney if you please."

' "Alas!" replies the old gentleman, "you don't understand us. My friend, inform him of his fate – I can't."

'The Gifted mustered up his voice, after many efforts, and

13

informed Tom that his nativity had been carefully cast, and he would expire at exactly thirty-five minutes, twenty-seven seconds, and five-sixths of a second past nine o'clock, a.m., on that day two months.

'Gentlemen, I leave you to judge what were Tom's feelings at this announcement, on the eve of matrimony and endless riches. "I think", he says in a trembling voice, "there must be a mistake in the working of that sum. Will you do me the favour to cast it up again?" – "There is no mistake," replies the old gentleman, "it is confirmed by Francis Moore, Physician. Here is the prediction for tomorrow two months." And he showed him the page, where sure enough were these words – "The decease of a great person may be looked for, about this time."

' "Which", says the old gentleman, "is clearly you, Mr Grig."

' "Too clearly," cries Tom, sinking into a chair, and giving one hand to the old gentleman, and one to the Gifted. "The orb of day has set on Thomas Grig for ever!"

'At this affecting remark, the Gifted shed tears again, and the other two mingled their tears with his, in a kind – if I may use the expression – of Mooney and Co.'s entire. But the old gentleman recovering first, observed that this was only a reason for hastening the marriage, in order that Tom's distinguished race might be transmitted to posterity; and requesting the Gifted to console Mr Grig during his temporary absence, he withdrew to settle the preliminaries with his niece immediately.

'And now, gentlemen, a very extraordinary and remarkable occurrence took place; for as Tom sat in a melancholy way in one chair, and the Gifted sat in a melancholy way in another, a couple of doors were thrown violently open, the two young ladies rushed in, and one knelt down in a loving attitude at Tom's feet, and the other at the Gifted's. So far, perhaps, as Tom was concerned – as he used to say – you will say there was nothing strange in this: but you will be of a different opinion when you understand that Tom's young lady was kneeling to the Gifted, and the Gifted's young lady was kneeling to Tom.

' "Halloa! stop a minute!" cries Tom, "Here's a mistake. I need condoling with by sympathising woman, under my afflicting circumstances; but we're out in the figure. Change partners, Mooney."

' "Monster!" cries Tom's young lady, clinging to the Gifted.

' "Miss!" says Tom. "Is *that* your manners?"

' "I abjure thee!" cries Tom's young lady. "I renounce thee. I never will be thine. Thou", she says to the Gifted, "art the object of my first and all-engrossing passion. Wrapt in thy sublime visions, thou hast not perceived my love; but, driven to despair, I now shake off the woman and avow it. Oh, cruel, cruel man!" With which reproach she laid her head upon the Gifted's breast, and put her arms about him in the tenderest manner possible, gentlemen.

' "And I," says the other young lady, in a sort of ecstasy, that made Tom start – "I hereby abjure my chosen husband too. Hear me, Goblin!" – this was to the Gifted – "Hear me! I hold thee in the deepest detestation. The maddening interview of this one night has filled my soul with love – but not for thee. It is for thee, for thee, young man," she cries to Tom. "As Monk Lewis finely observes, Thomas, Thomas, I am thine, Thomas, Thomas, thou art mine: thine for ever, mine for ever!" with which words, she became very tender likewise.

'Tom and the Gifted, gentlemen, as you may believe, looked at each other in a very awkward manner, and with thoughts not at all complimentary to the two young ladies. As to the Gifted, I have heard Tom say often, that he was certain he was in a fit, and had it inwardly.

' "Speak to me! Oh, speak to me!" cries Tom's young lady to the Gifted.

' "I don't want to speak to anybody," he says, finding his

voice at last, and trying to push her away. "I think I had better go. I'm – I'm frightened," he says, looking about as if he had lost something.

' "Not one look of love!" she cries. "Hear me while I declare—"

' "I don't know how to look a look of love," he says, all in a maze. "Don't declare anything. I don't want to hear anybody."

' "That's right!" cries the old gentleman (who it seems had been listening). "That's right! Don't hear her. Emma shall marry you tomorrow, my friend, whether she likes it or not, and *she* shall marry Mr Grig."

'Gentlemen, these words were no sooner out of his mouth than Galileo Isaac Newton Flamsteed (who it seems had been listening too) darts in, and spinning round and round, like a young giant's top, cries, "Let her. Let her. I'm fierce; I'm furious. I give her leave. I'll never marry anybody after this – never. It isn't safe. She is the falsest of the false," he cries, tearing his hair and gnashing his teeth; "and I'll live and die a bachelor!"

' "The little boy," observed the Gifted gravely, "albeit of tender years, has spoken wisdom. I have been led to the contemplation of woman-kind, and will not adventure on the troubled waters of matrimony."

' "What!" says the old gentleman, "not marry my daughter! Won't you, Mooney? Not if I make her? Won't you? Won't you?"

' "No," says Mooney, "I won't. And if anybody asks me any more, I'll run away, and never come back again."

' "Mr Grig," says the old gentleman, "the stars must be obeyed. You have not changed your mind because of a little girlish folly – eh, Mr Grig?"

'Tom, gentlemen, had had his eyes about him, and was pretty sure that all this was a device and trick of the waiting-maid, to put him off his inclination. He had seen her hiding and skipping about the two doors, and had observed that a very little whispering from her pacified the Salamander directly. "So," thinks Tom, "this is a plot – but it won't fit."

' "Eh, Mr Grig?" says the old gentleman.

' "Why, Sir," says Tom, pointing to the crucible, "if the soup's nearly ready—"

' "Another hour beholds the consummation of our labours," returned the old gentleman.

' "Very good," says Tom, with a mournful air. "It's only for two months, but I may as well be the richest man in the world even for that time. I'm not particular, I'll take her, Sir. I'll take her."

'The old gentleman was in a rapture to find Tom still in the same mind, and drawing the young lady towards him by little and little, was joining their hands by main force, when all of a sudden, gentlemen, the crucible blows up, with a great crash; everybody screams; the room is filled with smoke; and Tom, not knowing what may happen next, throws himself into a Fancy attitude, and says, "Come on, if you're a man!" without addressing himself to anybody in particular.

' "The labours of fifteen years", says the old gentleman, clasping his hands and looking down upon the Gifted, who was saving the pieces, "are destroyed in an instant!" – And I am told, gentlemen, by-the-bye, that this same philosopher's stone would have been discovered a hundred times at least, to speak within bounds, if it wasn't for the one unfortunate circumstance that the apparatus always blows up, when it's on the very point of succeeding.

'Tom turns pale when he hears the old gentleman expressing himself to this unpleasant effect, and stammers out that if it's quite agreeable to all parties, he would like to know exactly what has happened, and what change has really taken place in the prospects of that company.

' "We have failed for the present, Mr Grig," says the old gentleman, wiping his forehead. "And I regret it the more, because I have in fact invested my niece's five thousand pounds in this glorious speculation. But don't be cast down," he says, anxiously – "in another fifteen years, Mr Grig—"

' "Oh!" cries Tom, letting the young lady's hand fall. "Were the stars very positive about this union, Sir?"

' "They were," says the old gentleman.

' "I'm sorry to hear it," Tom makes answer, "for it's no go, Sir."

' "No what!" cries the old gentleman.

' "Go, Sir," says Tom, fiercely. "I forbid the banns." And with these words – which are the very words he used – he sat himself down in a chair, and, laying his head upon the table, thought with a secret grief of what was to come to pass on that day two months.

'Tom always said, gentlemen, that that waiting-maid was the artfullest minx he had ever seen; and he left it in writing in this country when he went to colonise abroad, that he was certain in his own mind she and the Salamander had blown up the philosopher's stone on purpose, and to cut him out of his property. I believe Tom was in the right, gentlemen; but whether or no, she comes forward at this point, and says, "May I speak, Sir?" and the old gentleman answering, "Yes, you may," she goes on to say that "the stars are no doubt quite right in every respect, but Tom is not the man." And she says, "Don't you remember, Sir, that when the clock struck five this afternoon, you gave Master Galileo a rap on the head with your telescope, and told him to get out of the way?" "Yes, I do," says the old gentleman. "Then," says the waiting-maid, "I say he's the man, and the prophecy is fulfilled."

'The old gentleman staggers at this, as if somebody had hit him a blow on the chest, and cries, "He! why he's a boy!" Upon that, gentlemen, the Salamander cries out that he'll be twenty-one next Lady-day; and complains that his father has always been so busy with the sun round which the earth revolves, that he has never taken any notice of the son that revolves round him; and that he hasn't had a new suit of clothes since he was fourteen; and that he wasn't even taken out of nankeen frocks and trousers till he was quite unpleasant in 'em; and touches on a good many more family matters to the same purpose. To make short of a long story, gentlemen, they all talk together, and cry together, and remind the old gentleman that as to the noble family, his own grandfather would have been lord mayor if he hadn't died at a dinner the year before; and they show him by all kinds of arguments that if the cousins are married, the prediction comes true every way. At last, the old gentleman being quite convinced, gives in; and joins their hands; and leaves his daughter to marry anybody she likes; and they are all well pleased; and the Gifted as well as any of them.

'In the middle of this little family party, gentlemen, sits Tom all the while, as miserable as you like. But, when everything else is arranged, the old gentleman's daughter says that their strange conduct was a little device of the waiting-maid's to disgust the lovers he had chosen for 'em, and will he forgive her? and if he will, perhaps he might even find her a husband – and when she says that, she looks uncommon hard at Tom. Then the waiting-maid says that, oh dear! she couldn't abear Mr Grig should think she wanted him to marry her; and that she had even gone so far as to refuse the last lamplighter, who was now a literary character (having set up as a bill-sticker); and that she hoped Mr Grig would not suppose she was on her last legs by any means, for the baker was very strong in his attentions at that moment, and as to the butcher, he was frantic. And I don't know how much more she might have said, gentlemen (for, as you know, this kind of young women are rare ones to talk), if the old gentleman hadn't cut in suddenly, and asked Tom if he'd have her, with ten pounds to recompense him for his loss of time and disappointment, and as a kind of bribe to keep the story secret.

' "It don't much matter, Sir," says Tom, "I ain't long for this world. Eight weeks of marriage, especially with this young woman, might reconcile me to my fate. I think", he says, "I could go off easy after that." With which he embraces her with a very dismal face, and groans in a way that might move a heart of stone – even of philosopher's stone.

' "Egad," says the old gentleman, "that reminds me – this bustle put it out of my head – there was a figure wrong. He'll live to a green old age – eighty-seven at least!"

' "How much, Sir?" cries Tom.

' "Eighty-seven!" says the old gentleman.

'Without another word, Tom flings himself on the old gentleman's neck; throws up his hat; cuts a caper; defies the waiting-maid; and refers her to the butcher.

' "You won't marry her!" says the old gentleman, angrily.

' "And live after it!" says Tom. "I'd sooner marry a mermaid with a small-tooth comb and looking-glass."

' "Then take the consequences," says the other.

'With those words – I beg your kind attention here, gentlemen, for it's worth your notice – the old gentleman wetted the forefinger of his right hand in some of the liquor from the crucible that was spilt on the floor, and drew a small triangle on Tom's forehead. The room swam before his eyes, and he found himself in the watch-house.'

'Found himself *where?*' cried the vice, on behalf of the company generally.

'In the watch-house,' said the chairman. 'It was late at night, and he found himself in the very watch-house from which he had been let out that morning.'

'Did he go home?' asked the vice.

'The watch-house people rather objected to that,' said the chairman; 'so he stopped there that night, and went before the magistrate in the morning. "Why, you're here again, are you?" says the magistrate, adding insult to injury; "we'll trouble you for five shillings more, if you can conveniently spare the money." Tom told him he had been enchanted, but it was of no use. He told the contractors the same, but they wouldn't believe him. It was very hard upon him, gentlemen, as he often said, for was it likely he'd go and invent such a tale? They shook their heads and told him he'd say anything but his prayers – as indeed he would; there's no doubt about that. It was the only imputation on his moral character that ever *I* heard of.'

Relics of General Chassé

A TALE OF ANTWERP

ANTHONY TROLLOPE

That Belgium is now one of the European kingdoms, living by its own laws, resting on its own bottom, with a king and court, palaces and parliament of its own, is known to all the world. And a very nice little kingdom it is; full of old towns, fine Flemish pictures, and interesting Gothic churches. But in the memory of very many of us who do not think ourselves old men, Belgium, as it is now called – in those days it used to be Flanders and Brabant – was a part of Holland, and it obtained its own independence by a revolution. In that revolution the most important military step was the siege of Antwerp, which was defended on the part of the Dutch by General Chassé, with the utmost gallantry, but nevertheless ineffectually.

After the siege Antwerp became quite a show place; and among the visitors who flocked there to talk of the gallant general, and to see what remained of the great effort which he had made to defend the place, were two Englishmen. One was the hero of this little history; and the other was a young man of considerably less weight in the world. The less I say of the latter the better; but it is necessary that I should give some description of the former.

The Rev. Augustus Horne was, at the time of my narrative, a beneficed clergyman of the Church of England. The profession which he had graced sat easily on him. Its external marks and signs were as pleasing to his friends as were its internal comforts to himself. He was a man of much quiet mirth, full of polished wit, and on some rare occasions he could descend to the more noisy hilarity of a joke. Loved by his friends, he loved all the world. He had known no care and seen no sorrow. Always intended for holy orders, he had entered them without a scruple, and remained within their pale without a regret. At twenty-four he had been a deacon, at twenty-seven a priest, at thirty a rector, and at thirty-five a prebendary; and as his rectory was rich and his prebendal stall well paid, the Rev. Augustus Horne was called by all, and called himself, a happy man. His stature was about six feet two, and his corpulence exceeded even those bounds which symmetry would have preferred as being most perfectly compatible even with such a height. But nevertheless Mr Horne was a well-made man; his hands and feet were small; his face was handsome, frank, and full of expression; his bright eyes twinkled with humour; his finely cut mouth disclosed two marvellous rows of well-preserved ivory; and his slightly aquiline nose was just such a projection as one would wish to see on the face of a well-fed, good-natured dignitary of the Church of England. When I add to all this that the reverend gentleman was as generous as he was rich – and the kind mother in whose arms he had been nurtured had taken care that he should never want – I need hardly say that I was blessed with a very pleasant travelling companion.

I must mention one more interesting particular. Mr Horne was rather inclined to dandyism, in an innocent way. His clerical starched neckcloth was always of the whitest, his cambric handkerchief of the finest, his bands adorned with the broadest border; his sable suit never degenerated to a rusty brown; it not only gave on all occasions glossy evidence of freshness, but also of the talent which the artisan had displayed in turning out a well-dressed clergyman of the Church of England. His hair was ever brushed with scrupulous attention, and showed in its regular waves the guardian care of each separate bristle. And all this was done with that ease and grace which should be the characteristics of a dignitary of the established English Church.

I had accompanied Mr Horne to the Rhine; and we had reached Brussels on our return, just at the close of that revolution which ended in affording a throne to the son-in-law of George the Fourth. At that moment General Chassé's name and fame were in every man's mouth, and, like other curious admirers of the brave, Mr Horne determined to devote two days to the scene of the late events at Antwerp. Antwerp, moreover, possesses perhaps the finest spire, and certainly one of the three or four finest pictures, in the world. Of General Chassé, of the cathedral, and of the Rubens, I had heard much, and was therefore well pleased that such should be his resolution. This accomplished, we were to return to Brussels; and thence, via Ghent, Ostend, and Dover, I to complete my legal studies in London, and Mr Horne to enjoy once more the peaceful retirement of Ollerton rectory. As we were to be absent from Brussels but one night we were enabled to indulge in the gratification of travelling without our luggage. A small *sac-de-nuit* was prepared; brushes, combs, razors, strops, a change of linen, &c. &c., were carefully put up; but our heavy baggage, our coats, waistcoats, and other wearing apparel were unnecessary. It was delightful to feel oneself so light-handed. The reverend gentleman, with my humble self by his side, left the portal of the Hôtel de Belle Vue at 7 a.m., in good humour with all the world. There were no railroads in those days; but a cabriolet, big enough to hold six persons, with rope traces and corresponding appendages, deposited us at the Golden Fleece in something less than six hours. The inward man was duly fortified, and we started for the castle.

It boots not here to describe the effects which gunpowder and grape-shot had had on the walls of Antwerp. Let the curious in these matters read the horrors of the siege of Troy, or the history of Jerusalem taken by Titus. The one may be found in Homer, and the other in Josephus. Or if they prefer doings of a later date there is the taking of Sebastopol, as narrated in the columns of *The Times* newspaper. The accounts are equally true, instructive, and intelligible. In the meantime allow the Rev. Augustus Horne and myself to enter the private chambers of the renowned though defeated general.

We rambled for a while through the covered way, over the glacis and along the counterscarp, and listened to the guide as he detailed to us, in already accustomed words, how the siege had gone. Then we got into the private apartments of the general, and, having dexterously shaken off our attendant, wandered at large among the deserted rooms.

'It is clear that no one ever comes here,' said I.

'No,' said the Rev. Augustus; 'it seems not; and to tell the truth, I don't know why anyone should come. The chambers in themselves are not attractive.'

What he said was true. They were plain, ugly, square, unfurnished rooms, here a big one and there a little one, as is usual in most houses – unfurnished, that is, for the most part. In one place we did find a table and a few chairs, in another a bedstead, and so on. But to me it was pleasant to indulge in those ruminations which any traces of the great or unfortunate create in softly sympathising minds. For a time we communicated our thoughts to each other as we roamed free as air through the apartments; and then I lingered for a few moments behind, while Mr Horne moved on with a quicker step.

At last I entered the bedchamber of the general, and there I overtook my friend. He was inspecting, with much attention, an article of the great man's wardrobe which he held in his hand. It was precisely that virile habiliment to which a well-known gallant captain alludes in his conversation with the posthumous appearance of Miss Bailey, as containing a Bank of England 5*l.* note.

'The general must have been a large man, George, or he would hardly have filled these,' said Mr Horne, holding up to the light the respectable leathern articles in question. 'He must have been a very large man – the largest man in

Antwerp, I should think; or else his tailor has done him more than justice.'

They were certainly large, and had about them a charming regimental military appearance. They were made of white leather, with bright metal buttons at the knees and bright metal buttons at the top. They owned no pockets, and were, with the exception of the legitimate outlet, continuous in the circumference of the waistband. No dangling strings gave them an appearance of senile imbecility. Were it not for a certain rigidity, sternness, and mental inflexibility – we will call it military ardour – with which they were imbued, they would have created envy in the bosom of a fox-hunter.

Mr Horne was no fox-hunter, but still he seemed to be irresistibly taken with the lady-like propensity of wishing to wear them. 'Surely, George,' he said, 'the general must have been a stouter man than I am' – and he contemplated his own proportions with complacency – 'these what's-the-names are quite big enough for me.'

I differed in opinion, and was obliged to explain that I thought he did the good living of Ollerton insufficient justice.

'I am sure they are large enough for me,' he repeated, with considerable obstinacy. I smiled incredulously, and then to settle the matter he resolved that he would try them on. Nobody had been in these rooms for the last hour, and it appeared as though they were never visited. Even the guide had not come on with us, but was employed in showing other parties about the fortifications. It was clear that this portion of the building was left desolate, and that the experiment might be safely made. So the sportive rector declared that he would for a short time wear the regimentals which had once contained the valorous heart of General Chassé.

With all decorum the Rev. Mr Horne divested himself of the work of the London artist's needle, and, carefully placing his own garments beyond the reach of dust, essayed to fit himself in military garb.

26

At that important moment – at the critical instant of the attempt – the clatter of female voices was heard approaching the chamber. They must have suddenly come round some passage corner, for it was evident by the sound that they were close upon us before we had any warning of their advent. At this very minute Mr Horne was somewhat embarrassed in his attempts, and was not fully in possession of his usual active powers of movement, nor of his usual presence of mind. He only looked for escape; and seeing a door partly open he with difficulty retreated through it, and I followed him. We found that we were in a small dressing-room; and as by good luck the door was defended by an inner bolt, my friend was able to protect himself.

'There shall be another siege, at any rate as stout as the last, before I surrender,' said he.

As the ladies seemed inclined to linger in the room it became a matter of importance that the above-named articles should fit, not only for ornament but for use. It was very cold, and Mr Horne was altogether unused to move in a Highland sphere of life. But alas, alas! General Chassé had not been nurtured in the classical retirement of Ollerton. The ungiving leather would stretch no point to accommodate the divine, though it had been willing to minister to the convenience of the soldier. Mr Horne was vexed and chilled; and throwing the now hateful garments into a corner and protecting himself from the cold as best he might by standing with his knees together and his body somewhat bent so as to give the skirts of his coat an opportunity of doing extra duty, he begged me to see if those jabbering females were not going to leave him in peace to recover his own property. I accordingly went to the door, and opening it to a small extent I peeped through.

Who shall describe my horror at the sight which I then saw? The scene, which had hitherto been tinted with comic effect, was now becoming so decidedly tragic that I did not dare at once to acquaint my worthy pastor with that which was occurring – and, alas! had already occurred.

Five country-women of our own – it was easy to know them by their dress and general aspect – were standing in the middle of the room; and one of them, the centre of the group, the senior of the lot, a maiden lady – I could have sworn to that – with a red nose, held in one hand a huge pair of scissors and in the other – the already devoted goods of my most unfortunate companion! Down from the waistband, through that goodly expanse, a fell gash had already gone through and through; and in useless, unbecoming disorder the broadcloth fell pendent from her arm on this side and on that. At that moment I confess that I had not the courage to speak to Mr Horne – not even to look at him.

I must describe that group. Of the figure next to me I could only see the back. It was a broad back done up in silk not of the newest. The whole figure, one may say, was dumpy. The black silk was not long, as dresses now are worn, nor wide in its skirts. In every way it was skimpy, considering the breadth it had to cover; and below the silk I saw the heels of two thick shoes, and enough to swear by of two woollen stockings. Above the silk was a red-and-blue shawl; and above that a ponderous, elaborate brown bonnet, as to the materials of which I should not wish to undergo an examination. Over and beyond this I could only see the backs of her two hands. They were held up as though in wonder at that which the red-nosed holder of the scissors had dared to do.

Opposite to this lady, and with her face fully turned to me, was a kindly-looking, fat motherly woman, with light-coloured hair not in the best order. She was hot and scarlet with exercise, being perhaps too stout for the steep steps of the fortress; and in one hand she held a handkerchief, with which from time to time she wiped her brow. In the other hand she held one of the extremities of my friend's property, feeling – good, careful soul! – what was the texture of the cloth. As she did so, I could see a glance of approbation pass across her warm features. I liked that lady's face, in spite of

her untidy hair, and felt that had she been alone my friend would not have been injured.

On either side of her there stood a flaxen-haired maiden, with long curls, large blue eyes, fresh red cheeks, an undefined lumpy nose, and large good-humoured mouth. They were as like as two peas, only that one was half an inch taller than the other; and there was no difficulty in discovering, at a moment's glance, that they were the children of that overheated matron who was feeling the web of my friend's cloth.

But the principal figure was she who held the centre place in the group. She was tall and thin, with fierce-looking eyes rendered more fierce by the spectacles which she wore; with a red nose as I said before; and about her an undescribable something which quite convinced me that she had never known – could never know – aught of the comforts of married life. It was she who held the scissors and the black garments. It was she who had given that unkind cut. As I looked at her she whisked herself quickly round from one companion to the other, triumphing in what she had done, and ready to triumph further in what she was about to do. I immediately conceived a deep hatred for that Queen of the Harpies.

'Well, I suppose they can't be wanted again,' said the mother, rubbing her forehead.

'Oh, dear, no!' said she of the red nose. 'They are relics!'

I thought to leap forth; but for what purpose should I have leaped? The accursed scissors had already done their work; and the symmetry, nay, even the utility of the vestment was destroyed.

'General Chassé wore a very good article; I will say that for him,' continued the mother.

'Of course he did!' said the Queen Harpy. 'Why should he not, seeing that the country paid for it for him? Well, ladies, who's for having a bit?'

'Oh, my! you won't go for to cut them up,' said the stout back.

'Won't I?' said the scissors; and she immediately made another incision. 'Who's for having a bit? Don't all speak at once.'

'I should like a morsel for a pin-cushion,' said flaxen-haired Miss No. 1, a young lady about nineteen, actuated by a general affection for all sword-bearing, fire-eating heroes. 'I should like to have something to make me think of the poor general!'

Snip, snip went the scissors with professional rapidity, and a round piece was extracted from the back of the calf of the left leg. I shuddered with horror; and so did the Rev. Augustus Horne with cold.

'I hardly think it's proper to cut them up,' said Miss No. 2.

'Oh, isn't it?' said the harpy. 'Then I'll do what's improper!' And she got her finger and thumb well through the holes in the scissors' handles. As she spoke resolution was plainly marked on her brow.

'Well, if they are to be cut up, I should certainly like a bit for a pen-wiper,' said No. 2. No. 2. was a literary young lady with a periodical correspondence, a journal, and an album. Snip, snip went the scissors again, and the broad part of the upper right division afforded ample materials for a pen-wiper.

Then the lady with the back, seeing that the desecration of the article had been completed, plucked up heart of courage and put in her little request: 'I think I might have a needle-case out of it,' said she, 'just as a *suvneer* of the poor general' – and a long fragment cut rapidly out of the waistband afforded her unqualified delight.

Mamma, with the hot face and untidy hair, came next. 'Well, girls,' she said, 'as you are all served, I don't see why I'm to be left out. Perhaps, Miss Grogram' – she was an old maid, you see – 'perhaps, Miss Grogram, you could get me as much as would make a decent-sized reticule.'

There was not the slightest difficulty in doing this. The harpy in the centre again went to work, snip, snip, and extracting from that portion of the affairs which usually sustained the greater portion of Mr Horne's weight two large round pieces of cloth, presented them to the well-pleased matron. 'The general knew well where to get a bit of good broadcloth, certainly,' said she, again feeling the pieces.

'And now for No. 1,' said she whom I so absolutely hated; 'I think there is still enough for a pair of slippers. There's nothing so nice for the house as good black cloth slippers that are warm to the feet and don't show the dirt.' And so saying, she spread out on the floor the lacerated remainders.

'There's a nice bit there,' said young lady No. 2, poking at one of the pockets with the end of her parasol.

'Yes,' said the harpy, contemplating her plunder. 'But I'm thinking whether I couldn't get leggings as well. I always wear leggings in the thick of the winter.' And so she concluded her operations, and there was nothing left but a melancholy skeleton of seams and buttons.

All this having been achieved, they pocketed their plunder and prepared to depart. There are people who have a wonderful appetite for relics. A stone with which Washington had broken a window when a boy – with which he had done so or had not, for there is little difference; a button that was on a coat of Napoleon's, or on that of one of his lackeys; a bullet said to have been picked up at Waterloo or Bunker's Hill; these and suchlike things are great treasures. And their most desirable characteristic is the ease with which they are attained. Any bullet or any button does the work. Faith alone is necessary. And now these ladies had made themselves happy and glorious with 'relics' of General Chassé cut from the ill-used habiliments of an elderly English gentleman!

They departed at last, and Mr Horne, for once in an ill-humour, followed me into the bedroom. Here I must be excused if I draw a veil over his manly sorrow at discovering what fate had done for him. Remember what was his position, unclothed in the castle of Antwerp! The nearest suitable change for those which had been destroyed was locked up in his portmanteau at the Hôtel de Belle Vue in Brussels! He had nothing left to him – literally nothing, in that Antwerp world. There was no other wretched being wandering then in that Dutch town so utterly denuded of the goods of life. For what is a man fit – for what can he be fit – when left in such a position? There are some evils which seem utterly to crush a man; and if there be any misfortune to which a man may be allowed to succumb without imputation on his manliness, surely it is such as this. How was Mr Horne to return to his hotel without incurring the displeasure of the municipality? That was my first thought.

He had a cloak, but it was at the inn; and I found that my friend was oppressed with a great horror at the idea of being left alone; so that I could not go in search of it. There is an old saying, that no man is a hero to his *valet de chambre* – the reason doubtless being this, that it is customary for his valet to see the hero divested of those trappings in which so much of the heroic consists. Who reverences a clergyman without his gown, or a warrior without his sword and *sabre-tasche*? What would even Minerva be without her helmet?

I do not wish it to be understood that I no longer reverenced Mr Horne because he was in an undress; but he himself certainly lost much of his composed, well-sustained dignity of demeanour. He was fearful and querulous, cold, and rather cross. When, forgetting his size, I offered him my own he thought that I was laughing at him. He began to be afraid that the story would get abroad, and he then and there exacted a promise that I would never tell it during his lifetime. I have kept my word; but now my old friend has been gathered to his fathers, full of years.

At last I got him to the hotel. It was long before he would leave the castle, cloaked though he was; not, indeed, till the shades of evening had dimmed the outlines of men and things, and made indistinct the outward garniture of those who passed to and fro in the streets. Then, wrapped in his cloak, Mr Horne followed me along the quays and through

32

the narrowest of the streets; and at length, without venturing
to return the gaze of anyone in the hotel court, he made his
way up to his own bedroom.

Dinnerless and supperless he went to his couch. But when
there he did consent to receive some consolation in the shape
of mutton cutlets and fried potatoes, a savoury omelet, and a
bottle of claret. The mutton cutlets and fried potatoes at the
Golden Fleece at Antwerp are – or were then, for I am speaking now of well-nigh thirty years since – remarkably good;
the claret, also, was of the best; and so, by degrees, the look of
despairing dismay passed from his face, and some scintilla-
tions of the old fire returned to his eyes.

'I wonder whether they find themselves much happier for
what they have got?' said he.

'A great deal happier,' said I. 'They'll boast of those things
to all their friends at home, and we shall doubtless see some
account of their success in the newspapers.'

'It would be delightful to expose their blunder – to show
them up. Would it not, George? To turn the tables on them?'

'Yes,' said I. 'I should like to have the laugh against them.'

'So would I, only that I should compromise myself by
telling the story. It wouldn't do at all to have it told at Oxford
with my name attached to it.'

To this also I assented. To what would I not have assented
in my anxiety to make him happy after his misery?

But all was not over yet. He was in bed now, but it was
necessary that he should rise again on the morrow. At home,
in England, what was required might perhaps have been
made during the night; but here, among the slow Flemings,
any such exertion would have been impossible. Mr Horne,
moreover, had no desire to be troubled in his retirement by a
tailor.

Now the landlord of the Golden Fleece was a very stout
man – a very stout man indeed. Looking at him as he stood
with his hands in his pockets at the portal of his own establishment, I could not but think that he was stouter even than

Mr Horne. But then he was certainly much shorter, and the want of due proportion probably added to his unwieldy appearance. I walked round him once or twice wishfully, measuring him in my eye, and thinking of what texture might be the Sunday best of such a man. The clothes which he then had on were certainly not exactly suited to Mr Horne's tastes.

He saw that I was observing him, and appeared uneasy and offended. I had already ascertained that he spoke a little English. Of Flemish I knew literally nothing, and in French, with which probably he was also acquainted, I was by no means voluble. The business which I had to transact was intricate, and I required the use of my mother-tongue.

It was intricate and delicate, and difficult withal. I began by remarking on the weather, but he did not take my remarks kindly. I am inclined to fancy that he thought I was desirous of borrowing money from him. At any rate he gave me no encouragement in my first advances.

'Vat misfortune?' at last he asked, when I had succeeded in making him understand that a gentleman upstairs required his assistance.

'He has lost these things,' and I took hold of my own garments. 'It's a long story, or I'd tell you how; but he has not a pair in the world till he gets back to Brussels – unless you can lend him one.'

'Lost hees br—?' and he opened his eyes wide, and looked at me with astonishment.

'Yes, yes, exactly so,' said I, interrupting him. 'Most astonishing thing, isn't it? But it's quite true.'

'Vas hees money in de pocket?' asked my suspicious landlord.

'No, no, no. It's not so bad as that. His money is all right. I had the money, luckily.'

'Ah, dat is better! But he have lost hees b—?'

'Yes, yes'; I was now getting rather impatient. 'There is no mistake about it. He has lost them as sure as you stand there.'

34

And then I proceeded to explain that as the gentleman in question was very stout, and as he, the landlord, was stout also, he might assist us in this great calamity by a loan from his own wardrobe.

When he found that the money was not in the pocket, and that his bill therefore would be paid, he was not indisposed to be gracious. He would, he said, desire his servant to take up what was required to Mr Horne's chamber. I endeavoured to make him understand that a sombre colour would be preferable; but he only answered that he would put the best that he had at the gentleman's disposal. He could not think of offering anything less than his best on such an occasion. And then he turned his back and went his way, muttering as he went something in Flemish, which I believed to be an exclamation of astonishment that any man should, under any circumstances, lose such an article.

It was now getting late; so when I had taken a short stroll by myself, I went to bed without disturbing Mr Horne again that night. On the following morning I thought it best not to go to him unless he sent for me; so I desired the boots to let him know that I had ordered breakfast in a private room, and that I would await him there unless he wished to see me. He sent me word back to say that he would be with me very shortly.

He did not keep me waiting above half an hour, but I confess that that half-hour was not pleasantly spent. I feared that his temper would be tried in dressing, and that he would not be able to eat his breakfast in a happy state of mind. So that when I heard his heavy footstep advancing along the passage my heart did misgive me, and I felt that I was trembling.

That step was certainly slower and more ponderous than usual. There was always a certain dignity in the very sound of his movements, but now this seemed to have been enhanced. To judge merely by the step one would have said that a bishop was coming that way instead of a prebendary.

And then he entered. In the upper half of his august person

35

no alteration was perceptible. The hair was as regular and as graceful as ever, the handkerchief as white, the coat as immaculate; but below his well-filled waistcoat a pair of red plush began to shine in unmitigated splendour, and continued from thence down to within an inch above his knee; nor, as it appeared, could any pulling induce them to descend lower. Mr Horne always wore black silk stockings – at least so the world supposed – but it was now apparent that the world had been wrong in presuming him to be guilty of such extravagance. Those, at any rate, which he exhibited on the present occasion were more economical. They were silk to the calf, but thence upwards they continued their career in white cotton. These then followed the plush; first two snowy, full-sized pillars of white, and then two jet columns of flossy silk. Such was the appearance, on that well-remembered morning, of the Rev. Augustus Horne, as he entered the room in which his breakfast was prepared.

I could see at a glance that a dark frown contracted his eyebrows, and that the compressed muscles of his upper lip gave a strange degree of austerity to his open face. He carried his head proudly on high, determined to be dignified in spite of his misfortunes, and advanced two steps into the room without a remark, as though he were able to show that neither red plush nor black cloth could disarrange the equal poise of his mighty mind!

And after all what are a man's garments but the outward husks in which the fruit is kept, duly tempered, from the wind?

> The rank is but the guinea stamp,
> The man's the gowd for a' that.

And is not the tailor's art as little worthy, as insignificant as that of the king who makes

> A marquis, duke, and a' that?

Who would be content to think that his manly dignity depended on his coat and waistcoat, or his hold on the world's esteem on any other garment of usual wear? That no such weakness soiled his mind Mr Horne was determined to prove; and thus he entered the room with measured tread and stern dignified demeanour.

Having advanced two steps his eye caught mine. I do not know whether he was moved by some unconscious smile on my part; for in truth I endeavoured to seem as indifferent as himself to the nature of his dress; or whether he was invincibly tickled by some inward fancy of his own, but suddenly his advancing step ceased, a broad flash of comic humour spread itself over his features, he retreated with his back against the wall, and then burst out into an immoderate roar of loud laughter.

And I – what else could I then do but laugh? He laughed, and I laughed. He roared, and I roared. He lifted up his vast legs to view till the rays of the morning sun shone through the window on the bright hues which he displayed; and he did not sit down to his breakfast till he had in every fantastic attitude shown off to the best advantage the red plush of which he had so recently become proud.

An Antwerp private cabriolet on that day reached the yard of the Hôtel de Belle Vue at about 4 p.m., and four waiters, in a frenzy of astonishment, saw the Rev. Augustus Horne descend from the vehicle and seek his chamber dressed in the garments which I have described. But I am inclined to think that he never again favoured any of his friends with such a sight.

It was on the next evening after this that I went out to drink tea with two maiden ladies, relatives of mine, who kept a seminary for English girls at Brussels. The Misses Macmanus were very worthy women, and earned their bread in an upright, painstaking manner. I would not for worlds have passed through Brussels without paying them this compliment. They were, however, perhaps a little dull, and I was aware that I should not probably meet in their drawing-room many of the fashionable inhabitants of the city. Mr Horne had declined to accompany me; but in doing so he was good enough to express a warm admiration for the character of my worthy cousins.

The elder Miss Macmanus, in her little note, had informed me that she would have the pleasure of introducing me to a few of my 'compatriots'. I presumed she meant Englishmen; and as I was in the habit of meeting such every day of my life at home, I cannot say that I was peculiarly elevated by the promise. When, however, I entered the room, there was no Englishman there – there was no man of any kind. There were twelve ladies collected together with the view of making the evening pass agreeably to me, the single virile being among them all. I felt as though I were a sort of Mohammed in Paradise; but I certainly felt also that the Paradise was none of my own choosing.

In the centre of the amphitheatre which the ladies formed sat the two Misses Macmanus – there, at least, they sat when they had completed the process of shaking hands with me. To the left of them, making one wing of the semicircle, were arranged the five pupils by attending to whom the Misses Macmanus earned their living; the other wing consisted of the five ladies who had furnished themselves with relics of General Chassé. They were my 'compatriots'.

I was introduced to them all, one after the other; but their names did not abide in my memory one moment. I was thinking too much of the singularity of the adventure, and could not attend to such minutiae. That the red-nosed harpy was Miss Grogram, that I remembered; that, I may say, I shall never forget. But whether the motherly lady with the somewhat blowsy hair was Mrs Jones or Mrs Green or Mrs Walker, I cannot now say. The dumpy female with the broad back was always called Aunt Sally by the young ladies.

Too much sugar spoils one's tea; I think I have heard that even prosperity will cloy when it comes in overdoses; and a schoolboy has been known to be overdone with jam. I myself have always been peculiarly attached to ladies' society, and have avoided bachelor parties as things execrable in their very nature. But on this special occasion I felt myself to be that schoolboy – I was literally overdone with jam. My tea was all sugar, so that I could not drink it. I was one among twelve. What could I do or say? The proportion of alloy was too small to have any effect in changing the nature of the virgin silver, and the conversation became absolutely feminine.

I must confess also that my previous experience as to these compatriots of mine had not prejudiced me in their favour. I regarded them with – I am ashamed to say so, seeing that they were ladies – but almost with loathing. When last I had seen them their occupation had reminded me of some obscene feast of harpies, or almost of ghouls. They had brought down to the verge of desperation the man whom of all men I most venerated. On these accounts I was inclined to be taciturn with reference to them – and then what could I have to say to the Misses Macmanus's five pupils?

My cousin at first made an effort or two in my favour, but these efforts were fruitless. I soon died away into utter unrecognised insignificance, and the conversation, as I have before said, became feminine. And indeed that horrid Miss Grogram, who was, as it were, the princess of the ghouls, nearly monopolised the whole of it. Mamma Jones – we will call her Jones for the occasion – put in a word now and then, as did also the elder and more energetic Miss Macmanus. The dumpy lady with the broad back ate tea-cake incessantly; the two daughters looked scornful, as though they were above their company with reference to the five pupils; and the five pupils themselves sat in a row with the utmost propriety, each with her hands crossed on her lap before her.

Of what they were talking at last I became utterly oblivious. They had ignored me, going into realms of muslin, questions of maid-servants, female rights, and cheap under-clothing;

and I therefore had ignored them. My mind had gone back to Mr Horne and his garments. While they spoke of their rights, I was thinking of his wrongs; when they mentioned the price of flannel I thought of that of broadcloth.

But of a sudden my attention was arrested. Miss Mac-manus had said something of the black silks of Antwerp, when Miss Grogram replied that she had just returned from that city and had there enjoyed a great success. My cousin had again asked something about the black silks, thinking, no doubt, that Miss Grogram had achieved some bargain; but that lady had soon undeceived her.

'Oh no,' said Miss Grogram, 'it was at the castle. We got such beautiful relics of General Chassé! Didn't we, Mrs Jones?'

'Indeed we did,' said Mrs Jones, bringing out from be-neath the skirts of her dress and ostensibly displaying a large black bag.

'And I've got such a beautiful needle-case,' said the broad-back, displaying her prize. 'I've been making it up all the morning.' And she handed over the article to Miss Mac-manus.

'And only look at this duck of a pen-wiper,' simpered flaxen-hair No. 2. 'Only think of wiping one's pens with relics of General Chassé!' and she handed it over to the other Miss Macmanus.

'And mine's a pin-cushion,' said No. 1, exhibiting the trophy.

'But that's nothing to what I've got,' said Miss Grogram. 'In the first place, there's a pair of slippers – a beautiful pair – they're not made up yet, of course; and then—'

The two Misses Macmanus and their five pupils were sit-ting open-eared, open-eyed, and open-mouthed. How all these sombre-looking articles could be relics of General Chassé did not at first appear clear to them.

'What are they, Miss Grogram?' said the elder Miss Mac-manus, holding the needle-case in one hand and Mrs Jones's bag in the other. Miss Macmanus was a strong-minded female, and I reverenced my cousin when I saw the decided way in which she intended to put down the greedy arrogance of Miss Grogram.

'They are relics.'

'But where do they come from, Miss Grogram?'

'Why, from the castle, to be sure; from General Chassé's own rooms.'

'Did anybody sell them to you?'

'No.'

'Or give them to you?'

'Why, no; at least not exactly give.'

'There they were, and she took 'em,' said the broad-back.

Oh, what a look Miss Grogram gave her! 'Took them! Of course I took them! That is, you took them as much as I did. They were things that we found lying about.'

'What things?' asked Miss Macmanus, in a peculiarly strong-minded tone.

Miss Grogram seemed to be for a moment silenced. I had been ignored, as I have said, and my existence forgotten; but now I observed that the eyes of the culprits were turned towards me – the eyes, that is, of four of them. Mrs Jones looked at me from beneath her fan; the two girls glanced at me furtively, and then their eyes fell to the lowest flounces of their frocks. Miss Grogram turned her spectacles right upon me, and I fancied that she nodded her head at me as a sort of answer to Miss Macmanus. The five pupils opened their mouths and eyes wider; but she of the broad back was nothing abashed. It would have been nothing to her had there been a dozen gentlemen in the room. 'We just found a pair of black ——.' The whole truth was told in the plainest possible language.

'Oh, Aunt Sally!' 'Aunt Sally, how can you?' 'Hold your tongue, Aunt Sally!'

'And then Miss Grogram just cut them up with her scissors,' continued Aunt Sally, not a whit abashed, 'and gave us

41

each a bit, only she took more than half for herself.' It was
clear to me that there had been some quarrel, some delicious
quarrel, between Aunt Sally and Miss Grogram. Through
the whole adventure I had rather respected Aunt Sally.
'She took more than half for herself,' continued Aunt Sally.
'She kept all the—'

'Jemima,' said the elder Miss Macmanus, interrupting the
speaker and addressing her sister, 'it is time, I think, for the
young ladies to retire. Will you be kind enough to see them to
their rooms?' The five pupils thereupon rose from their seats
and courtesied. They then left the room in file, the younger
Miss Macmanus showing them the way.

'But we haven't done any harm, have we?' asked Mrs
Jones, with some tremulousness in her voice.

'Well, I don't know,' said Miss Macmanus. 'What I'm
thinking of now is this: to whom, I wonder, did the garments
properly belong? Who had been the owner and wearer of
them?'

'Why, General Chassé, of course,' said Miss Grogram.

'They were the general's,' repeated the two young ladies;
blushing, however, as they alluded to the subject.

'Well, we thought they were the general's, certainly; and a
very excellent article they were,' said Mrs Jones.

'Perhaps they were the butler's?' said Aunt Sally. I certainly had not given her credit for so much sarcasm.

'Butler's!' exclaimed Miss Grogram, with a toss of her
head.

'Oh! Aunt Sally, Aunt Sally! How can you?' shrieked the
two young ladies.

'Oh, laws!' ejaculated Mrs Jones.

'I don't think that they could have belonged to the butler,'
said Miss Macmanus, with much authority, 'seeing that
domestics in this country are never clad in garments of that
description; so far my own observation enables me to speak
with certainty. But it is equally sure that they were never the
property of the general lately in command in Antwerp. Gen-

42

erals, when they are in full dress, wear ornamental lace upon their – their regimentals; and when . . .' So much she said, and something more, which it may be unnecessary that I should repeat; but such were her eloquence and logic that no doubt would have been left on the mind of any impartial hearer. If an argumentative speaker ever proved anything, Miss Macmanus proved that General Chassé had never been the wearer of the article in question.

'But I know very well they were his!' said Miss Grogram, who was not an impartial hearer. 'Of course they were; whose else's should they be?'

'I'm sure I hope they were his,' said one of the young ladies, almost crying.

'I wish I'd never taken it,' said the other.

'Dear, dear, dear!' said Mrs Jones.

'I'll give you my needle-case, Miss Grogram,' said Aunt Sally.

I had sat hitherto silent during the whole scene, meditating how best I might confound the red-nosed harpy. Now, I thought, was the time for me to strike in.

'I really think, ladies, that there has been some mistake,' said I.

'There has been no mistake at all, sir!' said Miss Grogram.

'Perhaps not,' I answered, very mildly; 'very likely not. But some affair of a similar nature was very much talked about in Antwerp yesterday.'

'Oh, laws!' again ejaculated Mrs Jones.

'The affair I allude to has been talked about a good deal, certainly,' I continued. 'But perhaps it may be altogether a different circumstance.'

'And what may be the circumstance to which you allude?' asked Miss Macmanus, in the same authoritative tone.

'I dare say it has nothing to do with these ladies,' said I; 'but an article of dress, of the nature they have described, was cut up in the castle of Antwerp on the day before yesterday. It belonged to a gentleman who was visiting the place; and I

43

was given to understand that he is determined to punish the people who have wronged him.'

'It can't be the same,' said Miss Grogram; but I could see that she was trembling.

'Oh, laws! What will become of us?' said Mrs Jones.

'You can all prove that I didn't touch them, and that I warned her not,' said Aunt Sally. In the meantime the two young ladies had almost fainted behind their fans.

'But how had it come to pass,' asked Miss Macmanus, 'that the gentleman had—'

'I know nothing more about it, cousin,' said I; 'only it does seem that there is an odd coincidence.'

Immediately after this I took my leave. I saw that I had avenged my friend, and spread dismay in the hearts of those who had injured him. I had learned in the course of the evening at what hotel the five ladies were staying; and in the course of the next morning I sauntered into the hall, and finding one of the porters alone, asked if they were still there. The man told me that they had started by the earliest diligence. 'And,' said he, 'if you are a friend of theirs, perhaps you will take charge of these things, which they have left behind them?' So saying, he pointed to a table at the back of the hall, on which were lying the black bag, the black needle-case, the black pin-cushion, and the black pen-wiper. There was also a heap of fragments of cloth which I well knew had been intended by Miss Grogram for the comfort of her feet and ankles.

I declined the commission, however. 'They were no special friends of mine,' I said; and I left all the relics still lying on the little table in the back hall.

'Upon the whole, I am satisfied!' said the Rev. Augustus Horne, when I told him the finale of the story.

The Model Millionaire

A NOTE OF ADMIRATION

OSCAR WILDE

Unless one is wealthy there is no use in being a charming fellow. Romance is the privilege of the rich, not the profession of the unemployed. The poor should be practical and prosaic. It is better to have a permanent income than to be fascinating. These are the great truths of modern life which Hughie Erskine never realised. Poor Hughie! Intellectually, we must admit, he was not of much importance. He never said a brilliant or even an ill-natured thing in his life. But then he was wonderfully good-looking, with his crisp, brown hair, his clear-cut profile, and his grey eyes. He was as popular with men as he was with women, and he had every accomplishment except that of making money. His father had bequeathed him his cavalry sword and a *History of the Peninsular War* in fifteen volumes. Hughie hung the first over his looking-glass, put the second on a shelf between *Ruff's Guide* and *Baily's Magazine*, and lived on two hundred a year that an old aunt allowed him. He had tried everything. He had gone on the Stock Exchange for six months; but what was a butterfly to do among bulls and bears? He had been a tea-merchant for a little longer, but had soon tired of pekoe and souchong. Then he had tried selling dry sherry. That did not answer; the sherry was a little too dry. Ultimately he became nothing, a delightful, ineffectual young man with a perfect profile and no profession.

To make matters worse, he was in love. The girl he loved was Laura Merton, the daughter of a retired colonel who had lost his temper and his digestion in India, and had never found either of them again. Laura adored him, and he was ready to kiss her shoe-strings. They were the handsomest couple in London, and had not a penny-piece between them. The colonel was very fond of Hughie, but would not hear of any engagement.

'Come to me, my boy, when you have got ten thousand pounds of your own, and we will see about it,' he used to say; and Hughie looked very glum in those days, and had to go to Laura for consolation.

One morning, as he was on his way to Holland Park, where the Mertons lived, he dropped in to see a great friend of his, Alan Trevor. Trevor was a painter. Indeed, few people escape that nowadays. But he was also an artist, and artists are rather rare. Personally he was a strange rough fellow, with a freckled face and a red, ragged beard. However, when he took up the brush he was a real master, and his pictures were eagerly sought after. He had been very much attracted by Hughie at first, it must be acknowledged, entirely on account of his personal charm. 'The only people a painter should know', he used to say, 'are people who are *bête* and beautiful, people who are an artistic pleasure to look at and an intellectual repose to talk to. Men who are dandies and women who are darlings rule the world, at least they should do so.' However, after he got to know Hughie better, he liked him quite as much for his bright, buoyant spirits and his generous, reckless nature, and had given him the permanent *entrée* to his studio.

When Hughie came in he found Trevor putting the finishing touches to a wonderful life-size picture of a beggar-man. The beggar himself was standing on a raised platform in a corner of the studio. He was a wizened old man, with a face like wrinkled parchment, and a most piteous expression. Over his shoulder was flung a coarse brown cloak, all tears and tatters; his thick boots were patched and cobbled, and with one hand he leant on a rough stick, while with the other he held out his battered hat for alms.

46

'What an amazing model!' whispered Hughie, as he shook hands with his friend.

'An amazing model?' shouted Trevor at the top of his voice; 'I should think so! Such beggars as he are not to be met with every day. A *trouvaille, mon cher*; a living Velasquez! My stars! what an etching Rembrandt would have made of him!'

'Poor old chap!' said Hughie, 'how miserable he looks! But I suppose, to you painters, his face is his fortune?'

'Certainly,' replied Trevor, 'you don't want a beggar to look happy, do you?'

'How much does a model get for sitting?' asked Hughie, as he found himself a comfortable seat on a divan.

'A shilling an hour.'

'And how much do you get for your picture, Alan?'

'Oh, for this I get two thousand!'

'Pounds?'

'Guineas. Painters, poets, and physicians always get guineas.'

'Well, I think the models should have a percentage,' cried Hughie, laughing; 'they work quite as hard as you do.'

'Nonsense, nonsense! Why, look at the trouble of laying on the paint alone, and standing all day long at one's easel! It's all very well, Hughie, for you to talk, but I assure you that there are moments when Art almost attains to the dignity of manual labour. But you mustn't chatter; I'm very busy. Smoke a cigarette, and keep quiet.'

After some time the servant came in, and told Trevor that the framemaker wanted to speak to him.

'Don't run away, Hughie,' he said, as he went out; 'I will be back in a moment.'

The old beggar-man took advantage of Trevor's absence to rest for a moment on a wooden bench that was behind him. He looked so forlorn and wretched that Hughie could not help pitying him, and felt in his pockets to see what money he had. All he could find was a sovereign and some coppers. 'Poor old fellow,' he thought to himself, 'he wants it more than I do, but it means no hansoms for a fortnight'; and he walked across the studio and slipped the sovereign into the beggar's hand.

The old man started, and a faint smile flitted across his withered lips. 'Thank you, sir,' he said, 'thank you.'

Then Trevor arrived, and Hughie took his leave, blushing a little at what he had done. He spent the day with Laura, got a charming scolding for his extravagance, and had to walk home.

That night he strolled into the Palette Club about eleven o'clock, and found Trevor sitting by himself in the smoking-room drinking hock and seltzer.

'Well, Alan, did you get the picture finished all right?' he said, as he lit his cigarette.

'Finished and framed, my boy!' answered Trevor; 'and, by the by, you have made a conquest. That old model you saw is quite devoted to you. I had to tell him all about you – who you are, where you live. What your income is, what prospects you have—'

'My dear Alan,' cried Hughie, 'I shall probably find him waiting for me when I go home. But, of course, you are only joking. Poor old wretch! I wish I could do something for him. I think it is dreadful that anyone should be so miserable. I have got heaps of old clothes at home – do you think he would care for any of them? Why, his rags were falling to bits.'

'But he looks splendid in them,' said Trevor. 'I wouldn't paint him in a frock coat for anything. What you call rags I call romance. What seems poverty to you is picturesqueness to me. However, I'll tell him of your offer.'

'Alan,' said Hughie seriously, 'you painters are a heartless lot.'

'An artist's heart is his head,' replied Trevor; 'and besides, our business is to realise the world as we see it, not to reform it as we know it. *A chacun son métier*. And now tell me how Laura is. The old model was quite interested in her.'

48

'You don't mean to say you talked to him about her?' said Hughie.

'Certainly I did. He knows all about the relentless colonel, the lovely Laura, and the £10,000.'

'You told that old beggar all my private affairs?' cried Hughie, looking very red and angry.

'My dear boy,' said Trevor, smiling, 'that old beggar, as you call him, is one of the richest men in Europe. He could buy all London tomorrow without overdrawing his account. He has a house in every capital, dines off gold plate, and can prevent Russia going to war when he chooses.'

'What on earth do you mean?' exclaimed Hughie.

'What I say,' said Trevor. 'The old man you saw today in the studio was Baron Hausberg. He is a great friend of mine, buys all my pictures and that sort of thing, and gave me a commission a month ago to paint him as a beggar. *Que voulez-vous? La fantaisie d'un millionnaire!* And I must say he made a magnificent figure in his rags, or perhaps I should say in my rags; they are an old suit I got in Spain.'

'Baron Hausberg!' cried Hughie. 'Good heavens! I gave him a sovereign!' and he sank into an armchair the picture of dismay.

'Gave him a sovereign!' shouted Trevor, and he burst into a roar of laughter. 'My dear boy, you'll never see it again. *Son affaire c'est l'argent des autres.*'

'I think you might have told me, Alan,' said Hughie sulkily, 'and not have let me make such a fool of myself.'

'Well, to begin with, Hughie,' said Trevor, 'it never entered my mind that you went about distributing alms in that reckless way. I can understand your kissing a pretty model, but your giving a sovereign to an ugly one – by Jove, no! Besides, the fact is that I really was not at home today to anyone; and when you came in I didn't know whether Hausberg would like his name mentioned. You know he wasn't in full dress.'

'What a duffer he must think me!' said Hughie.

'Not at all. He was in the highest spirits after you left; kept chuckling to himself and rubbing his old wrinkled hands together. I couldn't make out why he was so interested to know all about you; but I see it all now. He'll invest your sovereign for you, Hughie, pay you the interest every six months, and have a capital story to tell after dinner.'

'I am an unlucky devil,' growled Hughie. 'The best thing I can do is to go to bed; and, my dear Alan, you mustn't tell anyone. I shouldn't dare show my face in the Row.'

'Nonsense! It reflects the highest credit on your philanthropic spirit, Hughie. And don't run away. Have another cigarette, and you can talk about Laura as much as you like.'

However, Hughie wouldn't stop, but walked home, feeling very unhappy, and leaving Alan Trevor in fits of laughter.

The next morning, as he was at breakfast, the servant brought him up a card on which was written, 'Monsieur Gustave Naudin, *de la part de* M. le Baron Hausberg.' 'I suppose he has come for an apology,' said Hughie to himself; and he told the servant to show the visitor up.

An old gentleman with gold spectacles and grey hair came into the room, and said, in a slight French accent, 'Have I the honour of addressing Monsieur Erskine?'

Hughie bowed.

'I have come from Baron Hausberg,' he continued. 'The baron—'

'I beg, sir, that you will offer him my sincerest apologies,' stammered Hughie.

'The baron', said the old gentleman with a smile, 'has commissioned me to bring you this letter'; and he extended a sealed envelope.

On the outside was written, 'A wedding present to Hugh Erskine and Laura Merton, from an old beggar', and inside was a cheque for £10,000.

When they were married Alan Trevor was the best man, and the baron made a speech at the wedding breakfast.

'Millionaire models', remarked Alan, 'are rare enough; but, by Jove, model millionaires are rarer still!'

Poisson d'Avril

SOMERVILLE AND ROSS

The atmosphere of the waiting-room set at naught at a single glance the theory that there can be no smoke without fire. The stationmaster, when remonstrated with, stated, as an incontrovertible fact, that any chimney in the world would smoke in a south-easterly wind, and, further, said there wasn't a poker, and that if you poked the fire the grate would fall out. He was, however, sympathetic, and went on his knees before the smouldering mound of slack, endeavouring to charm it to a smile by subtle proddings with the handle of the ticket-punch. Finally, he took me to his own kitchen fire and talked politics and salmon-fishing, the former with judicious attention to my presumed point of view, and careful suppression of his own, the latter with no less tactful regard for my admission that for three days I had not caught a fish, while the steam rose from my wet boots, in witness of the ten miles of rain through which an outside car had carried me.

Before the train was signalled I realised for the hundredth time the magnificent superiority of the Irish mind to the trammels of officialdom, and the inveterate supremacy in Ireland of the Personal Element.

'You might get a foot-warmer at Carrig Junction,' said a species of lay porter in a knitted jersey, ramming my suitcase upside down under the seat. 'Sometimes they're in it, and more times they're not.'

The train dragged itself rheumatically from the station and a cold spring rain – the time was the middle of a most inclement April – smote it in flank as it came into the open. I pulled up both windows and began to smoke; there is, at least, a semblance of warmth in a thoroughly vitiated atmosphere.

It is my wife's habit to assert that I do not read her let-ters, and being now on my way to join her and my family in Gloucestershire, it seemed a sound thing to study again her latest letter of instructions.

I am starting today, as Alice wrote to say we must be there two days before the wedding, so as to have a rehearsal for the pages. Their dresses have come, and they look too delicious in them—
(I here omit profuse particulars not pertinent to this tale.)
It is sickening for you to have had such bad sport. If the worst comes to the worst couldn't you buy one?—

I smote my hand upon my knee. I had forgotten the infer-nal salmon! What a score for Philippa! If these contretemps would only teach her that I was not to be relied upon, they would have their uses, but experience is wasted upon her; I have no objection to being called an idiot, but, that being so, I ought to be allowed the privileges and exemptions proper to idiots. Philippa had, no doubt, written to Alice Hervey, and assured her that Sinclair would be only too delighted to bring her a salmon, and Alice Hervey, who was rich enough to find much enjoyment in saving money, would reckon upon it, to its final fin in mayonnaise.

Plunged in morose meditations, I progressed through a country parcelled out by shaky and crooked walls into a patchwood of hazel scrub and rocky fields, veiled in rain. About every six miles there was a station, wet and wind-swept; at one the sole occurrence was the presentation of a newspaper to the guard by the stationmaster; at the next the guard read aloud some choice excerpts from the same to the porter. The Personal Element was potent on this branch of the Munster and Connaught Railway. Routine, abhor-rent to all artistic minds, was sheathed in conversation; even the engine-driver, a functionary ordinarily as aloof as the

Mikado, alleviated his enforced isolation by sociable shrieks to every level crossing, while the long row of public-houses that formed, as far as I could judge, the town of Carrig, received a special and, as it seemed, humorous salutation.

The Time-Table decreed that we were to spend ten minutes at Carrig Junction; it was fifteen before the crowd of market people on the platform had been assimilated; finally, the window of a neighbouring carriage was flung open, and a wrathful English voice asked how much longer the train was going to wait. The stationmaster, who was at the moment engrossed in conversation with the guard and a man who was carrying a long parcel wrapped in newspaper, looked round, and said gravely:

'Well now, that's a mystery!'

The man with the parcel turned away, and convulsively studied a poster. The guard put his hand over his mouth.

The voice, still more wrathfully, demanded the earliest hour at which its owner could get to Belfast.

'Ye'll be asking me next when I take me breakfast,' replied the stationmaster, without haste or palpable annoyance.

The window went up again with a bang, the man with the parcel dug the guard in the ribs with his elbow, and the parcel slipped from under his arm and fell on the platform.

'Oh my! oh my! Me fish!' exclaimed the man, solicitously picking up a remarkably good-looking salmon that had slipped from its wrapping of newspaper.

Inspiration came to me, and I, in my turn, opened my window and summoned the stationmaster.

Would his friend sell me the salmon? The stationmaster entered upon the mission with ardour, but without success.

No; the gentleman was only just after running down to the town for it in the delay, but why wouldn't I run down and get one for myself? There was half-a-dozen more of them below at Coffey's, selling cheap; there would be time enough, the mail wasn't signalled yet.

I jumped from the carriage and doubled out of the station

53

at top speed, followed by an assurance from the guard that he would not forget me.

Congratulating myself on the ascendancy of the Personal Element, I sped through the soapy limestone mud towards the public-houses. *En route* I met a heated man carrying yet another salmon, who, without preamble, informed me that there were three or four more good fish in it, and that he was after running down from the train himself.

'Ye have whips o' time!' he called after me. 'It's the first house that's not a public-house. Ye'll see boots in the window – she'll give them for tenpence a pound if ye're stiff with her!'

I ran past the public-houses.

'Tenpence a pound!' I exclaimed inwardly, 'at this time of year! That's good enough.'

Here I perceived the house with boots in the window, and dived into its dark doorway.

A cobbler was at work behind a low counter. He mumbled something about Herself, through lengths of waxed thread that hung across his mouth, a fat woman appeared at an inner door, and at that moment I heard, appallingly near, the whistle of the incoming mail. The fat woman grasped the situation in an instant, and with what appeared but one movement, snatched a large fish from the floor of the room behind her and flung a newspaper round it.

'Eight pound weight!' she said swiftly. 'Ten shillings!'

A convulsive effort of mental arithmetic assured me that this was more than tenpence a pound, but it was not the moment for stiffness. I shoved a half-sovereign into her fishy hand, clasped my salmon in my arms, and ran.

Needless to say it was uphill, and at the steepest gradient another whistle stabbed me like a spur; above the station roof successive and advancing puffs of steam warned me that the worst had probably happened, but still I ran. When I gained the platform my train was already clear of it, but the Personal Element held good. Every soul in the station, or so it seemed to me, lifted up his voice and yelled. The stationmaster put

his fingers in his mouth and sent after the departing train an unearthly whistle, with a high trajectory and a serrated edge. It took effect; the train slackened, I plunged from the platform and followed it up the rails, and every window in both trains blossomed with the heads of deeply interested spectators. The guard met me on the line, very apologetic and primed with an explanation that the gentleman going for the boat-train wouldn't let him wait any longer, while from our rear came an exultant cry from the stationmaster: 'Ye *told* him ye wouldn't forget him!'

'There's a few countrywomen in your carriage, sir,' said the guard, ignoring the taunt, as he shoved me and my salmon up the side of the train, 'but they'll be getting out in a couple of stations. There wasn't another seat in the train for them!'

My sensational return to my carriage was viewed with the utmost sympathy by no less than seven shawled and cloaked countrywomen. In order to make room for me, one of them seated herself on the floor with her basket in her lap, another, on the seat opposite to me, squeezed herself under the central elbow flap that had been turned up to make room. The aromas of wet cloaks, turf smoke, and salt fish formed a potent blend. I was excessively hot, and the eyes of the seven women were fastened upon me with intense and unwearying interest.

'Move west a small piece, Mary Jack, if you please,' said a voluminous matron in the corner, 'I declare we're as throng as three in a bed this minute!'

'Why then, Julia Casey, there's little throubling yourself,' grumbled the woman under the flap. 'Look at the way meself is! I wonder is it to be putting humps on themselves the gentry has them things down on top o' them! I'd sooner be carrying a basket of turnips on me back than to be scrooged this way!'

The woman on the floor at my feet rolled up at me a glance of compassionate amusement at this rustic ignorance,

55

and tactfully changed the conversation by supposing that it was at Coffey's I got the salmon.

I said it was.

There was a silence, during which it was obvious that one question burnt in every heart.

'I'll go bail she axed him tinpence!' said the woman under the flap, as one who touches the limits of absurdity.

'It's a beautiful fish!' I said defiantly. 'Eight pounds weight. I gave her ten shillings for it.'

What is described in newspapers as 'sensation in court' greeted this confession.

'Look!' said the woman under the flap, darting her head out of the hood of her cloak, like a tortoise, ' 'tis what it is, ye haven't as much roguery in your heart as'd make ye a match for her!'

'Divil blow the ha'penny Eliza Coffey paid for that fish!' burst out the fat woman in the corner. 'Thim lads o' hers had a creel full o' thim snatched this morning before it was making day!'

'How would the gentleman be a match for her!' shouted the woman on the floor through a long-drawn whistle that told of a coming station. 'Sure a Turk itself wouldn't be a match for her! That one has a tongue that'd clip a hedge!'

At the station they clambered out laboriously, and with groaning. I handed down to them their monster baskets, laden, apparently, with ingots of lead; they told me in return that I was a fine *grauver* man, and it was a pity there weren't more like me; they wished, finally, that my journey might well thrive with me, and passed from my ken, bequeathing to me, after the agreeable manner of their kind, a certain comfortable mental sleekness that reason cannot immediately dispel. They also left me in possession of the fact that I was about to present the irreproachable Alice Hervey with a contraband salmon.

The afternoon passed cheerlessly into evening, and my journey did not conspicuously thrive with me. Somewhere in

56

the dripping twilight I changed trains, and again later on, and at each change the salmon moulted some more of its damp raiment of newspaper, and I debated seriously the idea of interring it, regardless of consequences, in my portmanteau. A lamp was banged into the roof of my carriage, half an inch of orange flame, poised in a large glass globe, like a goldfish, and of about as much use as an illuminant. Here also was handed in the dinner basket that I had wired for, and its contents, arid though they were, enabled me to achieve at least some measure of mechanical distension, followed by a dreary lethargy that was not far from drowsiness.

At the next station we paused long; nothing whatever occurred, and the rain drummed patiently upon the roof. Two nuns and some schoolgirls were in the carriage next door, and their voices came plaintively and in snatches through the partition; after a long period of apparent collapse, during which I closed my eyes to evade the cold gaze of the salmon through the netting, a voice in the next carriage said resourcefully:

'Oh, girls, I'll tell you what we'll do! We'll say the Rosary!'

'Oh, that will be lovely!' said another voice; 'well, who'll give it out? Theresa Condon, you'll give it out.'

Theresa Condon gave it out, in a not unmelodious monotone, interspersed with the responses, always in a lower cadence; the words were indistinguishable, but the rise and fall of the western voices was lulling as the hum of bees. I fell asleep.

I awoke in total darkness; the train was motionless, and complete and profound silence reigned. We were at a station, that much I discerned by the light of a dim lamp at the far end of a platform glistening with wet. I struck a match and ascertained that it was eleven o'clock, precisely the hour at which I was to board the mail train. I jumped out and ran down the platform; there was no one in the train; there was no one even on the engine, which was forlornly hissing to itself in the silence. There was not a human being anywhere.

57

Every door was closed, and all was dark. The name-board of the station was faintly visible; with a lighted match I went along it letter by letter. It seemed as if the whole alphabet were in it, and by the time I had got to the end I had forgotten the beginning. One fact I had, however, mastered, that it was not the junction at which I was to catch the mail.

I was undoubtedly awake, but for a moment I was inclined to entertain the idea that there had been an accident, and that I had entered upon existence in another world. Once more I assailed the station house and the appurtenances thereof, the ticket-office, the waiting-room, finally, and at some distance, the goods store, outside which the single lamp of the station commented feebly on the drizzle and the darkness. As I approached it a crack of light under the door became perceptible, and a voice was suddenly uplifted within.

'Your best now again that! Throw down your Jack!'

I opened the door with pardonable violence, and found the guard, the stationmaster, the driver, and the stoker, seated on barrels round a packing case, on which they were playing a game of cards.

To have too egregiously the best of a situation is not, to a generous mind, a source of strength. In the perfection of their overthrow I permitted the driver and stoker to wither from their places, and to fade away into the outer darkness without any suitable send-off; with the guard and the stationmaster I dealt more faithfully, but the pleasure of throwing water on drowned rats is not a lasting one. I accepted the statements that they thought there wasn't a Christian in the train, that a few minutes here or there wouldn't signify, that they would have me at the junction in twenty minutes, and it was often the mail was late.

Fired by this hope I hurried back to my carriage, preceded at an emulous gallop by the officials. The guard thrust in with me the lantern from the card table, and fled to his van.

'Mind the Goods, Tim!' shouted the stationmaster, as he slammed my door, 'she might be coming anytime now!'

The answer travelled magnificently back from the engine.

'Let her come! She'll meet her match!' A war-whoop upon the steam whistle fittingly closed the speech, and the train sprang into action.

We had about fifteen miles to go, and we banged and bucketed over it in what was, I should imagine, record time. The carriage felt as if it were galloping on four wooden legs, my teeth chattered in my head, and the salmon slowly churned its way forth from its newspaper, and moved along the netting with dreadful stealth.

All was of no avail.

'Well,' said the guard, as I stepped forth onto the deserted platform of Loughranny, 'that owld Limited Mail's th' un-punctualest thrain in Ireland! If you're a minute late she's gone from you, and may be if you were early you might be half an hour waiting for her!'

On the whole the guard was a gentleman. He said he would show me the best hotel in the town, though he feared I would be hard set to get a bed anywhere because of the *Feis* (a *feis*, I should explain, is a festival, devoted to competitions in Irish songs and dances). He shouldered my portmanteau, he even grappled successfully with the salmon, and, as we traversed the empty streets, he explained to me how easily I could catch the morning boat from Rosslare, and how it was, as a matter of fact, quite the act of Providence that my original scheme had been frustrated.

All was dark at the uninviting portals of the hotel favoured by the guard. For a full five minutes we waited at them, ringing hard: I suggested that we should try elsewhere.

'He'll come,' said the guard, with the confidence of the Pied Piper of Hamelin, retaining an implacable thumb upon the button of the electric bell. 'He'll come. Sure it rings in his room!'

The victim came, half awake, half dressed, and with an inch of dripping candle in his fingers. There was not a bed there, he said, nor in the town neither.

I said I would sit in the dining-room till the time for the early train.

'Sure there's five beds in the dining-room,' replied the Boots, 'and there's mostly two in every bed.'

His voice was firm, but there was a wavering look in his eye.

'What about the billiard-room, Mike?' said the guard, in wooing tones.

'Ah, God bless you! we have a mattress on the table this minute!' answered the Boots, wearily, 'and the fellow that got the First Prize for Reels asleep on top if it!'

'Well, and can't ye put the palliasse on the floor under it, ye omadhawn?' said the guard, dumping my luggage and the salmon in the hall, 'sure there's no snugger place in the house! I must run away home now, before Herself thinks I'm dead altogether!'

His retreating footsteps went lightly away down the empty street.

'Annything don't throuble *him*!' said the Boots bitterly.

As for me, nothing save the Personal Element stood between me and destitution.

It was in the dark of the early morning that I woke again to life and its troubles. A voice, dropping, as it were, over the edge of some smothering over-world, had awakened me. It was the voice of the First Prize for Reels, descending through a pocket of the billiard-table.

'I beg your pardon, sir, are ye going on the 5 to Cork?'

I grunted a negative.

'Well, if ye were, ye'd be late,' said the voice.

I received this useful information in indignant silence, and endeavoured to wrap myself again in the vanishing skirts of a dream.

'I'm going on the 6.30 meself,' proceeded the voice, 'and it's unknown to me how I'll put on me boots. Me feet is swelled the size o' three-pound loaves with the dint of the

60

little dancing-shoes I had on me in the competition last night. Me feet's delicate that way, and I'm a great epicure about me boots.'

I snored aggressively, but the dream was gone. So, for all practical purposes, was the night.

The First Prize for Reels arose, presenting an astonishing spectacle of grass-green breeches, a white shirt, and pearl-grey stockings, and accomplished a toilet that consisted of removing these and putting on ordinary garments, completed by the apparently excruciating act of getting into his boots. At any other hour of the day I might have been sorry for him. He then removed himself and his belongings to the hall, and there entered upon a resounding conversation with the Boots, while I crawled forth from my lair to renew the strife with circumstances and to endeavour to compose a telegram to Alice Hervey of explanation and apology that should cost less than seven and sixpence. There was also the salmon to be dealt with.

Here the Boots intervened, opportunely, with a cup of tea, and the intelligence that he had already done up the salmon in straw bottle-covers and brown paper, and that I could travel Europe with it if I liked. He further informed me that he would run up to the station with the luggage now, and that maybe I wouldn't mind carrying the fish myself; it was on the table in the hall.

My train went at 6.15. The Boots had secured for me one of many empty carriages, and lingered conversationally till the train started; he regretted politely my bad night at the hotel, and assured me that only for Jimmy Durkan having a little drink taken – Jimmy Durkan was the First Prize for Reels – he would have turned him off the billiard-table for my benefit. He finally confided to me that Mr Durkan was engaged to his sister, and was a rising baker in the town of Limerick. 'Indeed,' he said, 'any girl might be glad to get him. He dances like whalebone, and he makes grand bread!'

Here the train started.

It was late that night when, stiff, dirty, with tired eyes blinking in the dazzle of electric lights, I was conducted by the Herveys' beautiful footman into the Herveys' baronial hall, and was told by the Herveys' imperial butler that dinner was over, and the gentlemen had just gone into the drawing-room. I was in the act of hastily declining to join them there, when a voice cried –

'Here he is!'

And Philippa, rustling and radiant, came forth into the hall, followed in shimmers of satin, and flutterings of lace, by Alice Hervey, by the bride elect, and by the usual festive rout of exhilarated relatives, male and female, whose mission it is to keep things lively before a wedding.

'Is this a wedding present for me, Uncle Sinclair?' cried the bride elect, through a deluge of questions and commiserations, and snatched from under my arm the brown-paper parcel that had remained there from force of direful habit.

'I advise you not to open it!' I exclaimed; 'it's a salmon!'

The bride elect, with a shriek of disgust, and without an instant of hesitation, hurled it at her nearest neighbour, the head bridesmaid. The head bridesmaid, with an answering shriek, sprang to one side, and the parcel that I had cherished with a mother's care across two countries and a stormy channel fell, with a crash, on the flagged floor.

Why did it crash?

'A salmon!' screamed Philippa, gazing at the parcel, round which a pool was already forming, 'why that's whiskey! Can't you smell it?'

The footman here respectfully interposed, and kneeling down, cautiously extracted from folds of brown paper a straw bottle-cover full of broken glass and dripping with whiskey.

'I'm afraid the other things are rather spoiled, sir,' he said seriously, and drew forth, successively, a very large pair of high-low shoes, two long grey worsted stockings, and a pair of grass-green breeches.

They brought the house down, in a manner doubtless familiar to them when they shared the triumphs of Mr Jimmy Durkan, but they left Alice Hervey distinctly cold.

'You know, darling,' she said to Philippa afterwards, 'I don't think it was very clever of dear Sinclair to take the wrong parcel. I *had* counted on that salmon.'

The Man Higher Up

O. HENRY

Across our two dishes of spaghetti, in a corner of Provenzano's restaurant, Jeff Peters was explaining to me the three kinds of graft.

Every winter Jeff comes to New York to eat spaghetti, to watch the shipping in East River from the depths of his chinchilla overcoat, and to lay in a supply of Chicago-made clothing at one of the Fulton Street stores. During the other three seasons he may be found further west – his range is from Spokane to Tampa. In his profession he takes a pride which he supports and defends with a serious and unique philosophy of ethics. His profession is no new one. He is an incorporated, uncapitalized, unlimited asylum for the reception of the restless and unwise dollars of his fellow men.

In the wilderness of stone in which Jeff seeks his annual lonely holiday he is glad to palaver of his many adventures, as a boy will whistle after sundown in a wood. Wherefore, I mark on my calendar the time of his coming, and open a question of privilege at Provenzano's concerning the little wine-stained table in the corner between the rakish rubber plant and the framed palazzio della something on the wall.

'There are two kinds of grafts', said Jeff, 'that ought to be wiped out by law. I mean Wall Street speculation, and burglary.'

'Nearly everybody will agree with you as to one of them,' said I, with a laugh.

'Well, burglary ought to be wiped out, too,' said Jeff; and I wondered whether the laugh had been redundant.

'About three months ago,' said Jeff, 'it was my privilege

to become familiar with a sample of each of the aforesaid branches of illegitimate art. I was *sine qua grata* with a member of the housebreakers' union and one of the John D. Napoleons of finance at the same time.'

'Interesting combination,' said I, with a yawn. 'Did I tell you I bagged a duck and a ground squirrel at one shot last week over in the Ramapos?' I knew well how to draw Jeff's stories.

'Let me tell you first about these barnacles that clog the wheels of society by poisoning the springs of rectitude with their upas-like eye,' said Jeff, with the pure gleam of the muck-raker in his own.

'As I said, three months ago I got into bad company. There are two times in a man's life when he does this – when he's dead broke, and when he's rich.

'Now and then the most legitimate business runs out of luck. It was out in Arkansas I made the wrong turn at a cross-road, and drives into this town of Peavine by mistake. It seems I had already assaulted and disfigured Peavine the spring of the year before. I had sold $600 worth of young fruit trees there – plums, cherries, peaches and pears. The Peaviners were keeping an eye on the country road and hoping I might pass that way again. I drove down Main Street as far as the Crystal Palace drug-store before I realized I had committed ambush upon myself and my white horse Bill.

'The Peaviners took me by surprise and Bill by the bridle and began a conversation that wasn't entirely disassociated with the subject of fruit trees. A committee of 'em ran some trace-chains through the armholes of my vest and escorted me through their gardens and orchards.

'Their fruit trees hadn't lived up to their labels. Most of 'em had turned out to be persimmons and dogwoods, with a grove or two of blackjacks and poplars. The only one that showed any signs of bearing anything was a fine young cottonwood that had put forth a hornet's nest and half of an old corset-cover.

65

'The Peaviners protracted our fruitless stroll to the edge of town. They took my watch and money on account; and they kept Bill and the wagon as hostages. They said the first time one of them dogwood trees put forth an Amsden's June peach I might come back and get my things. Then they took off the trace-chains and jerked their thumbs in the direction of the Rocky Mountains; and I struck a Lewis and Clark lope for the swollen rivers and impenetrable forests.

'When I regained intellectualness I found myself walking into an unidentified town on the A., T. & S. F. railroad. The Peaviners hadn't left anything in my pockets except a plug of chewing – they wasn't after my life – and that saved it. I bit off a chunk and sits down on a pile of ties by the track to recogitate my sensations of thought and perspicacity.

'And then along comes a fast freight which slows up a little at the town; and off it drops a black bundle that rolls for twenty yards in a cloud of dust and then gets up and begins to spit soft coal and interjections. I see it is a young man broad across the face, dressed more for Pullmans than freights, and with a cheerful kind of smile in spite of it all that made Phoebe Snow's job look like a chimney-sweep's.

' "Fall off?" says I.

' "Nunk," says he. "Got off. Arrived at my destination. What town is this?"

' "Haven't looked it up on the map yet," says I. "I got in about five minutes before you did. How does it strike you?"

' "Hard," says he, twisting one of his arms around. "I believe that shoulder – no, it's all right."

'He stoops over to brush the dust off his clothes, when out of his pocket drops a fine, nine-inch burglar's steel jimmy. He picks it up and looks at me sharp, and then grins and holds out his hand.

' "Brother," says he, "greetings. Didn't I see you in Southern Missouri last summer selling colored sand at half-a-dollar a teaspoonful to put into lamps to keep the oil from exploding?"

' "Oil", says I, "never explodes. It's the gas that forms that explodes." But I shakes hands with him, anyway.

' "My name's Bill Bassett," says he to me, "and if you'll call it professional pride instead of conceit, I'll inform you that you have the pleasure of meeting the best burglar that ever set a gum-shoe on ground drained by the Mississippi River."

'Well, me and this Bill Bassett sits on the ties and exchanges brags as artists in kindred lines will do. It seems he didn't have a cent, either, and we went into close caucus. He explained why an able burglar sometimes had to travel on freights by telling me that a servant girl had played him false in Little Rock, and he was making a quick get-away.

' "It's part of my business", says Bill Bassett, "to play up to the ruffles when I want to make a riffle as Raffles. 'Tis loves that makes the bit go 'round. Show me a house with the swag in it and a pretty parlor-maid, and you might as well call the silver melted down and sold, and me spilling truffles and that Château stuff on the napkin under my chin, while the police are calling it an inside job just because the old lady's nephew teaches a Bible class. I first make an impression on the girl," says Bill, "and when she lets me inside I make an impression on the locks. But this one in Little Rock done me," says he. "She saw me taking a trolley ride with another girl, and when I came 'round on the night she was to leave the door open for me it was fast. And I had keys made for the doors upstairs. But, no sir. She had sure cut off my locks. She was a Delilah," says Bill Bassett.

'It seems that Bill tried to break in anyhow with his jimmy, but the girl emitted a succession of bravura noises like the top-riders of a tally-ho, and Bill had to take all the hurdles between there and the depot. As he had no baggage they tried hard to check his departure, but he made a train that was just pulling out.

' "Well," says Bill Bassett, when we had exchanged memoirs of our dead lives, "I could eat. This town don't look like it was kept under a Yale lock. Suppose we commit some mild atrocity that will bring in temporary expense money. I don't suppose you've brought along any hair tonic or rolled-gold watch-chains, or similar law-defying swindles that you could sell on the plaza to the pikers of the paretic populace, have you?"

' "No," says I, "I left an elegant line of Patagonian diamond earrings and rainy-day sunbursts in my valise at Peavine. But they're to stay there till some of them black-gum trees begin to glut the market with yellow clings and Japanese plums. I reckon we can't count on them unless we take Luther Burbank in for a partner."

' "Very well," says Bassett, "we'll do the best we can. Maybe after dark I'll borrow a hairpin from some lady, and open the Farmers' and Drovers' Marine Bank with it."

'While we were talking, up pulls a passenger train to the depot nearby. A person in a high hat gets off on the wrong side of the train and comes tripping down the track toward us. He was a little, fat man with a big nose and rat's eyes, but dressed expensive, and carrying a hand-satchel careful, as if it had eggs or railroad bonds in it. He passes by us and keeps on down the track, not appearing to notice the town.

' "Come on," says Bill Bassett to me, starting after him.

' "Where?" I asks.

' "Lordy!" says Bill, "had you forgot you was in the desert? Didn't you see Colonel Manna drop down right before your eyes? Don't you hear the rustling of General Raven's wings? I'm surprised at you, Elijah."

'We overtook the stranger in the edge of some woods, and, as it was after sundown and in a quiet place, nobody saw us stop him. Bill takes the silk hat off the man's head and brushes it with his sleeve and puts it back.

' "What does this mean, sir?" says the man.

' "When I wore one of these," says Bill, "and felt embarrassed, I always done that. Not having one now, I had to use yours. I hardly know how to begin, sir, in explaining our

68

business with you, but I guess we'll try your pockets first."

'Bill Bassett felt in all of them, and looked disgusted.

' "Not even a watch," he says. "Ain't you ashamed of yourself, you whited sculpture? Going about dressed like a head-waiter, and financed like a Count. You haven't even got carfare. What did you do with your transfer?"

'The man speaks up and says he has no assets or valuables of any sort. But Bassett takes his hand-satchel and opens it. Out comes some collars and socks and a half a page of a newspaper clipped out. Bill reads the clipping careful, and holds out his hand to the held-up party.

' "Brother," says he, "greetings! Accept the apologies of friends. I am Bill Bassett, the burglar. Mr Peters, you must make the acquaintance of Mr Alfred E. Ricks. Shake hands. Mr Peters", says Bill, "stands about halfway between me and you, Mr Ricks, in the line of havoc and corruption. He always gives something for the money he gets. I'm glad to meet you, Mr Ricks – you and Mr Peters. This is the first time I ever attended a full gathering of the National Synod of Sharks – housebreaking, swindling, and financiering all represented. Please examine Mr Ricks' credentials, Mr Peters."

'The piece of newspaper that Bill Bassett handed me had a good picture of this Ricks on it. It was a Chicago paper, and it had obloquies of Ricks in every paragraph. By reading it over I harvested the intelligence that said alleged Ricks had laid off all that portion of the State of Florida that lies under water into town lots and sold 'em to alleged innocent investors from his magnificently furnished offices in Chicago. After he had taken in a hundred thousand or so dollars one of these fussy purchasers that are always making trouble (I've had 'em actually try gold watches I've sold 'em with acid) took a cheap excursion down to the land where it is always just before supper to look at his lot and see if it didn't need a new paling or two on the fence, and market a few lemons in time for the Christmas present trade. He hires a surveyor to find his lot for him. They run the line out and find the flourishing town of Paradise Hollow, so advertised, to be about 40 rods and 16 poles S., 27° E. of the middle of Lake Okeechobee. This man's lot was under thirty-six feet of water, and, besides, had been preempted so long by the alligators and gars that his title looked fishy.

'Naturally, the man goes back to Chicago and makes it as hot for Alfred E. Ricks as the morning after a prediction of snow by the weather bureau. Ricks defied the allegation, but he couldn't deny the alligators. One morning the papers came out with a column about it, and Ricks came out by the fire-escape. It seems the alleged authorities had beat him to the safe-deposit box where he kept his winnings, and Ricks has to westward ho! with only feetwear and a dozen 15½ English pokes in his shopping bag. He happened to have some mileage left in his book, and that took him as far as the town in the wilderness where he was spilled out on me and Bill Bassett as Elijah III with not a raven in sight for any of us.

'Then this Alfred E. Ricks lets out a squeak that he is hungry, too, and denies the hypothesis that he is good for the value, let alone the price, of a meal. And so, there was the three of us, representing, if we had a mind to draw syllogisms and parabolas, labor and trade and capital. Now, when trade has no capital there isn't a dicker to be made. And when capital has no money there's a stagnation in steak and onions. That put it up to the man with the jimmy.

' "Brother bushrangers," says Bill Bassett, "never yet, in trouble, did I desert a pal. Hard by, in yon wood, I seem to see unfurnished lodgings. Let us go there and wait till dark."

'There was an old, deserted cabin in the grove, and we three took possession of it. After dark Bill Bassett tells us to wait, and goes out for half an hour. He comes back with a armful of bread and spare ribs and pies.

' "Panhandled 'em at a farmhouse on Washita Avenue," says he. "Eat, drink, and be leary."

'The full moon was coming up bright, so we sat on the

floor of the cabin and ate in the light of it. And this Bill Bassett begins to brag.

' "Sometimes", says he, with his mouth full of country produce, "I lose all patience with you people that think you are higher up in the profession than I am. Now, what could either of you have done in the present emergency to set us on our feet again? Could you do it, Ricksy?"

' "I must confess, Mr Bassett," says Ricks, speaking nearly inaudible out of a slice of pie, "that at this immediate juncture I could not, perhaps, promote an enterprise to relieve the situation. Large operations, such as I direct, naturally require careful preparation in advance. I—"

' "I know, Ricksy," breaks in Bill Bassett. "You needn't finish. You need $500 to make the first payment on a blonde typewriter, and four roomsful of quartered oak furniture. And you need $500 more for advertising contracts. And you need two weeks' time for the fish to begin to bite. Your line of relief would be about as useful in an emergency as advocating municipal ownership to cure a man suffocated by eighty-cent gas. And your graft ain't much swifter, Brother Peters," he winds up.

' "Oh," says I, "I haven't seen you turn anything into gold with your wand yet, Mr Good Fairy. 'Most anybody could rub the magic ring for a little leftover victuals."

' "That was only getting the pumpkin ready," says Bassett, braggy and cheerful. "The coach and six'll drive up to the door before you know it, Miss Cinderella. Maybe you've got some scheme under your sleeve-holders that will give us a start."

' "Son," says I, "I'm fifteen years older than you are, and young enough yet to take out an endowment policy. I've been broke before. We can see the lights of that town not half a mile away. I learned under Montague Silver, the greatest street man that ever spoke from a wagon. There are hundreds of men walking those streets this moment with grease spots on their clothes. Give me a gasoline lamp, a dry-goods box,

71

and a two-dollar bar of white castile soap, cut into little—"

' "Where's your two dollars?" snickered Bill Bassett into my discourse. There was no use arguing with that burglar.

' "No," he goes on; "you're both babes-in-the-wood. Finance has closed the mahogany desk, and trade has put the shutters up. Both of you look to labor to start the wheels going. All right. You admit it. Tonight I'll show you what Bill Bassett can do."

'Bassett tells me and Ricks not to leave the cabin till he comes back, even if it's daylight, and then he starts off toward town, whistling gay.

'This Alfred E. Ricks pulls off his shoes and his coat, lays a silk handkerchief over his hat, and lays down on the floor.

' "I think I will endeavor to secure a little slumber," he squeaks. "The day has been fatiguing. Good-night, my dear Mr Peters."

' "My regards to Morpheus," says I. "I think I'll sit up a while."

'About two o'clock, as near as I could guess by my watch in Peavine, home comes our laboring man and kicks up Ricks, and calls us to the streak of bright moonlight shining in the cabin door. Then he spreads out five packages of $1,000 each on the floor, and begins to cackle over the nest-egg like a hen.

' "I'll tell you a few things about that town," says he. "It's named Rocky Springs, and they're building a Masonic temple, and it looks like the Democratic candidate for mayor is going to get soaked by a Pop, and Judge Tucker's wife, who has been down with pleurisy, is some better. I had a talk on these lilliputian thesises before I could get a siphon in the fountain of knowledge that I was after. And there's a bank there called the Lumberman's Fidelity and Plowman's Savings Institution. It closed for business yesterday with $23,000 cash on hand. It will open this morning with $18,000 – all silver – that's the reason I didn't bring more. There you are, trade and capital. Now, will you be bad?"

' "My young friend," says Alfred E. Ricks, holding up his hands, "have you robbed this bank? Dear me, dear me!"

' "You couldn't call it that," says Bassett. " 'Robbing' sounds harsh. All I had to do was to find out what street it was on. That town is so quiet that I could stand on the corner and hear the tumblers clicking in that safe lock – 'right to 45; left twice to 80; right once to 60; left to 15' – as plain as the Yale captain giving orders in the football dialect. Now, boys," says Bassett, "this is an early rising town. They tell me the citizens are all up and stirring before daylight. I asked what for, and they said because breakfast was ready at that time. And what of merry Robin Hood? It must be Yoicks! and away with the tinkers' chorus. I'll stake you. How much do you want? Speak up, Capital."

' "My dear young friend," says this ground squirrel of a Ricks, standing on his hind legs and juggling nuts in his paws, "I have friends in Denver who would assist me. If I had $100 I—"

'Bassett unpins a package of the currency and throws five twenties to Ricks.

' "Trade, how much?" he says to me.

' "Put your money up, Labor," says I. "I never yet drew upon honest toil for its hard-earned pittance. The dollars I get are surplus ones that are burning the pockets of damfools and greenhorns. When I stand on a street corner and sell a solid gold diamond ring to a yap for $3.00, I make just $2.60. And I know he's going to give it to a girl in return for all the benefits accruing from a $125.00 ring. His profits are $122.00. Which of us is the biggest fakir?"

' "And when you sell a poor woman a pinch of sand for fifty cents to keep her lamp from exploding," says Bassett, "what do you figure her gross earnings to be, with sand at forty cents a ton?"

' "Listen," says I. "I instruct her to keep her lamp clean and well filled. If she does that it can't burst. And with the sand in it she knows it can't and she don't worry. It's kind of

Industrial Christian Science. She pays fifty cents, and gets both Rockefeller and Mrs Eddy on the job. It ain't everybody that can let the gold-dust twins do their work."

'Alfred E. Ricks all but licks the dust off of Bill Bassett's shoes.

' "My dear young friend," says he, "I will never forget your generosity. Heaven will reward you. But let me implore you to turn from your ways of violence and crime."

' "Mousie," says Bill, "the hole in the wainscoting for yours. Your dogmas and inculcations sound to me like the last words of a bicycle pump. What has your high moral, elevator-service system of pillage brought you to? Penuriousness and want. Even Brother Peters, who insists upon contaminating the art of robbery with theories of commerce and trade, admitted he was on the lift. Both of you live by the gilded rule. Brother Peters," says Bill, "you'd better choose a slice of this embalmed currency. You're welcome."

'I told Bill Bassett once more to put his money in his pocket. I never had the respect for burglary that some people have. I always gave something for the money I took, even if it was only some little trifle of a souvenir to remind 'em not to get caught again.

'And then Alfred E. Ricks grovels at Bill's feet again, and bids us adieu. He says he will have a team at a farmhouse, and drive to the station below, and take the train for Denver. It salubrified the atmosphere when that lamentable boll-worm took his departure. He was a disgrace to every non-industrial profession in the country. With all his big schemes and fine offices he had wound up unable even to get an honest meal except by the kindness of a strange and maybe unscrupulous burglar. I was glad to see him go, though I felt a little sorry for him, now that he was ruined forever. What could such a man do without a big capital to work with? Why, Alfred E. Ricks, as we left him, was as helpless as a turtle on its back. He couldn't have worked a scheme to beat a little girl out of a penny slate-pencil.

'When me and Bill Bassett was left alone I did a little sleight-of-mind turn in my head with a trade secret at the end of it. Thinks I, I'll show this Mr Burglar Man the difference between business and labor. He had hurt some of my professional self-adulation by casting his Persians upon commerce and trade.

' "I won't take any of your money as a gift, Mr Bassett," says I to him, "but if you'll pay my expenses as a travelling companion until we get out of the danger zone of the immoral deficit you have caused in this town's finances tonight, I'll be obliged."

'Bill Bassett agreed to that, and we hiked westward as soon as we could catch a safe train.

'When we got to a town in Arizona called Los Perros I suggested that we once more try our luck on terra-cotta. That was the home of Montague Silver, my old instructor, now retired from business. I knew Monty would stake me to web money if I could show him a fly buzzing 'round in the locality. Bill Bassett said all towns looked alike to him as he worked mainly in the dark. So we got off the train in Los Perros, a fine little town in the silver region.

'I had an elegant little sure thing in the way of a commercial slungshot that I intended to hit Bassett behind the ear with. I wasn't going to take his money while he was asleep, but I was going to leave him with a lottery ticket that would represent in experience to him $4,755 – I think that was the amount he had when we got off the train. But the first time I hinted to him about an investment, he turns on me and disencumbers himself of the following terms and expressions.

' "Brother Peters," says he, "it ain't a bad idea to go into an enterprise of some kind, as you suggest. I think I will. But if I do it will be such a cold proposition that nobody but Robert E. Peary and Charlie Fairbanks will be able to sit on the board of directors."

' "I thought you might want to turn your money over," says I.

' "I do," says he, "frequently. I can't sleep on one side all night. I'll tell you, Brother Peters," says he, "I'm going to start a poker room. I don't seem to care for the humdrum in swindling, such as peddling egg-beaters and working off breakfast food on Barnum and Bailey for sawdust to strew in their circus rings. But the gambling business", says he, "from the profitable side of the table is a good compromise between swiping silver spoons and selling penwipers at a Waldorf-Astoria charity bazaar."

' "Then," says I, "Mr Bassett, you don't care to talk over my little business proposition?"

' "Why," says he, "do you know, you can't get a Pasteur institute to start up within fifty miles of where I live. I bite so seldom."

'So, Bassett rents a room over a saloon and looks around for some furniture and chromos. The same night I went to Monty Silver's house, and he let me have $200 on my prospects. Then I went to the only store in Los Perros that sold playing cards and bought every deck in the house. The next morning when the store opened I was there bringing all the cards back with me. I said that my partner that was going to back me in the game had changed his mind; and I wanted to sell the cards back again. The storekeeper took 'em at half price.

'Yes, I was $75 loser up to that time. But while I had the cards that night I marked every one in every deck. That was labor. And then trade and commerce had their innings, and the bread I had cast upon the waters began to come back in the form of cottage pudding with wine sauce.

'Of course I was among the first to buy chips at Bill Bassett's game. He had bought the only cards there was to be had in town; and I knew the back of every one of them better than I know the back of my head when the barber shows me my haircut in the two mirrors.

'When the game closed I had the five thousand and a few odd dollars, and all Bill Bassett had was the wanderlust and a black cat he had bought for a mascot. Bill shook hands with me when I left.

' "Brother Peters," says he, "I have no business being in business. I was preordained to labor. When a No. 1 burglar tries to make a James out of his jimmy he perpetrates an improfundity. You have a well-oiled and efficacious system of luck at cards," says he. "Peace go with you." And I never afterward sees Bill Bassett again.'

'Well, Jeff,' said I, when the Autolycan adventurer seemed to have divulged the gist of his tale, 'I hope you took care of the money. That would be a respecta— that is a considerable working capital if you should choose some day to settle down to some sort of regular business.'

'Me?' said Jeff, virtuously. 'You can bet I've taken care of that five thousand.'

He tapped his coat over the region of his chest exultantly.

'Gold-mining stock,' he explained, 'every cent of it. Shares par value one dollar. Bound to go up 500 per cent within a year. Nonassessable. The Blue Gopher Mine. Just discovered a month ago. Better get in yourself if you've any spare dollars on hand.'

'Sometimes', said I, 'these mines are not—'

'Oh, this one's solid as an old goose,' said Jeff. '$50,000 worth of ore in sight, and 10 per cent monthly earnings guaranteed.'

He drew a long envelope from his pocket and cast it on the table.

'Always carry it with me,' said he. 'So the burglar can't corrupt or the capitalist break in and water it.'

I looked at the beautifully engraved certificate of stock.

'In Colorado, I see,' said I. 'And, by the way, Jeff, what was the name of the little man who went to Denver – the one you and Bill met at the station?'

'Alfred E. Ricks', said Jeff, 'was the toad's designation.'

'I see', said I, 'the president of this mining company

signs himself A. L. Fredericks. I was wondering—'

'Let me see that stock,' said Jeff quickly, almost snatching it from me.

To mitigate, even though slightly, the embarrassment I summoned the waiter and ordered another bottle of the Barbera. I thought it was the least I could do.

The Grey Parrot

W. W. JACOBS

The Chief Engineer and the Third sat at tea on the SS *Curlew* in the East India Docks. The small and not over-clean steward having placed everything he could think of upon the table, and then added everything the Chief could think of, had assiduously poured out two cups of tea and withdrawn by request. The two men ate steadily, conversing between bites, and interrupted occasionally by a hoarse and sepulchral voice, the owner of which, being much exercised by the sight of the food, asked for it, prettily at first, and afterwards in a way which at least compelled attention.

'That's pretty good for a parrot,' said the Third critically. 'Seems to know what he's saying too. No, don't give it anything. It'll stop if you do.'

'There's no pleasure to *me* in listening to coarse language,' said the Chief with dignity.

He absently dipped a piece of bread-and-butter in the Third's tea, and losing it chased it round and round the bottom of the cup with his finger, the Third regarding the operation with an interest and emotion which he was at first unable to understand.

'You'd better pour yourself out another cup,' he said thoughtfully as he caught the Third's eye.

'I'm going to,' said the other dryly.

'The man I bought it of', said the Chief, giving the bird the sop, 'said that it was a perfectly respectable parrot and wouldn't know a bad word if it heard it. I hardly like to give it to my wife now.'

'It's no good being too particular,' said the Third, regarding him with an ill-concealed grin; 'that's the worst of all you young married fellows. Seem to think your wife has got to be wrapped up in brown paper. Ten chances to one she'll be amused.'

The Chief shrugged his shoulders disdainfully. 'I bought the bird to be company for her,' he said slowly; 'she'll be very lonesome without me, Rogers.'

'How do you know?' enquired the other.

'She said so,' was the reply.

'When you've been married as long as I have,' said the Third, who having been married some fifteen years felt that their usual positions were somewhat reversed, 'you'll know that generally speaking they're glad to get rid of you.'

'What for?' demanded the Chief in a voice that Othello might have envied.

'Well, you get in the way a bit,' said Rogers with secret enjoyment; 'you see, you upset the arrangements. House-cleaning and all that sort of thing gets interrupted. They're glad to see you back at first, and then glad to see the back of you.'

'There's wives and wives,' said the bridegroom tenderly.

'And mine's a good one,' said the Third, 'registered A1 at Lloyd's, but she don't worry about me going away. Your wife's thirty years younger than you, isn't she?'

'Twenty-five,' corrected the other shortly. 'You see, what I'm afraid of is that she'll get too much attention.'

'Well, women like that,' remarked the Third.

'But I don't, damn it!' cried the Chief hotly. 'When I think of it I get hot all over. Boiling hot.'

'That won't last,' said the other reassuringly; 'you won't care twopence this time next year.'

'We're not all alike,' growled the Chief; 'some of us have got finer feelings than others have. I saw the chap next door looking at her as we passed him this morning.'

'Lor',' said the Third.

'I don't want any of your damned impudence,' said the

80

Chief sharply. 'He put his hat on straighter when he passed us. What do you think of that?'

'Can't say,' replied the other with commendable gravity; 'it might mean anything.'

'If he has any of his nonsense while I'm away I'll break his neck,' said the Chief passionately. 'I shall know it.'

The other raised his eyebrows.

'I've asked the landlady to keep her eyes open a bit,' said the Chief. 'My wife was brought up in the country, and she's very young and simple, so that it is quite right and proper for her to have a motherly old body to look after her.'

'Told your wife?' queried Rogers.

'No,' said the other. 'Fact is, I've got an idea about that parrot. I'm going to tell her it's a magic bird, and will tell me everything she does while I'm away. Anything the landlady tells me I shall tell her I got from the parrot. For one thing, I don't want her to go out after seven of an evening, and she's promised me she won't. If she does I shall know, and pretend that I know through the parrot. What do you think of it?'

'Think of it?' said the Third, staring at him. 'Think of it? Fancy a man telling a grown-up woman a yarn like that!'

'She believes in warnings and death-watches, and all that sort of thing,' said the Chief, 'so why shouldn't she?'

'Well, you'll know whether she believes in it or not when you come back,' said Rogers, 'and it'll be a great pity, because it's a beautiful talker.'

'What do you mean?' said the other.

'I mean it'll get its little neck wrung,' said the Third.

'Well, we'll see,' said Gannett. 'I shall know what to think if it does die.'

'I shall never see that bird again,' said Rogers, shaking his head as the Chief took up the cage and handed it to the steward, who was to accompany him home with it.

The couple left the ship and proceeded down the East India Dock Road side by side, the only incident being a hot argument between a constable and the engineer as to whether he could or could not be held responsible for the language in which the parrot saw fit to indulge when the steward happened to drop it.

The engineer took the cage at his door, and, not without some misgivings, took it upstairs into the parlour and set it on the table. Mrs Gannett, a simple-looking woman, with sleepy brown eyes and a docile manner, clapped her hands with joy.

'Isn't it a beauty?' said Mr Gannett, looking at it. 'I bought it to be company for you while I'm away.'

'You're too good to me, Jem,' said his wife. She walked all round the cage admiring it, the parrot, which was of a highly suspicious and nervous disposition, having had boys at its last place, turning with her. After she had walked round him five times he got sick of it, and in a simple sailorly fashion said so.

'Oh, Jem!' said his wife.

'It's a beautiful talker,' said Gannett hastily, 'and it's so clever that it picks up everything it hears, but it'll soon forget it.'

'It looks as though it knows what you are saying,' said his wife. 'Just look at it, the artful thing.'

The opportunity was too good to be missed, and in a few straightforward lies the engineer acquainted Mrs Gannett of the miraculous powers with which he had chosen to endow it.

'But you don't believe it?' said his wife, staring at him open-mouthed.

'I do,' said the engineer firmly.

'But how can it know what I'm doing when I'm away?' persisted Mrs Gannett.

'Ah, that's its secret,' said the engineer; 'a good many people would like to know that, but nobody has found out yet. It's a magic bird, and when you've said that, you've said all there is to say about it.'

Mrs Gannett, wrinkling her forehead, eyed the marvellous bird curiously.

'You'll find it's quite true,' said Gannett; 'when I come back that bird'll be able to tell me how you've been and all about you. Everything you've done during my absence.'

'Good gracious!' said the astonished Mrs Gannett.

'If you stay out after seven of an evening, or do anything else that I shouldn't like, that bird'll tell me,' continued the engineer impressively. 'It'll tell me who comes to see you, and in fact it will tell me everything you do while I'm away.'

'Well, it won't have anything bad to tell of me,' said Mrs Gannett composedly, 'unless it tells lies.'

'It can't tell lies,' said her husband confidently; 'and now, if you go and put your bonnet on, we'll drop in at the theatre for half an hour.'

It was a prophetic utterance, for he made such a fuss over the man next to his wife offering her his opera-glasses that they left, at the urgent request of the management, in almost exactly that space of time.

'You'd better carry me about in a bandbox,' said Mrs Gannett wearily as the outraged engineer stalked home beside her. 'What harm was the man doing?'

'You must have given him some encouragement,' said Mr Gannett fiercely – 'made eyes at him or something. A man wouldn't offer to lend a lady his opera-glasses without.'

Mrs Gannett tossed her head – and that so decidedly, that a passing stranger turned his head and looked at her. Mr Gannett accelerated his pace, and, taking his wife's arm, led her swiftly home with a passion too great for words.

By the morning his anger had evaporated, but his misgivings remained. He left after breakfast for the *Curlew*, which was to sail in the afternoon, leaving behind him copious instructions by following which his wife would be enabled to come down and see him off with the minimum exposure of her fatal charms.

Left to herself Mrs Gannett dusted the room, until, coming to the parrot's cage, she put down the duster and eyed its eerie occupant curiously. She fancied that she saw an evil glitter in the creature's eye, and the knowing way in which it drew the film over it was as near an approach to a wink as a bird could get.

She was still looking at it when there was a knock at the door, and a bright little woman – rather smartly dressed – bustled into the room and greeted her effusively.

'I just came to see you, my dear, because I thought a little outing would do me good,' she said briskly; 'and if you've no objection I'll come down to the docks with you to see the boat off.'

Mrs Gannett assented readily. It would ease the engineer's mind, she thought, if he saw her with a chaperon.

'Nice bird,' said Mrs Cluffins, mechanically bringing her parasol to the charge.

'Don't do that,' said her friend hastily.

'Why not?' said the other.

'Language!' said Mrs Gannett solemnly.

'Well, I must do something to it,' said Mrs Cluffins restlessly.

She held the parasol near the cage and suddenly opened it. It was a flaming scarlet, and for the moment the shock took the parrot's breath away.

'He don't mind that,' said Mrs Gannett.

The parrot, hopping to the farthest corner of the bottom of his cage, said something feebly. Finding that nothing dreadful happened, he repeated his remark somewhat more boldly, and, being convinced after all that the apparition was quite harmless and that he had displayed his craven spirit for nothing, hopped back on his perch and raved wickedly.

'If that was my bird,' said Mrs Cluffins, almost as scarlet as her parasol, 'I should wring its neck.'

'No, you wouldn't,' said Mrs Gannett solemnly. And having quieted the bird by throwing a cloth over its cage, she explained its properties.

'What!' said Mrs Cluffins, unable to sit still in her chair. 'You mean to tell me your husband said that!'

84

Mrs Gannett nodded.

'He's awfully jealous of me,' she said with a slight simper.

'I wish he was my husband,' said Mrs Cluffins in a thin, hard voice. 'I wish C. would talk to *me* like that. I wish somebody would try and persuade C. to talk to me like that.'

'It shows he's fond of me,' said Mrs Gannett, looking down.

Mrs Cluffins jumped up, and snatching the cover off the cage, endeavoured, but in vain, to get the parasol through the bars.

'And you believe that rubbish!' she said scathingly. 'Boo, you wretch!'

'I don't believe it,' said her friend, taking her gently away and covering the cage hastily just as the bird was recovering, 'but I let him think I do.'

'I call it an outrage,' said Mrs Cluffins, waving the parasol wildly. 'I never heard of such a thing; I'd like to give Mr Gannett a piece of my mind. Just about half an hour of it. He wouldn't be the same man afterwards – I'd parrot him!'

Mrs Gannett, soothing her agitated friend as well as she was able, led her gently to a chair and removed her bonnet, and finding that complete recovery was impossible while the parrot remained in the room, took that wonder-working bird outside.

By the time they had reached the docks and boarded the *Curlew* Mrs Cluffins had quite recovered her spirits. She roamed about the steamer asking questions, which savoured more of idle curiosity than a genuine thirst for knowledge, and was at no pains to conceal her opinion of those who were unable to furnish her with satisfactory replies.

'I shall think of you every day, Jem,' said Mrs Gannett tenderly.

'I shall think of you every minute,' said the engineer reproachfully.

He sighed gently and gazed in a scandalised fashion at Mrs Cluffins, who was carrying on a desperate flirtation with one of the apprentices.

'She's very light-hearted,' said his wife, following the direction of his eyes.

'She is,' said Mr Gannett curtly, as the unconscious Mrs Cluffins shut her parasol and rapped the apprentice playfully with the handle. 'She seems to be on very good terms with Jenkins, laughing and carrying on. I don't suppose she's ever seen him before.'

'Poor young things,' said Mrs Cluffins solemnly, as she came up to them. 'Don't you worry, Mr Gannett; I'll look after her and keep her from moping.'

'You're very kind,' said the engineer slowly.

'We'll have a jolly time,' said Mrs Cluffins. 'I often wish my husband was a seafaring man. A wife does have more freedom, doesn't she?'

'More what?' inquired Mr Gannett huskily.

'More freedom,' said Mrs Cluffins gravely. 'I always envy sailors' wives. They can do as they like. No husband to look after them for nine or ten months in the year.'

Before the unhappy engineer could put his indignant thoughts into words there was a warning cry from the gangway, and with a hasty farewell he hurried below. The visitors went ashore, the gangway was shipped, and in response to the clang of the telegraph the *Curlew* drifted slowly away from the quay and headed for the swing bridge slowly opening in front of her.

The two ladies hurried to the pier-head and watched the steamer down the river until a bend hid it from view. Then Mrs Gannett, with a sensation of having lost something, due, so her friend assured her, to the want of a cup of tea, went slowly back to her lonely home.

In the period of grass widowhood which ensued, Mrs Cluffins's visits formed almost the sole relief to the bare monotony of existence. As a companion the parrot was an utter failure, its language being so irredeemably bad that it spent most of its time in the spare room with a cloth over its cage, wondering when the days were going to lengthen a bit.

86

Mrs Cluffins suggested selling it, but her friend repelled the suggestion with horror, and refused to entertain it at any price, even that of the publican at the corner, who, having heard of the bird's command of language, was bent upon buying it.

'I wonder what that beauty will have to tell your husband,' said Mrs Cluffins, as they sat together one day some three months after the *Curlew*'s departure.

'I should hope that he has forgotten that nonsense,' said Mrs Gannett, reddening; 'he never alludes to it in his letters.'

'Sell it,' said Mrs Cluffins peremptorily. 'It's no good to you, and Hobson would give anything for it almost.'

Mrs Gannett shook her head. 'The house wouldn't hold my husband if I did,' she remarked with a shiver.

'Oh yes, it would,' said Mrs Cluffins; 'you do as I tell you, and a much smaller house than this would hold him. I told C. to tell Hobson he should have it for five pounds.'

'But he mustn't,' said her friend in alarm.

'Leave yourself right in my hands,' said Mrs Cluffins, spreading out two small palms and regarding them complacently. 'It'll be all right, I promise you.'

She put her arm round her friend's waist and led her to the window, talking earnestly. In five minutes Mrs Gannett was wavering, in ten she had given way, and in fifteen the energetic Mrs Cluffins was en route for Hobson's, swinging the cage so violently in her excitement that the parrot was reduced to holding on to its perch with claws and bill. Mrs Gannett watched the progress from the window, and with a queer look on her face sat down to think out the points of attack and defence in the approaching fray.

A week later a four-wheeler drove up to the door, and the engineer, darting upstairs three steps at a time, dropped an armful of parcels on the floor, and caught his wife in an embrace which would have done credit to a bear. Mrs Gannett, for reasons of which lack of muscle was only one, responded less ardently.

'Ha, it's good to be home again,' said Gannett, sinking into an easy-chair and pulling his wife on his knee. 'And how have you been? Lonely?'

'I got used to it,' said Mrs Gannett softly.

The engineer coughed. 'You had the parrot,' he remarked.

'Yes, I had the magic parrot,' said Mrs Gannett.

'How's it getting on?' said her husband, looking round. 'Where is it?'

'Part of it is on the mantelpiece,' said Mrs Gannett, trying to speak calmly, 'part of it is in a bonnet-box upstairs, some of it's in my pocket, and here is the remainder.'

She fumbled in her pocket and placed in his hand a cheap two-bladed clasp-knife.

'On the mantelpiece!' repeated the engineer, staring at the knife; 'in a bonnet-box!'

'Those blue vases,' said his wife.

Mr Gannett put his hand to his head. If he had heard aright, one parrot had changed into a pair of vases, a bonnet, and a knife. A magic bird with a vengeance!

'I sold it,' said Mrs Gannett suddenly.

The engineer's knee stiffened inhospitably, and his arm dropped from his wife's waist. She rose quietly and took a chair opposite.

'Sold it!' said Mr Gannett in awful tones. 'Sold my parrot!'

'I didn't like it, Jem,' said his wife. 'I didn't want that bird watching me, and I did want the vases, and the bonnet, and the little present for you.'

Mr Gannett pitched the little present to the other end of the room.

'You see, it mightn't have told the truth, Jem,' continued Mrs Gannett. 'It might have told all sorts of lies about me, and made no end of mischief.'

'It couldn't lie,' shouted the engineer passionately, rising from his chair and pacing the room. 'It's your guilty conscience that's made a coward of you. How dare you sell my parrot?'

88

'Because it wasn't truthful, Jem,' said his wife, who was somewhat pale.

'If you were half as truthful you'd do,' vociferated the engineer, standing over her. 'You, you deceitful woman.'

Mrs Gannett fumbled in her pocket again, and producing a small handkerchief applied it delicately to her eyes.

'I – I got rid of it for your sake,' she stammered. 'It used to tell such lies about you. I couldn't bear to listen to it.'

'About *me*!' said Mr Gannett, sinking into his seat and staring at his wife with very natural amazement. 'Tell lies about *me*! Nonsense! How could it?'

'I suppose it could tell me about you as easily as it could tell you about me?' said Mrs Gannett. 'There was more magic in that bird than you thought, Jem. It used to say shocking things about you. I couldn't bear it.'

'Do you think you're talking to a child or a fool?' demanded the engineer.

Mrs Gannett shook her head feebly. She still kept the handkerchief to her eyes, but allowed a portion to drop over her mouth.

'I should like to hear some of the stories it told about me – if you can remember them,' said the engineer with bitter sarcasm.

'The first lie,' said Mrs Gannett in a feeble but ready voice, 'was about the time you were at Genoa. The parrot said you were at some concert gardens at the upper end of the town.'

One moist eye coming mildly from behind the handkerchief saw the engineer stiffen suddenly in his chair.

'I don't suppose there even is such a place,' she continued.

'I – believe – there – is,' said her husband jerkily. 'I've heard – our chaps – talk of it.'

'But you haven't been there?' said his wife anxiously.

'*Never!*' said the engineer with extraordinary vehemence.

'That wicked bird said that you got intoxicated there,' said Mrs Gannett in solemn accents, 'that you smashed a little marble-topped table and knocked down two waiters, and that if it hadn't been for the captain of the *Pursuit*, who was in there and who got you away, you'd have been locked up. Wasn't it a wicked bird?'

'Horrible!' said the engineer huskily.

'I don't suppose there ever was a ship called the *Pursuit*,' continued Mrs Gannett.

'Doesn't sound like a ship's name,' murmured Mr Gannett.

'Well, then, a few days later it said the *Curlew* was at Naples.'

'I never went ashore all the time we were at Naples,' remarked the engineer casually.

'The parrot said you did,' said Mrs Gannett.

'I suppose you'll believe your own lawful husband before that damned bird?' shouted Gannett, starting up.

'Of course I didn't believe it, Jem,' said his wife. 'I'm trying to prove to you that the bird was not truthful, but you're so hard to persuade.'

Mr Gannett took a pipe from his pocket, and with a small knife dug with much severity and determination a hardened plug from the bowl, and blew noisily through the stem.

'There was a girl kept a fruit-stall just by the harbour,' said Mrs Gannett, 'and on this evening, on the strength of having bought three-pennyworth of green figs, you put your arm round her waist and tried to kiss her, and her sweetheart, who was standing close by, tried to stab you. The parrot said that you were in such a state of terror that you jumped into the harbour and were nearly drowned.'

Mr Gannett having loaded his pipe lit it slowly and carefully, and with tidy precision got up and deposited the match in the fireplace.

'It used to frighten me so with its stories that I hardly knew what to do with myself,' continued Mrs Gannett. 'When you were at Suez—'

The engineer waved his hand imperiously.

'That's enough,' he said stiffly.

'I'm sure I don't want to have to repeat what it told me about Suez,' said his wife. 'I thought you'd like to hear it, that's all.'

'Not at all,' said the engineer, puffing at his pipe. 'Not at all.'

'But you see why I got rid of the bird, don't you?' said Mrs Gannett. 'If it had told you untruths about me, *you* would have believed them, wouldn't you?'

Mr Gannett took his pipe from his mouth and took his wife in his extended arms. 'No, my dear,' he said brokenly, 'no more than you believe all this stuff about me.'

'And I did quite right to sell it, didn't I, Jem?'

'Quite right,' said Mr Gannett with a great assumption of heartiness. 'Best thing to do with it.'

'You haven't heard the worst yet,' said Mrs Gannett. 'When you were at Suez—'

Mr Gannett consigned Suez to its only rival, and, thumping the table with his clenched fist, forbade his wife to mention the word again, and desired her to prepare supper.

Not until he heard his wife moving about in the kitchen below did he relax the severity of his countenance. Then his expression changed to one of extreme anxiety, and he restlessly paced the room, seeking for light. It came suddenly.

'Jenkins!' he gasped. 'Jenkins and Mrs Cluffins, and I was going to tell Cluffins about him writing to his wife. I expect he knows the letter by heart.'

Bill, the Ventriloquial Rooster

HENRY LAWSON

'When we were up-country on the selection we had a rooster at our place named Bill,' said Mitchell; 'a big mongrel of no particular breed, though the old lady said he was a "brammer" – and many an argument she had with the old man about it too; she was just as stubborn and obstinate in her opinion as the governor was in his. But, anyway, we called him Bill, and didn't take any particular notice of him till a cousin of some of us came from Sydney on a visit to the country, and stayed at our place because it was cheaper than stopping at a pub. Well, somehow this chap got interested in Bill, and studied him for two or three days, and at last he says:

    ' "Why, that rooster's a ventriloquist!"

    ' "A what?"

    ' "A ventriloquist!"

    ' "Go along with yer!"

    ' "But he is. I've heard of cases like this before; but this is the first I've come across. Bill's a ventriloquist right enough."

'Then we remembered that there wasn't another rooster within five miles – our only neighbour, an Irishman named Page, didn't have one at the time – and we'd often heard another cock crow, but didn't think to take any notice of it. We watched Bill, and sure enough he *was* a ventriloquist. The "ka-cocka" would come all right, but the "co-ka-koo-oi-oo" seemed to come from a distance. And sometimes the whole crow would go wrong, and come back like an echo that had been lost for a year. Bill would stand on tiptoe, and hold his elbows out, and curve his neck, and go two or three times as if he was swallowing nest-eggs, and nearly break his neck and burst his gizzard; and then there'd be no sound at all where he was – only a cock crowing in the distance.

'And pretty soon we could see that Bill was in great trouble about it himself. You see, he didn't know it was himself – thought it was another rooster challenging him, and he wanted badly to find that other bird. He would get up on the woodheap, and crow and listen – crow and listen again – crow and listen, and then he'd go up to the top of the paddock, and get up on the stack, and crow and listen there. Then down to the other end of the paddock, and get up on the mullock-heap, and crow and listen there. Then across to the other side and up on a log among the saplings, and crow 'n' listen some more. He searched all over the place for that other rooster, but of course couldn't find him. Sometimes he'd be out all day crowing and listening all over the country, and then come home dead tired, and rest and cool off in a hole that the hens had scratched for him in a damp place under the water-cask sledge.

'Well, one day Page brought home a big white rooster, and when he let it go it climbed up on Page's stack and crowed, to see if there was any more roosters round there. Bill had come home tired; it was a hot day, and he'd routed out the hens, and was having a spell-oh under the cask when the white rooster crowed. Bill didn't lose any time getting out and on to the woodheap, and then he waited till he heard the crow again; then he crowed, and the other rooster crowed again, and they crowed at each other for three days, and called each other all the wretches they could lay their tongues to, and after that they implored each other to come out and be made into chicken soup and feather pillows. But neither'd come. You see, there were *three* crows – there was Bill's crow, and the ventriloquist crow, and the white rooster's crow – and each rooster thought that there was *two* roosters in the opposition camp, and that he mightn't get fair play, and, consequently, both were afraid to put up their hands.

93

'But at last Bill couldn't stand it any longer. He made up his mind to go and have it out, even if there was a whole agricultural show of prize and honourable-mention fighting-cocks in Page's yard. He got down from the woodheap and started off across the ploughed field, his head down, his elbows out, and his thick awkward legs prodding away at the furrows behind for all they were worth.

'I wanted to go down badly and see the fight, and barrack for Bill. But I daren't, because I'd been coming up the road late the night before with my brother Joe, and there was about three panels of turkeys roosting along on the top rail of Page's front fence; and we brushed 'em with a bough, and they got up such a blessed gobbling fuss about it that Page came out in his shirt and saw us running away; and I knew he was laying for us with a bullock-whip. Besides, there was friction between the two families on account of a thoroughbred bull that Page borrowed and wouldn't lend to us, and that got into our paddock on account of me mending a panel in the party fence, and carelessly leaving the top rail down after sundown while our cows was moving round there in the saplings.

'So there was too much friction for me to go down, but I climbed a tree as near the fence as I could and watched. Bill reckoned he'd found that rooster at last. The white rooster wouldn't come down from the stack, so Bill went up to him, and they fought there till they tumbled down the other side, and I couldn't see any more. Wasn't I wild? I'd have given my dog to have seen the rest of the fight. I went down to the far side of Page's fence and climbed a tree there, but of course I couldn't see anything, so I came home the back way. Just as I got home Page came round to the front and sung out, "Insoid there!" And me and Jim went under the house like snakes and looked out round a pile. But Page was all right – he had a broad grin on his face, and Bill safe under his arm. He put Bill down on the ground very carefully, and says he to the old folks:

94

' "Yer rooster knocked the stuffin' out of my rooster, but I bear no malice. 'Twas a grand foight."

'And then the old man and Page had a yarn, and got pretty friendly after that. And Bill didn't seem to bother about any more ventriloquism; but the white rooster spent a lot of time looking for that other rooster. Perhaps he thought he'd have better luck with him. But Page was on the look-out all the time to get a rooster that would lick ours. He did nothing else for a month but ride round and enquire about roosters; and at last he borrowed a game-bird in town, left five pounds deposit on him, and brought him home. And Page and the old man agreed to have a match – about the only thing they'd agreed about for five years. And they fixed it up for a Sunday when the old lady and the girls and kids were going on a visit to some relations, about fifteen miles away – to stop all night. The guv'nor made me go with them on horseback; but I knew what was up, and so my pony went lame about a mile along the road, and I had to come back and turn him out in the top paddock, and hide the saddle and bridle in a hollow log, and sneak home and climb up on the roof of the shed. It was an awful hot day, and I had to keep climbing backward and forward over the ridge-pole all the morning to keep out of sight of the old man, for he was moving about a good deal.

'Well, after dinner, the fellows from round about began to ride in and hang up their horses round the place till it looked as if there was going to be a funeral. Some of the chaps saw me, of course, but I tipped them the wink, and they gave me the office whenever the old man happened around.

'Well, Page came along with his game-rooster. Its name was Jim. It wasn't much to look at, and it seemed a good deal smaller and weaker than Bill. Some of the chaps were disgusted, and said it wasn't a game-rooster at all; Bill'd settle it in one lick, and they wouldn't have any fun.

'Well, they brought the game one out and put him down near the woodheap, and routed Bill out from under his cask.

He got interested at once. He looked at Jim, and got up on the woodheap and crowed and looked at Jim again. He reckoned *this* at last was the fowl that had been humbugging him all along. Presently his trouble caught him, and then he'd crow and take a squint at the game 'un, and crow again, and have another squint at gamey, and try to crow and keep his eye on the game-rooster at the same time. But Jim never committed himself, until at last he happened to gape just after Bill's whole crow went wrong, and Bill spotted him. He reckoned he'd caught him this time, and he got down off that woodheap and went for the foe. But Jim ran away – and Bill ran after him.

'Round and round the woodheap they went, and round the shed, and round the house and under it, and back again, and round the woodheap and over it and round the other way, and kept it up for close on an hour. Bill's bill was just within an inch or so of the game-rooster's tail feathers most of the time, but he couldn't get any nearer, do how he liked. And all the time the fellers kept chyakin' Page and singing out, "What price yer game 'un, Page! Go it, Bill! Go it, old cock!" and all that sort of thing. Well, the game-rooster went as if it was a go-as-you-please, and he didn't care if it lasted a year. He didn't seem to take any interest in the business, but Bill got excited, and by and by he got mad. He held his head lower and lower and his wings further and further out from his sides, and prodded away harder and harder at the ground behind, but it wasn't any use. Jim seemed to keep ahead without trying. They stuck to the woodheap towards the last. They went round first one way for a while, and then the other for a change, and now and then they'd go over the top to break the monotony; and the chaps got more interested in the race than they would have been in the fight – and bet on it, too. But Bill was handicapped with his weight. He was done up at last; he slowed down till he couldn't waddle, and then, when he was thoroughly knocked up, that game-rooster turned on him, and gave him the father of a hiding.

96

'And my father caught me when I'd got down in the excitement, and wasn't thinking, and *he* gave *me* the step-father of a hiding. But he had a lively time with the old lady afterwards, over the cock-fight.

'Bill was so disgusted with himself that he went under the cask and died.'

The Conjuror's Revenge

STEPHEN LEACOCK

'Now, ladies and gentlemen,' said the conjuror, 'having shown you that the cloth is absolutely empty, I will proceed to take from it a bowl of goldfish. Presto!'

All around the hall people were saying, 'Oh, how wonderful! How does he do it?'

But the Quick Man on the front seat said in a big whisper to the people near him, 'He – had – it – up – his – sleeve.'

Then the people nodded brightly at the Quick Man and said, 'Oh, of course'; and everybody whispered round the hall, 'He – had – it – up – his – sleeve.'

'My next trick', said the conjuror, 'is the famous Hindoostanee rings. You will notice that the rings are apparently separate; at a blow they all join (clang, clang, clang) – Presto!'

There was a general buzz of stupefaction till the Quick Man was heard to whisper, 'He – must – have – had – another – lot – up – his – sleeve.'

Again everybody nodded and whispered, 'The – rings – were – up – his – sleeve.'

The brow of the conjuror was clouded with a gathering frown.

'I will now', he continued, 'show you a most amusing trick by which I am enabled to take any number of eggs from a hat. Will some gentleman kindly lend me his hat? Ah, thank you – Presto!'

He extracted seventeen eggs, and for thirty-five seconds the audience began to think that he was wonderful. Then the Quick Man whispered along the front bench, 'He – has – a – hen – up – his – sleeve,' and all the people whispered

98

it on. 'He – has – a – lot – of – hens – up – his – sleeve.'

The egg trick was ruined.

It went on like that all through. It transpired from the whispers of the Quick Man that the conjuror must have concealed up his sleeve, in addition to the rings, hens, and fish, several packs of cards, a loaf of bread, a doll's cradle, a live guinea-pig, a fifty-cent piece, and a rocking-chair.

The reputation of the conjuror was rapidly sinking below zero. At the close of the evening he rallied for a final effort.

'Ladies and gentlemen,' he said, 'I will present to you, in conclusion, the famous Japanese trick recently invented by the natives of Tipperary. Will you, sir,' he continued, turning toward the Quick Man, 'will you kindly hand me your gold watch?'

It was passed to him.

'Have I your permission to put it into this mortar and pound it to pieces?' he asked savagely.

The Quick Man nodded and smiled.

The conjuror threw the watch into the mortar and grasped a sledge hammer from the table. There was a sound of violent smashing, 'He's – slipped – it – up – his – sleeve,' whispered the Quick Man.

'Now, sir,' continued the conjuror, 'will you allow me to take your handkerchief and punch holes in it? Thank you. You see, ladies and gentlemen, there is no deception; the holes are visible to the eye.'

The face of the Quick Man beamed. This time the real mystery of the thing fascinated him.

'And now, sir, will you kindly pass me your silk hat and allow me to dance on it? Thank you.'

The conjuror made a few rapid passes with his feet and exhibited the hat crushed beyond recognition.

'And will you now, sir, take off your celluloid collar and permit me to burn it in the candle? Thank you, sir. And will you allow me to smash your spectacles for you with my hammer? Thank you.'

By this time the features of the Quick Man were assuming a puzzled expression. 'This thing beats me,' he whispered, 'I don't see through it a bit.'

There was a great hush upon the audience. Then the conjuror drew himself up to his full height and, with a withering look at the Quick Man, he concluded:

'Ladies and gentlemen, you will observe that I have, with this gentleman's permission, broken his watch, burnt his collar, smashed his spectacles, and danced on his hat. If he will give me the further permission to paint green stripes on his overcoat, or to tie his suspenders in a knot, I shall be delighted to entertain you. If not, the performance is at an end.'

And amid a glorious burst of music from the orchestra the curtain fell, and the audience dispersed, convinced that there are some tricks, at any rate, that are not done up the conjuror's sleeve.

The Byzantine Omelette

SAKI

Sophie Chattel-Monkheim was a Socialist by conviction and a Chattel-Monkheim by marriage. The particular member of that wealthy family whom she had married was rich, even as his relatives counted riches. Sophie had very advanced and decided views as to the distribution of money: it was a pleasing and fortunate circumstance that she also had the money. When she inveighed eloquently against the evils of capitalism at drawing-room meetings and Fabian conferences she was conscious of a comfortable feeling that the system, with all its inequalities and iniquities, would probably last her time. It is one of the consolations of middle-aged reformers that the good they inculcate must live after them if it is to live at all.

On a certain spring evening, somewhere towards the dinner-hour, Sophie sat tranquilly between her mirror and her maid, undergoing the process of having her hair built into an elaborate reflection of the prevailing fashion. She was hedged round with a great peace, the peace of one who has attained a desired end with much effort and perseverance, and who has found it still eminently desirable in its attainment. The Duke of Syria had consented to come beneath her roof as a guest, was even now installed beneath her roof, and would shortly be sitting at her dining-table. As a good Socialist, Sophie disapproved of social distinctions, and derided the idea of a princely caste, but if there were to be these artificial gradations of rank and dignity she was pleased and anxious to have an exalted specimen of an exalted order included in her house-party. She was broad-minded enough to love the sinner while hating the sin – not that she entertained any warm feeling of personal affection for the Duke of Syria, who was a comparative stranger, but still, as Duke of Syria, he was very, very welcome beneath her roof. She could not have explained why, but no one was likely to ask her for an explanation, and most hostesses envied her.

'You must surpass yourself tonight, Richardson,' she said complacently to her maid; 'I must be looking my very best. We must all surpass ourselves.'

The maid said nothing, but from the concentrated look in her eyes and the deft play of her fingers it was evident that she was beset with the ambition to surpass herself.

A knock came at the door, a quiet but peremptory knock, as of someone who would not be denied.

'Go and see who it is,' said Sophie; 'it may be something about the wine.'

Richardson held a hurried conference with an invisible messenger at the door; when she returned there was noticeable a curious listlessness in place of her hitherto alert manner.

'What is it?' asked Sophie.

'The household servants have "downed tools", madame,' said Richardson.

'Downed tools!' exclaimed Sophie; 'do you mean to say they've gone on strike?'

'Yes, madame,' said Richardson, adding the information: 'It's Gaspare that the trouble is about.'

'Gaspare?' said Sophie wonderingly; 'the emergency chef! The omelette specialist!'

'Yes, madame. Before he became an omelette specialist he was a valet, and he was one of the strike-breakers in the great strike at Lord Grimford's two years ago. As soon as the household staff here learned that you had engaged him they resolved to "down tools" as a protest. They haven't got any grievance against you personally, but they demand that Gaspare should be immediately dismissed.'

'But', protested Sophie, 'he is the only man in England

who understands how to make a Byzantine omelette. I engaged him specially for the Duke of Syria's visit, and it would be impossible to replace him at short notice. I should have to send to Paris, and the Duke loves Byzantine omelettes. It was the one thing we talked about coming from the station.'

'He was one of the strike-breakers at Lord Grimford's,' reiterated Richardson.

'This is too awful,' said Sophie; 'a strike of servants at a moment like this, with the Duke of Syria staying in the house. Something must be done immediately. Quick, finish my hair and I'll go and see what I can do to bring them round.'

'I can't finish your hair, madame,' said Richardson quietly, but with immense decision. 'I belong to the union and I can't do another half-minute's work till the strike is settled. I'm sorry to be disobliging.'

'But this is inhuman!' exclaimed Sophie tragically; 'I've always been a model mistress and I've refused to employ any but union servants, and this is the result. I can't finish my hair myself; I don't know how to. What am I to do? It's wicked!'

'Wicked is the word,' said Richardson; 'I'm a good Conservative, and I've no patience with this Socialist foolery, asking your pardon. It's tyranny, that's what it is, all along the line, but I've my living to make, same as other people, and I've got to belong to the union. I couldn't touch another hairpin without a strike permit, not if you was to double my wages.'

The door burst open and Catherine Malsom raged into the room.

'Here's a nice affair,' she screamed, 'a strike of household servants without a moment's warning, and I'm left like this! I can't appear in public in this condition.'

After a very hasty scrutiny Sophie assured her that she could not.

'Have they *all* struck?' she asked her maid.

'Not the kitchen staff,' said Richardson, 'they belong to a different union.'

'Dinner at least will be assured,' said Sophie, 'that is something to be thankful for.'

'Dinner!' snorted Catherine, 'what on earth is the good of dinner when none of us will be able to appear at it? Look at your hair – and look at me! or rather, don't.'

'I know it's difficult to manage without a maid; can't your husband be any help to you?' asked Sophie despairingly.

'Henry? He's in worse case than any of us. His man is the only person who really understands that ridiculous new-fangled Turkish bath that he insists on taking with him everywhere.'

'Surely he could do without a Turkish bath for one evening,' said Sophie; 'I can't appear without hair, but a Turkish bath is a luxury.'

'My good woman,' said Catherine, speaking with a fearful intensity, 'Henry was *in* the bath when the strike started. *In* it, do you understand? He's there now.'

'Can't he get out?'

'He doesn't know how to. Every time he pulls the lever marked "release" he only releases hot steam. There are two kinds of steam in the bath, "bearable" and "scarcely bearable"; he has released them both. By this time I'm probably a widow.'

'I simply can't send away Gaspare,' wailed Sophie; 'I should never be able to secure another omelette specialist.'

'Any difficulty that I may experience in securing another husband is of course a trifle beneath anyone's consideration,' said Catherine bitterly.

Sophie capitulated. 'Go', she said to Richardson, 'and tell the Strike Committee, or whoever are directing this affair, that Gaspare is herewith dismissed. And ask Gaspare to see me presently in the library, when I will pay him what is due to him and make what excuses I can; and then fly back and finish my hair.'

Some half an hour later Sophie marshalled her guests in the Grand Salon preparatory to the formal march to the dining-room. Except that Henry Malsom was of the ripe raspberry tint that one sometimes sees at private theatricals representing the human complexion, there was little outward sign among those assembled of the crisis that had just been encountered and surmounted. But the tension had been too stupefying while it lasted not to leave some mental effects behind it. Sophie talked at random to her illustrious guest, and found her eyes straying with increasing frequency towards the great doors through which would presently come the blessed announcement that dinner was served. Now and again she glanced mirror-ward at the reflection of her wonderfully coiffed hair, as an insurance underwriter might gaze thankfully at an overdue vessel that had ridden safely into harbour in the wake of a devastating hurricane. Then the doors opened and the welcome figure of the butler entered the room. But he made no general announcement of a banquet in readiness, and the doors closed behind him; his message was for Sophie alone.

'There is no dinner, madame,' he said gravely; 'the kitchen staff have "downed tools". Gaspare belongs to the Union of Cooks and Kitchen Employees, and as soon as they heard of his summary dismissal at a moment's notice they struck work. They demand his instant reinstatement and an apology to the union. I may add, madame, that they are very firm; I've been obliged even to hand back the dinner rolls that were already on the table.'

After the lapse of eighteen months Sophie Chattel-Monkheim is beginning to go about again among her old haunts and associates, but she still has to be very careful. The doctors will not let her attend anything at all exciting, such as a drawing-room meeting or a Fabian conference; it is doubtful, indeed, whether she wants to.

Buried Treasure

P. G. WODEHOUSE

The situation in Germany had come up for discussion in the bar parlour of the Angler's Rest, and it was generally agreed that Hitler was standing at the crossroads and would soon be compelled to do something definite. His present policy, said a Whisky and Splash, was mere shilly-shallying.

'He'll have to let it grow or shave it off,' said the Whisky and Splash. 'He can't go on sitting on the fence like this. Either a man has a moustache or he has not. There can be no middle course.'

The thoughtful pause which followed these words was broken by a Small Bass.

'Talking of moustaches,' he said, 'you don't seem to see any nowadays, not what I call moustaches. What's become of them?'

'I've often asked myself the same question,' said a Gin and Italian Vermouth. 'Where, I've often asked myself, are the great sweeping moustaches of our boyhood? I've got a photograph of my grandfather as a young man in the album at home, and he's just a pair of eyes staring over a sort of quickset hedge.'

'Special cups they used to have,' said the Small Bass, 'to keep the vegetation out of their coffee. Ah, well, those days are gone for ever.'

Mr Mulliner shook his head.

'Not entirely,' he said, stirring his hot Scotch and lemon. 'I admit that they are rarer than they used to be, but in the remoter rural districts you will still find these curious growths flourishing. What causes them to survive is partly boredom and partly the good, clean spirit of amateur sport which has made us Englishmen what we are.'

The Small Bass said he did not quite get that.

'What I mean', said Mr Mulliner, 'is that life has not much to offer in the way of excitement to men who are buried in the country all the year round, so for want of anything better to do they grow moustaches at one another.'

'Sort of competitively, as it were?'

'Exactly. One landowner will start to try to surpass his neighbour in luxuriance of moustache, and the neighbour, inflamed, fights back at him. There is often a great deal of very intense feeling about these contests, with not a little wagering on the side. So, at least, my nephew Brancepeth, the artist, tells me. And he should know, for his present affluence and happiness are directly due to one of them.'

'Did he grow a moustache?'

'No. He was merely caught up in the whirlwind of the struggle for supremacy between Lord Bromborough, of Rumpling Hall, Lower Rumpling, Norfolk, and Sir Preston Potter, Bart., of Wapleigh Towers in the same county. Most of the vintage moustaches nowadays are to be found in Norfolk and Suffolk. I suppose the keen, moist sea air brings them on. Certainly it, or some equally stimulating agency, had brought on those of Lord Bromborough and Sir Preston Potter, for in the whole of England at that time there were probably no two finer specimens than the former's Joyeuse and the latter's Love in Idleness.'

It was Lord Bromborough's daughter Muriel (said Mr Mulliner) who had entitled these two moustaches in this manner. A poetic, imaginative girl, much addicted to reading old sagas and romances, she had adapted to modern conditions the practice of the ancient heroes of bestowing names on their favourite swords. King Arthur, you will remember, had his Excalibur, Charlemagne his Flamberge, Doolin of Mayence the famous Merveilleuse: and Muriel saw no reason

107

why this custom should be allowed to die out. A pretty idea, she thought, and I thought it a pretty idea when my nephew Brancepeth told me of it, and he thought it a pretty idea when told of it by Muriel.

For Muriel and Brancepeth had made one another's acquaintance some time before this story opens. The girl, unlike her father, who never left the ancestral acres, came often to London, and on one of these visits my nephew was introduced to her.

With Brancepeth it seems to have been a case of love at first sight, and it was not long before Muriel admitted to returning his passion. She had been favourably attracted to him from the moment when she found that their dance steps fitted, and when some little while later he offered to paint her portrait for nothing there was a look in her eyes which it was impossible to mistake. As early as the middle of the first sitting he folded her in his arms, and she nestled against his waistcoat with a low, cooing gurgle. Both knew that in the other they had found a soul-mate.

Such, then, was the relationship of the young couple, when one summer morning Brancepeth's telephone rang and, removing the receiver, he heard the voice of the girl he loved.

'Hey, cocky,' she was saying.

'What ho, reptile,' responded Brancepeth. 'Where are you speaking from?'

'Rumpling. Listen, I've got a job for you.'

'What sort of job?'

'A commission. Father wants his portrait painted.'

'Oh yes?'

'Yes. His sinister design is to present it to the local Men's Club. I don't know what he's got against them. A nasty jar it'll be for the poor fellows when they learn of it.'

'Why, is the old dad a bit of a gargoyle?'

'You never spoke a truer word. All moustache and eyebrows. The former has to be seen to be believed.'

'Pretty septic?'

'My dear! Suppurating. Well, are you on? I've told Father you're the coming man.'

'So I am,' said Brancepeth. 'I'm coming this afternoon.'

He was as good as his word. He caught the 3.15 train from Liverpool Street and at 7.20 alighted at the little station of Lower Rumpling, arriving at the Hall just in time to dress for dinner.

Always a rapid dresser, tonight Brancepeth excelled himself, for he yearned to see Muriel once more after their extended separation. Racing down to the drawing-room, however, tying his tie as he went, he found that his impetuosity had brought him there too early. The only occupant of the room at the moment of his entrance was a portly man whom, from the evidence submitted, he took to be his host. Except for a few outlying ears and the tip of a nose, the fellow was entirely moustache, and until he set eyes upon it, Brancepeth tells me, he had never really appreciated the full significance of those opening words of Longfellow's *Evangeline*, 'This is the forest primeval.'

He introduced himself courteously.

'How do you do, Lord Bromborough? My name is Mulliner.'

The other regarded him – over the zareba – with displeasure, it seemed to Brancepeth.

'What do you mean – Lord Bromborough?' he snapped curtly.

Brancepeth said he had meant Lord Bromborough.

'I'm not Lord Bromborough,' said the man.

Brancepeth was taken aback.

'Oh, aren't you?' he said. 'I'm sorry.'

'I'm glad,' said the man. 'Whatever gave you the silly idea that I was old Bromborough?'

'I was told that he had a very fine moustache.'

'Who told you that?'

'His daughter.'

The other snorted.

'You can't go by what a man's daughter says. She's biased. Prejudiced. Blinded by filial love, and all that sort of thing. If I wanted an opinion on a moustache, I wouldn't go to a man's daughter. I'd go to somebody who knew about moustaches. "Mr Walkinshaw," I'd say, or whatever the name might be . . . Bromborough's moustache a very fine moustache, indeed! Pshaw! Bromborough *has* a moustache – of a sort. He is not clean-shaven – I concede that . . . but fine? Pooh. Absurd. Ridiculous. Preposterous. Never heard such nonsense in my life.'

He turned pettishly away, and so hurt and offended was his manner that Brancepeth had no heart to continue the conversation. Muttering something about having forgotten his handkerchief, he sidled from the room and hung about on the landing outside. And presently Muriel came tripping down the stairs, looking more beautiful than ever.

She seemed delighted to see him.

'Hullo, Brancepeth, you old bounder,' she said cordially. 'So you got here? What are you doing parked on the stairs? Why aren't you in the drawing-room?'

Brancepeth shot a glance at the closed door and lowered his voice.

'There's a hairy bird in there who wasn't any too matey. I thought it must be your father and accosted him as such, and he got extraordinarily peevish. He seemed to resent my saying that I had heard your father had a fine moustache.'

The girl laughed.

'Golly! You put your foot in it properly. Old Potter's madly jealous of Father's moustache. That was Sir Preston Potter, of Wapleigh Towers, one of our better-known local Barts. He and his son are staying here.' She broke off to address the butler, a kindly, silver-haired old man who at this moment mounted the stairs. 'Hullo, Phipps, are you ambling up to announce the tea and shrimps? You're a bit early. I don't think Father and Mr Potter are down yet. Ah, here's Father,' she said, as a brilliantly moustached man of middle age appeared. 'Father, this is Mr Mulliner.'

Brancepeth eyed his host keenly as he shook hands, and his heart sank a little. He saw that the task of committing this man to canvas was going to be a difficult one. The recent slurs of Sir Preston Potter had been entirely without justification. Lord Bromborough's moustache was an extraordinarily fine one, fully as lush as that which barred the public from getting a square view of the Baronet. It seemed to Brancepeth, indeed, that the job before him was more one for a landscape artist than a portrait painter.

Sir Preston Potter, however, who now emerged from the drawing-room, clung stoutly to his opinion. He looked sneeringly at his rival.

'You been clipping your moustache, Bromborough?'

'Of course I have not been clipping my moustache,' replied Lord Bromborough shortly. It was only too plain that there was bad blood between the two men. 'What the dooce would I clip my moustache for? What makes you think I've been clipping my moustache?'

'I thought it had shrunk,' said Sir Preston Potter. 'It looks very small to me, very small. Perhaps the moth's been at it.'

Lord Bromborough quivered beneath the coarse insult, but his patrician breeding checked the hot reply which rose to his lips. He was a host. Controlling himself with a strong effort, he turned the conversation to the subject of early mangold-wurzels; and it was while he was speaking of these with eloquence and even fire that a young man with butter-coloured hair came hurrying down the stairs.

'Buck up, Edwin,' said Muriel impatiently. 'What's the idea of keeping us all waiting like this?'

'Oh, sorry,' said the young man.

'So you ought to be. Well, now you're here, I'd like to introduce you to Mr Mulliner. He's come to paint Father's portrait. Mr Mulliner . . . Mr Edwin Potter, my *fiancé.*'

'Dinner is served,' said Phipps the butler.

★

It was in a sort of trance that my nephew Brancepeth sat through the meal which followed. He toyed listlessly with his food and contributed so little to the conversation that a casual observer entering the room would have supposed him to be a deaf-mute who was on a diet. Nor can we fairly blame him for this, for he had had a severe shock. Few things are more calculated to jar an ardent lover and upset his poise than the sudden announcement by the girl he loves that she is engaged to somebody else, and Muriel's words had been like a kick in the stomach from an army mule. And in addition to suffering the keenest mental anguish, Brancepeth was completely bewildered.

It was not as if this Edwin Potter had been Clark Gable or somebody. Studying him closely, Brancepeth was unable to discern in him any of those qualities which win girls' hearts. He had an ordinary, meaningless face, disfigured by an eyeglass, and was plainly a boob of the first water. Brancepeth could make nothing of it. He resolved at the earliest possible moment to get hold of Muriel and institute a probe.

It was not until next day before luncheon that he found an opportunity of doing so. His morning had been spent in making preliminary sketches of her father. This task concluded, he came out into the garden and saw her reclining in a hammock slung between two trees at the edge of the large lawn.

He made his way towards her with quick, nervous strides. He was feeling jaded and irritated. His first impressions of Lord Bromborough had not misled him. Painting his portrait, he saw, was going to prove, as he had feared it would prove, a severe test of his courage and strength. There seemed so little about Lord Bromborough's face for an artist to get hold of. It was as if he had been commissioned to depict a client who, for reasons of his own, insisted on lying hid behind a haystack.

His emotions lent acerbity to his voice. It was with a

sharp intonation that he uttered the preliminary 'Hoy!'

The girl sat up.

'Oh, hullo,' she said.

'Oh, hullo, yourself, with knobs on,' retorted Brancepeth. 'Never mind the "Oh, hullo." I want an explanation.'

'What's puzzling you?'

'This engagement of yours.'

'Oh, that?'

'Yes, that. A nice surprise that was to spring on a chap, was it not? A jolly way of saying "Welcome to Rumpling Hall," I don't think.' Brancepeth choked. 'I came here thinking that you loved me . . .'

'So I do.'

'What!'

'Madly. Devotedly.'

'Then why the dickens do I find you betrothed to this blighted Potter?'

Muriel sighed.

'It's the old, old story.'

'What's the old, old story?'

'This is. It's all so simple, if you'd only understand. I don't suppose any girl ever worshipped a man as I worship you, Brancepeth, but Father hasn't a bean . . . you know what it's like owning land nowadays. Between ourselves, while we're on the subject, I'd stipulate for a bit down in advance on that portrait, if I were you . . .'

Brancepeth understood.

'Is this Potter rotter rich?'

'Rolling. Sir Preston was Potter's Potted Table Delicacies.'

There was a silence.

'H'm,' said Brancepeth.

'Exactly. You see now. Oh, Brancepeth,' said the girl, her voice trembling, 'why haven't you money? If you only had the merest pittance – enough for a flat in Mayfair and a little week-end place in the country somewhere and a couple of good cars and a villa in the South of France and a bit of trout fishing on some decent river, I would risk all for love. But as it is . . .'

Another silence fell.

'What you ought to do', said Muriel, 'is invent some good animal for the movies. That's where the money is. Look at Walt Disney.'

Brancepeth started. It was as if she had read his thoughts. Like all young artists nowadays, he had always held before him as the goal of his ambition the invention of some new comic animal for the motion pictures. What he burned to do, as Velasquez would have burned to do if he had lived today, was to think of another Mickey Mouse and then give up work and just sit back and watch the money roll in.

'It isn't so easy,' he said sadly.

'Have you tried?'

'Of course I've tried. For years I have followed the gleam. I thought I had something with Hilda the Hen and Bertie the Bandicoot, but nobody would look at them. I see now that they were lifeless, uninspired. I am a man who needs the direct inspiration.'

'Doesn't Father suggest anything to you?'

Brancepeth shook his head.

'No. I have studied your father, alert for the slightest hint . . .'

'Walter the Walrus?'

'No. Lord Bromborough looks like a walrus, yes, but unfortunately not a funny walrus. That moustache of his is majestic rather than diverting. It arouses in the beholder a feeling of awe, such as one gets on first seeing the pyramids. One senses the terrific effort behind it. I suppose it must have taken a lifetime of incessant toil to produce a cascade like that?'

'Oh, no. Father hadn't a moustache at all a few years ago. It was only when Sir Preston began to grow one and rather flaunt it at him at District Council meetings that he buckled down to it. But why', demanded the girl passionately, 'are we wasting time talking about moustaches? Kiss me, Brancepeth. We have just time before lunch.'

Brancepeth did as directed, and the incident closed.

I do not propose (resumed Mr Mulliner, who had broken off his narrative at this point to request Miss Postlethwaite, our able barmaid, to give him another hot Scotch and lemon) to dwell in detail on the agony of spirit endured by my nephew Brancepeth in the days that followed this poignant conversation. The spectacle of a sensitive artist soul on the rack is never a pleasant one. Suffice it to say that as each day came and went it left behind it an increased despair.

What with the brooding on his shattered romance and trying to paint Lord Bromborough's portrait and having his nerves afflicted by the incessant bickering that went on between Lord Bromborough and Sir Preston Potter and watching Edwin Potter bleating round Muriel and not being able to think of a funny animal for the movies, it is little wonder that his normally healthy complexion began to shade off to a sallow pallor and that his eyes took on a haunted look. Before the end of the first week he had become an object to excite the pity of the tender-hearted.

Phipps the butler was tender-hearted, and had been since a boy. Brancepeth excited his pity, and he yearned to do something to ameliorate the young man's lot. The method that suggested itself to him was to take a bottle of champagne to his room. It might prove a palliative rather than a cure, but he was convinced that it would, if only temporarily, bring the roses back to Brancepeth's cheeks. So he took a bottle of champagne to his room on the fifth night of my nephew's visit, and found him lying on his bed in striped pyjamas and a watered silk dressing-gown, staring at the ceiling.

The day that was now drawing to a close had been a particularly bad one for Brancepeth. The weather was unusually warm, and this had increased his despondency, so that he had found himself chafing beneath Lord Bromborough's moustache in a spirit of sullen rebellion. Before the afternoon sitting was over, he had become conscious of a vivid feeling of hatred for the thing. He longed for the courage to get at it with a hatchet after the manner of a pioneer in some wild country hewing a clearing in the surrounding jungle. When Phipps found him, his fists were clenched and he was biting his lower lip.

'I have brought you a little champagne, sir,' said Phipps, in his kindly, silver-haired way. 'It occurred to me that you might be in need of a restorative.'

Brancepeth was touched. He sat up, the hard glare in his eyes softening.

'That's awfully good of you,' he said. 'You are quite right. I could do with a drop or two from the old bin. I am feeling rather fagged. The weather, I suppose.'

A gentle smile played over the butler's face as he watched the young man put away a couple, quick.

'No, sir. I do not think it is the weather. You may be quite frank with me, sir. I understand. It must be a very wearing task, painting his lordship. Several artists have had to give it up. There was a young fellow here in the spring of last year who had to be removed to the cottage hospital. His manner had been strange and moody for some days, and one night we found him on a ladder, in the nude, tearing and tearing away at the ivy on the west wall. His lordship's moustache had been too much for him.'

Brancepeth groaned and refilled his glass. He knew just how his brother brush must have felt.

'The ironical thing', continued the butler, 'is that conditions would be just as bad, were the moustache non-existent. I have been in service at the Hall for a number of years, and I can assure you that his lordship was fully as hard on the eye when he was clean-shaven. Well, sir, when I tell you that I was actually relieved when he began to grow a moustache, you will understand.'

'Why, what was the matter with him?'

'He had a face like a fish, sir.'

'A fish?'

'Yes, sir.'

Something resembling an electric shock shot through Brancepeth, causing him to quiver in every limb.

'A funny fish?' he asked in a choking voice.

'Yes, sir. Extremely droll.'

Brancepeth was trembling like a saucepan of boiling milk at the height of its fever. A strange, wild thought had come into his mind. A funny fish . . .

There had never been a funny fish on the screen. Funny mice, funny cats, funny dogs . . . but not a funny fish. He stared before him with glowing eyes.

'Yes, sir, when his lordship began to grow a moustache, I was relieved. It seemed to me that it must be a change for the better. And so it was at first. But now . . . you know how it is, sir . . . I often find myself wishing those old, happy days were back again. We never know when we are well off, sir, do we?'

'You would be glad to see the last of Lord Bromborough's moustache?'

'Yes, sir. Very glad.'

'Right,' said Brancepeth. 'Then I'll shave it off.'

In private life, butlers relax that impassive gravity which the rules of their union compel them to maintain in public. Spring something sensational on a butler when he is chatting with you in your bedroom, and he will leap and goggle like any ordinary man. Phipps did so now.

'Shave it off, sir?' he gasped, quaveringly.

'Shave it off,' said Brancepeth, pouring out the last of the champagne.

'Shave off his lordship's moustache?'

'This very night. Leaving not a wrack behind.'

'But, sir . . .'

'Well?'

'The thought that crossed my mind, sir, was – how?'

Brancepeth clicked his tongue impatiently.

'Quite easy. I suppose he likes a little something last thing at night? Whisky or what not?'

'I always bring his lordship a glass of warm milk to the smoking-room.'

'Have you taken it to him yet?'

'Not yet, sir. I was about to do so when I left you.'

'And is there anything in the nature of a sleeping draught in the house?'

'Yes, sir. His lordship is a poor sleeper in the hot weather and generally takes a tablet of Slumberola in his milk.'

'Then, Phipps, if you are the pal I think you are, you will slip into his milk tonight not one tablet but four tablets.'

'But, sir . . .'

'I know, I know. What you are trying to say, I presume, is – What is there in it for you? I will tell you, Phipps. There is a packet in it for you. If Lord Bromborough's face in its stark fundamentals is as you describe it, I can guarantee that in less than no time I shall be bounding about the place trying to evade super-tax. In which event, rest assured that you will get your cut. You are sure of your facts? If I make a clearing in the tangled wildwood, I shall come down eventually to a face like a fish?'

'Yes, sir.'

'A fish with good comedy values?'

'Oh, yes, sir. Till it began to get me down, many is the laugh I have had at the sight of it.'

'That is all I wish to know. Right. Well, Phipps, can I count on your co-operation? I may add, before you speak, that this means my life's happiness. Sit in, and I shall be able to marry the girl I adore. Refuse to do your bit, and I drift through the remainder of my life a soured, blighted bachelor.'

The butler was plainly moved. Always kindly and silver-haired, he looked kindlier and more silver-haired than ever before.

'It's like that, is it, sir?'

'It is.'

'Well, sir, I wouldn't wish to come between a young gentleman and his life's happiness. I know what it means to love.'

'You do?'

'I do indeed, sir. It is not for me to boast, but there was a time when the girls used to call me Saucy George.'

'And so—?'

'I will do as you request, sir.'

'I knew it, Phipps,' said Brancepeth with emotion. 'I knew that I could rely on you. All that remains, then, is for you to show me which is Lord Bromborough's room.' He paused. A disturbing thought had struck him. 'I say! Suppose he locks his door?'

'It is quite all right, sir,' the butler reassured him. 'In the later summer months, when the nights are sultry, his lordship does not sleep in his room. He reposes in a hammock slung between two trees on the large lawn.'

'I know the hammock,' said Brancepeth tenderly. 'Well that's fine, then. The thing's in the bag. Phipps,' said Brancepeth, grasping his hand, 'I don't know how to express my gratitude. If everything develops as I expect it to; if Lord Bromborough's face gives me the inspiration which I anticipate and I clean up big, you, I repeat, shall share my riches. In due season there will call at your pantry elephants laden with gold, and camels bearing precious stones and rare spices. Also apes, ivory and peacocks. And . . . you say your name is George?'

'Yes, sir.'

'Then my eldest child shall be christened George. Or, if female, Georgiana.'

'Thank you very much, sir.'

'Not at all,' said Brancepeth. 'A pleasure.'

Brancepeth's first impression on waking next morning was that he had had a strange and beautiful dream. It was a vivid, lovely thing, all about stealing out of the house in striped pyjamas and a watered silk dressing-gown, armed with a pair of scissors, and stooping over the hammock where Lord Bromborough lay and razing his great moustache Joyeuse to its foundations. And he was just heaving a wistful sigh and wishing it were true, when he found that it was. It all came back to him – the furtive sneak downstairs, the wary passage of the lawn, the snip-snip-snip of the scissors blending with a strong man's snores in the silent night. It was no dream. The thing had actually occurred. His host's upper lip had became a devastated area.

It was not Brancepeth's custom, as a rule, to spring from his bed at the beginning of a new day, but he did so now. He was consumed with a burning eagerness to gaze upon his handiwork, for the first time to see Lord Bromborough steadily and see him whole. Scarcely ten minutes had elapsed before he was in his clothes and on his way to the breakfast-room. The other, he knew, was an early riser, and even so great a bereavement as he had suffered would not deter him from getting at the coffee and kippers directly he caught a whiff of them.

Only Phipps, however, was in the breakfast-room. He was lighting wicks under the hot dishes on the sideboard. Brancepeth greeted him jovially.

'Good morning, Phipps. What ho, what ho, with a hey nonny nonny and a hot cha-cha.'

The butler was looking nervous, like Macbeth interviewing Lady Macbeth after one of her visits to the spare room.

'Good morning, sir. Er – might I ask, sir . . .'

'Oh, yes,' said Brancepeth. 'The operation was a complete success. Everything went according to plan.'

'I am very glad to hear it, sir.'

'Not a hitch from start to finish. Tell me, Phipps,' said Brancepeth, helping himself buoyantly to a fried egg and a bit of bacon and seating himself at the table, 'what sort of a fish did Lord Bromborough look like before he had a moustache?'

The butler reflected.

'Well, sir, I don't know if you have seen Sidney the Sturgeon?'

'Eh?'

'On the pictures, sir. I recently attended a cinematographic performance at Norwich – it was on my afternoon off last week – and', said Phipps, chuckling gently at the recollection, 'they were showing a most entertaining new feature. "The Adventures of Sidney the Sturgeon." It came on before the big picture, and it was all I could do to keep a straight face. This sturgeon looked extremely like his lordship in the old days.'

He drifted from the room and Brancepeth stared after him, stunned. His air castles had fallen about him in ruins. Fame, fortune, and married bliss were as far away from him as ever. All his labour had been in vain. If there was already a funny fish functioning on the silver screen, it was obvious that it would be mere waste of time to do another. He clasped his head in his hands and groaned over his fried egg. And, as he did so, the door opened.

'Ha!' said Lord Bromborough's voice. 'Good morning, good morning.'

Brancepeth spun round with a sharp jerk which sent a piece of bacon flying off his fork as if it had been shot from a catapult. Although his host's appearance could not affect his professional future now, he was consumed with curiosity to see what he looked like. And, having spun round, he sat transfixed. There before him stood Lord Bromborough, but not a hair of his moustache was missing. It flew before him like a banner in all its pristine luxuriance.

'Eh, what?' said Lord Bromborough, sniffing. 'Kedgeree? Capital, capital.'

He headed purposefully for the sideboard. The door opened again, and Edwin Potter came in, looking more of a boob than ever.

In addition to looking like a boob, Edwin Potter seemed worried.

'I say,' he said, 'my father's missing.'

'On how many cylinders?' asked Lord Bromborough. He was a man who liked his joke of a morning.

'I mean to say,' continued Edwin Potter, 'I can't find him. I went to speak to him about something just now, and his room was empty and his bed had not been slept in.'

Lord Bromborough was dishing out kedgeree onto a plate.

'That's all right,' he said. 'He wanted to try my hammock last night, so I let him. If he slept as soundly as I did, he slept well. I came over all drowsy as I was finishing my glass of hot milk and I woke this morning in an arm-chair in the smoking-room. Ah, my dear,' he went on, as Muriel entered, 'come along and try this kedgeree. It smells excellent. I was just telling our young friend here that his father slept in my hammock last night.'

Muriel's face was wearing a look of perplexity.

'Out in the garden, do you mean?'

'Of course I mean out in the garden. You know where my hammock is. I've seen you lying in it.'

'Then there must be a goat in the garden.'

'Goat?' said Lord Bromborough, who had now taken his place at the table and was shovelling kedgeree into himself like a stevedore loading a grain ship. 'What do you mean, goat? There's no goat in the garden. Why should there be a goat in the garden?'

'Because something has eaten off Sir Preston's moustache.'

'What!'

'Yes. I met him outside, and the shrubbery had completely disappeared. Here he is. Look.'

What seemed at first to Brancepeth a total stranger was standing in the doorway. It was only when the newcomer folded his arms and began to speak in a familiar rasping voice that he recognised Sir Preston Potter, Bart., of Wapleigh Towers.

'So!' said Sir Preston, directing at Lord Bromborough a fiery glance full of deleterious animal magnetism.

Lord Bromborough finished his kedgeree and looked up.

'Ah, Potter,' he said. 'Shaved your moustache, have you? Very sensible. It would never have amounted to anything, and you will be happier without it.'

Flame shot from Sir Preston Potter's eyes. The man was plainly stirred to his foundations.

'Bromborough,' be snarled, 'I have only five things to say to you. The first is that you are the lowest, foulest fiend that ever disgraced the pure pages of Debrett; the second that your dastardly act in clipping off my moustache shows you a craven, who knew that defeat stared him in the eye and that only thus he could hope to triumph; the third that I intend to approach my lawyer immediately with a view to taking legal action; the fourth is good-bye for ever; and the fifth—'

'Have an egg,' said Lord Bromborough.

'I will not have an egg. This is not a matter which can be lightly passed off with eggs. The fifth thing I wish to say—'

'But, my dear fellow, you seem to be suggesting that I had something to do with this. I approve of what has happened, yes. I approve of it heartily. Norfolk will be a sweeter and better place to live in now that this has occurred. But it was none of my doing. I was asleep in the smoking-room all night.'

'The fifth thing I wish to say—'

'In an arm-chair. If you doubt me, I can show you the arm-chair.'

'The fifth thing I wish to say is that the engagement between my son and your daughter is at an end.'

'Like your moustache. Ha, ha!' said Lord Bromborough, who had many good qualities but was not tactful.

'Oh, but, Father!' cried Edwin Potter. 'I mean, dash it!'

'And *I* mean', thundered Sir Preston, 'that your engagement is at an end. You have my five points quite clear, Bromborough?'

'I think so,' said Lord Bromborough, ticking them off on his fingers. 'I am a foul fiend, I'm a craven, you are going to institute legal proceedings, you bid me good-bye for ever, and my daughter shall never marry your son. Yes, five in all.'

'Add a sixth. I shall see that you are expelled from all your clubs.'

'I haven't got any.'

'Oh?' said Sir Preston, a little taken aback. 'Well, if ever you make a speech in the House of Lords, beware. I shall be up in the gallery, booing.'

He turned and strode from the room, followed by Edwin, protesting bleatingly. Lord Bromborough took a cigarette from his case.

'Silly old ass,' he said. 'I expect that moustache of his was clipped off by a body of public-spirited citizens. Like the Vigilantes they have in America. It is absurd to suppose that a man could grow a beastly, weedy caricature of a moustache like Potter's without inflaming popular feeling. No doubt they have been lying in wait for him for months. Lurking. Watching their opportunity. Well, my dear, so your wedding's off. A nuisance in a way of course, for I'd just bought a new pair of trousers to give you away in. Still it can't be helped.'

'No, it can't be helped,' said Muriel. 'Besides there will be another one along in a minute.'

She shot a tender smile at Brancepeth, but on his lips there was no answering simper. He sat in silence, crouched over his fried egg.

What did it profit him, he was asking himself bitterly, that the wedding was off? He himself could never marry Muriel. He was a penniless artist without prospects. He would never invent a comic animal for the movies now. There had been an instant when he had hoped that Sir Preston's uncovered face might suggest one, but the hope had died at birth. Sir Preston Potter, without his moustache, had merely looked like a man without a moustache.

He became aware that his host was addressing him.

124

'I beg your pardon?'

'I said, "Got a light?"'

'Oh, sorry,' said Brancepeth.

He took out his lighter and gave it a twiddle. Then, absently, he put the flame to the cigarette between his host's lips.

Or, rather, for preoccupation had temporarily destroyed his judgement of distance, to the moustache that billowed above and around it. And the next moment there was a sheet of flame and a cloud of acrid smoke. When this had cleared away, only a little smouldering stubble was left of what had once been one of Norfolk's two most outstanding eyesores.

A barely human cry rent the air, but Brancepeth hardly heard it. He was staring like one in a trance at the face that confronted him through the shrouding mists, fascinated by the short, broad nose, the bulging eyes, the mouth that gaped and twitched. It was only when his host made a swift dive across the table with bared teeth and clutching hands that Prudence returned to its throne. He slid under the table and came out on the other side.

'Catch him!' cried the infuriated peer. 'Trip him up! Sit on his head!'

'Certainly not,' said Muriel. 'He is the man I love.'

'Is he!' said Lord Bromborough, breathing heavily as he crouched for another spring. 'Well, he's the man I am going to disembowel with my bare hands – when I catch him.'

'I think I should nip through the window, darling,' said Muriel gently.

Brancepeth weighed the advice hastily and found it good. The window, giving on to the gravel drive, was, he perceived, open at the bottom. The sweet summer air floated in, and an instant later he was floating out. As he rose from the gravel, something solid struck him on the back of the head. It was a coffee-pot.

But coffee-pots, however shrewdly aimed, mattered little to Brancepeth now. This one had raised a painful contusion, and he had in addition skinned both hands and one of his knees. His trousers, moreover, a favourite pair, had a large hole in them. Nevertheless, his heart was singing within him.

For Phipps had been wrong. Phipps was an ass. Phipps did not know a fish when he saw one. Lord Bromborough's face did not resemble that of a fish at all. It suggested something much finer, much fuller of screen possibilities, much more box-office than a fish. In that one blinding instant of illumination before he had dived under the table, Brancepeth had seen Lord Bromborough for what he was – Ferdinand the Frog.

He turned, to perceive his host in the act of hurling a cottage loaf.

'Muriel!' he cried.

'Hullo?' said the girl, who had joined her father at the window and was watching the scene with great interest.

'I love you, Muriel.'

'Same here.'

'But for the moment I must leave you.'

'I would,' said Muriel. She glanced over her shoulder. 'He's gone to get the kedgeree.' And Brancepeth saw that Lord Bromborough had left his butt. 'He is now', she added, 'coming back.'

'Will you wait for me, Muriel?'

'To all eternity.'

'It will not be necessary,' said Brancepeth. 'Call in six months or a year. By that time I shall have won fame and fortune.'

He would have spoken further, but at this moment Lord Bromborough reappeared, poising the kedgeree. With a loving smile and a wave of the hand, Brancepeth leaped smartly to one side. Then, turning, he made his way down the drive, gazing raptly into a future of Rolls-Royces, caviare and silk underclothing made to measure.

A Piece of Pie

DAMON RUNYON

On Boylston Street, in the city of Boston, Mass., there is a joint where you can get as nice a broiled lobster as anybody ever slaps a lip over, and who is in there one evening partaking of this tidbit but a character by the name of Horse Thief and me.

This Horse Thief is called Horsey for short, and he is not called by this name because he ever steals a horse but because it is the consensus of public opinion from coast to coast that he may steal one if the opportunity presents.

Personally, I consider Horsey a very fine character, because any time he is holding anything he is willing to share his good fortune with one and all, and at this time in Boston he is holding plenty. It is the time we make the race meeting at Suffolk Down, and Horsey gets to going very good, indeed, and in fact he is now a character of means, and is my host against the broiled lobster.

Well, at a table next to us are four or five characters who all seem to be well-dressed, and stout-set, and red-faced, and prosperous-looking, and who all speak with the true Boston accent, which consists of many 'ah's and very few 'r's. Characters such as these are familiar to anybody who is ever in Boston very much, and they are bound to be politicians, retired cops, or contractors, because Boston is really quite infested with characters of this nature.

I am paying no attention to them, because they are drinking local ale, and talking loud, and long ago I learn that when a Boston character is engaged in aleing himself up, it is a good idea to let him alone, because the best you can get out of him is maybe a boff on the beezer. But Horsey is in there on the old Ear-ie, and very much interested in their conversation, and finally I listen myself just to hear what is attracting his attention, when one of the characters speaks as follows:

'Well,' he says, 'I am willing to bet ten thousand dollars that he can outeat anybody in the United States any time.'

Now at this, Horsey gets right up and steps over to the table and bows and smiles in a friendly way on one and all, and says:

'Gentlemen,' he says, 'pardon the intrusion, and excuse me for billing in, but,' he says, 'do I understand you are speaking of a great eater who resides in your fair city?'

Well, these Boston characters all gaze at Horsey in such a hostile manner that I am expecting any one of them to get up and request him to let them miss him, but he keeps on bowing and smiling, and they can see that he is a gentleman, and finally one of them says:

'Yes,' he says, 'we are speaking of a character by the name of Joel Duffle. He is without doubt the greatest eater alive. He just wins a unique wager. He bets a character from Bangor, Me., that he can eat a whole window display of oysters in this very restaurant, and he not only eats all the oysters but he then wishes to wager that he can also eat the shells, but,' he says, 'it seems that the character from Bangor, Me., unfortunately taps out on the first proposition and has nothing with which to bet on the second.'

'Very interesting,' Horsey says. 'Very interesting, if true, but,' he says, 'unless my ears deceive me, I hear one of you state that he is willing to wager ten thousand dollars on this eater of yours against anybody in the United States.'

'Your ears are perfect,' another of the Boston characters says. 'I state it, although,' he says, 'I admit it is a sort of figure of speech. But I state it all right,' he says, 'and never let it be said that a Conway ever pigs it on a betting proposition.'

'Well,' Horsey says, 'I do not have a tenner on me at the moment, but,' he says, 'I have here a thousand dollars to put up as a forfeit that I can produce a character who will outeat your party for ten thousand, and as much more as you care to put up.'

And with this, Horsey outs with a bundle of coarse notes and tosses it on the table, and right away one of the Boston characters, whose name turns out to be Carroll, slaps his hand on the money and says:

'Bet.'

Well, now this is prompt action to be sure, and if there is one thing I admire more than anything else, it is action, and I can see that these are characters of true sporting instincts and I commence wondering where I can raise a few dibs to take a piece of Horsey's proposition, because of course I know that he has nobody in mind to do the eating for his side but Nicely-Nicely Jones.

And knowing Nicely-Nicely Jones, I am prepared to wager all the money I can possibly raise that he can outeat anything that walks on two legs. In fact, I will take a chance on Nicely-Nicely against anything on four legs, except maybe an elephant, and at that he may give the elephant a photo finish.

I do not say that Nicely-Nicely is the greatest eater in all history, but what I do say is he belongs up there as a contender. In fact, Professor D, who is a professor in a college out West before he turns to playing the horses for a livelihood, and who makes a study of history in his time, says he will not be surprised but what Nicely-Nicely figures one-two.

Professor D says we must always remember that Nicely-Nicely eats under the handicaps of modern civilization, which require that an eater use a knife and fork, or anyway a knife, while in the old days eating with the hands was a popular custom and much faster. Professor D says he has no doubt that under the old rules Nicely-Nicely will hang up a record that will endure through the ages, but of course maybe Professor D overlays Nicely-Nicely somewhat.

Well, now that the match is agreed upon, naturally Horsey

and the Boston characters begin discussing where it is to take place, and one of the Boston characters suggests a neutral ground, such as New London, Conn., or Providence, R.I., but Horsey holds out for New York, and it seems that Boston characters are always ready to visit New York, so he does not meet with any great opposition on this point.

They all agree on a date four weeks later so as to give the principals plenty of time to get ready, although Horsey and I know that this is really unnecessary as far as Nicely-Nicely is concerned, because one thing about him is he is always in condition to eat.

This Nicely-Nicely Jones is a character who is maybe five feet eight inches tall, and about five feet nine inches wide, and when he is in good shape he will weigh upward of two hundred and eighty-three pounds. He is a horse player by trade, and eating is really just a hobby, but he is undoubtedly a wonderful eater even when he is not hungry.

Well, as soon as Horsey and I return to New York, we hasten to Mindy's restaurant on Broadway and relate the bet Horsey makes in Boston, and right away so many citizens, including Mindy himself, wish to take a piece of the proposition that it is oversubscribed by a large sum in no time.

Then Mindy remarks that he does not see Nicely-Nicely Jones for a month of Sundays, and then everybody present remembers that they do not see Nicely-Nicely around lately, either, and this leads to a discussion of where Nicely-Nicely can be, although up to this moment if nobody sees Nicely-Nicely but once in the next ten years it will be considered sufficient.

Well, Willie the Worrier, who is a bookmaker by trade, is among those present, and he remembers that the last time he looks for Nicely-Nicely hoping to collect a marker of some years' standing, Nicely-Nicely is living at the Rest-Hotel in West Forty-ninth Street, and nothing will do Horsey but I must go with him over to the Rest to make inquiry for Nicely-Nicely, and there we learn that he leaves a forwarding address away up on Morningside Heights in care of somebody by the name of Slocum.

So Horsey calls a short, and away we go to this address, which turns out to be a five-story walk-up apartment, and a card downstairs shows that Slocum lives on the top floor. It takes Horsey and me ten minutes to walk up the five flights as we are by no means accustomed to exercise of this nature, and when we finally reach a door marked Slocum, we are plumb tuckered out, and have to sit down on the top step and rest a while.

Then I ring the bell at this door marked Slocum, and who appears but a tall young Judy with black hair who is without doubt beautiful, but who is so skinny we have to look twice to see her, and when I ask her if she can give me any information about a party named Nicely-Nicely Jones, she says to me like this:

'I guess you mean Quentin,' she says. 'Yes,' she says, 'Quentin is here. Come in, gentlemen.'

So we step into an apartment, and as we do so a thin, sickly looking character gets up out of a chair by the window, and in a weak voice says good evening. It is a good evening, at that, so Horsey and I say good evening right back at him, very polite, and then we stand there waiting for Nicely-Nicely to appear, when the beautiful skinny young Judy says:

'Well,' she says, 'this is Mr Quentin Jones.'

Then Horsey and I take another swivel at the thin character, and we can see that it is nobody but Nicely-Nicely, at that, but the way he changes since we last observe him is practically shocking to us both, because he is undoubtedly all shrunk up. In fact, he looks as if he is about half what he is in his prime, and his face is pale and thin, and his eyes are away back in his head, and while we both shake hands with him it is some time before either of us is able to speak. Then Horsey finally says:

'Nicely,' he says, 'can we have a few words with you in private on a very important proposition?'

Well, at this, and before Nicely-Nicely can answer aye, yes, or no, the beautiful skinny young Judy goes out of the room and slams a door behind her, and Nicely-Nicely says:

'My fiancée, Miss Hilda Slocum,' he says. 'She is a wonderful character. We are to be married as soon as I lose twenty pounds more. It will take a couple of weeks longer,' he says.

'My goodness gracious, Nicely,' Horsey says. 'What do you mean lose twenty pounds more? You are practically emaciated now. Are you just out of a sick bed, or what?'

'Why,' Nicely-Nicely says, 'certainly I am not out of a sick bed. I am never healthier in my life. I am on a diet. I lose eighty-three pounds in two months, and am now down to two hundred. I feel great,' he says. 'It is all because of my fiancée, Miss Hilda Slocum. She rescues me from gluttony and obesity, or anyway,' Nicely-Nicely says, 'this is what Miss Hilda Slocum calls it. My, I feel good. I love Miss Hilda Slocum very much,' Nicely-Nicely says. 'It is a case of love at first sight on both sides the day we meet in the subway. I am wedged in one of the turnstile gates, and she kindly pushes on me from behind until I wiggle through. I can see she has a kind heart, so I date her up for a movie that night and propose to her while the newsreel is on. But,' Nicely-Nicely says, 'Hilda tells me at once that she will never marry a fat slob. She says I must put myself in her hands and she will reduce me by scientific methods and then she will become my everloving wife, but not before.

'So,' Nicely-Nicely says, 'I come to live here with Miss Hilda Slocum and her mother, so she can supervise my diet. Her mother is thinner than Hilda. And I surely feel great,' Nicely-Nicely says. 'Look,' he says.

And with this, he pulls out the waistband of his pants, and shows enough spare space to hide the War Admiral in, but the effort seems to be a strain on him, and he has to sit down in his chair again.

'My goodness gracious,' Horsey says. 'What do you eat, Nicely?'

'Well,' Nicely-Nicely says, 'I eat anything that does not contain starch, but,' he says, 'of course everything worth eating contains starch, so I really do not eat much of anything whatever. My fiancée, Miss Hilda Slocum, arranges my diet. She is an expert dietician and runs a widely known department in a diet magazine by the name of *Let's Keep House.*'

Then Horsey tells Nicely-Nicely of how he is matched to eat against this Joel Duffle, of Boston, for a nice side bet, and how he has a forfeit of a thousand dollars already posted for appearance, and how many of Nicely-Nicely's admirers along Broadway are looking to win themselves out of all their troubles by betting on him, and at first Nicely-Nicely listens with great interest, and his eyes are shining like six bits, but then he becomes very sad, and says:

'It is no use, gentlemen,' he says. 'My fiancée, Miss Hilda Slocum, will never hear of me going off my diet even for a little while. Only yesterday I try to talk her into letting me have a little pumpernickel instead of toasted whole wheat bread, and she says if I even think of such a thing again, she will break our engagement. Horsey,' he says, 'do you ever eat toasted whole wheat bread for a month hand running? Toasted?' he says.

'No,' Horsey says. 'What I eat is nice, white French bread, and corn muffins, and hot biscuits with gravy on them.'

'Stop,' Nicely-Nicely says. 'You are eating yourself into an early grave, and, furthermore,' he says, 'you are breaking my heart. But,' he says, 'the more I think of my following depending on me in this emergency, the sadder it makes me feel to think I am unable to oblige them. However,' he says, 'let us call Miss Hilda Slocum in on an outside chance and see what her reactions to your proposition are.'

So we call Miss Hilda Slocum in, and Horsey explains our predicament in putting so much faith in Nicely-Nicely only to find him dieting, and Miss Hilda Slocum's reactions are to order Horsey and me out of the joint with instructions never to darken her door again, and when we are a block away we can still hear her voice speaking very firmly to Nicely-Nicely.

Well, personally, I figure this ends the matter, for I can see that Miss Hilda Slocum is a most determined character, indeed, and the chances are it does end it, at that, if Horsey does not happen to get a wonderful break.

He is at Belmont Park one afternoon, and he has a real good thing in a jump race, and when a brisk young character in a hard straw hat and eyeglasses comes along and asks him what he likes, Horsey mentions this good thing, figuring he will move himself in for a few dibs if the good thing connects.

Well, it connects all right, and the brisk young character is very grateful to Horsey for his information, and is giving him plenty of much-obliges, and nothing else, and Horsey is about to mention that they do not accept much-obliges at his hotel, when the brisk young character mentions that he is nobody but Mr McBurgle and that he is the editor of the *Let's Keep House* magazine, and for Horsey to drop in and see him any time he is around his way.

Naturally, Horsey remembers what Nicely-Nicely says about Miss Hilda Slocum working for this *Let's Keep House* magazine, and he relates the story of the eating contest to Mr McBurgle and asks him if he will kindly use his influence with Miss Hilda Slocum to get her to release Nicely-Nicely from his diet long enough for the contest. Then Horsey gives Mr McBurgle a tip on another winner, and Mr McBurgle must use plenty of influence on Miss Hilda Slocum at once, as the next day she calls Horsey up at his hotel before he is out of bed, and speaks to him as follows:

'Of course,' Miss Hilda Slocum says, 'I will never change my attitude about Quentin, but,' she says, 'I can appreciate that he feels very bad about you gentlemen relying on him and having to disappoint you. He feels that he lets you down, which is by no means true, but it weighs upon his mind. It is interfering with his diet.

'Now,' Miss Hilda Slocum says, 'I do not approve of your contest, because', she says, 'it is placing a premium on gluttony, but I have a friend by the name of Miss Violette Shumberger who may answer your purpose. She is my dearest friend from childhood, but it is only because I love her dearly that this friendship endures. She is extremely fond of eating,' Miss Hilda Slocum says. 'In spite of my pleadings, and my warnings, and my own example, she persists in food. It is disgusting to me but I finally learn that it is no use arguing with her.

'She remains my dearest friend,' Miss Hilda Slocum says, 'though she continues her practice of eating, and I am informed that she is phenomenal in this respect. In fact,' she says, 'Nicely-Nicely tells me to say to you that if Miss Violette Shumberger can perform the eating exploits I relate to him from hearsay she is a lily. Goodbye,' Miss Hilda Slocum says. 'You cannot have Nicely-Nicely.'

Well, nobody cares much about this idea of a stand-in for Nicely-Nicely in such a situation, and especially a Judy that no one ever hears of before, and many citizens are in favour of pulling out of the contest altogether. But Horsey has his thousand-dollar forfeit to think of, and as no one can suggest anyone else, he finally arranges a personal meet with the Judy suggested by Miss Hilda Slocum.

He comes into Mindy's one evening with a female character who is so fat it is necessary to push three tables together to give her room for her lap, and it seems that this character is Miss Violette Shumberger. She weighs maybe two hundred and fifty pounds, but she is by no means an old Judy, and by no means bad-looking. She has a face the size of a town clock and enough chins for a fire escape, but she has a nice smile and pretty teeth, and a laugh that is so hearty it knocks the whipped cream off an order of strawberry shortcake on a table fifty feet away and arouses the indignation of a customer by the name of Goldstein who is about to consume same.

Well, Horsey's idea in bringing her into Mindy's is to get some kind of line on her eating form, and she is clocked by many experts when she starts putting on the hot meat, and it is agreed by one and all that she is by no means a selling-plater. In fact, by the time she gets through, even Mindy admits she has plenty of class, and the upshot of it all is Miss Violette Shumberger is chosen to eat against Joel Duffle.

Maybe you hear something of this great eating contest that comes off in New York one night in the early summer of 1937. Of course eating contests are by no means anything new, and in fact they are quite an old-fashioned pastime in some sections of this country, such as the South and East, but this is the first big public contest of the kind in years, and it creates no little comment along Broadway.

In fact, there is some mention of it in the blats, and it is not a frivolous proposition in any respect, and more dough is wagered on it than any other eating contest in history, with Joel Duffle a 6 to 5 favourite over Miss Violette Shumberger all the way through.

This Joel Duffle comes to New York several days before the contest with the character by the name of Conway, and requests a meet with Miss Violette Shumberger to agree on the final details, and who shows up with Miss Violette Shumberger as her coach and adviser but Nicely-Nicely Jones. He is even thinner and more peaked-looking than when Horsey and I see him last, but he says he feels great, and that he is within six pounds of his marriage to Miss Hilda Slocum.

Well, it seems that his presence is really due to Miss Hilda Slocum herself, because she says that after getting her dearest friend Miss Violette Shumberger into this jackpot, it is only fair to do all she can to help her win it, and the only way she can think of is to let Nicely-Nicely give Violette the benefit of his experience and advice.

But afterward we learn that what really happens is that this editor, Mr McBurgle, gets greatly interested in the contest, and when he discovers that in spite of his influence, Miss Hilda Slocum declines to permit Nicely-Nicely to personally compete, but puts in a pinch eater, he is quite indignant and insists on her letting Nicely-Nicely school Violette.

Furthermore we afterward learn that when Nicely-Nicely returns to the apartment on Morningside Heights after giving Violette a lesson, Miss Hilda Slocum always smells his breath to see if he indulges in any food during his absence.

Well, this Joel Duffle is a tall character with stooped shoulders, and a sad expression, and he does not look as if he can eat his way out of a tea shoppe, but as soon as he commences to discuss the details of the contest, anybody can see that he knows what time it is in situations such as this. In fact, Nicely-Nicely says he can tell at once from the way Joel Duffle talks that he is a dangerous opponent, and he says while Miss Violette Shumberger impresses him as an improving eater, he is only sorry she does not have more seasoning.

This Joel Duffle suggests that the contest consist of twelve courses of strictly American food, each side to be allowed to pick six dishes, doing the picking in rotation, and specifying the weight and quantity of the course selected to any amount the contestant making the pick desires, and each course is to be divided for eating exactly in half, and after Miss Violette Shumberger and Nicely-Nicely whisper together a while, they say the terms are quite satisfactory.

Then Horsey tosses a coin for the first pick, and Joel Duffle says heads, and it is heads, and he chooses, as the first course, two quarts of ripe olives, twelve bunches of celery, and four pounds of shelled nuts, all this to be split fifty-fifty between them. Miss Violette Shumberger names twelve dozen cherry-stone clams as the second course, and Joel Duffle says two gallons of Philadelphia pepper-pot soup as the third.

Well, Miss Violette Shumberger and Nicely-Nicely whisper together again, and Violette puts in two five-pound striped bass, the heads and tails not to count in the eating, and Joel Duffle names a twenty-two-pound roast turkey.

Each vegetable is rated as one course, and Miss Violette Shumberger asks for twelve pounds of mashed potatoes with brown gravy. Joel Duffle says two dozen ears of corn on the cob, and Violette replies with two quarts of lima beans. Joel Duffle calls for twelve bunches of asparagus cooked in butter, and Violette mentions ten pounds of stewed new peas.

This gets them down to the salad, and it is Joel Duffle's play, so he says six pounds of mixed green salad with vinegar and oil dressing, and now Miss Violette Shumberger has the final selection, which is the dessert. She says it is a pumpkin pie, two feet across, and not less than three inches deep.

It is agreed that they must eat with knife, fork or spoon, but speed is not to count, and there is to be no time limit, except they cannot pause more than two consecutive minutes at any stage, except in case of hiccoughs. They can drink anything, and as much as they please, but liquids are not to count in the scoring. The decision is to be strictly on the amount of food consumed, and the judges are to take account of anything left on the plates after a course, but not of loose chewings on bosom or vest up to an ounce. The losing side is to pay for the food, and in case of a tie they are to eat it off immediately on ham and eggs only.

Well, the scene of this contest is the second-floor dining-room of Mindy's restaurant, which is closed to the general public for the occasion, and only parties immediately concerned in the contest are admitted. The contestants are seated on either side of a big table in the centre of the room, and each contestant has three waiters.

No talking and no rooting from the spectators is permitted, but of course in any eating contest the principals may speak to each other if they wish, though smart eaters never wish to do this, as talking only wastes energy, and about all they ever say to each other is please pass the mustard.

About fifty characters from Boston are present to witness the contest, and the same number of citizens of New York are admitted, and among them is this editor, Mr McBurgle, and he is around asking Horsey if he thinks Miss Violette Shumberger is as good a thing as the jumper at the race track.

Nicely-Nicely arrives on the scene quite early, and his appearance is really most distressing to his old friends and admirers, as by this time he is shy so much weight that he is a pitiful scene, to be sure, but he tells Horsey and me that he thinks Miss Violette Shumberger has a good chance.

'Of course,' he says, 'she is green. She does not know how to pace herself in competition. But,' he says, 'she has a wonderful style. I love to watch her eat. She likes the same things I do in the days when I am eating. She is a wonderful character, too. Do you ever notice her smile?' Nicely-Nicely says.

'But,' he says, 'she is the dearest friend of my fiancée, Miss Hilda Slocum, so let us not speak of this. I try to get Hilda to come to see the contest, but she says it is repulsive. Well, anyway,' Nicely-Nicely says, 'I manage to borrow a few dibs, and am wagering on Miss Violette Shumberger. By the way,' he says, 'if you happen to think of it, notice her smile.'

Well, Nicely-Nicely takes a chair about ten feet behind Miss Violette Shumberger, which is as close as the judges will allow him, and he is warned by them that no coaching from the corners will be permitted, but of course Nicely-Nicely knows this rule as well as they do, and furthermore by this time his exertions seem to have left him without any more energy.

There are three judges, and they are all from neutral territory. One of these judges is a party from Baltimore, Md., by the name of Packard, who runs a restaurant, and another is a party from Providence, R.I., by the name of Croppers, who is a sausage manufacturer. The third judge is an old Judy by the name of Mrs Rhubarb, who comes from Philadelphia, and once keeps an actors' boarding-house, and is considered an excellent judge of eaters.

Well, Mindy is the official starter, and at 8.30 p.m. sharp, when there is still much betting among the spectators, he outs with his watch, and says like this:

'Are you ready, Boston? Are you ready, New York?'

Miss Violette Shumberger and Joel Duffle both nod their heads, and Mindy says commence, and the contest is on, with Joel Duffle getting the jump at once on the celery and olives and nuts.

It is apparent that this Joel Duffle is one of these rough-and-tumble eaters that you can hear quite a distance off, especially on clams and soups. He is also an eyebrow eater, an eater whose eyebrows go up as high as the part in his hair as he eats, and this type of eater is undoubtedly very efficient.

In fact, the way Joel Duffle goes through the groceries down to the turkey causes the Broadway spectators some uneasiness, and they are whispering to each other that they only wish the old Nicely-Nicely is in there. But personally, I like the way Miss Violette Shumberger eats without undue excitement, and with great zest. She cannot keep close to Joel Duffle in the matter of speed in the early stages of the contest, as she seems to enjoy chewing her food, but I observe that as it goes along she pulls up on him, and I figure this is not because she is stepping up her pace, but because he is slowing down.

When the turkey finally comes on, and is split in two halves right down the middle, Miss Violette Shumberger looks greatly disappointed, and she speaks for the first time as follows:

'Why,' she says, 'where is the stuffing?'

Well, it seems that nobody mentions any stuffing for the turkey to the chef, so he does not make any stuffing, and Miss Violette Shumberger's disappointment is so plain to be seen that the confidence of the Boston characters is some-what shaken. They can see that a Judy who can pack away as much fodder as Miss Violette Shumberger has to date, and then beef for stuffing, is really quite an eater.

In fact, Joel Duffle looks quite startled when he observes Miss Violette Shumberger's disappointment, and he gazes at

her with great respect as she disposes of her share of the turkey, and the mashed potatoes, and one thing and another in such a manner that she moves up on the pumpkin pie on dead even terms with him. In fact, there is little to choose between them at this point, although the judge from Baltimore is calling the attention of the other judges to a turkey leg that he claims Miss Violette Shumberger does not clean as neatly as Joel Duffle does his, but the other judges dismiss this as a technicality.

Then the waiters bring on the pumpkin pie, and it is without doubt quite a large pie, and in fact it is about the size of a manhole cover, and I can see that Joel Duffle is observing this pie with a strange expression on his face, although to tell the truth I do not care for the expression on Miss Violette Shumberger's face, either.

Well, the pie is cut in two dead centre, and one half is placed before Miss Violette Shumberger and the other half before Joel Duffle, and he does not take more than two bites before I see him loosen his waistband and take a big swig of water, and thinks I to myself, he is now down to a slow walk, and the pie will decide the whole heat, and I am only wishing I am able to wager a little more dough on Miss Violette Shumberger. But about this moment, and before she as much as touches her pie, all of a sudden Violette turns her head and motions to Nicely-Nicely to approach her, and as he approaches, she whispers in his ear.

Now at this, the Boston character by the name of Conway jumps up and claims a foul and several other Boston characters join him in this claim, and so does Joel Duffle, although afterwards even the Boston characters admit that Joel Duffle is no gentleman to make such a claim against a lady.

Well, there is some confusion over this, and the judges hold a conference, and they rule that there is certainly no foul in the actual eating that they can see, because Miss Violette Shumberger does not touch her pie so far.

But they say that whether it is a foul otherwise all depends on whether Miss Violette Shumberger is requesting advice on the contest from Nicely-Nicely and the judge from Providence, R.I., wishes to know if Nicely-Nicely will kindly relate what passes between him and Violette so they may make a decision.

'Why,' Nicely-Nicely says, 'all she asks me is can I get her another piece of pie when she finishes the one in front of her.'

Now at this, Joel Duffle throws down his knife, and pushes back his plate with all but two bites of his pie left on it, and says to the Boston characters like this:

'Gentlemen,' he says, 'I am licked. I cannot eat another mouthful. You must admit I put up a game battle, but,' he says, 'it is useless for me to go on against this Judy who is asking for more pie before she even starts on what is before her. I am almost dying as it is, and I do not wish to destroy myself in a hopeless effort. Gentlemen,' he says, 'she is not human.'

Well, of course this amounts to throwing in the old napkin and Nicely-Nicely stands up on his chair, and says:

'Three cheers for Miss Violette Shumberger!'

Then Nicely-Nicely gives the first cheer in person, but the effort overtaxes his strength, and he falls off the chair in a faint just as Joel Duffle collapses under the table, and the doctors at the Clinic Hospital are greatly baffled to receive, from the same address at the same time, one patient who is suffering from undernourishment, and another patient who is unconscious from overeating.

Well, in the meantime, after the excitement subsides, and wagers are settled, we take Miss Violette Shumberger to the main floor in Mindy's for a midnight snack, and when she speaks of her wonderful triumph, she is disposed to give much credit to Nicely-Nicely Jones.

'You see,' Violette says, 'what I really whisper to him is that I am a goner. I whisper to him that I cannot possibly take one bite of the pie if my life depends on it, and if he has any bets down to try and hedge them off as quickly as possible.

'I fear,' she says, 'that Nicely-Nicely will be greatly disappointed in my showing, but I have a confession to make to him when he gets out of the hospital. I forget about the contest,' Violette says, 'and eat my regular dinner of pig's knuckles and sauerkraut an hour before the contest starts and', she says, 'I have no doubt this tends to affect my form somewhat. So,' she says, 'I owe everything to Nicely-Nicely's quick thinking.'

It is several weeks after the great eating contest that I run into Miss Hilda Slocum on Broadway and it seems to me that she looks much better nourished than the last time I see her, and when I mention this she says:

'Yes,' she says, 'I cease dieting. I learn my lesson,' she says. 'I learn that male characters do not appreciate anybody who tries to ward off surplus tissue. What male characters wish is substance. Why,' she says, 'only a week ago my editor, Mr McBurgle, tells me he will love to take me dancing if only I get something on me for him to take hold of. I am very fond of dancing,' she says.

'But,' I say, 'what of Nicely-Nicely Jones? I do not see him around lately.'

'Why,' Miss Hilda Slocum says, 'do you not hear what this cad does? Why, as soon as he is strong enough to leave the hospital, he elopes with my dearest friend, Miss Violette Shumberger, leaving me a note saying something about two souls with but a single thought. They are down in Florida running a barbecue stand, and,' she says, 'the chances are, eating like seven mules.'

'Miss Slocum,' I say, 'can I interest you in a portion of Mindy's chicken fricassee?'

'With dumplings?' Miss Hilda Slocum says. 'Yes,' she says, 'you can. Afterwards I have a date to go dancing with Mr McBurgle. I am crazy about dancing,' she says.

Homing Jane

BEN TRAVERS

I

After four long years he returned to her. And at his coming she veiled her face from him. He was Maurice Wincott, from Ceylon; she, his mother city. And even as he stepped from the train London wrapped herself in the shrouds of a thick November fog.

He deliberately accepted the challenge of the grumpy old metropolis. He booked a room at an hotel and indulged in a very prolonged and very warm bath. In this he reclined, lazily replenishing the hot-water supply with his big toe and forming dreamy plans for an enjoyable evening.

The first essential, of course, was company. Now who was there in London – excluding, naturally, relations and men? Was there no one he could discover and lug out to dinner – no pleasing female acquaintance of the past? And suddenly, in the bathroom vapours of luxurious indetermination, gleamed the half-forgotten features of Belle Bellamy.

Belle Bellamy, good Lord, yes!

He hadn't heard of her for four years, but she might still be living in that converted maisonette in those mews – No. 1 Something Mews, Knightsbridge. He left the bath and returned to his bedroom, where he ransacked a telephone directory.

Alas! there were no Miss Bellamys in mews. He tried what Miss Bellamys there were, but none of them was Belle. He would gladly, in his growing desperation, have struck up a chance acquaintance with any other of the Miss Bellamys and taken her to dinner, had she but known. But not one of the Miss Bellamys appeared to guess this.

Well, he'd have to go and investigate, that was all. He'd dress and find his way to the mews.

II

At No. 1 Radnor Mews, Knightsbridge, Mr Percival Thurlowe was in his dressing-room. His mirror reflected strange contortions of his plump face. He was battling with a white tie, and before him, propped against the hair-brush, was a leaflet of illustrated instructions in the correct tying of white ties, a stroke of commercial genius which has resulted in the destruction of thousands of white ties and the subsequent purchase of thousands more.

Mr Thurlowe, a man of fifty-five and capable of moments of strong passion, finally tore the tie from his collar and clenched it in a quivering fist. A very regrettable expression *re* white ties boiled to his lips.

This despairing toilet cry brought in his wife, who tied the tie for him and encouraged him into his tail-coat. He was dressing to attend a City banquet with the Worshipful Company of Flannel Vendors, but by this time he was grumbling against his tie, the fog and the very overrated pastime of banqueting in general. At which did the wife, who was only about half his age and little more than a bride, joyfully acquiesce and urge him to remain and keep her company? She did not.

'I should make an early start,' she said, and she called to the maid below: 'Florence, get a taxi!'

'No, Florence!' cried the husband. 'A taxi! All the way to the City? Think of the fare.'

'There are no taxis left in the mews, madam,' reported Florence. 'Only the old man at the far end with the horse-cab.'

'You needn't think I'm going to drive to the City in that broken-down cab.'

'Then take the Underground,' said Mrs Thurlowe.

She bore him to the front door, where he stood and scented the heavy atmosphere with foreboding.

145

'You'll stay in tonight, mind,' he said. 'I won't have you going over to Eileen's on a night like this.'

Eileen, who supplied Cora Thurlowe with a permanent excuse for evening excursions, was her stepdaughter, a girl in the early twenties, who occupied two rooms in a neighbouring block of flats and performed secretarial work by day. This made her too tired to visit the maisonette after working hours; so Cora would frequently pop over and see Eileen. Percival didn't mind much so long as she walked and didn't squander a shilling on a taxi.

Cora closed the front door on her gloomily departing spouse and hastened back to the telephone. To inform Eileen that she had been bidden to remain within doors? Not at all. To ask to speak to a Mr Morris.

'If,' says the French phrase-book in a passage of inspired philosophy, 'if one is not beautiful it is admirable to be good.' So, presumably, as one deviates from the straight and narrow path of utter virtue one may be expected to gain proportionately in good looks. Cora could not be termed actually beautiful, and she was by no means immoral. What perhaps robbed her of beauty was a certain piquancy of expression; you know, that cheekily tilted nose typical of some of our merry blondes whom gentlemen prefer. And a corresponding germ of mischief in her nature may have beckoned her occasionally from the stony path of rigorous probity to the smoother tracks of fun – though, indeed, she never wandered very far afield.

But fun has its reckoning; in this instance the payee being this Mr Morris. As Cora discoursed with him on the telephone that attractive smile which telephoning persons assume automatically – as though it could be observed by the interlocutor – played on her lips; but her eyes were widened and seemed to stare through the wall opposite at some visionary menace beyond.

'I know I said I'd pay tonight; but I can't. You shall have the money tomorrow, or quite soon . . . No, you can't possibly see my husband. He's out tonight; besides, he doesn't know about it, and if he did . . . What? Mr Morris, you wouldn't do a thing like that! . . . I know; I know. I thought I could raise it by tonight. I'm sorry, but you shall have it. You can trust me . . . No, you can't see him, you can't. He won't be in till late. Besides, you needn't think you'd get anything out of him . . . Not what? Not a large sum? Not to you, perhaps. All the more reason why you can afford to wait a little longer . . . You won't wait? . . . Hallo? Hallo?' But Mr Morris had rung off.

She sat deep in thought, her fingers tapping an aimless tune on the table. From somewhere, within the next hour or two, she must raise £300, or Percival would get to hear about it. What should she do? Her bank balance – well, she had had to nip into a taxi only yesterday to avoid meeting her bank manager in the street. Her few securities were in trust – curse this trust business. Who was there?

There was Ella Moone, for instance. She knew Ella well enough to confide in her; but look at the way Ella carried on if she lost half a crown at bridge! Still, Ella might be able to suggest something. Cora titivated hastily before her drawing-room mirror, hurried to the front door, and opened it to peer into the bland, expectant countenance of Maurice Wincott.

'Belle!' he cried. 'No. Dash! So sorry. I came to see a lady who lived here. She evidently doesn't. I beg your pardon. A Miss Bellamy. You don't happen to know?'

'Oh, she's gone to live at Brighton, I believe.'

'Oh. Sorry. You see, I've been abroad for four years, so I didn't know. This is my first night back in London. What a night for it, isn't it? Well, thank you.'

He raised his opera hat and turned, with perhaps just the smallest hint of reluctance, to depart. A well-dressed, well-spoken man with a pleasant, open smile. 'Hold him!' cried every instinct in Cora's constitution. 'Hold him! This may be your guardian angel unawares. Hold him; take him in and try him out.'

'Oh, but now you're here – won't you come in and warm yourself for a moment?' she said.

'Really? Oh, how kind! But you were going out.'

'No hurry.'

She led the way back to the little drawing-room and turned to face him again. They inspected each other in the better light with interest and, it appeared, mutual satisfaction. He was a bronzed, clean-shaven man of about forty. Not even the traces of fog could dim the benevolent gleam of admiration in his eyes.

'You know Miss Bellamy?' he asked.

'I met her when we took over the maisonette.'

'Yes; a plain – well, a comparatively plain woman, but a kind heart. I came to see her because I couldn't think of anyone else.'

'You've only just got back to London, you say?'

'Today. After four years in Ceylon. And look at London! Gloom and fog. I went out into Piccadilly. I've never felt so lonely in my life. I've been whole days and nights in the jungle with only the monkeys, but I found it twice as sociable as Piccadilly.'

'You wanted – company?'

'Company. Exactly. How quick of you!'

'Have a cigarette,' said Cora.

'You're more than kind,' he said. 'I'm getting warmer. Am I keeping you?'

'Not at all.'

'What were we saying? Oh, yes – company. Well, you know, everywhere I went in the fog in Piccadilly I saw or encountered couples. Happy little couples – sweethearts and wives – possibly someone's sweetheart who'd fallen in with someone else's wife in the fog – but no matter; anyhow, couples. Well, naturally I didn't feel like spending my first evening alone, so, in lieu of a better, I came to seek out Belle Bellamy.'

'And what will you do now?' asked Cora.

'Well, I certainly shan't go to Brighton. I must dine at

some lugubrious club, I suppose. And I'd pictured such a delightful little dinner in some lively restaurant; you know – sparkling wines, sparkling eyes – the soothing murmur of the saxophone – all that stuff. But, alas! it is not to be.' He sighed and examined the glow of his cigarette. 'I suppose,' he added wistfully.

She too displayed interest in her cigarette.

'Well, I really don't know what I can do to help you,' she said.

'Oh, nothing – naturally, nothing. But you so kindly asked me in and registered sympathy, that's all. You're married, I see.'

'Yes. I live here with my husband. He's gone out to a City dinner.'

'And left you to dine alone?'

'Yes.'

'Oh, why?' He spoke in a whisper so soft that it scarcely seemed more than a part of his smile.

She glanced at him quickly, and he plunged. Told her his name, his circumstances, advertised modestly his unimpeachable character. Sobering somewhat, paid restrained tribute to her infectious charm and its natural effect on one reclaimed from the rubber plantations.

'You must pardon me,' he urged, 'but, really, think of my case. For months together I haven't seen a white woman's face. Occasionally, perhaps, a little treat in the shape of a female missionary, and usually a very queer shape too. Well, you ask, how can you help me. And I tell you. You can help me by coming out with me to some tip-top restaurant and having a dashed good dinner.'

She crossed to the sofa. He remained standing in the centre of the room, looking like a patient awaiting the verdict of a specialist.

'It's funny', she said, 'that anyone should walk in here like this and ask me to help him, because if there's anyone in London who wants help tonight, it's me.'

He came deliberately to the sofa and sat beside her. 'Come on. Tell me,' he said.

'Look here,' she replied; 'I should think you're a pretty broadminded man.'

'Broadminded? I come from the island of Ceylon – a land where every prospect pleases and only man is vile. I tell you, you get broadminded soon enough, living among vile men with pleasing prospects.'

'All right, then. Listen . . .'

III

For a stepdaughter, Eileen was certainly a sport. She never let on that Cora's evening visits to her rooms were less frequent and of briefer duration than Percival supposed. Eileen perhaps found it easy to forgive a little harmless recreation to anyone who had married her father. She knew that Cora was wont to look in at Mr Morris's flat hard by and indulge in a taste for roulette, which Eileen personally considered a particularly footling form of amusement.

Cora, who had met Mr Morris through her bookmaker, became rather intrigued by the little parties in his rooms. They were admittedly below her social standard. She had lost steadily and had presented Mr Morris with IOUs. In short, this was Cora's folly; just as you and I have doubtless our own little follies carefully guarded and, with any luck, undreamt of at the other end of the dinner-table. Mr Morris was very suave and hand-lathering about the IOUs at first; then changed his demeanour. Cora's face when he threatened to apply to Mr Thurlowe told him that this was a very disagreeable idea to her; told him, moreover, that the fifth of November would be the most appropriate date for the revelation. So he told Mrs Thurlowe that unless she paid by the fifth he'd call on her husband. Only he didn't say 'your husband'. He said 'hubby'. Well, here was the fifth, and what had Cora done? Raised what ready money she could and tried to augment it by laying it on a sequence of disappointing racehorses. Such was the sad tale related, without elaboration or apology, to Maurice Wincott as she sat there in the midst of the poor little Jericho maisonette with Joshua Morris already tuning up his trumpet at the gates.

'I've come home with an almost indecent amount of cash,' he said. 'I'll let you have three hundred if you'll pay me back sometime.'

'You think', she expostulated, 'that I only told you because I wanted you to lend me the money?'

'Well, yes,' he answered obviously.

She looked at him searchingly, almost accusingly; then relapsed. 'Well, so I did,' she confessed.

He rose. 'Right. I'll wait while you dress. We'll dine. Then we'll call on this blighter and fix him. I've got my cheque-book in my pocket. I half guessed I might want it tonight.'

'Twenty minutes ago you'd never heard of me,' she said. 'You mean to say you'll lend me this money without security?'

'Yes. I can see exactly the sort of person you are. Of course I'll help you, with pleasure.'

'And you mean to say that it's possible for a man to do this for a woman without the faintest glimmer of an ulterior motive?'

'It is possible,' he replied. He looked at her and smiled briefly. 'It's difficult, but possible.'

Two minutes later she was dressing as light-heartedly as a schoolgirl on an outing. What elation is there in the world to compare with that which celebrates a menace parried? It is sufficient to supply a recreant philosopher with a handy excuse for seeking trouble.

IV

At 9.45 Cora brought him into Eileen's two-roomed quarters and introduced him to her – Mr Wincott, a friend of her youth just returned from Ceylon. Eileen took good stock of him, and liked the look of him very much. As for him, he sat positively staggered by the glory of Eileen, the sweet, graceful creature, with her trimly shingled brown locks and complexion of peaches.

By George, how delightful these girls appeared after a long sojourn in the sallow East! Cora could not fail to notice his keen appreciation of Eileen, but she didn't appear to resent it. On the contrary, she rather encouraged it.

The main object of the evening was still to be achieved. They had called at Mr Morris's, but he was out. There was no party there that night. They must call again, that was all. So they crossed the road to Eileen's rooms to pass the time.

It passed all too quickly for Wincott. At ten o'clock they went out and tried again. No luck; Mr Morris had not returned. There was no little roulette party that evening.

'What if he's done what he threatened and gone round to the mews?' said Cora.

'What if he has?' replied Wincott. 'He won't have found anyone there, and you don't expect a man like that to hang about indefinitely in mews in a fog.'

Cora shrugged. 'Anyhow, I must get back. Percival will be home soon. Hadn't I better perhaps have the money with me, just in case Morris should turn up? Then, if he doesn't, I could settle with him tomorrow.'

Wincott seated himself on a damp but convenient doorstep with his cheque-book and a fountain pen, and presented Cora with £300. Her expressions of gratitude were cut short, for a stray taxi came looming up, and taxis were not easy to find in the fog.

'Are you coming with me as far as the mews?' she asked.

'You bet I am.'

'Or would you rather go and take Eileen out to supper?'

'What?' he said quickly.

Cora laughed. 'There are not many ways in which I can show my gratitude, but if that's one of them, you carry on.'

As he hesitated she stepped into the taxi and stretched a hand out to him through its open doorway. He kissed it. She laughed again and drove away.

There met her, at the maisonette, a distracted Florence.

'Oh, madam, there's a strange man in the drawing-room. He insisted on coming in. Said he had very important business with the master and would wait.'

'What? He's really had the cheek? All right,' said Cora. 'I know about it. I'll see him.'

'Oh, but, madam! The master's been back. He came and went again just before this gentleman arrived. He thought you were at Miss Eileen's, and went to fetch you back.'

Cora bit her lip. Delicate business, this. 'How long ago when he went?'

'About a quarter of an hour'm.'

'Did he walk?'

'No'm. He wanted a taxi, but couldn't get one. That old cabman was just starting out looking for a fare in the fog, so he took him.'

'Oh, he'll be back pretty soon,' said Cora. 'All right, Florence.'

V

'Righto,' said Eileen; 'I'm on. We'll go to the Beaux Arts.'

'The Beaux Arts,' said Wincott. 'Splendid! Go into your bedroom and put on your prettiest evening frock. I'll wait here.'

For the second time that evening he reclined in a sitting-room while a feminine member of the Thurlowe family performed an adjacent toilet for his benefit. But suddenly there came a sharp rap at the outer door, and a thick masculine voice: 'Eileen!'

Eileen appeared from the bedroom. She was not entirely dressed, but near enough. Her pretty features were puckered in annoyance.

'It's father,' she said.

'Does that matter much?' he enquired.

'Not in the least,' said Eileen. 'Half a tick.'

She admitted a study in feasted and massive indignation. His greatcoat was open and flapping. He wore a tall hat at an imperious tilt. His ponderous jaw was working at some private rehearsal of wrathful remonstrance. It dropped, and he blinked in surprised challenge at Wincott, who rose and bowed ceremoniously. 'Father, I believe?' he said.

'Who the devil is this man, and what's he doing here, and where is your mother, and what are you in this half-clad condition for?' demanded Mr Thurlowe.

'Mr Wincott, from Ceylon. Because he's going to take me out to supper. Gone home. Because you can't go to the Beaux Arts in a blouse,' replied Eileen patiently.

'I was told your mother was here. What's she been up to? And what are you up to with this man?'

'Now, now, now,' said Wincott soothingly. 'Finish your dressing. Leave father to me.'

Eileen assented and withdrew. Wincott led the protesting parent to the sofa.

'Now, don't you worry about me,' he said. 'I'm a fine feller. So are you, I'm sure. Only just at the moment you're feeling – well, I know what it is; I've been through it myself. Only last time I was on leave I dined with the Worshipful Company of Milkmen. I remember it well. We all went home with each other.'

'You insinuate that I'm drunk?'

'Drunk? No, certainly not; not – not quite. But you mustn't trot about around town in a fog worrying about people. Do let me advise you to go home to bed.'

'Who are you, and how dare you—'

'I'm only trying to do you a kindness, sir. I ask you, look at yourself. Look at your tie – well, you can't, I suppose; but I mean, for instance, look here – what's this on your trousers? Horrible! A piece of pineapple.'

'I'm ready,' said Eileen, reappearing.

'I forbid you to go out with this man, whoever he is!' cried Mr Thurlowe.

'Nonsense,' said Eileen. 'He's a very nice man, as far as I know; and even if he isn't, I've enough sense to be able to look after myself.'

She escorted Wincott away. Mr Thurlowe remained on the sofa and drew a podgy hand across his brow.

The fog had doubled in intensity – a deepening blackness had stolen into it, shrouding everything outside a few yards radius.

'We shall never find a taxi,' said Eileen.

'Something's standing here,' said Wincott. 'I see lights.'

He advanced a step or two to the kerb. 'Here, I say, can you— Oh, good Lord, I'm talking to a horse!'

'Engaged,' said something in the darkness.

'But where? I can't find you. Is this you? With a beard? No, that's the other end of the horse.' An aged cabman floated into their ken.

'Can't take yer, sir. I brought a gent here from Radner Moos.'

'Father's cab,' said Eileen. 'That's all right. We'll take it on. He'll walk home.'

'Ah, but he said "Wait," ' said the cabman.

'Oh, but we're all in the family,' replied Wincott. 'Here you are. Here's your fare for bringing him here. Now take us to the Beaux Arts.'

'The bazaar?'

'No, no; the Beaux—'

'Rupert Street,' said Eileen, already inside the cab.

The cabman, somewhat reassured by five shillings, slowly turned his horse.

'I suppose your old horse can get there?' asked Wincott.

'Old Jane,' replied the cabman, 'she be better than any o' they taxis in a fog. But, you know, sir, that other gent, 'e said "Wait." '

'You're through with him, I tell you. Come on, now. Wake

Jane up and urge her to the Beaux Arts.' He got in beside Eileen and closed the door. 'Are you as comfortable as possible?' he enquired. 'I would suggest you sit fairly close, if only on account of the cold.'

The cabman mounted; but before Jane had gone a dozen paces he heard the voice of his ex-fare hailing him in no measured terms. Perplexed, he whoa'd Jane, slid from the box and returned to the pavement to argue the matter.

While he was yet searching, a group of overgrown boys, fresh from some fifth of November spree, passed Mr Thurlowe, jostling him in a very offensive manner. A few yards farther on they discovered an invaluable butt for their humour in the form of an apparently derelict growler. Jane, with a cracker leaping and exploding astern of her, awoke in earnest and lunged away into obscurity.

'We're off at last,' said Wincott.

The fog surged against the cab windows. In complete darkness they jogged contentedly along for some considerable time. Suddenly, and apparently for good, the cab came to rest. Maurice opened the door and peered out. He hailed the cabman, who made no reply. He turned with a puzzled smile to Eileen.

'Is this the Beaux Arts?' he asked.

'It doesn't look like it,' said Eileen, descending.

VI

'You mean', said Cora, 'you won't accept this cheque?'

'Not like it is now,' said Mr Morris. 'Your clever friend, whoever he is, has drawn it to "self" and forgotten to endorse it.'

Cora took the cheque, examined it with a frown, and replaced it in her handbag.

'Well, leave it till tomorrow. I'll get it endorsed.'

'No,' said Mr Morris. 'I'm through with all this, Mrs Thurlowe. Broken promises – useless cheques – no thanks. I'm going to wait and see your husband.'

156

'You needn't think you'll get a penny out of him.'

Mr Morris, five feet three inches of flaccid self-possession, eyed her dully.

'Go on,' he retorted. 'Why not admit straight out you'd give anything for hubby not to be told.'

Her pride rose in a wave of indignation.

'So I would,' she said. 'But he's got to be told, that's all. Now you can get out, please.'

'I shall only wait on the doorstep if I do,' replied Mr Morris.

She hesitated. After all, she'd better see Percival first and try to make what explanation she could. 'All right, stay where you are,' she said.

The imperturbable Mr Morris complied, and so they remained, he in the drawing-room, she in the dining-room, trying vaguely to formulate her unhappy confession.

At length she looked up quickly. She heard the sound of the cab returning to the mews outside. She rose and stood in the hall waiting for Percival to enter.

Whole minutes passed, and he made no appearance. Finally, unable to bear the suspense, she stepped forward and opened the front door. Again, like a recurring dream, in that doorway appeared Maurice Wincott, wearing an expression of bewildered amusement.

'Shall we come in,' he asked, 'Eileen and I? The most amazing thing has happened. We took father's cab. The cabby must have fallen off the box. And Jane homed.'

'What on earth do you mean?'

'You've heard of a homing pigeon?' he replied. 'Well, Jane is a homing horse. She homed through the fog to the mews.'

'Blessings on Jane!' exclaimed Cora. 'Because this is the one place in all the world where you're really wanted at this moment.'

Wincott and Eileen followed her into the dining-room. Five minutes later he opened the drawing-room door and confronted the intruder.

'Impossible!' he was saying as he entered. 'My wife guilty

of such a thing – incredible! Are you this man?'

'Yes, Mr Thurlowe. Sorry to have to cause a little flutter in the home circle.'

'But it's a lie. It's unbelievable. What proof have you got?'

Mr Morris produced his I O Us with a flourish. Wincott received them with trembling fingers. He moaned aloud as he examined them. 'My heavens!' he murmured. 'My wife!'

Cora hovered in the doorway. He rounded upon her.

'All this money!' he cried. 'Oh, you wicked woman! Oh, you rotten player!'

Then with a sudden gesture of loathing he cast the slips of paper into the back of the fire.

'Get out!' he said, and indicated the door very unmistakably to Mr Morris.

That gentleman raised a hand, less in protest than in defiance.

'Look here—' he began.

'No,' said Wincott. 'You look at me. You ran this beastly little roulette table and held the bank, and advanced my poor wife money to lose to you. Every bob you lent her you scooped back. You're not out of pocket a cent. And if you don't get out I shall have to kick you out. And then I shall ring up the police and report you for running a gaming saloon, you naughty little man.'

'I handed you those I O Us in good faith,' cried Mr Morris.

'Oh, ridiculous! You haven't any good faith to hand anyone anything in. Run away, now.'

Mr Morris, for once thoroughly roused, was not to be so easily ejected. It took over ten minutes to get him into the outer mews. The door had finally been closed upon him, and he was venting a few farewell threats as he departed, when he butted into the stomach of a stout gentleman who was being accompanied home by a cabless cabman. Mr Morris was, however, in small temper for apology and explanation.

'Keep it to yourself,' he snarled, 'can't you?' And he disappeared, fortunately, into the fog and was no more seen.

Percival Thurlowe unlocked and opened his front door. Then he stood back heavily on the toe of the cabman. His whole countenance seemed slowly to open. His opera hat fell with a thud.

'You!' he cried. 'Again! Here?'

Wincott advanced to meet him. The staring cabman supported himself by the doorpost and quoted a brief passage of Holy Writ.

Then Mr Thurlowe saw his wife leaving the drawing-room with Wincott, and swept forward across the narrow hall.

'Who and what is this infernal person?' he began. But she made so horrified a gesture that he paused.

'Really, Percival! Don't be so rude. How can you? This is a very old friend of mine, home from Ceylon. He came in just after you left tonight. He's been entertaining us most liberally.'

'But he took my cab—'

'Naturally. He had Eileen to look after in the fog.'

'But he left the cabman behind. Oh, what the devil is all this about?'

'Hush!' said Cora. 'You can't be yourself. Come in and sit down quietly.'

'Shan't we be going now?' suggested Eileen, emerging from the dining-room.

'Certainly,' replied Wincott. 'Come, cabman; pull yourself together! And tell Jane that this time we really must go to the Beaux Arts.'

He glanced back into the drawing-room. Mr Thurlowe had once more gained the welcome sanctuary of a sofa, where he sat with his ponderous cheeks buried in his hands. Cora raised her head from her ministrations and blew a good-night kiss into the hall.

Wincott returned it; then took the waiting arm of Eileen. As he passed out he linked up the still completely staggered cabman with his free arm and bore him down the length of the mews to Jane.

The Bishop's Handkerchief

RICHMAL CROMPTON

Until now William had taken no interest in his handkerchiefs as toilet accessories. They were greyish (once white) squares useful for blotting ink or carrying frogs or making lifelike rats to divert the long hours of afternoon school, but otherwise he had had no pride or interest in them.

But last week, Ginger (a member of the circle known to themselves as the Outlaws of which William was the leader) had received a handkerchief as a birthday present from an aunt in London. William, on hearing the news, had jeered, but the sight of the handkerchief had silenced him.

It was a large handkerchief, larger than William had conceived it possible for handkerchiefs to be. It was made of silk, and contained all the colours of the rainbow. Round the edge green dragons sported upon a red ground. Ginger displayed it at first deprecatingly, fully prepared for scorn and merriment, and for some moments the fate of the handkerchief hung in the balance. But there was something about the handkerchief that impressed them.

'Kinder – funny,' said Henry critically.

'Jolly big, isn't it?' said Douglas uncertainly.

' 'S more like a *sheet*,' said William, wavering between scorn and admiration.

Ginger was relieved. At any rate they had taken it seriously. They had not wept tears of mirth over it. That afternoon he drew it out of his pocket with a flourish and airily wiped his nose with it. The next morning Henry appeared with a handkerchief almost exactly like it, and the day after that Douglas had one. William felt his prestige lowered. He –

the born leader – was the only one of the select circle who did not possess a coloured silk handkerchief.

That evening he approached his mother.

'I don't think white ones is much use,' he said.

'Don't scrape your feet on the carpet, William,' said his mother placidly. 'I thought white ones were the only tame kind – not that I think your father will let you have any more. You know what he said when they got all over the floor and bit his finger.'

'I'm not talkin' about *rats*,' said William. 'I'm talkin' about handkerchiefs.'

'Oh – handkerchiefs! White ones are far the best. They launder properly. They come out a good colour – at least yours don't, but that's because you get them so black – but there's nothing better than white linen.'

'Pers'nally,' said William with a judicial air, 'I think silk's better than linen an' white's so tirin' to look at. I think a kind of colour's better for your eyes. My eyes do ache a bit sometimes. I think it's prob'ly with keep lookin' at white handkerchiefs.'

'Don't be silly, William. I'm not going to buy you silk handkerchiefs to get covered with mud and ink and coal as yours do.'

Mrs Brown calmly cut off her darning wool as she spoke, and took another sock from the pile by her chair. William sighed.

'Oh, I wouldn't do those things with a *silk* one,' he said earnestly. 'It's only because they're *cotton* ones I do those things.'

'Linen,' corrected Mrs Brown.

'Linen an' cotton's the same,' said William, 'it's not *silk*. I jus' want a *silk* one with colours an' so on, that's all. That's all I want. It's not much. Just a *silk* handkerchief with colours. Surely—'

'I'm *not* going to buy you another *thing*, William,' said Mrs Brown firmly. 'I had to get you a new suit and new collars only last month, and your overcoat's dreadful, because you *will* crawl through the ditch in it—'

William resented this cowardly change of attack.

'I'm not talkin' about suits an' collars an' overcoats an' so on –' he said; 'I'm talkin' about *handkerchiefs*. I simply ask you if—'

'If you want a silk handkerchief, William,' said Mrs Brown decisively, 'you'll have to buy one.'

'Well!' said William, aghast at the unfairness of the remark – 'Well, jus' fancy you sayin' that to me when you know I've not got any money, when you *know* I'm not even *going* to have any money for years an' years an' years.'

'You shouldn't have broken the landing-window,' said Mrs Brown.

William was pained and disappointed. He had no illusions about his father and elder brother, but he had expected more feeling and sympathy from his mother.

Determinedly, but not very hopefully, he went to his father, who was reading a newspaper in the library.

'You know, father,' said William confidingly, taking his seat upon the newspaper rack, 'I think white ones is all right for children – and so on. Wot I mean to say is that when you get older coloured ones is better.'

'Really?' said his father politely.

'Yes,' said William, encouraged. 'They wouldn't show dirt so, either – not like white ones do. An' they're bigger, too. They'd be cheaper in the end. They wouldn't cost so much for laundry – an' so on.'

'Exactly,' murmured his father, turning over to the next page.

'Well,' said William boldly, 'if you'd very kin'ly buy me some, or one would do, or I could buy them or it if you'd jus' give me—'

'As I haven't the remotest idea what you're talking about,' said his father, 'I don't see how I can. Would you be so very kind as to remove yourself from the newspaper rack for a minute and let me get the evening paper? I'm so sorry to trouble you. Thank you so much.'

'Handkerchiefs!' said William impatiently. 'I keep telling you. It's *handkerchiefs*. I jus' want a nice silk coloured one, 'cause I think it would last longer and be cheaper in the wash. That's all. I think the ones I have makes such a lot of trouble for the laundry. I jus'—'

'Though deeply moved by your consideration for other people,' said Mr Brown, as he ran his eye down the financial column, 'I may as well save you any further waste of your valuable time and eloquence by informing you at once that you won't get a halfpenny out of me if you talk till midnight.'

William went with silent disgust and slow dignity from the room.

Next he investigated Robert's bedroom. He opened Robert's dressing-table drawer and turned over his handkerchiefs. He caught his breath with surprise and pleasure. There it was beneath all Robert's other handkerchiefs – larger, silkier, more multi-coloured than Ginger's or Douglas's or Henry's. He gazed at it in ecstatic joy. He slipped it into his pocket and, standing before the looking-glass, took it out with a flourish, shaking its lustrous folds. He was absorbed in this occupation when Robert entered. Robert looked at him with elder-brother disapproval.

'I told you that if I caught you playing monkey tricks in my room again—' he began threateningly, glancing suspiciously at the bed, in the 'apple-pie' arrangements of which William was an expert.

'I'm not, Robert,' said William with disarming innocence. 'Honest I'm not. I jus' wanted to borrow a handkerchief. I thought you wun't mind lendin' me a handkerchief.'

'Well, I would,' said Robert shortly, 'so you can jolly well clear out.'

'It was this one I thought you wun't mind lendin' me,' said William. 'I wun't take one of your nice white ones, but I thought you wun't mind me having this ole coloured dirty-looking one.'

'Did you? Well, give it back to me.'

Reluctantly William handed it back to Robert.

'How much'll you give it me for?' he said shortly.

'Well, how much have you?' said Robert ruthlessly.

'Nothin' – not jus' at present,' admitted William. 'But I'd *do* something for you for it. I'd do anythin' you want done for it. You just tell me what to do for it, an' I'll *do* it.'

'Well, you can – you can get the Bishop's handkerchief for me, and then I'll give mine to you.'

The trouble with Robert was that he imagined himself a wit.

The trouble with William was that he took things literally.

The Bishop was expected in the village the next day. It was the great event of the summer. He was a distant relation of the Vicar's. He was to open the Sale of Work, address a large meeting on Temperance, spend the night at the Vicarage, and depart the next morning.

The Bishop was a fatherly, simple-minded old man of seventy. He enjoyed the Sale of Work except for one thing. Wherever he looked he met the gaze of a freckled untidy frowning small boy. He could not understand it. The boy seemed to be everywhere. The boy seemed to follow him about. He came to the conclusion that it must be his imagination, but it made him feel vaguely uneasy.

Then he addressed the meeting on Temperance, his audience consisting chiefly of adults. But, in the very front seat, the same earnest frowning boy fixed him with a determined gaze. When the Bishop first encountered this gaze he became slightly disconcerted, and lost his place in his notes. Then he tried to forget the disturbing presence and address his remarks to the middle of the hall. But there was something hypnotic in the small boy's gaze. In the end the Bishop yielded to it. He fixed his eyes obediently upon William. He harangued William earnestly and forcibly upon the necessity of self-control and the effect of alcohol upon the liver. And William returned his gaze unblinkingly.

After the meeting William wandered down the road to the Vicarage. He pondered gloomily over his wasted afternoon. Fate had not thrown the Bishop's handkerchief in his path. But he did not yet despair.

On the way he met Ginger. Ginger drew out his interminable coloured handkerchief and shook it proudly.

'D'ye mean to *say*,' he said to William, 'that you still use those old *white* ones?'

William looked at him with cold scorn.

'I'm too busy to bother with you jus' now,' he said.

Ginger went on.

William looked cautiously through the Vicarage hedge. Nothing was to be seen. He crawled inside the garden and round to the back of the house, which was invisible from the road. The Bishop was tired after his address. He lay outstretched upon a deckchair beneath a tree.

Over the head and face of His Lordship was stretched a large superfine linen handkerchief. William's set stern expression brightened. On hands and knees he began to crawl through the grass towards the portly form, his tongue protruding from his pursed lips.

Crouching behind the chair, he braced himself for the crime; he measured the distance between the chair and the garden gate.

One, two, three – then suddenly the portly form stirred, the handkerchief was firmly withdrawn by a podgy hand, and a dignified voice yawned and said: 'Heigh-ho!'

At the same moment the Bishop sat up. William, from his refuge behind the chair, looked wildly round. The door of the house was opening. There was only one thing to do. William was as nimble as a monkey. Like a flash of lightning he disappeared up the tree. It was a very leafy tree. It completely concealed William, but William had a good bird's eye view of the world beneath him. The Vicar came out rubbing his hands.

'You rested, my Lord?' he said.

'I'm afraid I've had forty winks,' said His Lordship pleasantly. 'Just dropped off, you know. I dreamt about that boy who was at the meeting this afternoon.'

'What boy, my Lord?' asked the Vicar.

'I noticed him at the Sale of Work and the meeting – he looked – he looked a soulful boy. I daresay you know him.'

The Vicar considered.

'I can't think of any boy round here like that,' he said.

The Bishop sighed.

'He may have been a stranger, of course,' he said meditatively. 'It seemed an earnest *questing* face – as if the boy wanted something – *needed* something. I hope my little talk helped him.'

'Without doubt it did, my Lord,' said the Vicar politely. 'I thought we might dine out here – the days draw out so pleasantly now.'

Up in his tree, William with smirks and hand-rubbing and mincing (though soundless) movements of his lips kept up a running imitation of the Vicar's speech, for the edification apparently of a caterpillar which was watching him intently.

The Vicar went in to order dinner in the garden. The Bishop drew the delicate handkerchief once more over his rubicund features. In the tree William abandoned his airy pastime, and his face took on again the expression of soulful earnestness that had pleased the Bishop.

The breast of the Bishop on the lawn began to rise and sink. The figure of the Vicar was visible at the study window as he gazed with fond pride upon the slumbers of his distinguished guest. William dared not descend in view of that watching figure. Finally it sat down in a chair by the window and began to read a book.

Then William began to act. He took from his pocket a bent pin attached to a piece of string. This apparatus lived

166

permanently in his pocket, because he had not given up hope of catching a trout in the village stream. He lowered this cautiously and drew the bent pin carefully on to the white linen expanse.

It caught – joy!

'Phut!' said the Bishop, bringing down his hand heavily, not on the pin, but near it.

The pin was loosened – William drew it back cautiously up into the tree, and the Bishop settled himself once more to his slumbers.

Again the pin descended – again it caught.

'Phut!' said the Bishop, testily shaking the handkerchief, and again loosening the pin.

Leaning down from his leafy retreat William made one last desperate effort. He drew the bent pin sharply across. It missed the handkerchief and it caught the Bishop's ear. The Bishop sat up with a scream. William, pin and string withdrew into the shade of the branches. 'Crumbs!' said William desperately to the caterpillar, 'talk about bad *luck!*'

The Vicar ran out from the house, full of concern at the sound of the Bishop's scream.

'I've been badly stung in the ear by some insect,' said the Bishop in a voice that was pained and dignified. 'Some virulent tropical insect, I should think – very painful. Very painful indeed—'

'My Lord,' said the Vicar, 'I am so sorry – so very sorry – a thousand pardons – can I procure some remedy for you – Vaseline, ammonia – er – cold cream—?' Up in the tree the pantomimic imitation of him went on much to William's satisfaction.

'No, no, no, no,' snapped the Bishop. 'This must be a bad place for insects, that's all. Even before that some heavy creatures came banging against my handkerchief. I put my handkerchief over my face for a protection. If I had failed to do that I should have been badly stung.'

'Shall we dine indoors, then, my Lord?' said the Vicar.

'Oh, no, no, NO!' said the Bishop impatiently.

The Vicar sat down upon his chair. William collected a handful of acorns and began to drop them one by one upon the Vicar's bald head. He did this simply because he could not help it. The sight of the Vicar's bald head was irresistible. Each time an acorn struck the Vicar's bald head it bounced up into the air, and the Vicar put up his hand and rubbed his head. At first he tried to continue his conversation on the state of the parish finances with the Bishop, but his replies became distrait and incoherent. He moved his chair slightly. William moved the position of his arm and continued to drop acorns.

At last the Bishop noticed it.

'The acorns seem to be falling,' he said.

The Vicar rubbed his head again.

'Don't they?' he said.

'Rather early,' commented the Bishop.

'Isn't it?' he said as another acorn bounced upon his head.

The Bishop began to take quite an interest in the unusual phenomenon.

'I shouldn't be surprised if there was some sort of blight in that tree,' he said. 'It would account for the premature dropping of the acorns and for the insects that attacked me.'

'Exactly,' said the Vicar irritably, as yet another acorn hit him. William's aim was unerring.

Here a diversion was caused by the maid who came out to lay the table. They watched her in silence. The Vicar moved his chair again, and William, after pocketing his friend the caterpillar, shifted his position in the tree again to get a better aim.

'Do you know,' said the Bishop, 'I believe that there is a cat in the tree. Several times I have heard a slight rustling.'

It would have been better for William to remain silent, but William's genius occasionally misled him. He was anxious to prevent investigation; to prove once for all his identity as a cat.

168

He leant forward and uttered a re-echoing 'Mi-*aw-aw-aw!*'

As imitations go it was rather good.

There was a slight silence. Then:

'It *is* a cat,' said the Bishop in triumph.

'Excuse me, my Lord,' said the Vicar.

He went softly into the house and returned holding a shoe.

'This will settle his feline majesty,' he smiled.

Then he hurled the shoe violently into the tree.

'Sh! Scoot!' he said as he did it.

William was annoyed. The shoe narrowly missed his face. He secured it and waited.

'I hope you haven't lost the shoe,' said the Bishop anxiously.

'Oh, no. The gardener's boy or someone will get it for me. It's the best thing to do with cats. It's probably scared it on to the roof.'

He settled himself in his chair comfortably with a smile.

William leant down, held the shoe deliberately over the bald head, then dropped it.

'*Damn!*' said the Vicar. 'Excuse me, my Lord.'

'H'm,' said the Bishop. 'Er – yes – most annoying. It lodged in a branch for a time probably, and then obeyed the force of gravity.'

The Vicar was rubbing his head. William wanted to enjoy the sight of the Vicar rubbing his head. He moved a little further up the branch. He forgot all caution. He forgot that the branch on which he was was not a very secure branch, and that the further up he moved the less secure it became.

There was the sound of a rending and a crashing, and on to the table between the amazed Vicar and Bishop descended William's branch and William.

The Bishop gazed at him. 'Why, that's the boy,' he said.

William sat up among the debris of broken glasses and crockery. He discovered that he was bruised and that his hand was cut by one of the broken glasses. He extricated himself from the branch and the table, and stood rubbing his bruises and sucking his hand.

'Crumbs!' was all he said.

The Vicar was gazing at him speechlessly.

'You know, my boy,' said the Bishop in mild reproach, 'that's a very curious thing to do – to hide up there for the purpose of eavesdropping. I know that you are an earnest, well-meaning little boy, and that you were interested in my address this afternoon, and I daresay you were hoping to listen to me again, but this is my time for relaxation, you know. Suppose the Vicar and I had been talking about something we didn't want you to hear? I'm sure you wouldn't like to listen to things people didn't want you to hear, would you?'

William stared at him in unconcealed amazement. The Vicar, with growing memories of acorns and shoes and 'damns' and with murder in his heart, was picking up twigs and broken glass. He knew that he could not, in the Bishop's presence, say the things to William and do the things to William that he wanted to do and say. He contented himself with saying:

'You'd better go home now. Tell your father I'll be coming to see him tomorrow.'

'A well-meaning little boy, I'm sure,' said the Bishop kindly, 'well-meaning, but unwise – er – unwise – but your attentiveness during the meeting did you credit, my boy – did you credit.'

William, for all his ingenuity, could think of no remark suitable to the occasion.

'Hurry up,' said the Vicar.

William turned to go. He knew when he was beaten. He had spent a lot of time and trouble and had not even secured the episcopal handkerchief. He had bruised himself and cut himself. He understood the Vicar's veiled threat. He saw his already distant chances of pocket-money vanish into nothingness when the cost of the Vicar's glasses and plates was added to the landing-window. He wouldn't have minded if he'd got the handkerchief. He wouldn't have minded any-thing if—

'Don't suck your hand, my boy,' said the Bishop. 'An open cut like that is most dangerous. Poison works into the system by it. You remember I told you how the poison of alcohol works into the system – well, any kind of poison can work into it by a cut – don't suck it; keep it covered up – haven't you a handkerchief? – here, take mine. You needn't trouble to return it. It's an old one.'

The Bishop was deeply touched by what he called the 'bright spirituality' of the smile with which William thanked him.

William, limping slightly, his hand covered by a grimy rag, came out into the garden, drawing from his pocket with a triumphant flourish an enormous violently coloured silk handkerchief. Robert, who was weeding the rose-bed, looked up. 'Here,' he called, 'you can jolly well go and put that hand-kerchief of mine back.'

William continued his limping but proud advance.

' 'S all right,' he called airily, 'the Bishop's is on your dressing-table.'

Robert dropped the trowel.

'Gosh!' he gasped, and hastened indoors to investigate.

William went down to the gate, smiling very slightly to himself.

'The days are drawing out so pleasantly,' he was saying to himself in a mincing accent. 'Vaseline – ammonia – er – or cold cream— Damn!'

He leant over the gate, took out his caterpillar, satisfied himself that it was still alive, put it back and looked up and down the road. In the distance he caught sight of the figure of his friend.

'Gin–*ger*,' he yelled in hideous shrillness.

He waved his coloured handkerchief carelessly in greeting as he called. Then he swaggered out into the road . . .

Dusk Before Fireworks

DOROTHY PARKER

He was a very good-looking young man indeed, shaped to be annoyed. His voice was intimate as the rustle of sheets, and he kissed easily. There was no tallying the gifts of Charvet handkerchiefs, *art moderne* ash-trays, monogrammed dressing-gowns, gold key-chains, and cigarette-cases of thin wood, inlaid with views of Parisian comfort stations, that were sent him by ladies too quickly confident and were paid for with the money of unwitting husbands, which is acceptable any place in the world. Every woman who visited his small, square apartment promptly flamed with the desire to assume charge of its redecoration. During his tenancy, three separate ladies had achieved this ambition. Each had left behind her, for her brief monument, much too much glazed chintz.

The glare of the latest upholstery was dulled, now, in an April dusk. There was a soft blur of mauve and gray over chairs and curtains, instead of the daytime pattern of heroic-sized double poppies and small, sad elephants. (The most recent of the volunteer decorators was a lady who added interest to her ways by collecting all varieties of elephants save those alive or stuffed; her selection of the chintz had been made less for the cause of contemporary design than in the hope of keeping ever present the wistful souvenirs of her hobby and, hence, of herself. Unhappily, the poppies, those flowers for forgetfulness, turned out to be predominant in the pattern.)

The very good-looking young man was stretched in a long chair, legless and short in the back. It was a strain to see in that chair any virtue save the speeding one of modernity. Certainly it was a peril to all who dealt with it; they were far from their best within its arms, and they could never have wished to be remembered as they appeared while easing into its depths or struggling out again. All, that is, save the young man. He was a long young man, broad at the shoulders and chest and narrow everywhere else, and his muscles obeyed him at the exact instant of command. He rose and lay, he moved and was still, always in beauty. Several men disliked him, but only one woman really hated him. She was his sister. She was stump-shaped, and she had straight hair.

On the sofa opposite the difficult chair there sat a young woman, slight and softly dressed. There was no more to her frock than some dull, dark silk and a little chiffon, but the recurrent bill for it demanded, in bitter black and white, a sum well on toward the second hundred. Once the very good-looking young man had said that he liked women in quiet and conservative clothes, carefully made. The young woman was of those unfortunates who remember every word. This made living peculiarly trying for her when it was later demonstrated that the young man was also partial to ladies given to garments of slap-dash cut and color like the sound of big brass instruments.

The young woman was temperately pretty in the eyes of most beholders; but there were a few, mainly hand-to-mouth people, artists and such, who could not look enough at her. Half a year before, she had been sweeter to see. Now there was tension about her mouth and unease along her brow, and her eyes looked puzzled and beseeching. The gentle dusk became her. The young man who shared it with her could not see these things.

She stretched her arms and laced her fingers high above her head.

'Oh, this is nice,' she said. 'It's nice being here.'

'It's nice and peaceful,' he said. 'Oh, Lord. Why can't

173

people just be peaceful? That's little enough to ask, isn't it? Why does there have to be so much hell, all the time?'

She dropped her hands to her lap.

'There doesn't have to be at all,' she said. She had a quiet voice, and she said her words with every courtesy to each of them, as if she respected language. 'There's never any need for hell.'

'There's an awful lot of it around, sweet,' he said.

'There certainly is,' she said. 'There's just as much hell as there are hundreds of little shrill, unnecessary people. It's the second-raters that stir up hell; first-rate people wouldn't. You need never have another bit of it in your beautiful life if – if you'll pardon my pointing – you could just manage to steel yourself against that band of spitting hell-cats that is in- cluded in your somewhat overcrowded acquaintance, my lamb. Ah, but I mean it, Hobie, dear. I've been wanting to tell you for so long. But it's so rotten hard to say. If I say it, it makes me sound just like one of them – makes me seem inex- pensive and jealous. Surely you know, after all this time, I'm not like that. It's just that I worry so about you. You're so fine, you're so lovely, it nearly kills me to see you just eaten up by a lot of things like Margot Wadsworth and Mrs Holt and Evie Maynard and those. You're so much better than that. You know that's why I'm saying it. You know I haven't got a stitch of jealousy in me. Jealous! Good heavens, if I were going to be jealous, I'd be it about someone worth while, and not about any silly, stupid, idle, worthless, selfish, hysterical, vul- gar, promiscuous, sex-ridden—'

'Darling!' he said.

'Well, I'm sorry,' she said. 'I guess I'm sorry. I didn't really mean to go into the subject of certain of your friends. Maybe the way they behave isn't their fault,' said she, lying in her teeth. 'After all, you can't expect them to know what it's about. Poor things, they'll never know how sweet it can be, how lovely it always is when we're alone together. It is, isn't it? Ah, Hobie, isn't it?'

The young man raised his slow lids and looked at her. He smiled with one end of his beautiful curly mouth.

'Uh-huh,' he said.

He took his eyes from hers and became busy with an ash-tray and a spent cigarette. But he still smiled.

'Ah, don't,' she said. 'You promised you'd forget about – about last Wednesday. You said you'd never remember it again. Oh, whatever made me do it! Making scenes. Having tantrums. Rushing out into the night. And then coming crawling back. Me, that wanted to show you how different a woman could be! Oh, please, please don't let's think about it. Only tell me I wasn't as terrible as I know I was.'

'Darling,' he said, for he was often a young man of simple statements, 'you were the worst I ever saw.'

'And doesn't that come straight from Sir Hubert!' she said. 'Oh, dear. Oh, dear, oh, dear. What can I say? "Sorry" isn't nearly enough. I'm broken. I'm in little bits. Would you mind doing something about putting me together again?'

She held out her arms to him.

The young man rose, came over to the sofa, and kissed her. He had intended a quick, good-humored kiss, a moment's stop on a projected trip out to his little pantry to mix cocktails. But her arms clasped him so close and so gladly that he dismissed the plan. He lifted her to her feet, and did not leave her.

Presently she moved her head and hid her face above his heart.

'Listen,' she said, against cloth. 'I want to say it all now, and then never say it any more. I want to tell you that there'll never, never be anything like last Wednesday again. What we have is so much too lovely ever to cheapen. I promise, oh, I promise you, I won't ever be like – like anybody else.'

'You couldn't be, Kit,' he said.

'Ah, think that always,' she said, 'and say it sometimes. It's so sweet to hear. Will you, Hobie?'

'For your size,' he said, 'you talk an awful lot.' His fingers

slid to her chin and he held her face for his greater convenience.

After a while she moved again.

'Guess who I'd rather be, right this minute, than anybody
in the whole world,' she said.

'Who?' he said.

'Me,' she said.

The telephone rang.

The telephone was in the young man's bedroom, standing
in frequent silence on the little table by his bed. There was no
door to the bed-chamber; a plan which had disadvantages,
too. Only a curtained archway sequestered its intimacies from
those of the living-room. Another archway, also streaming
chintz, gave from the bedroom upon a tiny passage, along
which were ranged the bathroom and the pantry. It was only
by entering either of these, closing the door behind, and
turning the faucets on to the full that any second person in
the apartment could avoid hearing what was being said over
the telephone. The young man sometimes thought of removing to a flat of more sympathetic design.

'There's that damn telephone,' the young man said.

'Isn't it?' the young woman said. 'And wouldn't it be?'

'Let's not answer it,' he said. 'Let's let it ring.'

'No, you mustn't,' she said. 'I must be big and strong.
Anyway, maybe it's only somebody that just died and left you
twenty million dollars. Maybe it isn't some other woman at
all. And if it is, what difference does it make? See how sweet
and reasonable I am? Look at me being generous.'

'You can afford to be, sweetheart,' he said.

'I know I can,' she said. 'After all, whoever she is, she's
'way off on an end of a wire, and I'm right here.'

She smiled up at him. So it was nearly half a minute
before he went away to the telephone.

Still smiling, the young woman stretched her head back,
closed her eyes and flung her arms wide. A long sigh raised
her breast. Thus she stood, then she went and settled back on

176

the sofa. She essayed whistling softly, but the issuing sounds would not resemble the intended tune and she felt, though interested, vaguely betrayed. Then she looked about the dusk-filled room. Then she pondered her finger nails, bringing each bent hand close to her eyes, and could find no fault. Then she smoothed her skirt along her legs and shook out the chiffon frills at her wrists. Then she spread her little handkerchief on her knee and with exquisite care traced the 'Katherine' embroidered in script across one of its corners. Then she gave it all up and did nothing but listen.

'Yes?' the young man was saying. 'Hello? Hello. I *told* you this is Mr Ogden. Well, I *am* holding the wire. I've *been* holding the wire. *You're* the one that went away. Hello? Ah, now listen— Hello? Hey. Oh, what the hell *is* this? Come back, will you? Operator! Hello. *Yes*, this is Mr Ogden. Who? Oh, hello, Connie. How are you, dear? What? You're what? Oh, that's too bad. What's the matter? Why can't you? Where are you, in Greenwich? Oh, I see. When, now? Why, Connie, the only thing is I've got to go right out. So if you come in to town now, it really wouldn't do much— Well, I couldn't very well do that, dear, I'm keeping these people waiting as it is. I say I'm late now, I was just going out the door when you called. Why, I'd better not say that, Connie, because there's no telling when I'll be able to break away. Look, why don't you wait and come in to town tomorrow some time? What? Can't you tell me now? Oh— Well— Oh, Connie, there's no reason to talk like that. Why, of course I'd do anything in the world I could, but I tell you I can't tonight. No, no, no, no, no, it isn't that at all. No, it's nothing like that, I tell you. These people are friends of my sister's, and it's just one of those things you've got to do. Why don't you be a good girl and go to bed early, and then you'll feel better tomorrow? Hm? Will you do that? What? Of course I do, Connie. I'll try to later on if I can, dear. Well, all right, if you want to, but I don't know what time I'll be home. Of course I do. Of course I do. Yes, I *do*, Connie. You be a good girl, won't you? 'By, dear.'

The young man returned, through the chintz. He had a rather worn look. It was, of course, becoming to him.

'God,' he said, simply.

The young woman on the sofa looked at him as if through clear ice.

'And how *is* dear Mrs Holt?' she said.

'Great,' he said. 'Corking. 'Way up at the top of her form.' He dropped wearily into the low chair. 'She says she has something she wants to tell me.'

'It can't be her age,' she said.

He smiled without joy. 'She says it's too hard to say over the wire,' he said.

'Then it may be her age,' she said. 'She's afraid it might sound like her telephone number.'

'About twice a week,' he said, 'Connie has something she must tell you right away, that she couldn't possibly say over the telephone. Usually it turns out she's caught the butler drinking again.'

'I see,' she said.

'Well,' he said. 'Poor little Connie.'

'Poor little Connie,' she said. 'Oh, my God. That saber-toothed tigress. Poor little Connie.'

'Darling, why do we have to waste time talking about Connie Holt?' he said. 'Can't we just be peaceful?'

'Not while that she-beast prowls the streets,' she said. 'Is she coming in to town tonight?'

'Well, she was,' he said, 'but then she more or less said she wouldn't.'

'Oh, she will,' she said. 'You get right down out of that fool's paradise you're in. She'll shoot out of Greenwich like a bat out of hell, if she thinks there's a chance of seeing you. Ah, Hobie, you don't really want to see that old thing, do you? Do you? Because if you do— Well, I suppose maybe you do. Naturally, if she has something she must tell you right away, you want to see her. Look, Hobie, you know you can see me any time. It isn't a bit important, seeing me

178

tonight. Why don't you call up Mrs Holt and tell her to take the next train in? She'd get here quicker by train than by motor, wouldn't she? Please go ahead and do it. It's quite all right about me. Really.'

'You know,' he said, 'I knew that was coming. I could tell it by the way you were when I came back from the telephone. Oh, Kit, what makes you want to talk like that? You know damned well the last thing I want to do is see Connie Holt. You know how I want to be with you. Why do you want to work up all this? I watched you just sit there and deliberately talk yourself into it, starting right out of nothing. Now what's the idea of that? Oh, good Lord, what's the matter with women, anyway?'

'Please don't call me "women",' she said.

'I'm sorry, darling,' he said. 'I didn't mean to use bad words.' He smiled at her. She felt her heart go liquid, but she did her best to be harder won.

'Doubtless,' she said, and her words fell like snow when there is no wind, 'I spoke ill-advisedly. If I said, as I must have, something to distress you, I can only beg you to believe that that was my misfortune, and not my intention. It seemed to me as if I were doing only a courteous thing in suggesting that you need feel no obligation about spending the evening with me, when you would naturally wish to be with Mrs Holt. I simply felt that— Oh, the hell with it! I'm no good at this. Of course I didn't mean it, dearest. If you had said, "All right," and had gone and told her to come in, I should have died. I just said it because I wanted to hear you say it was me you wanted to be with. Oh, I need to hear you say that, Hobie. It's – it's what I live on, darling.'

'Kit,' he said, 'you ought to know, without my saying it. You know. It's this feeling you *have* to say things – that's what spoils everything.'

'I suppose so,' she said. 'I suppose I know so. Only – the thing is, I get so mixed up, I just – I just can't go on. I've got to be reassured, dearest. I didn't need to be at first, when everything was gay and sure, but things aren't – well, they aren't the same now. There seem to be so many others that— So I need so terribly to have you tell me that it's me and not anybody else. Oh, I *had* to have you say that, a few minutes ago. Look, Hobie. How do you think it makes me feel to sit here and hear you lie to Connie Holt – to hear you say you have to go out with friends of your sister's? Now why couldn't you say you had a date with me? Are you ashamed of me, Hobie? Is that it?'

'Oh, Kit,' he said, 'for heaven's sake! I don't know why I did it. I did it before I even thought. I did it – well, sort of instinctively I guess, because it seemed to be the easiest thing to do. I suppose I'm just weak.'

'No!' she said. 'You weak? Well! And is there any other news tonight?'

'I know I am,' he said. 'I know it's weak to do anything in the world to avoid a scene.'

'Exactly what', she said, 'is Mrs Holt to you and you to her that she may make a scene if she learns that you have an engagement with another woman?'

'Oh, God!' he said. 'I told you I don't give a damn about Connie Holt. She's nothing to me. Now will you for God's sake let it drop?'

'Oh, she's nothing to you,' she said. 'I see. Naturally, that would be why you called her "dear" every other word.'

'If I did,' he said, 'I never knew I was saying it. Good Lord, that doesn't mean anything. It's simply a – a form of nervousness, I suppose. I say it when I can't think what to call people. Why, I call telephone operators "dear".'

'I'm sure you do!' she said.

They glared. It was the young man who gave first. He went and sat close to her on the sofa, and for a while there were only murmurs. Then he said, 'Will you stop? Will you stop it? Will you always be just like this – just sweet and the way you're meant to be and no fighting?'

'I will,' she said. 'Honest, I mean to. Let's not let anything come between us again ever. Mrs Holt, indeed! Hell with her.'

'Hell with her,' he said. There was another silence, during which the young man did several things that he did extraordinarily well.

Suddenly the young woman stiffened her arms and pushed him away from her.

'And how do I know', she said, 'that the way you talk to me about Connie Holt isn't just the way you talk to her about me when I'm not here? How do I know that?'

'Oh, my Lord,' he said. 'Oh, my dear, sweet Lord. Just when everything was all right. Ah, stop it, will you, ba-bay? Let's just be quiet. Like this. See?'

A little later he said, 'Look, sweet, how about a cocktail? Mightn't that be an idea? I'll go make them. And would you like the lights lighted?'

'Oh, no,' she said. 'I like it better in the dusk, like this. It's sweet. Dusk is so personal, somehow. And this way you can't see those lampshades. Hobie, if you knew how I hate your lampshades!'

'Honestly?' he said, with less injury than bewilderment in his voice. He looked at the shades as if he saw them for the first time. They were of vellum, or some substance near it, and upon each was painted a panorama of the right bank of the Seine, with the minute windows of the buildings cut out, under the direction of some master mind, so that light might come through. 'What's the matter with them, Kit?'

'Dearest, if you don't know, I can't ever explain it to you,' she said. 'Among other things, they're banal, inappropriate, and unbeautiful. They're exactly what Evie Maynard *would* have chosen. She thinks, just because they show views of Paris, that they're pretty darned sophisticated. She is that not uncommon type of woman that thinks any reference to *la belle France* is an invitation to the waltz. "Not uncommon." If that isn't the mildest word-picture that ever was painted of that—'

'Don't you like the way she decorated the apartment?' he said.

'Sweetheart,' she said, 'I think it's poisonous. You know that.'

'Would you like to do it over?' he said.

'I should say not,' she said. 'Look, Hobie, don't you remember me? I'm the one that doesn't want to decorate your flat. Now do you place me? But if I ever *did*, the first thing I should do would be to paint these walls putty color – no, I guess first I'd tear off all this chintz and fling it to the winds, and then I'd—'

The telephone rang.

The young man threw one stricken glance at the young woman and then sat motionless. The jangles of the bell cut the dusk like vicious little scissors.

'I think', said the young woman, exquisitely, 'that your telephone is ringing. Don't let me keep you from answering it. As a matter of fact, I really must go powder my nose.'

She sprang up, dashed through the bedroom, and into the bathroom. There was the sound of a closed door, the grind of a firmly turned key, and then immediately the noise of rushing waters.

When she returned, eventually, to the living-room, the young man was pouring a pale, cold liquid into small glasses. He gave one to her, and smiled at her over it. It was his wistful smile. It was of his best.

'Hobie,' she said, 'is there a livery stable anywhere around here where they rent wild horses?'

'What?' he said.

'Because if there is,' she said, 'I wish you'd call up and ask them to send over a couple of teams. I want to show you they couldn't drag me into asking who that was on the telephone.'

'Oh,' he said, and tried his cocktail. 'Is this dry enough, sweet? Because you like them dry, don't you? Sure it's all right? Really? Ah, wait a second, darling. Let *me* light your cigarette. There. Sure you're all right?'

'I can't stand it,' she said. 'I just lost all my strength of purpose – maybe the maid will find it on the floor in the morning. Hobart Ogden, who was that on the telephone?'

'Oh, that?' he said. 'Well, that was a certain lady who shall be nameless.'

'I'm sure she should be,' she said. 'She doubtless has all the other qualities of a— Well. I didn't quite say it, I'm keeping my head. Ah, dearest, was that Connie Holt again?'

'No, that was the funniest thing,' he said. 'That was Evie Maynard. Just when we were talking about her.'

'Well, well, well,' she said. 'Isn't it a small world? And what's on her mind, if I may so flatter her? Is *her* butler tight, too?'

'Evie hasn't got a butler,' he said. He tried smiling again, but found it better to abandon the idea and concentrate on refilling the young woman's glass. 'No, she's just dizzy, the same as usual. She's got a cocktail party at her apartment, and they all want to go out on the town, that's all.'

'Luckily,' she said, 'you had to go out with these friends of your sister's. You were just going out the door when she called.'

'I never told her any such thing!' he said. 'I said I had a date I'd been looking forward to all week.'

'Oh, you didn't mention any names?' she said.

'There's no reason why I should, to Evie Maynard,' he said. 'It's none of her affair, any more than what she's doing and who she's doing it with is any concern of mine. She's nothing in my life. You know that. I've hardly seen her since she did the apartment. I don't care if I never see her again. I'd *rather* I never saw her again.'

'I should think that might be managed, if you've really set your heart on it,' she said.

'Well, I do what I can,' he said. 'She wanted to come in now for a cocktail, she and some of those interior decorator boys she has with her, and I told her absolutely no.'

'And you think that will keep her away?' she said. 'Oh, no.

183

She'll be here. She and her feathered friends. Let's see – they ought to arrive just about the time that Mrs Holt has thought it over and come in to town. Well. It's shaping up into a lovely evening, isn't it?'

'Great,' he said. 'And if I may say so, you're doing everything you can to make it harder, you little peach.' He poured more cocktails. 'Oh, Kit, why are you being so nasty? Don't do it, darling. It's not like you. It's so unbecoming to you.'

'I know it's horrible,' she said. 'It's – well, I do it in defense, I suppose, Hobie. If I didn't say nasty things, I'd cry. I'm afraid to cry; it would take me so long to stop. I – oh, I'm so hurt, dear. I don't know what to think. All these women. All these awful women. If they were fine, if they were sweet and gentle and intelligent, I shouldn't mind. Or maybe I should. I don't know. I don't know much of anything, any more. My mind goes round and round. I thought what we had was so different. Well – it wasn't. Sometimes I think it would be better never to see you any more. But then I know I couldn't stand that. I'm too far gone now. I'd do anything to be with you! And so I'm just another of those women to you. And I used to come first, Hobie – oh, I did! I did!'

'You did!' he said. 'And you do!'

'And I always will?' she said.

'And you always will,' he said, 'as long as you'll only be your own self. Please be sweet again, Kit. Like this, darling. Like this, child.'

Again they were close, and again there was no sound.

The telephone rang.

They started as if the same arrow had pierced them. Then the young woman moved slowly back.

'You know,' she said, musingly, 'this is my fault. I did this. It was me. I was the one that said let's meet here, and not at my house. I said it would be quieter, and I had so much I wanted to talk to you about. I said we could be quiet and alone here. Yes. I said that.'

'I give you my word,' he said, 'that damn thing hasn't rung in a week.'

'It was lucky for me, wasn't it?' she said, 'that I happened to be here last time it did it. I am known as Little Miss Horse-shoes. Well. Oh, please do answer it, Hobie. It drives me even crazier to have it ring like this.'

'I hope to God,' the young man said, 'that it's a wrong number.' He held her to him, hard. 'Darling,' he said. Then he went to the telephone.

'Hello,' he said into the receiver. 'Yes? Oh, hello there. How are you, dear—how are you? Oh, did you? Ah, that's too bad. Why, you see I was out with these friends of my— I was out till quite late. Oh, you did? Oh, that's too bad, dear, you waited up all that time. No, I did *not* say that, Margot, I said I'd come if I possibly could. That's exactly what I said. I did so. Well, then you misunderstood me. Well, you must have. Now, there's no need to be unreasonable about it. Listen, what I said, I said I'd come if it was pos-sible, but I didn't think there was a chance. If you think hard, you'll remember, dear. Well, I'm terribly sorry, but I don't see what you're making so much fuss about. It was just a misunderstanding, that's all. Why don't you calm down and be a good little girl? Won't you? Why, I can't tonight, dear. Because I *can't*. Well, I have a date I've had for a long time. Yes. Oh, no, it isn't anything like that! Oh, now, please, Margot! Margot, please don't! Now don't do that! I tell you I won't be here. All right, come ahead, but I won't be in. Listen, I can't talk to you when you're like this. I'll call you tomorrow, dear. I tell you I won't be IN, dear! Please be good. Certainly I do. Look, I have to run now. I'll call you, dear. 'By.'

The young man came back to the living-room, and sent his somewhat shaken voice ahead of him.

'How about another cocktail, sweet?' he said. 'Don't you think we really ought—' Through the thickening dark, he saw the young woman. She stood straight and tense. Her fur scarf was knotted about her shoulders, and she was drawing on her second glove.

'What's this about?' the young man said.

'I'm so sorry,' the young woman said, 'but I truly must go home.'

'Oh, really?' he said. 'May I ask why?'

'It's sweet of you', she said, 'to be interested enough to want to know. Thank you so much. Well, it just happens, I can't stand any more of this. There is somewhere, I think, some proverb about a worm's eventually turning. It is doubtless from the Arabic. They so often are. Well, good night, Hobie, and thank you so much for those delicious cocktails. They've cheered me up wonderfully.'

She held out her hand. He caught it tight in both of his.

'Ah, now listen,' he said. 'Please don't do this, Kit. Please don't, darling. Please. This is just the way you were last Wednesday. Remember?'

'Yes,' she said. 'And for exactly the same reason. Please give me back my hand. Thank you. Well, good night, Hobie, and good luck, always.'

'All right,' he said. 'If this is what you want to do.'

'Want to do!' she said. 'It's nothing *I* want. I simply felt it would be rather easier for you if you could be alone, to receive your telephone calls. Surely you cannot blame me for feeling a bit *de trop*.'

'My Lord, do you think I want to talk to those fools?' he said. 'What can I do? Take the telephone receiver off? Is that what you want me to do?'

'It's a good trick of yours,' she said. 'I gather that was what you did last Wednesday night, when I kept trying to call you after I'd gone home, when I was in holy agony there.'

'I did not!' he said. 'They must have been calling the wrong number. I tell you I was alone here all the time you were gone.'

'So you said,' she said.

'I don't lie to you, Kit,' he said.

186

'That', she said, 'is the most outrageous lie you have ever told me. Good night, Hobie.'

Only from the young man's eyes and voice could his anger be judged. The beautiful scroll of his mouth never straightened. He took her hand and bowed over it.

'Good night, Kit,' he said.

'Good night,' she said. 'Well, good night. I'm sorry it must end like this. But if you want – other things – well, they're what you want. You can't have both them and me. Good night, Hobie.'

'Good night, Kit,' he said.

'I'm sorry,' she said. 'It does seem too bad. Doesn't it?'

'It's what you want,' he said.

'I?' she said. 'It's what *you* do.'

'Oh, Kit, can't you understand?' he said. 'You always used to. Don't you know how I am? I just say things and do things that don't mean anything, just for the sake of peace, just for the sake of not having a feud. That's what gets me in trouble. You don't have to do it, I know. You're luckier than I am.'

'Luckier?' she said. 'Curious word.'

'Well, stronger, then,' he said. 'Finer. Honester. Decenter. All those. Ah, don't do this, Kit. Please. Please take those things off, and come sit down.'

'Sit down?' she said. 'And wait for the ladies to gather?'

'They're not coming,' he said.

'How do you know?' she said. 'They've come here before, haven't they? How do you know they won't come tonight?'

'I don't know!' he said. 'I don't know what the hell they'll do. I don't know what the hell you'll do, any more. And I thought you were different!'

'I was different,' she said, 'just so long as you thought I was different.'

'Ah, Kit,' he said, 'Kit. Darling. Come and be the way we were. Come and be sweet and peaceful. Look. Let's have a cocktail, just to each other, and then let's go out to some quiet place for dinner, where we can talk. Will you?'

'Well—' she said. 'If you think—'

'I think,' he said.

The telephone rang.

'Oh, my *God*!' shrieked the young woman. 'Go answer it, you damned – you damned *stallion*!'

She rushed for the door, opened it, and was gone. She was, after all, different. She neither slammed the door nor left it stark open.

The young man stood, and he shook his remarkable head slowly. Slowly, too, he turned and went into the bedroom.

He spoke into the telephone receiver drearily at first, then he seemed to enjoy both hearing and speaking. He used a woman's name in address. It was not Connie; it was not Evie; it was not Margot. Glowingly he besought the unseen one to meet him; tepidly he agreed to await her coming where he was. He besought her, then, to ring his bell first three times and then twice, for admission. No, no, no, he said, this was not for any reason that might have occurred to her; it was simply that some business friend of his had said something about dropping in, and he wanted to make sure there would be no such intruders. He spoke of his hopes, indeed his assurances, of an evening of sweetness and peace. He said 'good by,' and he said 'dear.'

The very good-looking young man hung up the receiver, and looked long at the dial of his wrist-watch, now delicately luminous. He seemed to be calculating. So long for a young woman to reach her home, and fling herself upon her couch, so long for tears, so long for exhaustion, so long for remorse, so long for rising tenderness. Thoughtfully he lifted the receiver from its hook and set it on end upon the little table.

Then he went into the living-room, and sped the dark before the tiny beams that sifted through the little open windows in the panoramas of Paris.

The Curb in the Sky

JAMES THURBER

When Charlie Deshler announced that he was going to marry Dorothy, someone said he would lose his mind post-haste. 'No,' said a wit who knew them both, 'post hoc.' Dorothy had begun, when she was quite young, to finish sentences for people. Sometimes she finished them wrongly, which annoyed the person who was speaking, and sometimes she finished them correctly, which annoyed the speaker even more.

'When William Howard Taft was—' some guest in Dorothy's family's home would begin.

'President!' Dorothy would pipe up. The speaker may have meant to say 'President' or he may have meant to say 'young', or 'Chief Justice of the Supreme Court of the United States'. In any case, he would shortly put on his hat and go home. Like most parents, Dorothy's parents did not seem to be conscious that her mannerism was a nuisance. Very likely they thought that it was cute, or even bright. It is even probable that when Dorothy's mother first said 'Come, Dorothy, eat your—' and Dorothy said 'Spinach, dear,' the former telephoned Dorothy's father at the office and told him about it, and he told everybody he met that day about it – and the next day and the day after.

When Dorothy grew up she became quite pretty and so even more of a menace. Gentlemen became attracted to her and then attached to her. Emotionally she stirred them, but mentally she soon began to wear them down. Even in her late teens she began correcting their English. 'Not "was", Arthur,' she would say, ' "were". "Were prepared."'

189

See?' Most of her admirers tolerated this habit because of their interest in her lovely person, but as time went on and her interest in them remained more instructive than sentimental, they slowly drifted away to less captious, if dumber, girls.

Charlie Deshler, however, was an impetuous man, of the sweep-them-off-their-feet persuasion, and he became engaged to Dorothy so quickly and married her in so short a time that, being deaf to the warnings of friends, whose concern he regarded as mere jealousy, he really didn't know anything about Dorothy except that she was pretty and bright-eyed and (to him) desirable.

Dorothy as a wife came, of course, into her great flowering: she took to correcting Charlie's stories. He had travelled widely and experienced greatly and was a truly excellent *raconteur*. Dorothy was, during their courtship, genuinely interested in him and in his stories, and since she had never shared any of the adventures he told about, she could not know when he made mistakes in time or in place or in identities. Beyond suggesting a change here and there in the number of a verb, she more or less let him alone. Charlie spoke rather good English, anyway – he knew when to say 'were' and when to say 'was' after 'if' – and this was another reason he didn't find Dorothy out.

I didn't call on them for quite a while after they were married, because I liked Charlie and I knew I would feel low if I saw him coming out of the anaesthetic of her charms and beginning to feel the first pains of reality. When I did finally call, conditions were, of course, all that I had feared. Charlie began to tell, at dinner, about a motor trip the two had made to this town and that – I never found out for sure what towns, because Dorothy denied almost everything that Charlie said. 'The next day,' he would say, 'we got an early start and drove two hundred miles to Fairview—' 'Well,' Dorothy would say, 'I wouldn't call it *early*. It wasn't as early as the first day we set out, when we got up about *seven*. And we only drove a hundred and eighty miles, because I remember looking at that mileage thing when we started.'

'Anyway, when we got to Fairview—' Charlie would go on. But Dorothy would stop him. 'Was it Fairview that day, darling?' she would ask. Dorothy often interrupted Charlie by asking him if he were right, instead of telling him that he was wrong, but it amounted to the same thing, for if he would reply: 'Yes, I'm sure it was Fairview,' she would say: 'But it *wasn't*, darling,' and then go on with the story herself. (She called everybody that she differed from 'darling'.)

Once or twice, when I called on them or they called on me, Dorothy would let Charlie get almost to the climax of some interesting account of a happening and then, like a tackler from behind, throw him just as he was about to cross the goal-line. There is nothing in life more shocking to the nerves and to the mind than this. Some husbands will sit back amiably – almost, it seems, proudly – when their wives interrupt, and let them go on with the story, but these are beaten husbands. Charlie did not become beaten. But his wife's tackles knocked the wind out of him, and he began to realize that he would have to do something. What he did was rather ingenious. At the end of the second year of their marriage, when you visited the Deshlers, Charlie would begin some outlandish story about a dream he had had, knowing that Dorothy could not correct him on his own dreams. They became the only life he had that was his own.

'I thought I was running an airplane,' he would say, 'made out of telephone wires and pieces of old leather. I was trying to make it fly to the moon, taking off from my bedroom. About halfway up to the moon, however, a man who looked like Santa Claus, only he was dressed in the uniform of a customs officer, waved at me to stop – he was in a plane made of telephone wires, too. So I pulled over to a cloud. "Here," he said to me, "you can't go to the moon, if you are the man who invented these wedding cookies." Then he showed me a cookie made in the shape of a man and woman being married – little images of a man and a woman and a minister, made of dough and fastened firmly to a round, crisp cookie base.' So he would go on.

Any psychiatrist will tell you that at the end of the way Charlie was going lies madness in the form of monomania. You can't live in a fantastic dream world, night in and night out and then day in and day out, and remain sane. The substance began to die slowly out of Charlie's life, and he began to live entirely in shadow. And since monomania of this sort is likely to lead in the end to the reiteration of one particular story, Charlie's invention began to grow thin and he eventually took to telling, over and over again, the first dream he had ever described – the story of his curious flight toward the moon in an airplane made of telephone wires. It was extremely painful. It saddened us all.

After a month or two, Charlie finally had to be sent to an asylum. I was out of town when they took him away, but Joe Fultz, who went with him, wrote me about it. 'He seemed to like it up here right away,' Joe wrote. 'He's calmer and his eyes look better.' (Charlie had developed a wild, hunted look.) 'Of course,' concluded Joe, 'he's finally got away from that woman.'

It was a couple of weeks later that I drove up to the asylum to see Charlie. He was lying on a cot on a big screened-in porch, looking wan and thin. Dorothy was sitting on a chair beside his bed, bright-eyed and eager. I was somehow surprised to see her there, having figured that Charlie had, at least, won sanctuary from his wife. He looked quite mad. He began at once to tell me the story of his trip to the moon. He got to the part where the man who looked like Santa Claus waved at him to stop. 'He was in a plane made of telephone wires, too,' said Charlie. 'So I pulled over to a curb—'

'No. You pulled over to a *cloud*,' said Dorothy. 'There

aren't any curbs in the *sky*. There *couldn't* be. You pulled over to a cloud.'

Charlie sighed and turned slightly in his bed and looked at me. Dorothy looked at me, too, with her pretty smile.

'He always gets that story wrong,' she said.

Shoes

AN INTERNATIONAL EPISODE

ELIZABETH BOWEN

Their room was in morning disorder. To keep the french window open at its widest an armchair smothered in clothes had been pushed up, a curtain tied back with one of Mrs Aherne's stockings. She had stripped the beds – one could never be certain hotel femmes-de-chambre did this thoroughly – and two great scrolls of bedclothes toppled over the room like baroque waves. The two had breakfasted; the coffee-tray, lodged on a table-edge among brushes, collars and maps, was littered with cigarette-ends, stained beet sugar and crumbs of roll. Mr Aherne did not care for the crumby part and had an untidy habit of scooping this out with his thumb.

Outside, the pale glare of morning, unreal like midsummer sunshine remembered at Christmas, painted garden tree-tops, blond tiled roofs, and polished some green glass balls cemented onto a wall till one wanted to reach out and touch them.

Mrs Aherne, feeling French and sophisticated, wandered round in her dressing-gown smoking a cigarette. Her husband bowing forward into the looking-glass carefully parted his hair. It was exquisite to be leisurely. Her chemise, back from a French laundress, was delicate on her skin.

'All the same,' she said, 'I wish you would hurry up with that glass. What about *my* hair?'

'You look lovely the way you are,' said Mr Aherne, studying himself sympathetically.

She felt she did. She really was a pretty thing; blonde, brown, vigorous. She said:

'I should hate them to think all Englishwomen were frumpy.'

'You may be certain they don't. I saw two of them turn and have a good look at you going out of the dining-room—'

'Really? . . . Oh, don't be so silly!'

Mr Aherne, in shirt-sleeves, looking like one of those nice advertisements of shaving-soap, dived out into the passage to bring in the shoes. He reappeared, put them down and looked at them with a smile. These two pairs of shoes, waiting outside for him every morning, still seemed a formal advertisement to the world of their married state.

'Nice little couple,' said Edward Aherne.

Dillie didn't notice the shoes at once; she, in possession of the looking-glass, was powdering over the sunburn at the base of her throat. But when she turned round she said sharply:

'Edward, what are *these* doing in here? They're not mine!'

The female shoes, uncertainly balanced because of their high heels, listed towards the strong shoes of Edward timidly and lackadaisically. They were fawn kid, very clean inside (so probably new), low at the insteps, with slim red heels and a pattern in scarlet leather across the strap and over the toe-cap. They were tiny (size three or three-and-a-half) and looked capable solely of an ineffectual, somehow alluring totter.

'These are *not* my shoes,' repeated Mrs Aherne ominously.

Edward, incredulous, came to look at the shoes. His face went into stiff lines, conscious of being searched.

'*I* never—'

'I didn't suppose you did . . .' She flashed with anger. 'Oh, but what little horrors! How *could* they think—!'

'They didn't think; they got muddled up about rooms.'

'There was no mistake about *your* shoes.'

'I wonder', said Edward archly, 'who yours have been spending the night with!'

Not feeling French any longer, she wasn't amused. She threw her cigarette out of the window – to smoke more than one after breakfast made her feel stuffy, anyhow.

Dillie was an advanced, intelligent girl who had married Edward two years ago. Since then they had travelled a good deal. She had been constant to the good resolutions made on her honeymoon: not to be insular, not to behave like a 'dear little thing'. She never grumbled at rich cooking, at having no egg for breakfast and no pudding; when Latins ogled she frowned in the other direction but did not complain to Edward. She tried to share Edward's elation when café waiters brought her *La Vie Parisienne*. 'They wouldn't bring *that* to most Englishwomen!' Edward used to exclaim: she wondered why they didn't bring it to Frenchwomen either. She walked about France in good brogues and didn't mind if her feet looked a shade powerful. She took six-and-a-halfs for ordinary wear and, when she wanted to be really comfortable, sevens.

To be annoyed by the simpering shoes was unworthy; she said reasonably: 'Well, find mine, and put those wherever mine were.'

'Everyone else's have been taken in, I noticed; ours were the last.'

He was *too* helpless; she snorted. 'Then give them to me!'

The passage outside was stuffy and panelled with doors. Dillie paced up and down, swinging the shoes by their straps, raging. Those doors were cynical. She looked at the numbers each side of their own; No. 19 clicked open and a man with no collar looked out at her ardently, but with a shake of the head shut the door again in discouragement. Dillie bristled. She was now quite certain the horrors belonged to his wife, or at any rate (one couldn't blink at these things) to the lady in there with him. If he hadn't put the matter on such a basis she would have knocked and presented them. She jumped as door No. 11 opened behind her and a lady in red crêpe-de-chine came out on a gust of geranium powder.

'*Ceux sont à vous, peut-être?*' said Dillie, advancing the shoes nervously and forgetting '*Madame*'. The lady said '*Merci*,' and went by in repudiation, chillingly. The shoes were in no worse taste than her own and, at least, cleaner. Dillie, now on the defensive, returned to her room. 'Better ring, I suppose,' she said stormily.

The worst, at any crisis, of these jolly little hotels is that the *sommelier* is the waiter and disappears between ten and eleven, delegating upstairs business to the femme-de-chambre who is sympathetic but irrational. The femme-de-chambre, on appearance, was desolated for Madame but knew nothing. She dangled the horrors temptingly; they were '*des jolies chaussures . . . mignonnes.*'

'*Je ne pourrais pas même les porter. Aussi, je les deteste. Enlevez-les.*'

The femme-de-chambre languished at Edward.

'*Enlevez-les*,' Edward said sternly. '*Et allez demander. Les chaussures de Madame . . .*'

'*C'est ça!*' agreed the femme-de-chambre, inspired. She vanished and did not return.

Meanwhile it was half-past ten. 'We meant to have done that *jubé* before lunch and if we do it now we won't get back till one. By that time the *hors d'œuvres* will have been picked over and we shall get nothing but those beastly little bits of sausage. How greedy the French are. And I always did think this hotel was sinister. I told you so at the time, Edward.'

'Oh, my darling . . .'

'Well, not last night, but I had that cherry brandy and there was the moon.'

They went out, finally, into the hardening brilliance. Dillie, unwillingly elegant in snakeskins she'd been keeping for the Americans in Carcassonne, tottered over the *pavé*. Edward turned down his panama over his eyes and assumed with his chin a subdued expression. It really *was* annoying for Dillie. They went unseeingly through the market: he offered Dillie peaches. 'How', she said scornfully, 'can we possibly eat peaches in a cathedral?'

'Oh . . . we *are* going there?' said Edward deferentially.

'Well, we don't want to waste a morning absolutely, I suppose. We will at least', she said vindictively, '*begin* the *jubé*.'

As they turned down the Rue des Deux Croix towards the cathedral bold in sunshine, somebody swept off a hat ineffably. It was the collarless man with the expression, now in a very low, tight collar over which his neck hung out voluptuously. Dillie wore one of the local hats of thin, limp, peach-coloured straw; Edward side-glanced vainly under the drooping brim. She did not speak; he said nothing.

The cathedral mounted over them, they blinked, incredulous, up at the façade. Lost to one another, they went silently into the pointed, chilly darkness.

After half an hour the back of Edward's neck was aching from much admiration; he said he would like a drink. Dillie, who had pinned back the flap of her hat, looked through him ethereally. She supposed men were like that. '*I'll* just sit here,' she said. 'Edward . . .?'

'Dearest?'

'Has one got a terribly little soul? How could one have felt shoes mattered!'

He couldn't imagine, either. 'But you're sure', he said respectfully, 'you wouldn't care for a *little* drink?'

She couldn't even bring the idea into focus, so he went out alone to the café. He thought how much more spiritual women were. But before his drink arrived she came limping across the square. She thought perhaps she had better have something to pick her up. 'You see, my feet are rather hurting. I can't – absorb. It's these high heels on the *pavé*.'

He ordered another mixed vermouth, and a syphon. 'Just think how you'd feel if you were wearing things like those . . . like the horrors.'

198

'Just think of wearing them always. Oh, Edward, what a conception of women!'

'What a conception!' echoed Edward with vehemence, looking round for the waiter. He laid a hand for a moment on the hand of his wife and companion, but she, relentlessly intelligent, slipped hers away. She was waiting for something, she had planned a discussion. The vermouths arrived; Edward looked at his wisely. 'Queer thing, life,' he said, marking time.

'Queer,' accepted Dillie. 'Of course they *were* pretty,' she said, and looked at him sideways.

'*I* thought so—' said Edward rashly.

'I knew you did! Why couldn't you say so? Oh, Edward, do I deserve that kind of thing? Can't you be frank? I could see that at once by the way you looked at them. You are so transparent. Why *can't* you be frank?'

'It seems rather a waste to be frank if I'm transparent.'

'I suppose no men really want to respect women. Frenchmen are franker, that's all. What men really want—'

'My darling, I do wish you needn't generalise about men".' She was ignoring her vermouth; he felt constrained to put down his glass.

'I do sometimes wonder how really modern you are.'

'Darling—'

'Don't keep on calling me "darling"; it's like being patted. Would I have come out all this way with you and be staying in this stuffy embarrassing dishonest hotel eating unwholesome food, miles from all my friends, if I were simply a little wifie?'

'I knew you really wanted to go to the seaside with the Phippses.'

This was too much. 'If I had wanted to go to the seaside with the Phippses I'd have gone. You know we believe in freedom.'

'Of course I know. I think we do nearly always mean the same thing, only sometimes one of us expresses it unhappily.

I *did* think you liked the food here; you agreed that half the fun of a morning abroad was wondering what there would be for lunch.'

'There are no vitamins. The salads are so oily. However,' said Dillie, 'we needn't go on like this, need we, just outside the cathedral?' She had a nice sense of locality and was most particular as to where they quarrelled and where they made love. Smiling at him with a calculated amiability, she began sipping her vermouth.

At lunch, when they had finished with the *hors d'œuvres*, Edward asked the waiter, who seemed to be influential, about Dillie's shoes. The waiter, surprised and interested, admitted someone must have deceived himself. It was curious.

'*C'est ennuyant pour Madame*,' Edward said accusingly.

Dillie said in an undertone: 'Can't you possibly think of anything stronger?' Edward frowned at her. '*Très ennuyant*,' he said with a Gallic gesticulation: Dillie guarded the wine-bottle. The waiter watched in surprise, as though it occurred to him that foreigners gesticulated a good deal. He would make enquiries; without doubt some lady had also deceived herself. Reassuringly, he swept away the *hors d'œuvres*.

'*Quelque dame* couldn't possibly have *se trompéed*,' said Dillie, furious. 'Somebody in this hotel is definitely dishonest.'

'As a matter of fact,' Edward said, 'this *is* rather interesting. I had heard the best type of French were becoming increasingly Anglophile. Someone will send your brogues along certainly; they're probably back by now, but meanwhile someone will have been taking note of them, to copy.' Any sign of a theory justifying itself gave Edward a happy, fulfilled feeling. He smiled: 'She will certainly get them copied.'

'Oh, do you really think so? Do you think p'raps it was one of those women who turned last night when I went out of the dining-room?'

Edward said he should not be at all surprised.

'O-oh . . . Then I do hope we haven't seemed unpleasant.

I shouldn't like them to think one at all grudging. It *is* remarkable, isn't it, how we seem to be setting the tone. You know, I'm quite sure if brogue shoes came to be worn over here generally, there'd be quite a change in the Latin attitude towards women – I do wish you'd *listen*, Edward, and not keep looking furtively at the menu. If you want to read it, read it; I don't mind you being greedy so long as you're sincere about it.'

'I only wanted to see what was coming next – My darling, you know your husband lives to be sincere with you! – As a matter of fact, it's *vol-au-vent:* you like that, don't you? Now *do* go on about the Latin attitude . . .'

They were lunching half out of doors, under a roof that covered part of the garden. Now and then, lizards flickered over the tiles at their feet. Just beyond, shadow came to an end with an edge like metal; there was a glare of gravel, palm trees leaned languid together, creeper poured flaming over a wall, and a row of young orange trees in bright glazed vases swaggered along a balustrade. Balanced in the hot stillness, the green glass balls on the wall-top snatched one's attention with their look of precariousness. At the garden's end, impermanent yellow buildings, fit to go down at a puff; intense and feverish, like a memory of Van Gogh's. A long cat, slipping from vase to vase, fawned on its reflection in an unnatural ecstasy.

Dillie looked at all this, sideways. 'You do like this?' said Edward, anxious.

'If only it weren't so hot; I hate being hot after lunch. And the glare is so awful. Everything one looks at has – has an echo.'

'That's rather clever. I do wish you'd write, Dillie.'

Dillie liked being told she ought to write; she replied with complacency that she lacked the creative imagination. 'I'm afraid I'm too critical. I do wish one could be more imposed upon.'

'Yes, I do wish one could!'

'Oh, but *you* are,' said Dillie firmly. That disposed of Edward; she brushed some crumbs from under her elbows and settled down to explain why. They had coffee brought out, and liqueurs, and remained talking after the last of the other guests had stared and gone. They both felt they *analysed* better in France; and of course wine did intensify the personality. They discussed Edward and Dillie, Dillie in relation to Edward, Edward to Dillie, Edward and Dillie to Dillie's shoes, and Dillie's shoes to the Latin attitude. They discussed sex. They vaguely glowed at each other with admiration. The waiter hung round, flicking at empty tables; they saw him as a tree, dimly; they had no idea how aggravating they were. Clasped hands supporting their flushed faces, they looked mistily past the waiter.

When he broke into their circle of consciousness they were surprised. The shoes, he was more than delighted to say, had been traced. A lady had found them outside her door and taken them into her room in mistake for her own. She had returned them to No. 20; they awaited Madame above. Dillie said 'There!' in triumph, got up and went out carefully between the tables. She had a pleasant feeling of extension, as though she were everywhere, on the table-tops, in the wine-bottles, in the waiter; wise with all of them. Every experience meant something; each had its place. She groped down the corridor, blind in the sudden darkness, singing.

Their room was still darker; the shutters were latched. Dillie kicked the snakeskin shoes off her aching feet, then let daylight in with a bang and a blast of hot air. She turned to look for her brogues.

Reflected, swan-like, into the waxy floor, the Horrors awaited her. Heel to heel, they radiated sex-consciousness; dangling their little scarlet straps. '*Les chaussures de Madame*' – shoes attributed to Dillie Aherne, the frank and equal companion of Edward. 'You *damned*!' said Dillie. 'You absolutely *damned* damned!' Then she picked them up (she could never explain what came to her) and threw them one by one out of the window, aiming very carefully at a particular point in the sky. One struck the dining-room roof and ricocheted off it. The other spun on the sky with a flash of bright heel and dropped into a palm tree. Dillie grinned fearfully after them; then, shocked unutterably, buried her face in the curtain. Tears came on; she was caught in them, helpless, as in a thunder-shower.

Edward and she were both interested in her temper and in a kind of way proud of it. It was an anachronism but rather distinctive. But it sometimes came on her unprepared and so frightened and really hurt her. 'Oh!' she cried, trembling. 'Oh oh *oh!*' The curtain tore.

At the sound of the shoe on the roof Edward ran out, looked down at the shoe and up at the window. He saw his Dillie back in the darkness, hiding her face in the curtain.

'A shoe's just come down . . . Oh?'

Dillie wound herself up in the curtain.

Edward swallowed. 'Shall – shall I come up?' he said loyally.

Dillie unwound, and leant out to give emphasis. 'You can tell them the other's up in a palm tree – it has as much business there as in my room. Tell them they're vilely cynical and that we shall be leaving tonight.' She slammed the shutter.

'Scene in the best French manner,' Edward admitted. Several other shutters opened an inch or two; he felt people looking out at him sympathetically. He hurried across to the foot of a likely palm: up there, sure enough, was the little siren, lodged at the base of two fronds. It looked as though a shake of the tree should bring it down easily: he tried two or three and they didn't. He walked round the tree, looking up; he bombarded the shoe with pebbles; it faintly wobbled. He eyed it, without prejudice . . . it *was* rather a nice little shoe. Perhaps it belonged to the girl in pleated green organdie, with the gazelle eyes . . . (An ultra-feminine type, Dillie and he had agreed.) It would look rather jolly with pleated green organdie . . . The scarlet straps would compete with the scarlet hat –

under which the gazelle eyes looked out deprecatingly, mysteriously. He wondered what she would think of him, trying to rout her shoe out of a palm with a piece of bamboo – the bamboo was too short. He might have swarmed up the trunk, but that would look silly and ruin his trousers. When she appeared, he would say to that girl . . .

He hoped Dillie wouldn't summon him. Her tempers, once over the crying stage, were very explicit. Hypnotically, the sky glittered through the fronds; caressing one shoe, gazing up at the other, Edward remained in a dream.

Dillie sat on her bed in the smothering darkness, wondering what to do now. She thought that, to keep her word at its present high value with Edward, she should pull the suitcases out and begin packing. She sighed; she did hope Edward would rush in and over-persuade her before she had put in the first layer. 'It's nothing personal,' she repeated, 'it's just that I cannot tolerate cynical inefficiency. I'm sorry, Edward; I just happen to be made like that.' She felt that if she could not say this to somebody soon it would lose its first edge of conviction; she peeped through the shutters, but Edward was standing stupidly under a palm-tree and *she* wasn't going to call him. Reluctantly, she rolled up two jumpers. It really was queer how men failed one; one looked to them at a crisis, and they just walked away and stood under a tree with their legs apart. She tossed some paper out of a suitcase, trying to think of the French for 'inefficiency'.

Somebody knocked. Dillie stood still a moment; her lips moved. She powdered her nose which, still flushed with anger, felt larger than usual, then opened the door fiercely. An arch little boy in a blouse, called Anatole, stood outside with her brogues. '*V'là les chaussures de Monsieur*,' said Anatole, putting them down briskly. And he had been sent, he said, to look for the shoes that Madame had taken this morning, that did not belong to Madame at all, that belonged to another lady who now searched for them everywhere. He looked at Dillie, severely.

Dillie faltered, '*Comment?*'

Anatole very politely shrugged. '*Mais voilà les chaussures de Monsieur,*' he repeated, and held out her brogues encouragingly.

'– *de Monsieur.*' It was the moment, certainly, for Dillie to make a demonstration. *Now* she could show them. '*Ceux ne sont pas—*' began Dillie. But she went scarlet and stopped. *Was* Anatole worth it – so small, so sleek, already so irreclaimable? She looked down; her good brogues sat there stodgily, square on the parquet. There was no nonsense about them. '*Les chaussures de Monsieur . . .*'

'*Allez-vous-en!*' snapped Dillie, and slammed the door.

Ten minutes later, felt hat pulled on jauntily, she clattered happily to and fro on the parquet, brogued once more to resume the day. She was loth to waste an hour. She must make Edward feel how he was forgiven. She parted the shutters and looked out; a curious group intrigued her.

Edward, crossing the garden, was followed by the waiter at one end of a ladder and Anatole at the other. A girl in green ruffles was supported in indignation by two men, one in a Homburg, one in a flat cap. She was just the sort of girl for the shoes, Dillie observed with triumph. Edward was pink; it was trying for him, but one must not be sentimental. The waiter propped the ladder against the palm and after some discussion began to go up it; Anatole held the bottom and Edward directed.

'*Je ne sais pas comment c'est arrivé,*' Edward kept explaining. '*A gauche, un peu plus à gauche! Là – secouez-le . . . Je ne sais pas comment c'est arrivé. Ça a l'air, n'est-ce pas, d'être tombé! Oui, c'est tombé, sans doute.*'

It was painful, in fact, to listen to the lying of Edward. Dillie, hot to the very back-bone, turned from the window; she even shut the shutters defensively. She kept moving about the room, jerked her hat off and came to a full-stop in front of the glass. Her eyes in the half-dark were haggard and rather profound; she looked startled. She tried to see Edward's

Dillie: her thoughts raced round and round till one half suspected, inside this whirlwind of thought, there was nothing
at all! She remembered the two Ahernes, vis-à-vis, at happy
lunchtime, analysing each other; she envied them now like
strangers. Such assurance, such a *right* kind of self-sufficiency
. . . Goaded, Dillie pulled her hat on again, seized her stick
and made for the door – then, in a queer kind of panic, returned and stood waiting for something, someone. The travelling clock loudly, officiously ticked.

Edward at last came up. He rippled a tap and entered,
ruefully smiling. He was still rather warm.

'Well?' said Dillie.

'Squared 'em all. Wasn't it like a French farce though – not
the improper kind. See us?'

'Partly. That terrible girl with the hips. Aren't French
women *hard*, Edward!'

'Oh no, she was wonderfully sporting. Once she got her
shoe back, she seemed rather amused. After all, Dillie, allow-
ing for tastes, one does value one's shoes. I liked the two men
she was with, too; of course they began by being rather ag-
gressive – the French have a strong sense of property – but
they finished up quite sympathetic and nice. You know, I
always think—'

'– Did they *guess*?'

They looked at each other a moment in naked discomfort.
Edward blinked. '*I* don't know: didn't ask them. Of course,
the shoes had been traced to our room . . .'

'I dare say', Dillie said, unconcerned, 'she thought you
looked like the Prince of Wales. You do, in that suit.'

'Do I? Good!'

Dillie steeled herself. Edward *was* rather pathetic. If one
had been a 'wee wifie' sort of a person one would have clung
to his chest, stroked the back of his nice neck and dithered:
'Oh, Edward, I've been such a beast, such a fool!' Dillie was
glad she wasn't going to do this: it would have lowered her in
Edward's eyes. It would have been shocking to drop the thing

206

to the emotional plane and let it remain there, unanalysed, undiscussed.

'Queer,' she said bravely, 'what one gains with these people by an apparent access of uncontrol . . . They'd admire hysterics – Don't you agree?' she said sharply.

Edward went to the basin and made a loud noise with the tap. He rubbed water up his face. He gurgled into the water.

'What *do* you think – really, Edward?'

'Can't think now – I'm too hot.'

'Edward, you *don't* think I—? Surely, Edward—'

'Coming out?' said Edward, looking round for his hat.

Dillie felt quite hollow. What was Edward thinking? How dare he! . . . 'Edward, kiss me . . . You *do* believe in me? *Edward!* Kiss me!'

But Edward still seemed bothered about his hat. She supposed this might well be the end of their marriage.

Then a kiss from Edward, uncertainly placed, began to be prolonged with some ardour in the dark room.

'You poor little angel!'

'You know, I did throw them out of the window.'

'You take things too hard, darling.'

'You do see I was right?' she said anxiously. She heard Edward breathe hard, considering.

'Under these particular circumstances – yes, I'm sure you were.'

'You weren't ashamed of me?' She couldn't let go of his coat-sleeve till he had answered.

'It was awful for you.'

'It was just', she said, 'that I *cannot* tolerate cynical inefficiency.'

'You were quite right . . . Shall we go out now and have a rather long, cool drink before we look at any more of the cathedral? *Bière blonde* or something . . . Coming?'

'Yes,' she said, 'if you really must.' With infinite patronage, infinite affection, she took his arm.

Mr and Mrs Aherne, free, frank, on terms of perfect

equality, clattered down the corridor, disturbing some dozen siestas. Talking loudly together about the Latin mentality, they passed with a blink and a gasp into the reeling glare of the afternoon.

The Key to My Heart

V. S. PRITCHETT

When Father dropped dead and Mother and I were left to run the business on our own, I was twenty-four years old. It was the principal bakery in our town, a good little business, and Father had built it up from nothing. Father used to wink at me when Mother talked about their 'first wedding'. 'How many times have you been married? Who was it that time?' he used to say to her. She was speaking of the time they first ventured out of the bakery into catering for weddings and local dances. For a long time, when I was a child, we lived over the shop; then Mother made Father take a house down the street. Later still, we opened a café next door but two to the shop, and our idea was to buy up the two little places in between. But something went wrong in the last years of Father's life. Working at night in the heat and getting up at the wrong time of day disorganised him. And then the weddings were his downfall. There is always champagne left over at weddings, and Father got to like it and live on it. And then brandy followed. When Mr Pickering, the solicitor, went into the will and the accounts, there was muddle everywhere, and bills we had never heard of came in.

'Father kept it all in his head,' Mother said, very proud of him for that. Mr Pickering and I had to sort it all out, and one of the things we discovered was that what we owed was nothing to what people owed us. Mother used to serve in the shop and do the books. She did it, we used to say, for the sake of the gossip – to day-dream about why the school-mistress ordered crumpets only on Thursdays, or guessing, if someone ordered more of this kind of cake or that, who

209

was going to eat it with them. She was generally right, and she knew more about what was going on in the town than anyone else. As long as the daily and weekly customers paid their books, she didn't bother; she hated sending bills, and she was more pleased than upset when Mr Pickering told her there was a good six hundred pounds owing by people who either hadn't been asked to pay or who were simply not troubling themselves. In a small business, this was a lot of money. It was the rich and the big pots in the county who were the worst of these debtors. Dad and Mother never minded being owed by the rich. They had both grown up in the days when you were afraid of offending people, and to hear my mother talk you would have thought that by asking the well-off to fork out you were going to kill the goose that lays the golden egg, knock the bottom out of society, and let a Labour government in.

'Think of what they have to pay in taxes,' she would say, pitying them. 'And the death duties!' And when I did what Mr Pickering said, and sent out accounts to these people, saying politely that it had no doubt been overlooked, Mother looked mournful and said getting a commission in the Army had turned my head. The money came in, of course. When Colonel Williams paid up and didn't dispute it, Mother looked at his cheque as if it were an insult from the old gentleman and, in fact, 'lost' it in her apron pocket for a week. Lady Littlebank complained, but she paid all the same. A few did not answer, but when I called at their houses they paid at once. Though the look on Mother's face was as much as to say I was a son ruining her lifework and destroying her chances of holding her head up in society. At the end of two or three months, there was only one large account outstanding – a Mrs Brackett's. Mrs Brackett did not answer, and you can guess Mother made the most of this. Mother spoke highly of Mrs Brackett, said she was 'such a lady', came of a wonderful family, and once even praised her clothes. She was the richest woman in the county, and young. She became my mother's ideal.

Mrs Brackett was married to a pilot and racing motorist known in the town as Noisy Brackett; it was she, as my mother said, nodding her head up and down, who 'had the money'. Noisy was given a couple of cars and his pocket money, but, having done that, Mrs Brackett paid as little as she could, as slowly as she could, to everyone else. When I talked about her account to other shopkeepers in the town, they put on their glasses, had a look at their books, sniffed, and said nothing. Every shopkeeper, my father used to say, woke up in the early hours of the morning thinking of how much she owed him, and dreaming of her fortune. You can work out how long her bill with us had run on when I say it was nearly two hundred and thirty pounds. The exact sum was two hundred and twenty-eight pounds fourteen and fourpence. I shall always remember it.

The first time I made out Mrs Brackett's bill, I gave it to Noisy. He often came into the café to flirt with the girls, or to our shop to see Mother and get her to cash cheques for him. He was a thin little man, straight as a stick and looked as brittle, and covered (they said) with scars and wounds from his crashes. He had curly shining black hair, the face of a sick gipsy, and the lines of a charmer all over it. His smiles quickly ended in a sudden, stern twitching of his left cheek and eye, like the crack of a whip, which delighted the women. He was a dandy, and from Mother he had the highest praise she could give to any man. He was, she said, 'snobby'.

When I gave Noisy our bill, he handed it back to me at once. 'Be a sweetie-pie,' he said, 'and keep it under your hat until the day after tomorrow. Tomorrow's my pay-day, and I don't want the Fairy Queen to get her mind taken off it – d'you follow? Good! Fine! Splendid fellow! Bang on!' And, with a twitch, he was back in his long white Bentley. 'Bring it yourself,' he said, looking me up and down. I am a very tall man, and little Noisy had a long way to look. 'It'll do the trick.'

Noisy did not hide his dependence on his wife. Everyone except the local gentry liked him.

So on the Thursday, when the shop was closed and I could leave the café to the waitresses – a good pair of girls, and Rosie, the dark one, very pretty – I took the station wagon and drove up to Heading Mount, four miles out of the town. It was June; they were getting the hay in. The land in the valley fetches its price – you wouldn't believe it if I told you what a farm fetches there. Higher up, the land is poor, where the oak woods begin, and all that stretch belonged to old Mr Lucas, Mrs Brackett's father, who had made a fortune out of machine tools. The estate was broken up when he died. I came out of the oak woods and turned in to the drive, which winds between low stone walls and tall rhododendron bushes, so that it is like a damp, dark, sunken lane, and very narrow. Couples often walked up on Sundays in June to see the show of rhododendrons on the slopes at Heading; the bushes were in flower as I drove by. I was speeding to the sharp turn at the end of the drive, before you come to the house, when I had to brake suddenly. Mrs Brackett's grey Bentley was drawn broadside across it, blocking the drive completely. I ought to have seen this was a bad omen.

To leave a car like that, anywhere, was typical of Mrs Brackett. If there was a traffic jam in the town, or if someone couldn't get into the market, nine times out of ten Mrs Brackett's car was the cause. She just stepped out of it wherever it was, as if she were dropping her coat off for someone else to pick up. The police did nothing. As she got back in, she would smile at them, raise one eyebrow, wag her hips, and let them see as much of her legs as she thought fit for the hour of the day, and drive off with a small wave of her hand that made them swell with apologies and blow up someone else. Sometimes she went into a rage that was terrifying coming from so small a person.

Now, in her driveway, I left my wagon and walked round her car towards the house. It was an old L-shaped house, sheltered by sycamores and built in the grey flaking stone of our part of the country. They say her father paid only twelve thousand pounds for it, and that included two or three cottages and farm buildings. The kitchens and servants' rooms and garages were at one side of the L – modern buildings, screened by laurels. Not that there were often any servants there. There was a small circle of lawn in the front of the house, with a statue in the middle of it.

As I walked across the lawn, I realised I had missed the back lane to the house, and that I ought to have driven along a wire-fenced road across the fields to the farm and the kitchen, where the housekeeper lived. But I had not been up there for several years, and had forgotten it. As I walked towards the white front door, I kicked a woman's shoe – a shoe for a very small foot. I picked it up. I was a few yards from the door when Mrs Brackett marched out, stopped on the steps, and then, as sharp as a sergeant, shouted, 'Jimmy!' She was looking up at the sky, as though she expected to bring her husband down out of it.

She was barefooted, wearing a blue-and-white checked shirt and dusty jeans, and her short fair hair untidy, and she was making an ugly mouth, like a boy's, on her pretty face. I was holding out the shoe as I went forward. There was no answer to her shout. Then she saw me and stared at the shoe.

'Who are you? What are you doing with that?' she asked. 'Put it down.'

But before I could answer, from the other side of the buildings there was the sound of a car starting and driving off on the back road. Mrs Brackett heard this. She turned and marched into the house again, but in a few seconds she returned, running past me across the lawn. She jumped into her car, backed – and then she saw mine blocking the drive. She sounded her horn, again and again. A dog barked, and she jumped out and bawled at me. 'You bloody fool!' she shouted. 'Get that van of yours out of the way!'

The language that came out of her small mouth was like

what you hear in the cattle market on Fridays. I slowly went up and got into my van. I could hear her swearing and the other car tearing off; already it must have turned in to the main road. I got into mine, and there we sat, face to face, scowling at each other through our windscreens. I reversed down the long, winding drive, very fast, keeping one eye on her all the time, and turned sharply off the road at the entrance. I don't mind saying that I was showing off. I can reverse a car at speed and put it anywhere to within an inch of where I want to. I saw her face change as she came on, for in her temper she was coming fast down the drive straight at me, radiator to radiator. At the end, she gave one glance of surprise at me, and I think held back a word she had ready as she drove past. At any rate, her mouth was open. Half a dozen cows started from under the trees and went trotting round the field in panic as she went, and the rooks came out of the elms like bits of black paper.

By bad luck, you see, I had arrived in the middle of one of the regular Brackett rows. They were famous in the neighbourhood. The Bracketts chased each other round the house, things came out of windows – clothes, boots, anything. Our roundsman said he had once seen a portable radio, playing full on, come flying out, and that it had fallen, still playing, in the roses. Servants came down to the town and said they had had enough of it. Money was usually at the bottom of the trouble. There was a tale going round that when a village girl who worked there got married, Mrs Brackett gave her a three-shilling alarm clock for a wedding present.

The rows always went the same way. A car would race out of the drive with Noisy in it, and five minutes later Mrs Brackett would be in her car chasing him, and no one was safe on the roads for twenty miles around. Sometimes it might end quietly in a country pub, with Mrs Brackett in one bar and Noisy in the other, white-faced and playing hymns on the piano to mock her until she gave in. Other times, it might go on through the night. Noisy, who raced cars, was

the better driver, but she was wilder. She would do anything
– she once cut through the footpath of the cemetery to catch
him on the other side. She sometimes caught him, but more
than once her meanness about money would leave her standing. There would be a telephone call to Briggs' garage: Mrs
Brackett had run out of petrol. She was too mean ever to
have much more than a gallon in the tank.

'Bless her,' Noisy used to say if anyone mentioned these
chases to him. 'I always rely on the Fairy Queen to run out
of gas.'

Noisy was a woman-hater. His trouble was his habit of
saying 'Bless you' to the whole female sex.

'Well, I hope you're satisfied,' my mother said when I got
home. I put Mrs Brackett's shoe on the table.

'I've made some progress,' I said.

My mother looked at the shoe for a long time. Now that I
had got something out of Mrs Brackett, Mother began to
think a little less of her. 'You'd think a woman with feet like
that would dress better,' she said.

But what annoyed me was that at some stage in the afternoon's chase Noisy had slipped in and got Mother to cash
him a cheque for twenty pounds.

June is the busy time of the year for us. There are all the June
weddings. Noisy and Mrs Brackett must have settled down
again somehow, because I saw them driving through the
town once or twice. I said to myself, 'You wait till the rush
is over.'

In July, I went up to the Bracketts' house a second time.
Rosie, the dark girl who works in our café, came with me,
because she wanted to meet her aunt at the main-line station
three or four miles over the hill beyond Heading Mount, and
I was taking her on there after I had spoken to Mrs Brackett.
I drove up to the house. The rhododendrons had died, and
there were pods on them already going brown. The sun
struck warm in front of the house. It was wonderfully quiet.

I left the girl in the car, reading a book, and was working out a sentence to say, when I saw Mrs Brackett kneeling by a goldfish pond, at the far side of the great lawn. She turned and saw me. I did not know whether to go over the lawn to her or to wait where I was. I decided to go over, and she got up and walked to me. Mother was right about her clothes. This time she was wearing a gaudy tomato-coloured cotton dress that looked like someone else's, and nothing on underneath it. I do not know why it was – whether it was because I was standing on the grass she was walking over, whether it was my anxiety about how to begin the conversation, or whether it was because of her bare white arms, the dawdling manner of her walk, and the inquisitiveness of her eyes – but I thought I was going to faint. When she was two yards away, my heart jumped, my throat closed, and my head was swimming. Although I had often seen her driving through the town, and though I remembered our last meeting all too well, I had never really looked at her before. She stopped, but I had the feeling that she had not stopped but was invisibly walking on until she walked clean through me. My arms went weak. She was amused by the effect she had on me.

'I know who you are,' she said. 'You are Mr Fraser's son. Do you want to speak to me?'

I did, but I couldn't. I forgot all the sentences I had prepared. 'I've come about our cheque,' I said at last. I shouted it. Mrs Brackett was as startled by my shout as I was. She blushed at the loudness and shock of it – not a light blush but a dark, red, flooding blush on her face and her neck that confused her and made her lower her head like a child caught stealing. She put her hands behind her back like a child. I blushed, too. She walked up and down a yard or two, her head still down, thinking. Then she walked away to the house.

'You'd better come inside,' she called back in an offhand way.

You could have put our house into the hall and sitting-room of Heading Mount. I had been in that room when I was a boy, helping the waitress when my father was there doing the catering for a party. I do not know what you'd have to pay for the furniture there – thousands, I suppose. She led me through the room to a smaller room beyond it, where there was a desk. I felt I was slowly walking miles. I have never seen such a mess of papers and letters. They were even spread on the carpet. She sat down at the desk.

'Can you see the bill?' she muttered, not looking at me and pointing to the floor.

'I've got it here,' I said, taking the bill out of my pocket. She jerked her head. The flush had gone, and now she looked as keen as needles at me.

'Well, sit down,' she said.

She took the bill from me and looked at it. Now I could see that her skin was not white but was really pale and clay-coloured, with scores of little cracks in it, and that she was certainly nearer forty than thirty, as Mother always said.

'I've paid this,' she said, giving the bill a mannish slap. 'I pay every quarter.'

'It has been running for three and a half years,' I said, more at ease now.

'What?' she said. 'Oh, well, I paid something, anyway. This isn't a bill. It's a statement.'

'Yes,' I said. 'We have sent you the bills.'

'Where's the date? This hasn't got any date on it.'

I got up and pointed to the date.

'It ought to be at the top,' she said.

My giddiness had gone. Noisy came into the room. 'Hullo, Bob,' he said. 'I've just been talking to that beautiful thing you've got in the car.' He always spoke in an alert, exhausted way about women, like someone at a shoot waiting for the birds to come over. 'Have you seen Bob's girl, darling?' he said to her. 'I've just offered her the key to my heart.' And he lifted the silk scarf he was wearing in the neck of his canary-coloured pullover, and there was a piece of string round his neck with a heavy old door key hanging from it. Noisy gave a twitch to one side of his face.

'Oh God, that old gag,' said Mrs Brackett.

'Not appreciated, old boy,' said Noisy to me.

'Irresistible,' said Mrs Brackett, with an ugly mouth. She turned and spoke to me again, but glanced shrewdly at Noisy as she did so. 'Let me try this one on you,' she said. 'You've already got my husband's cheques for this bill. I send him down to pay you, and he just cashes them?'

'I'm afraid not, Mrs Brackett,' I said. 'That wouldn't be possible.'

'You can't get away with that one, my pet,' said Noisy. 'Are you ready to go out?' He looked at her dress, admiring her figure. 'What a target, Bob,' he said.

'I don't think we will ask Mr Fraser's opinion,' she said coldly, but very pleased. And she got up and started out of the room, with Noisy behind her.

'You had better send me the bills,' she called back to me, turning round from the door.

I felt very, very tired. I left the house and slammed the car door when I got in. 'Now she wants the damn bills,' I said to Rosie as I drove her up to Tolton station. I did not speak to her the rest of the way. She irritated me, sitting there.

When I got home and told my mother, she was short with me. That was the way to lose customers, she said. I was ruining all the work she and Dad had put into the business. I said if Mrs Brackett wanted her bills she could come and get them herself. Mother was very shocked.

She let it go for a day or two, but she had to bring it up again. 'What are you sulking about?' she said to me one afternoon. 'You upset Rosie this morning. Have you done those bills for Mrs Brackett yet?'

I made excuses, and got in the car and went over to the millers and to the people who make our boxes, to get away from the nagging. Once I was out of the town, in the open country, Mrs Brackett seemed to be somewhere just ahead of me, round a corner, over a hill, beyond a wood. There she was, trying to make me forget she owed us two hundred and twenty-eight pounds fourteen and fourpence. The moment she was in my head, the money went out of it. When I got back, late in the evening, Mother was on to me again. Noisy had been in. She said he had been sent down by his wife to ask why I had not brought the bills.

'The poor Wing Commander,' my mother said. 'Another rumpus up there.' (She always gave him his rank if there was a rumour of another quarrel at Heading.) 'She never gives him any peace. He's just an errand boy. She does what she likes with him.'

'He's been offering you the key to his heart, Mother,' I said.

'I don't take any stock of him,' Mother said. 'Or that pansy "sweetheart" stuff. Dad was the one and only for me. I don't believe in second marriages. I've no time for jealous women; they're always up to something, like Mrs Doubleday thinking I spoke to her husband in the bank and she was caught with the chemist, but you always think the Fairy Prince will turn up – it's natural.'

It always took a little time getting at what was in Mother's mind, yet it was really simple. She was a good church-woman, and she thought Noisy was not really married to Mrs Brackett, because he had been divorced by his first wife. She did not blame Noisy for this – in fact, she admired it, in a romantic way – but she blamed Mrs Brackett, because, by Mother's theories, Mrs Brackett was still single. And Mother never knew whether to admire single women for holding out or to suspect them of being on the prowl. One thing she was certain of. 'Money talks,' she said. The thing that made Noisy respectable for her, and as good as being married in church, was that he had married Mrs Brackett for her money.

She talked like this the night we sat up and did that

month's bills, but the next day – and this was the trouble with Mother – it ended in a row. I sent the bills up to Mrs Brackett by our delivery van.

'That is not the way to behave,' Mother said. 'You should have taken them yourself.'

And before the day was out, Mother was in a temper again. Mrs Brackett had spoken to her on the telephone and said she had been through the bills and that we had charged her for things she hadn't had, because she'd been in the South of France at the time.

'I told you to go,' Mother said to me.

I was angry, too, at being called dishonest. I got out the van and said I was going up at once.

'Oh, that's how it is,' said my mother, changing round again. 'Her Ladyship snaps her fingers and you go up at once. She's got you running about for her like Noisy. If I ask you to do anything, you don't pay any attention to me. But Mrs Brackett – she's the Queen of England. Two of you running after her.'

Mother was just like that with Father when he was alive. He took no notice. Neither did I. I went up to Heading. A maid let me in, and I sat there waiting in the drawing-room. I waited a long time, listening to the bees coming down the chimney, circling lower and lower and then roaring out into the room, like Noisy's car. I could hear Mrs Brackett talking on the telephone in her study. I could hear now and then what she was saying. She was a great racing woman, and from words she said here and there I would say she was speaking to a bookmaker. One sentence I remember, because I think it had the name of a horse in it, and when I got back home later I looked up the racing news to see if I could find it. 'Tray Pays On,' she said. She came out into the room with the laughter of her telephone call still on her face. I was standing up, with our account book in my hand, and when she saw me the laughter went.

I was not afraid of her any more. 'I hear there is some

trouble about the bills,' I said. 'If you've got them, you can check them with the book. I've brought it.'

Mrs Brackett was a woman who watched people's faces. She put on her dutiful, serious, and obedient look, and led me again to the little room where the papers were. She sat down and I stood over her while we compared the bills and the book. I watched the moving of her back as she breathed. I pointed to the items, one by one, and she nodded and ticked the bills with a pencil. We checked for nearly half an hour. The only thing she said was in the middle of it – 'You've got a double-jointed thumb. So have I' – but she went right on.

'I can see what it is,' I said at the end. 'You've mistaken 1953 for '54.'

She pushed the book away, and leaned back in the chair against my arm, which was resting on it.

'No, I haven't,' she said, her small, unsmiling face looking up into mine. 'I just wanted you to come up.'

She gazed at me a long time. I thought of all the work Mother and I had done, and then that Mother was right about Mrs Brackett. I took my hand from the chair and stepped back.

'I wanted to ask you one or two things,' she said, confidingly, 'about that property next to the shop. I'll be fair with you. I'm interested in it. Are you? All right, don't answer. I see you are.'

My heart jumped. Ever since I could remember, Father and Mother had talked of buying this property. It was their day-dream. They simply liked little bits of property everywhere, and now I wanted it so that we could join the shop and the café.

'I asked because . . .' She hesitated. 'I'll be frank with you. The bank manager was talking about it to me today.'

My fright died down. I didn't believe that the bank manager – he was Mr Pickering's brother-in-law – would let my mother down and allow the property to go to Mrs Brackett without giving us the offer first.

'We want it, of course,' I said. And then I suspected this was one of her tricks. 'That is why I have been getting our bills in,' I said.

'Oh, I didn't think that was it,' she said. 'I thought you were getting married. My husband says you are engaged to the girl you brought up here. He said he thought you were. Has she any money?'

'Engaged!' I said. 'I'm not. Who told him that?'

'Oh,' she said, and then a thought must have struck her. I could read it at once. In our town, if you cough in the High Street the chemist up at the Town Hall has got a bottle of cough mixture wrapped up and waiting for you; news travels fast. She must have guessed that when Noisy came down dangling the key to his heart, he could have been round the corner all the time, seeing Rosie.

'I'm glad to hear you're not engaged,' Mrs Brackett said tenderly. 'I like a man who works. You work like your father did – God, what an attractive man! You're like him. I'm not flattering you. I saw it when you came up the first time.'

She asked me a lot of questions about the shop and who did the baking now. I told her I didn't do it and that I wanted to enlarge the restaurant. 'The machine bakeries are getting more and more out into the country,' I said. 'And you've got to look out.'

'I don't see why you shouldn't do catering for schools,' she said. 'And there's the Works.' (Her father's main factory.) 'Why don't you get hold of the catering there?'

'You can only do that if you have capital. We're not big enough,' I said, laughing.

'How much do you want?' she said. 'Two thousand? Three? I don't see why we couldn't do something.'

The moment she said 'we', I came to my senses. Here's a funny turnout, I thought. She won't pay her bills, but first she's after these shops, and now she's waving two thousand pounds in my face. Everyone in our town knew she was art- ful. I suppose she thought I was green.

'Not as much as two thousand,' I said. 'Just the bill,' I said, nodding at it.

Mrs Brackett smiled. 'I like you. You're interested in money. Good. I'll settle it.' And, taking her cheque-book from the top of the desk, she put it in her drawer. 'I never pay these accounts by cheque. I pay in cash. I'll get it tomorrow at the bank. I'll tell you what I'll do. You've got a shoe of mine. Bring it up tomorrow evening at, say, half past eight. I'll be back by then and you can have it.' She paused, and then, getting up, added quickly, 'Half tomorrow, half in October.'

It was like dealing with the gipsies that come to your door.

'No, Mrs Brackett,' I said. 'I'd like all of it. Now.' We stared at each other. It was like that moment months ago when she had driven at me in her car and I had reversed down the drive with one eye watching her and one on the road as I shot back. That was the time, I think, I first noticed her – when she opened her mouth to shout a word at me and then did not shout. I could have stayed like this, looking into her small, pretty, miser's blue eyes, at her determined head, her chopped-off fair hair, for half an hour. It was a struggle.

She was the first to speak, and that was a point gained to me. Her voice shook a little. 'I don't keep that amount of money in the house,' she said.

I knew that argument. Noisy said she always had two or three hundred pounds in the safe in the wall of her study, and whether this was so or not, I could not help glancing towards it.

'I don't like being dictated to,' she said, catching my glance. 'I have told you what I will do.'

'I think you could manage it, Mrs Brackett,' I said.

I could see she was on the point of flying into one of her tempers, and as far as I was concerned (I don't know why), I hoped she would. Her rows with Noisy were so famous that I must have wanted to see one for myself. And I didn't see why she should get away with it. At the back of my mind, I thought of all the others down in the town and how they would look when I said I had got my money out of Mrs Brackett.

Yet I wasn't really thinking about the money at all, at this moment. I was looking at her pretty shoulders.

But Mrs Brackett did not fly into a temper. She considered me, and then she spoke in a quiet voice that took me off my guard. 'Actually,' she said, lowering her eyes, 'you haven't been coming up here after money at all, have you?'

'Well—' I began.

'Sh-h-h!' she said, jumping up from her chair and putting her hand on my mouth. 'Why didn't you ring me and tell me you were coming? I am often alone.'

She stepped to the door and bawled out, 'Jimmy!' as if he were a long way off. He was – to my surprise, and even more to hers – very near.

'Yes, ducky?' Noisy called back from the hall.

'Damn,' she said to me. 'You must go.' And, squeezing my hand, she went through the drawing-room into the hall.

'What time do we get back tomorrow evening?' she said boldly to Noisy. 'Half-past eight? Come at half-past eight,' she said, turning to me, for I had followed her. 'I'll bring back the cash.'

The sight of Noisy was a relief to me, and the sound of the word 'cash' made Noisy brighten.

'Not lovely little bits of money!' he exclaimed.

'Not you,' said Mrs Brackett, glaring at him.

'How did you work it, old boy?' said Noisy later, giving me one of his most quizzical twitches as he walked with me to my van. When I drove off, I could see him still standing there, watching me out of sight.

I drove away very slowly. My mind was in confusion. About half a mile off, I stopped the car and lit a cigarette. All the tales I had heard about Mrs Brackett came back into my mind. It was one thing to look at her, another thing to know about her. The one person I wished I had with me was Noisy. He seemed like a guarantor of safety, a protection. To have

224

had my thoughts read like that by her filled me with fear.

I finished my cigarette. I decided not to go straight home, and I drove slowly all along the lower sides of the oak woods, so slowly and carelessly that I had to swerve to avoid oncoming cars. I was making, almost without knowing it, for the Green Man, at Mill Cross. There was a girl there I had spoken to once or twice. No one you would know. I went in and asked for a glass of beer. I hardly said a word to her, except about the weather, and then she left the bar to look after a baby in the kitchen at the back. That calmed me. I think the way she gave me my change brought me back to earth and made me feel free of Mrs Brackett's spell. At any rate, I put the threepence in my pocket and swallowed my beer. I laughed at myself. Mrs Brackett had gypped me again.

When I got home it was late, and my mother was morose. She was wearing a black dress she often wore when she was alone, dressed up and ready to go out, yet not intending to, as if now that my father was dead she was free if someone would invite her. Her best handbag was beside her. She was often waiting like this, sitting on the sofa, doing nothing but listening to the clock tick, and perhaps getting up to give a touch to some flowers on the table and then sitting down again. Her first words shook me.

'Mrs Brackett was down here looking for you,' she said sharply. 'I thought you were with her. She wants you to be sure to go up tomorrow evening to collect some money when she comes back from Tolton. Where have you been?'

'Let the old bitch post it or bring it in,' I said.

Mother was horrified at the idea of Mrs Brackett soiling her hands with money.

'You'll do as I tell you,' she said. 'You'll go up and get it. If you don't, Noisy will get his hands on it first. You'd think a woman with all that money would go to a decent hairdresser. It's meanness, I suppose.'

And then, of course, I saw I was making a lot of fuss about nothing. Noisy would be there when I went up to Heading. Good old Noisy, I thought; thank God for that. And he'll see I get the money, because she said it in front of him.

So the next evening I went. I put my car near the garage, and the first person I saw was Noisy, standing beside his own car. He had a suitcase in his hand. I went over to him.

'Fairy Queen's been at work,' he said. He nodded at his tyres. They were flat. 'I'm doing some quick thinking.'

At that moment, a top window of the house was opened and someone emptied a suitcase of clothes out of it, and then a shower of cigarettes came down.

'She's tidying,' he said. 'I've got a quarter of an hour to catch the London train. Be a sweetie-pie and run me over there.'

I had arrived once more in the middle of one of the Brackett rows. Only this time Noisy was leaving it to me. That is how I felt about it. 'Hop in,' I said.

And when we were off and a mile from Heading, he sat up in the seat and looked round. 'Nothing on our tail,' he said.

'Have you ever heard of a horse called Tray?' I asked him. 'Tray Pays something? Tray Pays On – that can't be it.'

'Tray Pays On?' repeated Noisy. 'Is it a French horse?'

'I don't know,' I said.

'Bloody peasant? Could be,' said Noisy. 'Sounds a bit frog to me.'

We got to Tolton station. Noisy was looking very white and set with hatred. Not until he was standing in the queue getting his ticket did it occur to me what Noisy was doing.

'The first time I've travelled by train for fifteen years,' he called to me across from the queue. 'Damned serious. You can tell her if you see her' – people stared – 'the worm has turned. I'm packing it in for good.'

And as he went off to the train he called, 'I suppose you're going back? No business of mine, but I'll give you a tip. If you do, you won't find anything in the kitty, Bob.' He gave me his stare and his final twitch. It was like the crack of a shot. Bang on, as he would have said. A bull's-eye.

I walked slowly away as the London train puffed out. I took his advice. I did not go back to Heading.

There were rows and rows between the Bracketts, but there was none like this one. It was the last. The others were a chase. This was not. For only Mrs Brackett was on the road that night. She was seen, we were told, in all the likely places. She had been a dozen times through the town. Soon after ten o'clock she was hooting outside our house. Mother peeped through the curtains, and I went out. Mrs Brackett got out of her car and marched at me. 'Where have you been?' she shouted. 'Where is my husband?'

'I don't know,' I said.

'Yes, you do,' she said. 'You took him to Tolton, they told me.'

'I think he's gone to London,' I said.

'Don't be a damn liar,' she said. 'How can he have? His car is up there.'

'By train,' I said.

'By train,' she repeated. Her anger vanished. She looked at me with astonishment. The rich are very peculiar. Mrs Brackett had forgotten people travel by train. I could see she was considering the startling fact. She was not a woman to waste time staying in one state of mind for long. Noisy used to say of her, 'That little clock never stops ticking.'

'I see,' she said to me sarcastically, nodding out the words. 'That's what you and Jimmy have been plotting.' She gave a shake to her hair and held her chin up. 'You've got your money and you don't care,' she said.

'What money is that?' I said.

'What money!' she exclaimed sharply, going over each inch of my face. What she saw surprised her at first. Until then she had been fighting back, but now a sly look came to her; it grew into a smile; the smile got wider and wider, and then her eyes became two curved lines, like crow's wings in the sky, and she went into shouts of laughter. It sounded all down the empty street. She rocked with it.

'Oh no!' she laughed. 'Oh no, that's too good! That's a winner. He didn't give you a penny! He swiped the lot!'

And she looked up at the sky in admiration of that flying man. She was still grinning at me when she taunted breathlessly, 'I mean to say – I mean to say—'

I let her run on.

'It was all or nothing with you, wasn't it?' she said. 'And you get nothing, don't you?'

I am not sure what I did. I may have started to laugh it off and I may have made a step towards her. Whatever I did, she went hard and prim, and if ever a woman ended anything, she did then. She went over to the car, got in, and slammed the door.

'You backed the wrong horse when you backed Jimmy,' she called out to me.

That was the last of her. No more Mrs Brackett at the shop. 'You won't hear another word from her,' my mother said.

'What am I supposed to do – get her husband back?' I said.

By the end of the week, everyone in the town was laughing and winking at me.

'You did the trick, boy,' the grocer said.

'You're a good-looking fellow, Bob,' the ironmonger said.

'Quite a way with the girls,' the butcher said. 'Bob's deep.'

For when Mrs Brackett went home that night, she sat down and paid every penny she owed to every shopkeeper in the town. Paid everyone, I say. Bar me.

The Great Mammoth Story

STELLA GIBBONS

'And don't make the mistake of thinkin' your Dad's money and his being an MP means anything to Cosmos Publicity, Mr Field. Once you step inside this building of a morning, you're an employee of this firm, and nothing more.'

There was a pause, while the departmental manager turned his attention angrily to the ringing telephone.

Claude Field sat staring at the tip of his shoe and swinging it gently to and fro, exactly as he had sat since Mr Sprott began to talk ten minutes ago.

He did not resent this dressing-down; he admitted that he was indolent, inefficient and unpunctual. But he was also bored; a state of mind unknown to the personnel which laboured to make Cosmos Publicity, Limited, even larger, richer and more public than it already was.

'Ants, my dear soul, positive ants,' was how he had described the staff of Cosmos Publicity to a younger sister on his return from his first day there. 'All toiling and moiling (whatever moiling may be) and laying up hay for the rainy day and all the rest of it. Very exhausting. I'm not at all sure that I shall be able to cope.'

His prophecy was fulfilled. After six months with the firm, Claude was invited to see Mr Sprott in his office.

The receiver was slammed angrily down.

'. . . and it all reflects on the firm, Mr Field,' resumed Mr Sprott, turning on Claude a long North-country face bitter as an east wind. 'You may think that your duties are slight, and so they are, but the life of a machine, Mr Field, is dependent upon the efficiency of the smallest cog in that machine, and details are important . . . as you may one day learn. I take a serious view of this matter. I am warning you, Mr Field. This is not the first time, I believe, that you have received a hint that Cosmos is dissatisfied with your work. Unless you can make a drastic change in your methods, Cosmos has no further use for you.'

He leant forward, his forefinger on a bell push, and looked full with his frosty eyes into Claude's mild young face.

'Oh I say, sir,' protested Claude, as he stood up, 'that's a bit thick, isn't it? I mean to say . . . well, the trouble is, you know, I'm not cut out for routine work. I'd much sooner have a stab at the creative side of the business; copy-writing and thinking up stunts and all that. I feel sure I could do that sort of thing, you know. More scope and all that.'

Mr Sprott smiled bitterly as his secretary entered with her notebook.

'It won't do, Mr Field,' was his last word. 'Stunts, as you call them, and copy-writing need Flair. They aren't everybody's work. Learn to be punctual, and write a good business letter, and talk sense on the telephone; that'll be enough to keep you busy for the next year or so. Good morning. Miss Bruce, take a letter, please.'

He leant back as Claude shut the door and began to dictate in an absent-minded snarl.

Claude wandered along the corridor to his own little office, kicked the door open, and went moodily in. He looked out of place among the chromium and pale wood of the fierce modernist furniture, for he had the long narrow head of an eighteenth-century portrait, and he seemed half asleep. His light suit, tea-coloured hair and pale face suggested neither efficiency nor a desire to Get On.

Among his letters was one from a firm of breakfast-food manufacturers, with their trademark stamped at the head of the paper. It was at this that Claude sat staring for nearly half an hour, while his cigarette burned peacefully to ash on the rim of the tray.

★

230

The preparations for the General Election, which began some three weeks later, increased the conversation between those who frequented the Rest in Peace, near Hurling Gap, in Sussex, but did not increase their number. It was a quiet little pub, visited by the same moderate drinkers year in and year out; and Miss Clipper, the landlady's niece and barmaid, often threatened to go off and get a job at Brightbourne, a large and noisy seaside town some eight miles away.

This evening the bar was quiet as usual. It was getting on for seven o'clock. A clear May twilight covered the Downs. Mr Rose had been in for his glass and gone out again. Now there was a lull until eight o'clock or so, when the men would begin to drift in after their suppers.

Miss Clipper leant her elbows upon the bar, and sighed. Nothing ever 'appens, reflected Miss Clipper. Not what you might call anything, that is. She glanced at the faded face of an old clock which ticked loudly in a corner, sighed again, and took a duster and began flicking spitefully among the bottles.

It was precisely as Miss Clipper began to flick that she heard an unusual noise outside.

Someone was running down the chalk road which led up to Hurling Down.

Miss Clipper heard the footsteps coming nearer and nearer. She glanced at the dark rim of the mighty Down, which she could see against the yellow sky through the window of the Rest in Peace. It's them kids of Dowler's, thought Miss Clipper, flicking. Ought to be in bed.

Suddenly the monotony of which Miss Clipper complained was broken.

The door flew open.

An old man staggered in, waving his arms above his head, and collapsed across the bar, choking.

'Brandy, me dear, brandy,' he gasped. 'I run all the way from the Gap and I'm near dead. I see an elephant – oh, my

231

dear heart, I see a great hairy elephant nigh as big as a house and I run all the way and I'm near dead.'

Miss Clipper drew herself virtuously away from the old man.

'Mr Mitson,' said Miss Clipper, 'I'm surprised at you, that I am. You ought to be ashamed of yourself. Where've you been? That nasty Red Lion, I suppose; bad beer and worse company. Elephants, indeed!'

Her homily ended in a shriek. Mr Mitson had gained a point by fainting.

'What's all this?' demanded Mrs Wilson, landlady of the Rest in Peace, sailing into the bar. 'What elephants?'

'Mr Mitson's dead,' announced Miss Clipper, pointing.

'Nonsense,' said Mrs Wilson. 'He's only fainted. Here, Nellie, get some brandy, and be quick about it.'

At the fiery touch of the brandy, shudderingly administered by Miss Clipper while Mrs Wilson supported him, Mr Mitson recovered enough to sit up and drain the glass, not without a glance of triumph at the barmaid.

'Now, Mr Mitson, just you tell us all about it,' said Mrs Wilson comfortably. 'You were in a state, weren't you? Have a drop more – well, perhaps sherry 'ud be better this time. Nellie, get Mr Mitson a small sherry.'

A pause. The sherry was drunk, and Mr Mitson began to breathe more calmly. He wiped his forehead with a trembling hand and glanced from one concerned face to the other. Miss Clipper still looked a little indignant, but Mrs Wilson was plainly all agog.

'Well, Mrs Wilson, me dear, and you, miss,' began Mr Mitson, 'I was coming home along from a day's work up at New Hurling in Major Fortescue's garden, rolling his lawn and doing a bit o' pruning and I see an elephant.'

He paused, and nodded. The expressions on two faces looking down at him changed a little.

'I see an elephant,' repeated Mr Mitson, more loudly. 'Just as I were coming up by Long Barrow Wood. A great elephant he were, true as I lie here, all over long black hair and he had

great big tusks and a trunk as long as this bar, Mrs Wilson, me dear. And when I see him a standing there, waving his trunk and as big as a house, I were fair horrified and I run all the way down from Hurling Gap wi'out stopping and here I be.'

Mrs Wilson shook her head.

'Now, now, Danny Mitson! Remember you and me have known each other since I was so-high. Don't you come into the Rest in Peace with tales like that. You and your hairy elephants! Liker it was a cow.'

'It were an elephant,' repeated Mr Mitson obstinately. 'Mind you, I don't say as it were a *real* elephant. Maybe it were a ghost-elephant out of Long Barrow where all them old heathen soldiers is buried. Come to think of it, 'e glided along like a ghost. But I saw him, plain as your hand.'

Mrs Wilson and Miss Clipper exchanged glances, which said, 'Poor old man, his wits are failing at last. We must humour him.'

'Well, he can't get you now, whatever he was,' said Mrs Wilson soothingly. 'You just sit by the fire and rest a bit, and when Jim Wykes comes in, you can go along home with him. Just you take it easy, now.'

She rose from her kneeling position beside the old man, and was holding out her hand playfully to help him rise from the floor, when a gasp from Miss Clipper made her look round.

'Look!' whispered Miss Clipper.

Three pairs of eyes turned towards the long ridge of Hurling Down, black against the fading light, which could be seen through the window.

A vast shaggy shape, enormous even at that distance, passed leisurely across the skyline, swinging a great trunk!

It disappeared beyond the edge of the window; and there was an intense stillness.

Mr Mitson broke it.

'I told yer so,' nodded Mr Mitson complacently.

★

'Hooper,' said the news editor of the *Morning Star* in the reporters' room of that paper, a week later, 'take a run down to Sussex and see if there's anything in this Mammoth story, will you? Don't handle it too seriously, of course. Strike the "Silly Sussex" note . . . but don't strike it too hard or we shall get let in for a long correspondence with that old ass Sir John Field. He's a nasty customer when he's roused, and he loves Sussex like a father. He's a cert for Brightbourne, too; they've returned him for the last ten years. Don't do too much; half a column at the most. See how it works out.'

Hooper, sceptical, but fond of fresh air and looking forward to a day in the country, ran into his young friend Claude Field while he was starting up his car.

'How's Cosmos?' asked Hooper.

Claude shook his head. He was not unlike a fish, decided Hooper, except that fishes had more spine and were not all so elaborately dressed.

'Very irksome. I envy you, Hooper. You do see life, anyway. Where are you beetling off to?'

'Mammoth-chasing,' grinned Hooper. 'Our correspondent at Brightbourne has sent in a yarn about some local worthies seeing a hairy elephant on the Downs. Marvellous what beer can do, aided by imagination.'

Claude looked at him pensively.

'I wonder, Hooper? The Downs are jolly ancient, you know, and all that. Prehistoric and what-not. I shouldn't be at all surprised if there's something in it.'

'I should,' said Hooper, driving away. 'Very.'

So it happened that Hooper was responsible for the Great Mammoth Story, which burst over England on the following morning and drove the General Election News off the front page for nearly a fortnight.

Hooper saw the Mammoth.

At least, he saw something more like a mammoth than anything he had ever seen before; a huge dark shape moving across a twilight valley half a mile away, its trunk rooting

234

among the fresh shoots of the furze bushes. He stood on the hillside, staring down into the dusk, suddenly very aware how vast and lonely were the hills rolling on all sides, and how empty the darkening sky.

Suddenly the thing disappeared.

He realised that he was staring at a dark patch of bushes. The moving shape had apparently sunk into the earth.

Hooper hesitated, standing on the hillside and gazing doubtfully down into the dim valley. He knew that he ought to go down there and have a look round. It was his duty, as a newspaper man, to trail the Mammoth to its lair and secure the biggest scoop in history. But he did not go, because he was afraid; and he did not mind confessing as much to the scoffing news editor of the *Morning Star* later.

There was a contrast between that bulk, and its stealthy gliding movement which was so strong as to be horrible.

There should have been the noise of tearing undergrowth and cracking branches to accompany the monstrous size of the brute, but there had not been a sound. Like a ghost, thought Hooper, staring down into the valley. It moved like a ghost.

The *Morning Star* splashed his story on the front page with a photograph of a different Sussex valley, explaining that this was the type of country where the Mammoth had been seen.

By the afternoon the evening papers were on the trail, and the Rest in Peace had sold out of gin.

The *Morning Star* was fond of speculating in its columns about probable conditions in the next world; and it took the Mammoth story from a supernatural angle. It pointed out in a brightly written leader that mammoths had at one time roamed England from Scotland to Cornwall. There was scarcely a county in England which might not contain their fossilised remains (it was safe to say this, as anyone who wrote in to say that there were no fossilised mammoths in their part of the world could be floored by telling them that

235

their part of the world was one of the few counties where there were no fossilised mammoths). The article ended on a pious 'Who knows?' note. The leader writer refrained from quoting Hamlet but afterwards inserted the quotation on a hint from the editor.

This leader brought a letter from Professor Pinchell Wain-flete, F.Z.S., B.Sc., Ph.D.

'I cannot say that I am surprised at the *nature* of the article in your paper,' wrote the Professor. 'I ceased some years ago to be surprised at the nature of *any* item printed by the daily Press. But I must confess that your leader has revealed to me depths which I had hitherto not suspected. I marvel, sir. I stand like a little child, and I marvel. Of all the barbarous, inaccurate, mischievous and positively harmful . . .' etc.

The President of the Spiritists Society, invited by telephone to say what he thought about Professor Wainflete's letter, coughed up handsomely by calling the Professor an old-fashioned materialist. He quoted Sir James Jeans. He also suggested that the Mammoth might be an emanation or earth-bound herd-spirit, given off by some part of the Downs where huge herds of mammoths had once grazed.

'I don't care if it's Gary Cooper in disguise,' crooned the news editor of the *Morning Star*. 'This is the best story since that chap killed his wife with a pencil-sharpener.'

The Mammoth Story rioted over the front pages of the Press for a fortnight; even *The Times* gave it eight lines at the bottom of a column and a veiled reference in a third leader.

It would not be true to say that people talked about nothing else; but they certainly talked about it a great deal. Society hostesses gave Mammoth Luncheons. Comedians made jokes about it. Mammoth hunting parties were organised and Carr, the famous barman at the Sheridan, invented a new cocktail which he called Tusker.

But Hooper was not satisfied.

He was the only other man in England who had seen the

236

Mammoth; and therefore he was the only man who believed that it was real. Mr Mitson agreed with the President of the Spiritists Society in believing it to be a ghost. As for Mrs Wilson and Miss Clipper, they were dismissed as hysterical females who probably imagined things.

Mr Mitson and Hooper had many a long talk about the Mammoth. Hooper was still down in Sussex, covering the story from that end, and he spent his evenings in the bar of the Rest in Peace.

Mr Mitson took the Mammoth very seriously indeed. He had temporarily retired on the money earned by two articles signed by himself and entitled: 'When I saw the Mammoth' and 'The Mammoth: What it Means'. These had been judiciously sub-edited by Hooper.

'The Mammoth: What it Means' had been a bit difficult to do because, if the matter were looked squarely in the face, the Mammoth did not seem to mean anything in particular except better trade for the cottages near Hurling which sold teas to motorists. But Hooper had a chat with the President of the Spiritists Society and spent one afternoon in the Natural History Museum and another in the reading-room of the British Museum library; and then turned out an article in a pure yet racy style which was, as even the news editor had to admit, 'pure Mitson in his later, and better, manner'.

But Hooper was puzzled.

He compared notes with Mr Mitson, and they agreed that it was queer that the Mammoth should restrict his appearances to the hour of dusk.

'Almost as though he didn't want to be seen,' mused Mr Mitson, who now assumed the airs of a connoisseur in mammoths. 'Funny kind of a walk he's got, too. Kind of a glide. Not 'uman, if you come to think of it. But then, come to think of it again, that's only natural.'

'Why?' demanded Miss Clipper, polishing a glass.

'Because he *ain't* human,' said Mr Mitson triumphantly.

237

'Well, if you ask me I think it's someone playing a joke,' said Mrs Wilson.

No one took any notice of this.

Three nights later two young men, driving home across the Downs after a party in Seacove, saw the Mammoth by bright moonlight, 'tossing its trunk in the air as though it were playing'. They telephoned the *Morning Star* just as the paper was going to bed, and the front page lay-out had to be altered. The General Election news was huddled into a corner. England awoke to read of 'Mammoth at Play on the Downs by Moonlight'. In the lunch edition of the evening papers this had changed to 'Mammoth's Moonlight Gambol on Downs'.

But Hooper, lounging in the bar of the Rest in Peace, was shaking his head. The Mammoth Story had gone just a little too far. Hooper smelt a rat, and fancied he knew its name.

He was studying a paragraph from a London paper's gossip column which stated that Sir Sam Range, the famous big-game-hunter, had taken Hurling House near Mammoth Wood (as Long Barrow Wood was now called) for the season.

'Is this mighty hunter hoping to get a pot at the Mammoth?' archly demanded the gossip-writer.

Hooper slipped the cutting into his pocket-book, and glanced out through the window at the slowly darkening sky.

'A perfect mammoth evening,' thought Hooper. 'I think I'll run up and see Sir Sam about the possibilities of a mammoth-shooting season on the South Downs.'

But when Hooper arrived at Hurling House he was not pleased to find a fellow-newspaperman, Jorrocks of the *Comet*, standing at the gate, silently listening to Sir Sam Range giving instructions to a couple of game-keepers who carried rifles. Sir Sam was armed with a heavier type of gun.

He glanced round as Hooper approached, and made a brief sign of welcome. He knew the reporter fairly well, who was himself a fair shot, as Hooper had interviewed him several times.

Hooper looked coldly at Jorrocks.

'We're going mammoth-hunting,' murmured Jorrocks. 'All of us. I came up here on the trail of that paragraph in the *Clarion* and walked into this peach of a story. Hooper . . . when I think that if I had been half an hour later I should have missed it, I almost believe in God.'

Hooper looked at him with distaste, and asked where they were to begin the search for their quarry?

'By Long Barrow Wood, I understand, where old Mitson first saw the brute . . . or thought he did. Oh, beg pardon, you saw it too, of course, didn't you? Sir Sam and the keepers are going to fire at sight. And if we don't see anything tonight we're coming out every night until we do see something.'

'Will he mind the publicity?'

'He'll eat it. And think of the kudos for him if he shoots the first mammoth on English soil.'

Hooper studied Jorrocks in silence, then shook his head.

'If you're not careful,' he said kindly, 'you'll find yourself seeing the Mammoth, too.'

The light had almost gone by the time the little party reached Long Barrow Wood. They approached Long Barrow itself from the wood side, so that the great mound was visible against the skyline between the trunks of the trees.

'If he's anywhere, he's about here somewhere,' breathed Sir Sam as they cautiously entered the wood, 'and this is the time to get him. The light couldn't be worse for shooting, of course, but he's big enough to hit at a mile if the stories are true.'

They paused among the last thin barrier of trees before the wood ended, full in face of Long Barrow itself.

'Now we'll lie down,' whispered Sir Sam, 'and wait. There's nothing else to be done. The odds are a million to one against our seeing anything, of course. Still, now we're here, we may as well stay.'

Contempt, scepticism and excitement were oddly mixed in his low, grumbling tones. He settled himself among the undergrowth with the noiselessness of an old hunter, and the other men did the same.

They had been waiting perhaps three-quarters of an hour, and Hooper was beginning to feel that he must smoke or shriek, when Jorrocks put out his hand stealthily and touched Sir Sam's arm.

Against the shadows, no more than a deepening of their darkness, another shadow was rearing up, between the watchers and the Long Barrow!

It was an enormous bulk, moving with a peculiar gliding motion.

There was not a sound. Not a leaf stirred.

Jorrocks felt the hair rising on his scalp as the enormous shadow began to move slowly up Long Barrow towards the skyline, and he saw a long trunk swaying before it, and the glimmer of its tusks.

Sir Sam was shaking with excitement. He wormed his way forward, followed by the others, until they left the trees behind them and were advancing over the turf towards the Barrow, towering black and ominous against the sky.

But Hooper, who was the least moved of the party, was listening hard, as they advanced, to catch a peculiar intermittent creaking noise which seemed to come from the direction of the mighty shadow.

It was exactly like the whine of an unoiled wheel.

And surely there was a peculiar stiffness about the lower part of the brute's body? The legs scarcely seemed to move; the bulk jerked, rather than glided, over the ground.

It was now towering on the twilight skyline scarcely fifty feet away.

Hooper's reflections were cut short by the splitting report of Sir Sam's rifle, followed, before the echoes had stopped tearing through the wood, by a second and a third.

'Fire, you fools, fire!' yelled Sir Sam, running forward (with insane courage, considering the situation) and the keepers, scarcely stopping to take aim, obeyed.

240

If the Mammoth doesn't get us, the keepers will, thought Hooper, dodging a bullet.

Then he saw an amazing sight.

The upper part of the Mammoth's body was shrinking!

Even as they advanced, encouraged by the curious stillness of that enormous shape, the great body collapsed between the pedestals of the legs with a long, sustained whistling sound like that made by escaping air.

'Fooled!' exclaimed Sir Sam grimly, and his torch flashed over the legs of painted canvas mounted on collapsible wire hoops, mounted on a wheeled stand. Between them sagged the body of black balloon silk, hung with coarse black hair.

'The biggest practical joke of the century, by gad! Look –' he smartly struck one of the legs with the butt of his gun, 'they collapse at a touch. You could pack the thing into a side-car.'

But Hooper had seen something else – the figures of two men running like hares across the dim turf towards the Hurling road, and with a shout he set off in pursuit, followed by the two keepers.

'Take a look at this, will you?' demanded Sir Sam, pursuing investigations with his torch.

'This' was a placard slung across the Mammoth's shapeless forehead.

EAT MAMMOTH WHEATNUTS AND VOTE
FOR SIR JOHN FIELD.

And across the bottom of the placard:

This is a Cosmos Advertisement.

Hooper, after a fierce chase and a battle, found himself sitting on the chest of his young friend Claude Field.

'You great fool, it's me,' said Claude coldly. 'Let me get up, can't you.'

'I thought as much,' said Hooper. 'As soon as you and

241

young Brabazon sent in that pretty tale about the Mammoth playing ball by moonlight, I began to wonder.'

'Get off my bosom, you big piece of cheese, and I'll tell you all about it.'

There was not much to tell. The Great Mammoth Story was rapidly dwindling into prose: and the story of how young Claude revived the Edwardian mania for practical joking on a Homeric scale, and won his small but secure place in the records of the social historians, is another story, spread over many years.

'Brabazon and I made Belisha (that's his name) in Brabazon's studio in Brightbourne. It was quite easy for us to slip out in the evening in the car, wait till it got dark, and then blow Belisha up. He was as easy to pull along as a toy motorcar; you just got behind one of his legs and hauled away. It was child's play. Honestly, I never thought it would go down half as well as it has.'

He paused. They were strolling back towards the forlorn, deflated mass of silk and hair that was Belisha. Brabazon had escaped the keepers, and driven off in Claude's car.

'You see,' pursued Claude, 'I was tired of being told at Cosmos that I couldn't think up stunts. I hope this will show the people there that I'm not cut out for routine.'

He paused again. When he spoke again his tone was a little less complacent.

'It's just father I'm thinking about, as a matter of fact. He may think it an undignified way of securing votes.'

He sighed.

'Older people are so amazingly rabid about their dignity, aren't they? Oh well . . . it was a good stunt, though I says it as shouldn't.'

And thus ended the Great Mammoth Story.

Excursion in Reality

EVELYN WAUGH

I

The commissionaire at Espinoza's restaurant seems to maintain under his particular authority all the most decrepit
taxicabs in London. He is a commanding man; across his
great chest the student of military medals may construe a tale
of heroism and experience; Boer farms sink to ashes, fanatical Fuzzi-wuzzies hurl themselves to paradise, supercilious
mandarins survey the smashing of their porcelain and rending of fine silk, in that triple row of decorations. He has only
to run from the steps of Espinoza's to call to your service a
vehicle as crazy as all the enemies of the King-Emperor.

Half-a-crown into the white cotton glove, because Simon
Lent was too tired to ask for change. He and Sylvia huddled
into the darkness on broken springs, between draughty windows. It had been an unsatisfactory evening. They had sat
over their table until two because it was an extension night.
Sylvia would not drink anything because Simon had said he
was broke. So they sat for five or six hours, sometimes silent,
sometimes bickering, sometimes exchanging listless greetings with the passing couples. Simon dropped Sylvia at her
door; a kiss, clumsily offered, coldly accepted; then back to
the attic flat, over a sleepless garage, for which Simon paid
six guineas a week.

Outside his door they were sluicing a limousine. He
squeezed round it and climbed the narrow stairs, that had
once echoed to the whistling of ostlers, stamping down to the
stables before dawn. (Woe to young men in Mewses! Oh woe,
to bachelors half in love, living on £800 a year!) There was a
small heap of letters on his dressing-table, which had arrived

243

that evening while he was dressing. He lit his gas fire and began to open them. Tailor's bill £56, hosier £43; a reminder that his club subscription for that year had not yet been paid; his account from Espinoza's with a note informing him that the terms were strict, net cash monthly, and that no further credit would be extended to him; it 'appeared from the books' of his bank that his last cheque overdrew his account £10 16s. beyond the limit of his guaranteed overdraft; a demand from the income-tax collector for particulars of his employees and their wages (Mrs Shaw, who came in to make his bed and orange juice for 4s. 6d. a day); small bills for books, spectacles, cigars, hair lotion and Sylvia's last four birthday presents. (Woe to shops that serve young men in Mewses!)

The other part of his mail was in marked contrast to this. There was a box of preserved figs from an admirer in Fresno, California; two letters from young ladies who said they were composing papers about his work for their college literary societies, and would he send a photograph; press cuttings describing him as a 'popular', 'brilliant', 'meteorically successful', and 'enviable' young novelist; a request for the loan of two hundred pounds from a paralysed journalist; an invitation to luncheon from Lady Metroland; six pages of closely reasoned abuse from a lunatic asylum in the North of England. For the truth, which no one who saw into Simon Lent's heart could possibly have suspected, was that he was in his way and within his limits quite a famous young man.

There was a last letter with a typewritten address which Simon opened with little expectation of pleasure. The paper was headed with the name of a Film Studio in one of the suburbs of London. The letter was brief and businesslike.

Dear Simon Lent [a form of address, he had noted before, largely favoured by the theatrical profession],

I wonder whether you have ever considered writing for the Films. We should value your angle on a picture we are now making. Perhaps you would meet me for luncheon tomorrow at the Garrick Club and let me know your reactions to this. Will you leave a message with my night-secretary some time before 8 a.m. tomorrow morning or with my day-secretary after that hour.

Cordially yours,

Below this were two words written in pen and ink which seemed to be *Jewee Mecceee* with below them the explanatory typescript (*Sir James Macrae*).

Simon read this through twice. Then he rang up Sir James Macrae and informed his night-secretary that he would keep the luncheon appointment next day. He had barely put down the telephone before the bell rang.

'This is Sir James Macrae's night-secretary speaking. Sir James would be very pleased if Mr Lent would come round and see him this evening at his house in Hampstead.'

Simon looked at his watch. It was nearly three. 'Well . . . it's rather late to go so far tonight . . .'

'Sir James is sending a car for you.'

Simon was no longer tired. As he waited for the car the telephone rang again. 'Simon,' said Sylvia's voice; 'are you asleep?'

'No, in fact I'm just going out.'

'*Simon* . . . I say, was I beastly tonight?'

'Lousy.'

'Well, I thought you were lousy too.'

'Never mind. See you sometime.'

'Aren't you going to go on talking?'

'Can't, I'm afraid. I've got to do some work.

'*Simon*, what *can* you mean?'

'Can't explain now. There's a car waiting.'

'When am I seeing you – tomorrow?'

'Well, I don't really know. Ring me up in the morning. Good night.'

A quarter of a mile away, Sylvia put down the telephone, rose from the hearthrug, where she had settled herself in the

expectation of twenty minutes' intimate explanation, and
crept disconsolately into bed.

Simon bowled off to Hampstead through deserted streets.
He sat back in the car in a state of pleasant excitement. Presently they began to climb the steep little hill and emerged
into an open space with a pond and the tops of trees, black
and deep as a jungle in the darkness. The night-butler admitted him to the low Georgian house and led him to the library, where Sir James Macrae was standing before the fire,
dressed in ginger-coloured plus-fours. A table was laid with
supper.

'Evening, Lent. Nice of you to come. Have to fit in business when I can. Cocoa or whisky? Have some rabbit pie, it's
rather good. First chance of a meal I've had since breakfast.
Ring for some more cocoa, there's a good chap. Now what
was it you wanted to see me about?'

'Well, I thought *you* wanted to see *me*.'

'Did I? Very likely. Miss Bentham'll know. She arranged the
appointment. You might ring the bell on the desk, will you?'

Simon rang and there instantly appeared the neat night-
secretary.

'Miss Bentham, what did I want to see Mr Lent about?'

'I'm afraid I couldn't say, Sir James. Miss Harper is
responsible for Mr Lent. When I came on duty this evening I
merely found a note from her asking me to fix an appointment as soon as possible.'

'Pity,' said Sir James. 'We'll have to wait until Miss Harper
comes on tomorrow.'

'I think it was something about writing for films.'

'Very likely,' said Sir James. 'Sure to be something of the
kind. I'll let you know without delay. Thanks for dropping in.'
He put down his cup of cocoa and held out his hand with
unaffected cordiality. 'Good night, my dear boy.' He rang the
bell for the night-butler. 'Sanders, I want Benson to run Mr
Lent back.'

246

'I'm sorry, sir. Benson has just gone down to the studio to fetch Miss Grits.'

'Pity,' said Sir James. 'Still, I expect you'll be able to pick up a taxi or something.'

II

Simon got to bed at half-past four. At ten minutes past eight the telephone by his bed was ringing.

'Mr Lent? This is Sir James Macrae's secretary speaking. Sir James's car will call for you at half-past eight to take you to the studio.'

'I shan't be ready as soon as that, I'm afraid.'

There was a shocked pause; then, the day-secretary said: 'Very well, Mr Lent. I will see if some alternative arrangement is possible and ring you in a few minutes.'

In the intervening time Simon fell asleep again. Then the bell woke him once more and the same impersonal voice addressed him.

'Mr Lent? I have spoken to Sir James. His car will call for you at eight forty-five.'

Simon dressed hastily. Mrs Shaw had not yet arrived, so there was no breakfast for him. He found some stale cake in the kitchen cupboard and was eating it when Sir James's car arrived. He took a slice down with him, still munching.

'You needn't have brought that,' said a severe voice from inside the car. 'Sir James has sent you some breakfast. Get in quickly; we're late.'

In the corner, huddled in rugs, sat a young woman in a jaunty red hat; she had bright eyes and a very firm mouth.

'I expect that you are Miss Harper.'

'No. I'm Elfreda Grits. We're working together on this film, I believe. I've been up all night with Sir James. If you don't mind I'll go to sleep for twenty minutes. You'll find a thermos of cocoa and some rabbit pie in the basket on the floor.'

'Does Sir James live on cocoa and rabbit pie?'

247

'No; those are the remains of his supper. Please don't talk. I want to sleep.'

Simon disregarded the pie, but poured some steaming cocoa into the metal cap of the thermos flask. In the corner, Miss Grits composed herself for sleep. She took off the jaunty red hat and laid it between them on the seat, veiled her eyes with two blue-pigmented lids and allowed the firm lips to relax and gape a little. Her platinum-blonde wind-swept head bobbed and swayed with the motion of the car as they swept out of London through converging and diverging tram lines. Stucco gave place to brick and the façades of the tube stations changed from tile to concrete; unoccupied building plots appeared and newly planted trees along unnamed avenues. Five minutes exactly before their arrival at the studio, Miss Grits opened her eyes, powdered her nose, touched her lips with red, and pulling her hat on to the side of her scalp, sat bolt upright, ready for another day.

Sir James was at work on the lot when they arrived. In a white-hot incandescent hell two young people were carrying on an infinitely tedious conversation at what was presumably the table of a restaurant. A dozen emaciated couples in evening dress danced listlessly behind them. At the other end of the huge shed some carpenters were at work building the façade of a Tudor manor house. Men in eye-shades scuttled in and out. Notices stood everywhere. *Do not Smoke. Do not Speak. Keep away from the high-power cable.*

Miss Grits, in defiance of these regulations, lit a cigarette, kicked some electric apparatus out of her path, said, 'He's busy. I expect he'll see us when he's through with this scene,' and disappeared through a door marked *No admittance.*

Shortly after eleven o'clock Sir James caught sight of Simon. 'Nice of you to come. Shan't be long now,' he called out to him. 'Mr Briggs, get a chair for Mr Lent.'

At two o'clock he noticed him again. 'Had any lunch?'

248

'No,' said Simon.

'No more have I. Just coming.'

At half-past three Miss Grits joined him and said: 'Well, it's been an easy day so far. You mustn't think we're always as slack as this. There's a canteen across the yard. Come and have something to eat.'

An enormous buffet was full of people in a variety of costume and make-up. Disappointed actresses in languorous attitudes served cups of tea and hard-boiled eggs. Simon and Miss Grits ordered sandwiches and were about to eat them when a loud-speaker above their heads suddenly announced with alarming distinctness, 'Sir James Macrae calling Mr Lent and Miss Grits in the Conference Room.'

'Come on, quick,' said Miss Grits. She bustled him through the swing doors, across the yard, into the office buildings and up a flight of stairs to a solid oak door marked *Conference. Keep out.*

Too late.

'Sir James has been called away,' said the secretary. 'Will you meet him at the West End office at five-thirty.'

Back to London, this time by tube. At five-thirty they were at the Piccadilly office ready for the next clue in their treasure hunt. This took them to Hampstead. Finally at eight they were back at the studio. Miss Grits showed no sign of exhaustion.

'Decent of the old boy to give us a day off,' she remarked. 'He's easy to work with in that way – after Hollywood. Let's get some supper.'

But as they opened the canteen doors and felt the warm breath of light refreshments, the loud-speaker again announced: 'Sir James Macrae calling Mr Lent and Miss Grits in the Conference Room.'

This time they were not too late. Sir James was there at the head of an oval table; round him were grouped the chiefs of his staff. He sat in a greatcoat with his head hung forward, elbows on the table and his hands clasped behind his neck.

The staff sat in respectful sympathy. Presently he looked up, shook himself and smiled pleasantly.

'Nice of you to come,' he said. 'Sorry I couldn't see you before. Lots of small things to see to on a job like this. Had dinner?'

'Not yet.'

'Pity. Have to eat, you know. Can't work at full pressure unless you eat plenty.'

Then Simon and Miss Grits sat down and Sir James explained his plan. 'I want, ladies and gentlemen, to introduce Mr Lent to you. I'm sure you all know his name already and I daresay some of you know his work. Well, I've called him in to help us and I hope that when he's heard the plan he'll consent to join us. I want to produce a film of *Hamlet*. I daresay you don't think that's a very original idea – but it's Angle that counts in the film world. I'm going to do it from an entirely new angle. That's why I've called in Mr Lent. I want him to write dialogue for us.'

'But, surely,' said Simon, 'there's quite a lot of dialogue there already?'

'Ah, you don't see my angle. There have been plenty of productions of Shakespeare in modern dress. We are going to produce him in modern speech. How can you expect the public to enjoy Shakespeare when they can't make head or tail of the dialogue. D'you know I began reading a copy the other day and blessed if *I* could understand it. At once I said, "What the public wants is Shakespeare with all his beauty of thought and character translated into the language of everyday life." Now Mr Lent here was the man whose name naturally suggested itself. Many of the most high-class critics have commended Mr Lent's dialogue. Now my idea is that Miss Grits here shall act in an advisory capacity, helping with the continuity and the technical side, and that Mr Lent shall be given a free hand with the scenario . . .'

The discourse lasted for a quarter of an hour; then the chiefs of staff nodded sagely; Simon was taken into another room and given a contract to sign by which he received £50 a week retaining fee and £250 advance.

'You had better fix up with Miss Grits the times of work most suitable to you. I shall expect your first treatment by the end of the week. I should go and get some dinner if I were you. Must eat.'

Slightly dizzy, Simon hurried to the canteen where two languorous blondes were packing up for the night.

'We've been on since four o'clock this morning,' they said, 'and the supers have eaten everything except the nougat. Sorry.'

Sucking a bar of nougat Simon emerged into the now deserted studio. On three sides of him, to the height of twelve feet, rose in appalling completeness the marble walls of the scene-restaurant; at his elbow a bottle of imitation champagne still stood in its pail of melted ice; above and beyond extended the vast gloom of rafters and ceiling.

'*Fact*,' said Simon to himself, 'the world of action . . . the pulse of life . . . Money, hunger . . . *Reality*.'

Next morning he was called with the words, 'Two young ladies waiting to see you.'

'Two?'

Simon put on his dressing-gown and, orange juice in hand, entered his sitting-room. Miss Grits nodded pleasantly.

'We arranged to start at ten,' she said. 'But it doesn't really matter. I shall not require you very much in the early stages. This is Miss Dawkins. She is one of the staff stenographers. Sir James thought you would need one. Miss Dawkins will be attached to you until further notice. He also sent two copies of *Hamlet*. When you've had your bath, I'll read you my notes for our first treatment.'

But this was not to be; before Simon was dressed Miss Grits had been recalled to the studio on urgent business.

'I'll ring up and tell you when I am free,' she said.

Simon spent the morning dictating letters to everyone he

could think of; they began – *Please forgive me for dictating this, but I am so busy just now that I have little time for personal correspondence . . .*' Miss Dawkins sat deferentially over her pad. He gave her Sylvia's number.

'Will you get on to this number and present my compliments to Miss Lennox and ask her to luncheon at Espinoza's . . . And book a table for two there at one forty-five.'

'Darling,' said Sylvia, when they met, 'why were you out all yesterday and *who* was that voice this morning?'

'Oh, that was Miss Dawkins, my stenographer.'

'Simon, what *can* you mean?'

'You see, I've joined the film industry.'

'*Darling*. Do give me a job.'

'Well, I'm not paying much attention to casting at the moment – but I'll bear you in mind.'

'Goodness. How you've changed in two days!'

'Yes!' said Simon, with great complacency. 'Yes, I think I have. You see, for the first time in my life I have come into contact with Real Life. I'm going to give up writing novels. It was a mug's game anyway. The written word is dead – first the papyrus, then the printed book, now the film. The artist must no longer work alone. He is part of the age in which he lives; he must share (only of course, my dear Sylvia, in very different proportions) the weekly wage envelope of the proletarian. Vital art implies a corresponding set of social relationships. Co-operation . . . co-ordination . . . the hive endeavour of the community directed to a single end . . .'

Simon continued in this strain at some length, eating meantime a luncheon of Dickensian dimensions, until, in a small, miserable voice, Sylvia said: 'It seems to me that you've fallen for some ghastly film star.'

'O God,' said Simon, 'only a virgin could be as vulgar as that.'

They were about to start one of their old, interminable quarrels when the telephone boy brought a message that Miss Grits wished to resume work instantly.

'So that's her name,' said Sylvia.

'If you only knew how funny that was,' said Simon, scribbling his initials on the bill and leaving the table while Sylvia was still groping with gloves and bag.

As things turned out, however, he became Miss Grits's lover before the week was out. The idea was hers. She suggested it to him one evening at his flat as they corrected the typescript of the final version of their first treatment.

'No, really,' Simon said aghast. 'No, really. It would be quite impossible. I'm sorry, but . . .'

'Why? Don't you like women?'

'Yes, but . . .'

'Oh, come along,' Miss Grits said briskly. 'We don't get much time for amusement . . .' And later, as she packed their manuscripts into her attaché case, she said, 'We must do it again if we have time. Besides I find it's so much easier to work with a man if you're having an *affaire* with him.'

III

For three weeks Simon and Miss Grits (he always thought of her by this name in spite of all subsequent intimacies) worked together in complete harmony. His life was redirected and transfigured. No longer did he lie in bed, glumly preparing himself for the coming day; no longer did he say every morning, 'I *must* get down to the country and finish that book,' and every evening find himself slinking back to the same urban flat; no longer did he sit over supper tables with Sylvia, idly bickering; no more listless explanations over the telephone. Instead he pursued a routine of incalculable variety, summoned by telephone at all hours to conferences which rarely assembled; sometimes to Hampstead, sometimes to the studios, once to Brighton. He spent long periods of work pacing up and down his sitting-room, with Miss Grits pacing backwards and forwards along the other wall and Miss Dawkins obediently perched between them, as the

253

two dictated, corrected and redrafted their scenario. There were meals at improbable times and vivid, unsentimental passages of love with Miss Grits. He ate irregular and improbable meals, bowling through the suburbs in Sir James's car, pacing the carpet dictating to Miss Dawkins, perched in deserted lots upon scenery which seemed made to survive the collapse of civilisation. He lapsed, like Miss Grits, into brief spells of death-like unconsciousness, often awakening, startled, to find that a street or desert or factory had come into being about him while he slept.

The film meanwhile grew rapidly, daily putting out new shoots and changing under their eyes in a hundred unexpected ways. Each conference produced some radical change in the story. Miss Grits in her precise, unvariable voice would read out the fruits of their work. Sir James would sit with his head in his hand, rocking slightly from side to side and giving vent to occasional low moans and whimpers; round him sat the experts – production, direction, casting, continuity, cutting and costing managers, bright eyes, eager to attract the great man's attention with some apt intrusion.

'Well,' Sir James would say, 'I think we can OK that. Any suggestions, gentlemen?'

There would be a pause, until one by one the experts began to deliver their contributions . . . 'I've been thinking, sir, that it won't do to have the scene laid in Denmark. The public won't stand for travel stuff. How about setting it in Scotland – then we could have some kilts and clan gathering scenes?'

'Yes, that's a very sensible suggestion. Make a note of that, Lent . . .'

'I was thinking we'd better drop this character of the Queen. She'd much better be dead before the action starts. She hangs up the action. The public won't stand for him abusing his mother.'

'Yes, make a note of that, Lent.'

254

'How would it be, sir, to make the ghost the Queen instead of the King . . .'

'Yes, make a note of that Lent . . .'

'Don't you think, sir, it would be better if Ophelia were Horatio's sister. More poignant, if you see what I mean.'

'Yes, make a note of that . . .'

'I think we are losing sight of the essence of the story in the last sequence. After all, it is first and foremost a Ghost Story, isn't it?. . .'

And so from simple beginnings the story spread majestically. It was in the second week that Sir James, after, it must be admitted, considerable debate, adopted the idea of incorporating with it the story of *Macbeth*. Simon was opposed to the proposition at first, but the appeal of the three witches proved too strong. The title was then changed to *The White Lady of Dunsinane*, and he and Miss Grits settled down to a prodigious week's work in rewriting their entire scenarios.

IV

The end came as suddenly as everything else in this remarkable episode. The third conference was being held at an hotel in the New Forest where Sir James happened to be staying; the experts had assembled by train, car and motor-bicycle at a moment's notice and were tired and unresponsive. Miss Grits read the latest scenario; it took some time, for it had now reached the stage when it could be taken as 'white script' ready for shooting. Sir James sat sunk in reflection longer than usual. When he raised his head, it was to utter the single word:

'No.'

'No?'

'No, it won't do. We must scrap the whole thing. We've got much too far from the original story. I can't think why you need introduce Julius Caesar and King Arthur at all.'

'But, sir, they were your own suggestions at the last conference.'

'Were they? Well, I can't help it. I must have been tired and not paying full attention . . . Besides, I don't like the dialogue. It misses all the poetry of the original. What the public wants is Shakespeare, the whole of Shakespeare and nothing but Shakespeare. Now this scenario you've written is all very well in its way – but it's not Shakespeare. I'll tell you what we'll do. We'll use the play exactly as he wrote it and record from that. Make a note of it, Miss Grits.'

'Then you'll hardly require my services any more?' said Simon.

'No, I don't think I shall. Still, nice of you to have come.'

Next morning Simon woke bright and cheerful as usual and was about to leap from his bed when he suddenly remembered the events of last night. There was nothing for him to do. An empty day lay before him. No Miss Grits, no Miss Dawkins, no scampering off to conferences or dictating of dialogue. He rang up Miss Grits and asked her to lunch with him.

'No, quite impossible, I'm afraid. I have to do the continuity for a scenario of St John's Gospel before the end of the week. Pretty tough job. We're setting it in Algeria so as to get the atmosphere. Off to Hollywood next month. Don't suppose I shall see you again. Good-bye.'

Simon lay in bed with all his energy slowly slipping away. Nothing to do. Well, he supposed, now was the time to go away to the country and get on with his novel. Or should he go abroad? Some quiet café-restaurant in the sun where he could work out those intractable last chapters. That was what he would do . . . sometime . . . the end of the week perhaps.

Meanwhile he leaned over on his elbow, lifted the telephone and, asking for Sylvia's number, prepared himself for twenty-five minutes' acrimonious reconciliation.

The Xerox in the Lost Room

ROBERTSON DAVIES

Those of you who have attended several of these Christmas Parties are aware how extensively, indeed extravagantly, this College is haunted. Every year a ghost; sometimes more than one. I cannot explain how a new building in a new country – or a country that pretends it is new, although in reality it is very old – comes to be so afflicted with what our university sociologists call 'spectral density'. I suspect it has something to do with the concentration of our College community, senior and junior, on intellectual things. There is in Nature a need for balance, a compensating principle which demands in our case that where there is too much rationality there should be occasional outbreaks of irrationality. I offer my explanation tentatively, because I am no philosopher and certainly no scientist, and detractors have said that rationality is a quality by which I am seldom overwhelmed.

It could also be that there is a housing shortage in the World Beyond, just as there is here below. Everybody is aware of the alarming rate at which the world's population is increasing. In the lifetime of some of us it has very nearly doubled. More people and thus, inevitably, more ghosts. Where are they to put themselves? Many of them are emigrating from the lands of their origin and coming to Canada, which is still comparatively open, especially in the spiritual aspect of things. That may be the explanation.

Over the years our ghosts have tended to be from the upper ranks of the spirit world; it is an odd fact that the poor and humble rarely have ghosts. Celebrated people have haunted us; now and then we have bagged a spectral crowned head, but as a general thing our ghosts are drawn from the intelligentsia. I confess with shame that this has betrayed me into a measure of vanity. I catch myself wondering, early in January, 'Who will it be this year?' And then I consult a list of anniversaries falling in the year to come. Ghosts, you know, are not always tied to the places where their earthly life was passed; now and then they are granted a freedom of movement which is called a Witches' Sabbatical.

Last January I looked eagerly to see who would be on tour, so to speak, and my eye fell upon the name of Henrik Ibsen. It was the 150th anniversary of his birth, and all over the world a good deal of fuss was going to be made. Ibsen! My mouth watered. To be visited by that mighty dramatist, considered by so many people to be the greatest of his kind since Shakespeare – what a cultural *coup* that would be! Why would he visit us? Canada reflects the social world of Ibsen as much as any country in the world today. Surely he would come to Canada, if only to sneer. And, as you know, we contain within our walls the University's Centre for the Study of Drama, and I knew that Ibsen would be in their minds, and on their tongues. Surely the great man would favour us with a few morose words. But then I reproached myself. It is stupid to count your ghosts before they are manifested. Down, vanity! Down, worldly aspiration, I cried; and they downed. But not totally. From time to time I surprised, at the back of my mind, an unworthy hankering.

When December arrived, I was nervously aware that time was getting on. Henrik Ibsen was late. It was not like him. All through his life he was known for his punctiliousness about appointments. If he said he would do a thing, he would do it, especially if it were something disagreeable. But then I came to my senses; Ibsen had promised nothing; this whole business of his visit was a foolish whimwham of my own. You should be ashamed of yourself, I said; and I was obediently ashamed of myself. Nevertheless, deep in the undisciplined abyss of my mind, that hankering continued.

258

The resolution of the affair came, as it so often does, on the night of our College Dance. It has long been my custom, after the supper which is a feature of our dance, to go out into the quad and take a few turns up and down. It is then that I often see ghosts. Nothing to do with the supper, I assure you, because I never take anything but a cup of coffee. Perhaps it has something to do with the excitement of seeing this quiet place turned, for one evening, into a palace of delights. So, as I paced the familiar flagstones in the chill air, I was not surprised to see a stranger standing – lurking, to be more precise – in a dark corner.

My heart leapt within me. Was it he? The figure was slight for Henrik Ibsen who, as you know from his photographs, was built rather like a barrel encased in a frock coat. And the hat – where was the resplendent silk hat which was the great man's invariable outdoor wear? As I drew nearer it was plain that the figure was wrapped in a cloak, which, even in darkness, looked shabby. And the hat was quite wrong; it was a three-cornered hat. Unless Ibsen had chosen for some inexplicable reason to get himself up as a figure from the early eighteenth century, this was the wrong ghost. I was disappointed and annoyed and perhaps I spoke abruptly. What I said was 'Well?' with that upward intonation that makes it clear that it is not at all well.

'If you please,' said the ghost, 'I am looking for a modest, dry lodging in quiet surroundings.'

'This is an odd time to be looking for a room,' said I. 'You should come back in daylight and speak to the Bursar. If you are able to appear in daylight,' I added, nastily.

'Please don't be severe with me,' said the ghost in such a pitiful tone that I felt ashamed of myself. 'My need is very great, and I must find a place tonight, or terrible things will happen to me.' He was almost weeping.

'I have no wish to be severe,' said I, 'but you must understand that this college has a purpose to fulfil in the university, and that purpose makes no provision for—'

'For people in my situation?' said the ghost. 'But you are famous for your hospitality toward ghosts. Ah, but I see,' he continued, 'you are only interested in famous ghosts, and I am a sadly obscure person. That has been the pathos of my life. If I were not such a failure, I would use a stronger word than pathos; I would say tragedy.'

Poor fellow! I felt thoroughly ashamed of myself. Here I was, hankering after the ghost of a world-famous dramatist and behaving with abominable callousness to a poor phantom whose life had been a tragedy perhaps deeper than any Ibsen had conceived. Tears filled my eyes.

I should have known better. Ghosts are all rampaging egotists – forces of egotism that refuse to accept death as a fact. The ghost before me was now fixing me with a baleful glare, and I felt its hand laid with icy firmness on my sleeve.

'List, list to me,' said the ghost; 'I could a tale unfold whose lightest word would harrow up thy soul, freeze thy young blood—'

'All right, all right,' I said impatiently. 'If you must – and believe me I know how communicative you ghosts can be – let me have it as briefly as possible, and without poetry. I'm very well up in *Hamlet*. Who are you?'

'That is my trouble,' said the ghost. 'I'm a private person, but not therefore utterly without poetry and feeling. In life I was that particular type of gentleperson called a Poor Relation.'

'Whose Poor Relation were you?' said I.

'A Rich Relation's, of course. He was a country squire in Gloucestershire. Not an ill-natured fellow. He knew I had no prospects and no luck, and he let me live in his manor house in a subordinate position, helping with the estate accounts, writing letters, teaching the children a little Latin, and sometimes drawing scale plans for his drainage projects, while he and the Vicar were out shooting. You know the kind of things Poor Relations do. I had been something of a scholar, you see, and I had hoped for a college fellowship, but I had no

influential friends; I had hoped to enter the Church, but the Bishop had too many nephews, and altogether I was a failure and a dependant. I didn't complain. Not very much, that is to say. But I was a cousin of the squire, and it irked me that the servants treated me so badly.'

This was the sorriest excuse for a ghost I had ever met. Failure in the spirit world is particularly chilling, and I was beginning to shiver. But I couldn't break away. It would have been unfeeling.

'But you have apparently achieved some success after death,' said I. 'You are a ghost, and you are far from home. How have you got leave to travel?'

'That is the saddest part of my story,' said he. 'But you must hear me out. Don't bustle me.'

I groaned, but I had not the heart to leave him.

'It came to a head this very night, two hundred and fifty years ago,' said the ghost. 'It was on December the ninth, in 1728. Our good King George II had just entered the eleventh year of his long reign—'

'Yes, yes,' said I; 'I know a little history myself. Do make haste.'

'What a fidget you are,' said the ghost, rather sharply I thought for a Poor Relation. 'Then hear me. My cousin, the squire, and his lady had gone to Sudeley Castle, to a ball. I was not invited. Of course not. I was a nobody and I had no fine clothes. I was left at home without even a word of apology. Nor had any dinner been ordered. My cousin's wife, who was inclined to be mean, said that doubtless I could get something in the kitchen with the servants.

'That would not have been so bad, because the servants saw to it that they ate very well, but it meant that I had to brave my greatest enemy, the butler; he took every chance to make me feel my position as a Poor Relation. And that night he was particularly tyrannous, because he was drunk. We quarrelled. He killed me.'

'Stabbed you?' I asked.

'No.'

'Shot you? The great kitchen blunderbuss, kept above the chimney, loaded in case of burglars? In his drunken rage the butler tore it from its place and shot you while the women-folk screamed?'

'You have been seeing too much television,' said the ghost. 'The eighteenth century wasn't like that at all.'

I continued to be hopeful and romantic. 'But the quarrel,' I said; 'he insulted you, spoke slightingly of your birth, and your good blood was aroused. You lunged at him with your sword, but lost your footing, and he seized the sword and stabbed you to the heart. Please say it was like that.'

'I never owned a sword in my life,' said the ghost. 'Nasty, dangerous things. No: I'll tell you exactly how it was. I was rather drunk myself, you see, and we were having a dispute about how to make boot-blacking. I had complained that the blacking he used had too much brown sugar in it. You know, the secret of good boot-blacking is the proportion of brown sugar to the amount of soot and vinegar. It's the butler's work to make it. And I said he put in too much brown sugar. I said my boots were always sticky. He said I lied. I said he forgot himself in the presence of his betters. He said what betters, and I was no more than a servant myself and begged the Squire's old wigs. Then I absent-mindedly picked up a table fork and stuck it into his right buttock. He must have had very soft flesh because it went much farther in than I had expected. Right up to the handle. Then he picked up a pewter tankard and hit me over the head, and to my surprise and indignation I fell to the floor, dead as a nit.'

This was the lowest ghost I had ever been pestered by. A wearer of second-hand wigs! Brained in a kitchen brawl with a pewter pot! And he had the gall to haunt Massey College! Nevertheless, as a tale of low-life, this had its interest.

'What happened then?' I asked.

'That was the cream of the whole thing,' said the ghost, as near to laughter as a ghost can get. 'You see, as soon as the

262

butler hit me with that pot, I found myself about nine inches above the ground, watching everything – myself stretched out on the floor, the cook trying to staunch the blood from my head with a towel, all the maids in hysterics, the footman saying he knew it would come to this some day, and the butler, as white as a sheet, blubbering: "Oh zur, come back I beg 'ee. I never went fur to do it, zur. Come back and I'll go light on the brown sugar as long as I live, indeed zur, I will." But it was hopeless. I was gone, so far as they were concerned. The butler ran off and became a highwayman, but he was too fat and stupid for the work, and he was caught and hanged within a year.

'But there was one thing about the affair that was truly impressive. The cook was a wise woman, in her fashion, and before the butler ran off she begged him to taste my blood – just a little, just to dip his finger in the blood and lick it. He refused. She took a few licks herself, to show him that there was nothing really unpleasant about it, but of course she was professionally accustomed to tasting uncooked substances. Why? Because, you see, she knew that if he did that my ghost would never be able to appear. Now you remember that, if ever you kill anybody; swallow some of his blood, or you'll be sorry. But of course in these days so many murderers are careless and ignorant that what I am telling you has almost been forgotten. I have always been glad that butler was thoroughly stupid; otherwise my fine career, my real achievement, would have been impossible.'

The ghost was markedly more cheerful, now. 'Do you know, that was the best thing that ever happened to me? From being a Poor Relation, I was suddenly promoted to Family Ghost. My cousin and his wife were proud of me, and as succeeding generations appeared in the manor I became quite a celebrity. I was once investigated by the Society for Psychical Research, and Harry Price himself gave me the coveted three-star rating: Accredited Spectre, First Class.'

I continued to be patient, under difficulties. 'But what brings you here?' I asked. A ghost from Gloucestershire with a nice little local reputation – what sent him travelling?

He groaned. All ghosts groan, and it is a very disquieting sound. This ghost was a first-rate groaner.

'You read the newspapers, I suppose?' he said.

'Unfailingly,' I replied.

'Zena Cherry?' said he.

'Religiously,' said I, and made the sign of the gossip columnist – one hand cupped to the ear, the other reaching for the pencil.

'Then surely you remember her account of the old English manor house that had been bought by a Toronto entrepreneur and re-built, stone by stone, in Don Mills, near the Bridle Path?'

I did remember it.

'It was, literally, an uprooting,' said the ghost. 'But I took it philosophically. The trouble with a ghost's situation, you see, is the sameness of it. After two hundred and fifty years I was beginning to feel housebound, and I thought a new country, new people to frighten, new people to boast about me, would be an adventure. So I didn't mind the move to Toronto; the journey by airline freight wasn't bad, in spite of the delays by strikes. But when I arrived at last, all sorts of terrible things began to happen.'

'Climate unfavourable, I suppose?' said I, sympathetically.

'Not that, so much as the structural changes,' said the ghost. 'Our splendid old manor-house kitchen was thought too big for a Canadian dwelling. To begin, it was a good hundred and forty feet from the dining-room, and there was a flight of stone stairs on the way. You should have heard what the real-estate people had to say about that! And it had a flagstone floor, which was hard and cold to Canadian feet. Further, our house was a proper gentleman's residence, and without a butler and a footman and six maids and a cook and a scullion nothing more ambitious than sandwiches could be managed. So the real-estate people decided that an entirely new kitchen should be built, and the old kitchen should become something called a rumpus room, where the children of the family could be at a suitable distance from their elders. I gather that "rumpus" is the modern word for what in my day was called hullabaloo.

'To accommodate the new kitchen, the contractor bought in England and transferred to Don Mills an object that would never be seen attached to a respectable manor. It was an oasthouse. You know what an oast-house is?'

I didn't.

'It's a kiln for drying hops, a great tower-like building with a pointed roof. An unseemly object. But they stuck it to the side of the manor, right by the dining-room, and put a modern kitchen in it.

'A modern kitchen is no place for a ghost. Crackling with electric current, cold things, hot things, and cramped so that one miserable servant can do the work of five. Where is the inglenook, where visiting grooms and coachmen can dry themselves in bad weather? Where is the cheerful fire, and the spit, the dogs, the cat and her kittens, the hens running in and out, the ducks peeping in at the door, and, in winter, the shadowy corners for haunting? But the worst thing of all was that the builders and the contractor couldn't get the name right, and they called the horrid thing an oaf-house. Who wants to haunt an oaf-house, I ask you? A Poor Relation I may have been, but an oaf – never!

'Nevertheless, I determined to make the best of it. All immigrants have a hard time in a new country, for a few hundred years. I decided to divide my time between the oaf-house, on the housekeeper's day off, and the rumpus room when the children weren't doing whatever children do in a rumpus room, which is something I never found out.

'Because, you see, the house didn't sell. Even with all the tinkering and destruction and costly misery and modern convenience it somehow failed to catch on. So the people who were trying to sell it hit on a great idea; they would let the public visit it.

'That was the end, for me. We phantoms have our feelings, and I never undertook to haunt wholesale, so to speak. Servants I will frighten – yes, gladly. Gentlefolk of my own kindred I will provide with the thrill of a true family phantom, though I have always drawn the line at manifesting myself to more than two at a time – usually a man and his wife or, better still, somebody who ought to be his wife. But haunt I must. It is part of my condition of existence, you see. Unless I make an appearance at least once a year, I am in serious trouble with – well, never you mind who. But appearing to people who have paid admission on behalf of a charity – no, no, the thing is not to be thought of.'

'I suppose a great many people visited the house?' said I. I knew what had happened, but I wanted to hear his version of it.

'They came by scores and hundreds,' said he. 'And what they did to our family manor beggars description, as Old Shakespeare says. They invited Toronto decorators to refurbish it, a room to each decorator, and the decorators themselves made my eyes start out of my head. They were men of an affected elegance – what in my day might have been called exquisites or beaux, except that these were not gentlemen – they worked for their living, and what they sold was Taste. As if anyone of any consequence ever had taste, or wanted any! They filled our comfortable old manor with spindly walnut and mahogany that might have done well enough in a fashionable bawdy-house in London, but was not to be compared with our comfortable old oak and chairs stuffed with the wool of our own sheep. They brought in pictures of people nobody had ever heard of, and declared they were by Sir Peter Lely and later masters. They stuck up curtains and threw down carpets of horrid gaudy colours, as if brown were not the only colour a lady of good family would endure in her rooms. But there was worse to come, much worse.

266

'They did up some of the rooms in what they called "contemporary taste" and that was Chaos and Old Night, I assure you. They papered the floors, and stuck fur to the walls, and hung pictures by madmen, and set out furniture in which even I, as a weightless spectre, could not have sat with any comfort. And when all this was done the procession of viewers appeared. They were the friends of the Women's Committees of the charities that were to be benefited by this dreadful rape of my dear old manor, and they tramped everywhere and poked into everything.

'They seemed to have no idea of the comforts of an eighteenth-century house, and so they admired all the po-boxes in the bedrooms and said what charming little bedside tables they were, and they admired the silver chamber-pot my cousin had kept in the dining-room sideboard, for his convenience after dinner, and to my shame it was kept in full sight, filled with flowers. They loved all the modern rooms because they reminded them of their own homes. Best of all they liked the new kitchen, and said how wonderful it was that an inconvenient old manor could be so elegantly adapted for really civilized living. There were blue-haired ladies who came in aid of the Art Gallery and there were ladies with hair of improbable shades who came in aid of the Ballet, and noisy stout ladies who were patrons of Opera, and there were garden ladies who came to see the dreadful tropical plants that the decorators called "growies" which were stuck up everywhere -- as if garden rubbish didn't belong outside a respectable gentleman's house.'

'And you couldn't bear it?' said I, sympathetically.

'I could bear everything,' said he, and I swear that if ever a ghost had tears in his eyes, it was at that moment. 'Everything, that is, except the air-conditioning. Would you believe that they filled the fine old walls with metal guts that conveyed jets of air that stank of mice to every part of that dear old place – jets that squirted out where one least expected, blowing me about like a leaf in a storm and playing merry hell with my ectoplasm until I developed the worst case of phantom arthritis that has ever been seen at any of our Hallowe'en meetings. That was the finish. That settled the matter for ever. I had to leave or I should have become a mere knotted bundle of malice, and would probably have dwindled into a Poltergeist of the lowest class. It was leave my home or lose countenance irreparably in the phantom world.

'So will you take me in? You are a modern foundation, I know, but your College has some of what I regard as the comforts of home. Draughts, mostly; I miss normal, healthy draughts more than you can imagine.'

I pondered, and that is always fatal, for when I ponder my resolution leaks away. He was a humble creature, as ghosts go, but his story had gone to my heart. Still – where on earth was I to put him?

'I could make myself useful,' he said, wistfully. 'I have heard that a trade flourishes on this continent – that of a Ghost Writer, and I know a lot of writing is done here. Yourself, for instance. I know you write romances, and though I despise romances, perhaps, in time, I could grind out a three-volume novel about an unfortunate young man who wanted to be a college fellow, and then wanted to take holy orders, but who was slain untimely in an affair of honour with an aristocratic adversary. I promise to put in lots of theology. You could sign it, of course.'

'No,' I said firmly, 'that wouldn't do at all.'

He looked very forlorn, and he seemed to grow more transparent as grief overcame him. 'Could I copy manuscripts?' he pleaded.

I had a flash of illumination! Our Xerox machine in the College is terribly inadequate, and a copyist would be a great benefit to us – especially a copyist who was cheap.

But where was I to put him? I cudgelled my brains and then – another flash – I had the answer.

Years ago, when this College building was completed, the architect, Mr Thom, presented me with a set of plans. I

268

counted the rooms for occupation by Junior Fellows – and I paused. Then I went through the College with the Bursar and we counted, and counted again, and however carefully we counted there were three rooms in the plan which could not be found in the building. I made enquiry of Mr Thom. 'Yes,' he said, in the abstracted manner which is characteristic of architects, 'when I had made all the alterations the founders called for, three rooms somehow got mislaid. Walls were moved, and jogs and corners were eliminated, and somehow or other three rooms disappeared. They are there, in a way, and yet in another way they aren't there.'

Without a word, I led the ghost up to the top of staircase number three, until we confronted a blank wall. 'Here is your room,' said I; 'I don't pretend that I can see it myself, but perhaps you can.'

It was a risk on my part, and it worked. The ghost vanished through the wall, but I could hear his voice, and for the first time since we met, its tone was cheerful.

'Of course,' he cried; 'the very thing I've always wanted. Commodious, a charming view of the quad, several strong draughts, and no modern conveniences whatever. Bless you, sir, bless you.'

I was rid of him, for the moment. I made a chalk mark on the wall where his door seemed to be. In a day or two I would hunt him up and instruct him in his new duties as an unseen and unrequited Xerox.

As I walked back through the quad with a light heart I suddenly saw – my heart leapt into my mouth – I suddenly saw a figure, familiar to me from a score of nineteenth-century photographs, standing near the gate, looking about him with an air of deep disapproval. That barrel-shaped body in the impeccable frock coat; that tall silk hat of surpassing splendour. It must be he! I was to be rewarded for my good deed! I rushed forward, my hand outstretched.

'Dr Ibsen!' I cried; 'you have come at last. Do stay a while! Do come inside! Have a glass of aquavit! Let us have a really

269

splendid talk about your work! And will you honour me by inscribing my copy of your great drama, *Ghosts*?'

Ibsen – for indeed it was he – bent upon me a gaze that was like being transfixed by two little knives. His thin lips parted, and a single word escaped the prison-house of his formidable countenance.

'Tvertimot,' said he, and without another word he vanished through the bars of our gate.

Tvertimot! Tvertimot – that supremely characteristic utterance had been the last word he spoke on his deathbed! I rushed into my study, dragged down my great Dictionary of the Norwegian Tongue and looked it up with trembling hands.

'Tvertimot', said the entry: 'Quite the contrary, or colloquially, Not on your Nellie.'

Well, I reflected, not a bad year for ghosts after all. We had acquired an additional Xerox, and Ibsen had dropped in for a sneer.

The 2003 Claret

KINGSLEY AMIS

'How long to go now?' the Director asked for the tenth time.

I compared the main laboratory chronometer with the dial on the TIOPEPE (Temporal Integrator, Ordinal Predictor and Electronic Propulsion Equipment). 'He should be taking the trance-pill in a few seconds, sir,' I said. 'Then there's only the two minutes for it to take effect, and we can bring him back.'

'Supposing he hasn't taken the pill?'

'I'm sure he'd survive the time-shift even if he were fully conscious, sir. It's instantaneous, after all.'

'I know, but being snatched back from fifty years in the future can't do a man's mind any good, can it? We just don't know what we're up against, Baker. I wish those blasted politicians had let us go slow on this project. But no, there mustn't be any delay or the Russians will have developed time-travel before the Atlantic Powers, so we bundle Simpson off to the year 2010 and if we lose him or he turns up a raving lunatic it's our fault.' The Director sat moodily down on a work-bench. 'What happens if he gets tight?'

'He won't have done that, sir. Simpson's one of the Knights of Bordeaux. They never get drunk – isn't it a rule of the society?'

'I believe so, yes.' The Director cheered up a little. 'He'll probably have a good deal to tell us, with any luck. The Douro growers are saying that last year was the best since 1945, you know, Baker. Imagine what that stuff must be like where Simpson is. Just one glass—'

'Did you actually tell Simpson to sample the wines in 2010?'

The Director coughed. 'Well, I did just make the suggestion to him. After all, part of our terms of reference was to report on social conditions, in addition to the political situation. And drinking habits are a pretty good guide to the social set-up, aren't they? Find out how people treat their port and you've found out a lot about the kind of people they are.'

'Something in that, sir.' I'm a beer man myself, which made me a bit of an outsider in the team. There were only the four of us in the lab that night – the VIPs and the press boys had been pushed into the Conference Room, thank heaven – and all the other three were wine-bibbers of one sort or another. The Director, as you will have gathered, was fanatical about port; Rabaiotti, my senior assistant, belonged to a big Chianti family; and Schneider, the medical chap, had written a book on hock. Simpson was reputedly on the way to becoming a sound judge of claret, though I had sometimes wondered whether perhaps tactical considerations played their part in his choice of hobby. Anyway, I considered I was lucky to have got the job of Chief Time-Engineer, against competition that included a force-field expert who doubled as an amateur of old Madeira, and an electronics king named Gilbey – no relation, it turned out, but the Director couldn't have known that at the time.

'The receiver is tuned, Dr Baker.'

'Thank you, Dr Rabaiotti. Would you like to operate the recall switch, sir?'

'Why, that's extremely kind of you, Baker.' The Director was shaking with excitement. 'It's this one here, isn't it?' His hand brushed the trigger of a relay that would have sent Simpson shooting back to about the time of Victoria's accession. This may have been half-deliberate: the Director often got wistful about what pre-phylloxera stuff might or might not have tasted like.

'No, this one, sir. Just press it gently down.'

The switch clicked and instantly the figure of Simpson –

tallish, forty-ish, baldish – appeared in the receiver. We all gave a shout of triumph and relief. Rabaiotti killed the power. Schneider hurried forward and there was tension again. 'I'd give a case of Dow 1919 to see him conscious and mentally sound,' the Director muttered at my side.

'Everything all right so far,' Schneider called. 'I've given him a shot that'll pull him round in a minute or two.'

We lit cigarettes. 'Pity conditions wouldn't allow of him bringing anything back,' the Director said. 'Just think of a forty-year-old 1970 all ready to drink. But I suppose it would have cost too much anyway. Next time we must find a better way of handling the currency problem. Very risky giving him raw gold to pawn. And we're restricted to a lump small enough not to arouse too much suspicion. Oh, well, he should have been able to afford a few glasses. I hope that champagne's all right, by the way?'

'Oh, yes, I put it in the molecular-motion-retarder myself, with the setting at point-three. It'll be nicely chilled by now.'

'Splendid. I do want the dear boy to get a decent livener inside him before he faces all those cameras and interviews. I should have preferred a dry port myself, or possibly a Bittall, but I know what the occasion demands, of course. It's a Lambert 1952 I've got for him. I don't understand these things myself, but the Director of Lunar Projectiles swears by it.'

'He's coming round now,' Schneider shouted, and we all pressed forward.

There was an intense silence while Simpson blinked at us, sat up and yawned. His face was absolutely impassive. Very slowly he scratched his ear. He looked like a man with a bad hangover.

'Well?' the Director demanded eagerly. 'What did you see?'

'Everything. At least, I saw enough.'

'Had there been a war? Is there going to be a war?'

'No. Russia joined the Western Customs Union in 1993,

China some time after 2000. The RAF's due to be disbanded in a few months.'

Then everyone hurled questions at once: about flying saucers, the Royal Family, the sciences, the arts, interplanetary travel, climatic conditions in the Rheingau – all sorts of things. Simpson seemed not to hear. He just sat there with the same blank look on his face, wearily shaking his head.

'What's the matter?' I asked finally. 'What was wrong?'

After a moment, he said in a hollow voice, 'Better if there had been a war. In some ways. Yes. Much better.'

'What on earth do you mean?'

Simpson gave a deep sigh. Then, hesitantly, to a silent audience and with the bottle of champagne quite forgotten, he told the following story.

The landing went off perfectly. Hyde Park was the area selected, with a thousand-square-yard tolerance to prevent Simpson from materialising inside a wall or halfway into a passer-by. Nobody saw him arrive. He changed his gold into currency without difficulty, and in a few minutes was walking briskly down Piccadilly, looking into shop-windows, studying dress and behaviour, buying newspapers and magazines, and writing busily in his notebook. He had several fruitful conversations, representing himself according to plan as a native of Sydney. This brought him some commiseration, for England had just beaten Australia at Lord's by an innings and 411 runs. Yes, everything seemed normal so far.

His political report and much of his social report were complete by six-thirty, and his thoughts started turning to drink: after all, it was a positive duty. As he strolled up Shaftesbury Avenue he began looking out for drink advertisements. The beer ones had much in common with those of 1960, but were overshadowed in prominence by those recommending wines. MOUTON ROTHSCHILD FOR POWER, BREEDING AND GRANDEUR, one said. ASK FOR OESTRICHER PFAFFENBERG – THE HOCK WITH THE CLEAN FINISH, enjoined another. MY GOLLY, MY ST GYOERGHYHEGYI FURMINT, bawled a third. Well, practical experiment would soon establish what was what. Simpson slipped quietly through the doorway of an establishment clearly devoted to drink.

The interior was surprising. If some French provincial café had not been gutted of décor and furnishings to get this place up, then a good job of duplication had been done. Men in neat, sombre clothing sat at the tables talking in low tones, wine-glasses and wine-bottles before them, while aproned waiters moved silently about. One of them was decanting a red wine from a bottle that was thick with dust and cobwebs, watched critically by all the nearby drinkers. Simpson crept to a seat in an unfrequented part of the room.

A waiter approached. 'What can I bring you, monsieur?'

Here it must be explained that Simpson was not quite the claret-fancier the Director thought him. He enjoyed claret all right, but he also enjoyed other French wines, and German wines, and Italian wines, and Iberian wines, and Balkan wines, and fortified wines, and spirits, and liqueurs, and *apéritifs*, and cocktails, and draught beer, and bottled beer, and stout, and cider, and perry – all the way down to Fernet Branca. (There were some drinks he had never drunk – *arak*, *kava*, Gumpoldskirchner Rotgipfler, methylated spirits – but they were getting fewer all the time.) Anyway, feeling dehydrated after his walk round the streets, he unreflectingly ordered a pint of bitter.

'I'm sorry, monsieur, I don't understand. What is this bitter?'

'Bitter beer, ale; you know. Haven't you got any?'

'Beer, monsieur?' The waiter's voice rose in contempt. '*Beer?* I'm afraid you're in the wrong district for that.'

Several men turned round, nudged one another and stared at Simpson, who blushed and said, 'Well . . . a glass of wine, then.'

'France, Germany, Luxembourg, Austria . . .'

Simpson tried to think. 'A claret, please. Let's say – a nice St Emilion.'

'Château Le Couvent, Château Puyblanquet, Château Bellefore Belcier, Château Grand Corbin d'Espagne . . .'

'Oh . . . I leave it to you.'

'*Bien*, monsieur. And the year? Will you leave that to me too?'

'If you don't mind.'

The waiter swept away. Conscious that all eyes were upon him, Simpson tried to sink into his chair. Before he could compose himself, a middle-aged man from a nearby table had come over and sat down next to him. 'Well, who are you?' this man asked.

'A – a traveller. From Sydney.'

'These days that's no excuse for not knowing your wines, friend. Some of them Rubicons and malbecs are as firm and fully rounded as all bar the greatest Burgundies. And I found a Barossa Riesling on holiday this year that was pretty near as gay as a Kreuznacher Steinweg. You well up on the Barossas, friend?'

'No, not really, I'm afraid.'

'Thought not, somehow. Otherwise you wouldn't stalk in here and screech out for *beer*. Ger, ought to be ashamed of yourself, you ought.'

'I'm awfully sorry.'

'Should hope so and all. Now, I'm an honest working man, see? I'm a DRIP, I am.'

'A drip?'

'Domestic Reactor Installation Patentee. Don't they go in for them down under? Now you listen to me. When I come in here to meet my colleagues and crack a bottle or two after the daily round, I don't want my palate soured by some toff yelling out about beer, especially not when we got a really elegant Gevrey Chambertin or Chambolle Musigny or something of that in front of us. It's psychosomatic, like. Just the

276

idea of beer's enough to cut off some of the subtler overtones, get me?'

'I'm sorry,' Simpson said again. 'I didn't realise. But tell me: don't you eat while you're drinking these wines?'

'What, and foul up the taste-buds with fat and sauces and muck? You got a nerve even mentioning food in a place like this. We're oenophiles in here, I'll have you know, not a bunch of pigs. Ah, here's your claret.' The stranger held the glass up to the light, then sniffed it delicately. 'Right, now let's see what you got to say about this. And get on with it.'

Simpson drank. It was the most wonderful wine he had ever known, with a strange warm after-taste that seemed to seep upwards and flood his olfactory centres. He sighed deeply. 'Superb,' he said at last.

'Come on, come on, we want more than that; you got to do better than that. Give us a spot of imagery, kind of style, a reference to art, that type of stuff.'

'It's – I don't know – it's the richness of summer, all the glory of . . . of love and lyric poetry, a whole way of life, profound and . . . some great procession of—'

'Ah, you turn me up,' the man said violently. 'This is a 2003 Château La Bouygue, reconstituted pre-phylloxera of course. Now, light and free, not rich in association but perfectly assured without any insincerity, instrumental where the '01s are symphonic, the gentleness of a Braque rather than the bravura of a Matisse. That's as far as you can go with it. Love and lyric poetry indeed. I never heard such slop in my life. You aren't fit to come in here, friend. You get off out to one of the pubs with your boss-class pals, that's where you belong.'

Simpson threw down some coins and ran, a gust of ill-natured laughter sounding in his ears. He felt like walking the streets for the two hours in 2010 that still remained to him, but a nagging curiosity emboldened him to ask to be directed to a pub.

The place he finally made his way to was on the corner of

a narrow street on the edge of Soho. It was a red-brick affair like a miniature grammar school or a suburban bank. As he approached, a bus drew up and a crowd of young people got off, chattering loudly to one another in what Simpson made out as a version of the upper-class tones current in his own time. He was more or less swept in through the front door of the pub, and had no time to puzzle out the significance of a notice above the entrance, painted by hand with what seemed deliberate inelegance, and bearing the legend: CRACKED UP BY THE WALLOP AND SCOFF MOB.

He found himself in a large, ill-lighted and crowded room of which the main feature was a long counter that ran from end to end zig-zag-wise, as if to accommodate as many as possible of the tall stools that were closely packed along it. What were evidently glass sandwich cupboards stood every couple of feet along the red plastic top. A group of people, half-crowd, half-queue, was clustered round the entrance, and Simpson mingled with them. He noticed that most of the stools were occupied by persons drinking beer or some such liquid out of pint glasses and eating rolls or sandwiches. Conversations were bawling away around him.

'My dear, simply nobody goes to the Crown these days. Simon and I were given fresh crisps the last time we went.'

'It doesn't surprise me. We had some mustard that couldn't have been more than a day old.'

'The wallop's first-class down at the George, and as for the scoff – the bluest piece of ham you ever saw. A really memorable thrash. I'm getting the secretary of the Mob to crack them up in the next issue of the *Boozer Rag*.'

'Have you bagged stools, sir?'

'I beg your pardon?'

'Sorry, mate. Have you bagged, mate?'

'No, I'm afraid not. May I see the head potman?'

'I'll get him over directly, mate.'

'Shall we start thinking about what we're going to have? Pickled onions to start? With a glass of mild?'

278

'Nuts for me. Mixed and salted.'

'Right, that's three onions, one nuts. And then I can recommend the cheese rolls. They know me here and always see
that I get the three-day-old, with plenty of rind.'

After some time, Simpson obtained a stool and ordered a
pint of bitter from the grubby barmaid.

'Certainly, love. A fresh barrel has just come on.'

'Oh, I'll have mild instead, then.'

'By all means, love, if you wish for it. Your taste is your
own. And what will you have in the way of scoff, love?'

'Oh, er – nothing to eat, thank you.'

'If I may say so, love, with all due respect, you might perhaps do better at the wine-bar if you don't wish for any scoff.
We have standards to maintain here, love.'

'I'm awfully sorry. What . . . scoff do you recommend?'

'Our gherkins have frequently been cracked up, love. Not
a dish is sold till it's two days old.'

'They sound delightful. One dish, please.'

'Very good, love. With cigarette-ash garnishings, of
course.'

The beer came. It was horrible. The gherkins came. Simpson took no notice of them. Dazedly he watched and listened
to those around him. A kind of ritual seemed to be being
enacted by a group of four immediately next to him. The
two couples raised their pints in concert, intoned the word
'Cheers' in a liturgical manner, poured a few drops on to
the front of their greasy pullovers, and sank their drinks in
one swallow. Afterwards they all sighed loudly, wiped their
mouths with their hands, banged the empty glasses down on
the counter, and spoke in turn.

'Lovely drop of wallop.'

'First today.'

'I needed that.'

'Lays the dust.'

'You can't beat a decent pint.'

'Full of goodness.'

'Keeps your insides working.'

'It's a real drink.'

When this point was reached, all four shouted 'Let's have another' in unison, and were immediately served with fresh drinks and small plates of sandwiches. The bread on these was curled up at the corners, revealing purple strips of meat criss-crossed with gristle. One of the men felt the texture of the bread and nodded approvingly. 'I told you this place was good,' his friend said. Then the party got down to what was clearly the *pièce de résistance*, alternately biting at the sandwiches and taking pulls of beer, chewing the resulting mush with many a belch of appreciation. Simpson lowered his head into his hands. The talk went on.

'What's the fighting like here?'

'Oh, excellent. The governor of the boozer gets it under way at ten-thirty sharp, just outside on the corner. I did hear a whisper that he's going to allow broken bottles for the last five minutes tonight. The police should be with us by then. They're very keen round here.'

'At the Feathers, you know, they kick off at ten-fifteen inside the bar. Don't know whether I agree with that.'

'No. After all, it's only the finale of the evening.'

'Absolutely. Shouldn't make it too important.'

'Definitely not. Getting tight's the object of the exercise.'

'Quite. By the way, who's that fellow next to you?'

'No idea. Wine-bar type, if you ask me.'

'Hasn't touched his gherkins. Refused fresh bitter. Shouldn't be here at all.'

'Couldn't agree more. I mean, look at his clothes.'

'Wonder how long since they were slept in.'

'If they ever have been.'

'Disgusting.'

'And what would you like to follow, love?'

This last was the barmaid. Simpson raised his head and gave a long yell of fury, bewilderment, horror and protest. Then he ran from the room and went on running until he was back at the point where the TIOPEPE was to pick him up. With shaking fingers he put the trance-pill into his mouth.

The Director broke the silence that followed the end of Simpson's story. 'Well, it's a long time ahead, anyway,' he said with an attempt at cheerfulness.

'Is it?' Simpson shouted. 'Do you think that sort of situation develops in a couple of weeks? It's starting to happen already. Wine-snobbery spreading, more and more of this drinking what you ought to drink instead of what you like. Self-conscious insistence on the virtues of pubs and beer because the wrong people are beginning to drink wine. It'll be here in our time, don't you worry. You just wait.'

'Ah, now, Simpson, you're tired and overwrought. A glass of champagne will soon make you see things in a different light.'

'Slip away with me afterwards,' I murmured. 'We'll have a good go at the beer down in town.'

Simpson gave a long yell – much like the one, probably, he vented at the end of his visit to 2010. Springing to his feet, he rushed away down the lab to where Schneider kept the medical stores.

'What's he up to?' the Director puffed as we hurried in pursuit. 'Is he going to try and poison himself?'

'Not straight away, sir, I imagine.'

'How do you mean, Baker?'

'Look at that bottle he's got hold of, sir. Can't you see what it is?'

'But . . . I can't believe my eyes. Surely it's . . .'

'Yes, sir. Surgical spirit.'

Miss Pinkerton's Apocalypse

MURIEL SPARK

One evening, a damp one in February, something flew in at the window. Miss Laura Pinkerton, who was doing something innocent to the fire, heard a faint throbbing noise overhead. On looking up, 'George! come here! come quickly!'

George Lake came in at once, though sullenly because of their quarrel, eating a sandwich from the kitchen. He looked up at the noise then sat down immediately.

From this point onward their story comes in two versions, his and hers. But they agree as to the main facts; they agree that it was a small round flattish object, and that it flew.

'It's a flying object of some sort,' whispered George eventually.

'It's a saucer,' said Miss Pinkerton, keen and loud, 'an antique piece. You can tell by the shape.'

'It can't be an antique, that's absolutely certain,' George said.

He ought to have been more tactful, and would have been, but for the stress of the moment. Of course it set Miss Pinkerton off, she being in the right.

'I know my facts,' she stated as usual, 'I should hope I know my facts. I've been in antique china for twenty-three years in the autumn,' which was true, and George knew it.

The little saucer was cavorting round the lamp.

'It seems to be attracted by the light,' George remarked, as one might distinguish a moth.

Promptly, it made as if to dive dangerously at George's head. He ducked, and Miss Pinkerton backed against the

wall. As the dish tilted on its side, skimming George's shoulder, Miss Pinkerton could see inside it.

'The thing might be radio-active. It might be dangerous.' George was breathless. The saucer had climbed, was circling high above his head, and now made for him again, but missed.

'It is not radio-active,' said Miss Pinkerton, 'it is Spode.'

'Don't be so damn silly,' George replied, under the stress of the occasion.

'All right, very well,' said Miss Pinkerton, 'it is not Spode. I suppose you are the expert, George, I suppose you know best. I was only judging by the pattern. After the best part of a lifetime in china—'

'It must be a forgery,' George said unfortunately. For, unfortunately, something familiar and abrasive in Miss Pinkerton's speech began to grind within him. Also, he was afraid of the saucer.

It had taken a stately turn, following the picture rail in a steady career round the room.

'Forgery, ha!' said Miss Pinkerton. She was out of the room like a shot, and in again carrying a pair of steps.

'I will examine the mark,' said she, pointing intensely at the saucer. 'Where are my glasses?'

Obligingly, the saucer settled in a corner; it hung like a spider a few inches from the ceiling. Miss Pinkerton adjusted the steps. With her glasses on she was almost her sunny self again, she was ceremonious and expert.

'Don't touch it, don't go near it!' George pushed her aside and grabbed the steps, knocking over a blue glass bowl, a Dresden figure, a vase of flowers and a decanter of sherry; like a bull in a china shop, as Miss Pinkerton exclaimed. But she was determined, and struggled to reclaim the steps.

'Laura!' he said desperately. 'I believe it is Spode. I take your word.'

The saucer then flew out of the window.

They acted quickly. They telephoned to the local paper. A reporter would come right away. Meanwhile, Miss Pinkerton telephoned to her two scientific friends – at least, one was interested in psychic research and the other was an electrician. But she got no reply from either. George had leaned out of the window, scanning the rooftops and the night sky. He had leaned out of the back windows, had tried all the lights and the wireless. These things were as usual.

The news man arrived, accompanied by a photographer.

'There's nothing to photograph,' said Miss Pinkerton excitably. 'It went away.'

'We could take a few shots of the actual spot,' the man explained.

Miss Pinkerton looked anxiously at the result of George and the steps.

'The place is a wreck.'

Sherry from the decanter was still dripping from the sideboard.

'I'd better clear the place up. George, help me!' She fluttered nervously, and started to pack the fire with small coals.

'No, leave everything as it is,' the reporter advised her. 'Did the apparition make this mess?'

George and Miss Pinkerton spoke together.

'Well, indirectly,' said George.

'It wasn't an apparition,' said Miss Pinkerton.

The reporter settled on the nearest chair, poising his pencil and asking, 'Do you mind if I take notes?'

'Would you mind sitting over here?' said Miss Pinkerton. 'I don't use the Queen Annes, normally. They are very frail pieces.'

The reporter rose as if stung, then perched on a table which Miss Pinkerton looked at uneasily.

'You see, I'm in antiques,' she rattled on, for the affair was beginning to tell on her, as George told himself. In fact he sized up that she was done for; his irritation abated, his confidence came flooding back.

'Now, Laura, sit down and take it easy.' Solicitously he pushed her into an easy chair.

284

'She's overwrought,' he informed the pressmen in an audible undertone.

'You say this object actually flew in this window?' suggested the reporter.

'That is correct,' said George.

The camera-man trained his apparatus on the window.

'And you were both here at the time?'

'No,' Miss Pinkerton said. 'Mr Lake was in the kitchen and I called out, of course. But he didn't see inside the bowl, only the outside, underneath where the manufacturer's mark is. I saw the pattern so I got the steps to make sure. That's how Mr Lake knocked my things over. I saw inside.'

'I am going to say something,' said George.

The men looked hopefully towards him. After a pause, George continued, 'Let us begin at the beginning.'

'Right,' said the reporter, breezing up.

'It was like this,' George said. 'I came straight in when Miss Pinkerton screamed, and there was a white convex disc, you realise, floating around up there.'

The reporter contemplated the spot indicated by George.

'It was making a hell of a racket like a cat purring,' George told him.

'Any idea what it really was?' the reporter enquired.

George took his time to answer. 'Well, yes,' he said, 'and no.'

'Spode ware,' said Miss Pinkerton.

George continued, 'I'm not up in these things. I'm extremely sceptical as a rule. This was a new experience to me.'

'That's just it,' said Miss Pinkerton. 'Personally, I've been in china for twenty-three years. I recognised the thing immediately.'

The reporter scribbled and enquired, 'These flying discs appear frequently in China?'

'It was a saucer. I've never seen one flying before,' Miss Pinkerton explained.

'I am going to ask a question,' George said.

Miss Pinkerton continued, 'Mr Lake is an art framer. He handles old canvases but next to no antiques.'

'I am going to ask. Are you telling the story or am I?' George said.

'Perhaps Mr Lake's account first and then the lady's,' the reporter ventured.

Miss Pinkerton subsided crossly while he turned to George.

'Was the object attached to anything? No wires or anything? I mean, someone couldn't have been having a joke or something?'

George gave a decent moment to the possibility.

'No,' he then said. 'It struck me, in fact, that there was some sort of Mind behind it, operating from outer space. It tried to attack me, in fact.'

'Really, how was that?'

'Mr Lake was not attacked,' Miss Pinkerton stated. 'There was no danger at all. I saw the expression on the pilot's face. He was having a game with Mr Lake, grinning all over his face.'

'Pilot?' said George. 'What are you talking about – pilot!'

Miss Pinkerton sighed. 'A tiny man half the size of my finger,' she declared. 'He sat on a tiny stool. He held the little tiny steering-wheel with one hand and waved with the other. Because, there was something like a sewing-machine fixed near the rim, and he worked the tiny treadle with his foot. Mr Lake was not attacked.'

'Don't be so damn silly,' said George.

'You don't mean this?' the reporter asked her with scrutiny.

'Of course I do.'

'I would like to know something,' George demanded.

'You only saw the underside of the saucer, George.'

'You said nothing about any pilot at the time,' said George. 'I saw no pilot.'

'Mr Lake got a fright when the saucer came at him. If he

hadn't been dodging he would have seen for himself.'

'You mentioned no pilot,' said George. 'Be reasonable.'

'I had no chance,' said she. She appealed to the camera-man. 'You see, I know what I'm talking about. Mr Lake thought he knew better, however. Mr Lake said, "It's a forgery." If there's one thing I do know, it's china.'

'It would be most unlikely,' said George to the reporter. 'A steering-wheel and a treadle machine these days, can you credit it?'

'The man would have fallen out,' the camera-man reflected.

'I must say,' said the reporter, 'that I favour Mr Lake's long-range theory. The lady may have been subject to some hallucination, after the shock of the saucer.'

'Quite,' said George. He whispered something to the photographer. 'Women!' Miss Pinkerton heard him breathe.

The reporter heard him also. He gave a friendly laugh. 'Shall we continue with Mr Lake's account, and then see what we can make of both stories?'

But Miss Pinkerton had come to a rapid decision. She began to display a mood hitherto unknown to George. Leaning back, she gave way to a weak and artless giggling. Her hand fluttered prettily as she spoke between gurgles of mirth. 'Oh, what a mess! What an evening! We aren't accustomed to drink, you see, and now oh dear, oh dear!'

'Are you all right, Laura?' George enquired severely.

'Yes, yes, yes,' said Miss Pinkerton, drowsy and amiable. 'We really oughtn't to have done this, George. Bringing these gentlemen out. But I can't keep it up, George. Oh dear, it's been fun though.'

She was away into her giggles again. George looked bewildered. Then he looked suspicious.

'It's definitely the effect of this extraordinary phenomenon,' George said firmly to the Press.

'It was my fault, all my fault,' spluttered Miss Pinkerton.

The reporter looked at his watch. 'I can quite definitely

say you saw a flying object?' he asked. 'And that you were both put out by it?'

'Put down that it was a small, round, flattish object. We both agree to that,' George said.

A spurt of delight arose from Miss Pinkerton again.

'Women, you know! It always comes down to women in the finish,' she told them. 'We had a couple of drinks. Mr Lake had rather more than I did,' she added triumphantly.

'I assure you,' said George to the reporter.

'We might be fined for bringing the Press along, George. It might be an offence,' she put in.

'I assure you', George insisted to the photographer, 'that we had a flying saucer less than an hour ago in this room.'

Miss Pinkerton giggled.

The reporter looked round the room with new eyes; and with the air of one to whom to understand all is to forgive all, he folded his notebook. The camera-man stared at the pool of sherry, the overturned flowers, the broken glass and china. He packed up his camera, and they went away.

George gave out the tale to his regular customers. He gave both versions, appealing to their reason to choose. Further up the road at her corner shop, Miss Pinkerton smiled tolerantly when questioned. 'Flying saucer? George is very artistic,' she would say, 'and allowances must be made for imaginative folk.' Sometimes she added that the evening had been a memorable one, 'Quite a party!'

It caused a certain amount of tittering in the neighbourhood. George felt this; but otherwise, the affair made no difference between them. Personally, I believe the story, with a preference for Miss Pinkerton's original version. She is a neighbour of mine. I have reason to believe this version because, not long afterwards, I too received a flying visitation from a saucer. The little pilot, in my case, was shy and inquisitive. He pedalled with all his might. My saucer was Royal Worcester, fake or not I can't say.

288

Acknowledgements

Every effort has been made to contact copyright holders; in the event of an inadvertent omission or error, the editorial department should be notified at The Folio Society Ltd, 44 Eagle Street, London, WC1R 4FS.

The Folio Society wishes to thank the following writers, publishers and literary representatives for their permission to use copyright material:

Amis, Kingsley: 'The 2003 Claret' from *The Collected Short Stories of Kingsley Amis* (Hutchinson, 1980) reproduced by permission of The Random House Group Ltd and Jonathan Clowes Ltd, London, on behalf of The Literary Estate of Sir Kingsley Amis.

Bowen, Elizabeth: 'Shoes' from *Joining Charles and Other Stories* (Constable, 1929) reproduced by permission of Constable & Robinson Ltd.

Crompton, Richmal: 'The Bishop's Handkerchief' from *Still William* (George Newnes, 1925) reproduced by permission of A. P. Watt Ltd on behalf of The Royal Literary Fund.

Davies, Robertson: 'The Xerox in the Lost Room' from *High Spirits: A Collection of Ghost Stories* (Penguin, 1982) © Robertson Davies, 1982. Reproduced by permission of Penguin Group (UK), Penguin Group (Canada), a division of Pearson Penguin Canada Inc., and Viking Penguin, a division of Penguin Group (USA) Inc.

Gibbons, Stella: 'The Great Mammoth Story' reproduced by permission of Curtis Brown Group Ltd, London, on behalf of the Estate of Stella Gibbons. Copyright © Stella Gibbons.

Jacobs, W. W.: 'The Grey Parrot' (1908) reproduced by permission of The Society of Authors as the Literary Representative of the Estate of W. W. Jacobs.

Acknowledgements

Parker, Dorothy: 'Dusk Before Fireworks' from *The Portable Dorothy Parker*, edited by Brendan Gill, © 1928, renewed © 1956 by Dorothy Parker. Reproduced by permission of Viking Penguin, a division of Penguin Group (USA) Inc., and Gerald Duckworth & Co. Ltd.

Pritchett, V. S.: 'The Key to My Heart' from *The Complete Short Stories* (Chatto & Windus, 1990) © 1990 by V. S. Pritchett. Reproduced by permission of The Random House Group Ltd & Random House, Inc.

Runyon, Damon: 'A Piece of Pie' from *Broadway Stories* (Constable & Co., 1954) reproduced by permission of Constable & Robinson Ltd.

Spark, Muriel: 'Miss Pinkerton's Apocalypse' from *The Collected Stories* (Macmillan, 1967) reproduced by permission of David Higham Associates.

Thurber, James: 'The Curb in the Sky' from *The Middle-Aged Man on the Flying Trapeze* (Harper & Bros, 1935). Copyright © 1935 James Thurber and 1963 Rosemary A. Thurber. Reproduced by arrangement with Rosemary A. Thurber and The Barbara Hogenson Agency, Inc. All rights reserved.

Travers, Ben: 'Homing Jane' reproduced by permission of PFD (www.pfd.co.uk) on behalf of the Estate of Ben Travers.

Waugh, Evelyn: 'Excursion in Reality' from *Work Suspended and Other Stories* (Chapman & Hall, 1947). Copyright © Evelyn Waugh Settlement Trust 1943. Reproduced by permission of PFD on behalf of the Evelyn Waugh Settlement Trust.

Wodehouse, P. G.: 'Buried Treasure' from *Lord Emsworth and Others* (Barrie & Jenkins, 1937) reproduced by permission of The Random House Group Ltd and by A. P. Watt Ltd on behalf of The Trustees of the Wodehouse Estate.